THE HUNGRY HORIZON

PIRATES OF THE PACIFIC

Book One

MIKE HAWTHORNE

Cover design by Samuel Fernandez
Interior design by Jacqueline Cook

ISBN: 978-1-61179-363-5 (Paperback)
ISBN: 978-1-61179-364-2 (e-book)

10 9 8 7 6 5 4 3 2 1

BISAC Subject Headings:
FIC002000 FICTION / Action & Adventure
FIC014000 FICTION / Historical
FIC047000 FICTION / Sea Stories

Address all correspondence to:
Fireship Press, LLC
P.O. Box 68412
Tucson, AZ 85737
fireshipinfo@gmail.com

Or visit our website at:
www.fireshippress.com

ACKNOWLEDGEMENTS

With thanks to:

English & Creative Writing Department, Roehampton University,
London, UK

Caird Library and Archive at the National Maritime Museum,
Greenwich, London, UK

The National Archives, Twickenham, Surrey, UK

THE HUNGRY HORIZON

PIRATES OF THE PACIFIC

Book One

MIKE HAWTHORNE

FIRESHIP
PRESS

1
PORT ROYAL

The weathered planks and trampled dirt floor of the hut dissolved in steam as the slave woman washed Tom's back. The various stenches of Port Royal no longer bothered him.

Yesterday, he had moored the heavily laden boat in Chocoletta Hole, tucked behind Fort Charles at the harbor mouth in Jamaica. The shallow pool nestled a short walk from his usual lodgings at The Three Mariners Inn. When Tom stepped onto the quayside, the stink nearly knocked him back into the water. An evening land breeze, seeking the sea from the island's hot interior, picked up all the odors and hit him like an invisible wall. He staggered, retching. His mates propped him up.

"Steady now, Tom," said Joseph. The tall Irishman was almost motherly. "Take it slow."

The Scottish joker, Malcolm, shook his dark ringlets and brandished a gull's feather. "Poo! Shall I tickle yer throat for ye, Master Sheppard?"

Tom felt as if he'd swallowed a cactus. It came in layers; first the shit from the tannery beyond the harbor, then the fish from the market, and finally the concentrated poison wafting out of a Guinea trader at the North Docks. Pure death, stewed in the very bowels of

1

Satan, clawed at his tonsils and made his gorge rise.

It was not so bad this morning. A light breeze came from the sea. Having discharged her human cargo into the Royal Africa Company pens under Fort James, the Guinea ship crossed the bay to the mouth of the Rio Cobre, to have her shelves removed and her hold scrubbed. That took the edge off it. Compared to the stench of the slaver's filth, the other smells were bearable. Some were even pleasant. Roast cocoa, tobacco, and sour wine drifted across the yard from the back door of The Three Mariners taproom. A bundle of Palo Santo twigs smoldered in a corner of the hut. Oily incense filtered into the palm thatch. It gave the sweat from Theodora's armpits a musky flavor. Her nipples stroked his shoulders.

Tom felt as if he was melting. His tanned limbs dangled over the side of the laundry tub. Theodora had picked up heated rocks with a spade and dropped them into the water. He leaned forward to let her sponge his back.

"Lobsta too big fe pot," she laughed.

He was snug as a fetus in the womb, but with a barnacle-hard erection. Fine scars criss-crossed his back like the lines on a nautical chart. Her tongue traced them along his spine.

"Salty lobsta," she whispered.

"More like an upside-down tortoise," he sighed. "Lower, girl. All kinds of clinker down there."

"Blue mark fe face, Massa Thomas," she said, "nebber come off."

"Powder burn," he said, and remembered his panic when he had over-primed the touchhole of his matchlock in his haste to aim at the Spanish lancer. He was lucky to have escaped with a singed beard and the indigo stain along his right cheekbone.

The trips were becoming riskier and less profitable. Frenchmen swarmed over the western end of Hispaniola. The Spaniards were trying to kill all the stray cattle in the center while they concentrated their defenses around Santo Domingo. Rotting cow carcasses buzzed with bluebottles in the fields and bushes. That meant fewer hides and less food. Tom had grown heartily sick of eating turtles. The price of their shells was plummeting too, but the scarcity of shallow oyster beds galled him the most. Indian divers, worked to death by the Dons, had stripped the easy beds. Pearls were Tom's passion. They often lay too deep to reach. Malcolm, who did virtually all the diving, complained that he would soon rupture a lung. He was terrified that one scratch on a sharp coral would make the deadly shark fins appear. Joseph, the third partner in the boat, had begun to mutter about joining the Brethren of the Coast in a raid on the main. It had been a long, hard twelve weeks. Tom would be thirty-six years old in May; a tough old bird in a climate where Englishmen died young.

The sponge probed. Tom closed his eyes and emptied his mind. This was no time to fret about work. He was pure sensation now. The hot tub gave him a hint of eternal peace. He surrendered to the luxury like a Turkish sultan. Among the islands, whenever he found a spring near a volcano, he stewed his skin in the prickly bubbles and imagined the air smelled of Theodora's hut instead of bad eggs. On hostile territory, at the end of a forest trail, he took care not to fall asleep in the thermals. More than one exhausted bather had succumbed to the fumes to meet his Maker like a parboiled chicken under the vault of the giant trees. Here, in Thea's shack, with a clean shirt and breeches hanging on a nail by the door, Tom let all the tension drain out of his muscles. His cock threatened to explode with the pressure inside it, without any effort at all. It felt like a separate object in the water, a truncheon or belaying pin, until the sponge casually brushed the knob and searing pleasure shot from his groin up to his scalp and down to his toes.

He half-opened his eyes. A tiny lizard with turquoise stripes nodded at him from the wall. It loomed as big as a dragon and then vanished in blurred trickles of sweat. He closed his eyes again. Spots swam in the glow behind the lids. Air, water, and blood were all at the same temperature. His skin did not exist except where Thea touched it. A nipple brushed his lips. He sucked it eagerly. The sponge popped to the surface as her fingers closed around his balls. The second part of the ritual began. It did not take long.

Afterwards, Tom dressed and strutted across the yard to the

back door of the inn. Bedclothes on the washing line hung like slack sails in his path, barely moving. He paused to smooth the red parrot feathers in his hat, angled the brim low against the glare, and glanced at his turtle shells stacked on raw hides in a handcart by the gate. Jupiter, a muscular Ibo slave with vertical cheek scars, sat in the shade, sharpening a machete. The rasping noise unsettled the chickens. They clucked and crowded behind Thea's shack as if their little brains remembered decapitated relatives racing in bloody circles before yesterday's lunchtime. Jupiter kept an eye on things. He watched the rear of the three-story brick building. Jupiter was Thea's man, but displayed no more emotion than if she'd just milked a goat. Slimy mango kernels lay in the dust at his feet. He nodded at Tom without interrupting the rhythm of the stone against the blade. It was already sharper than a barber's razor.

Tom hesitated before climbing the stairs to the garret. He heard raised voices coming from the taproom beyond the scullery. Peering round the corner into the public bar, he looked in vain for Joseph and Malcolm. Long Ben, the doorman, had a filthy sailor by the collar. The man's face glistened unnaturally yellow beneath his moldy woolen cap, crawling with lice. His breeches hung open at the knees, encrusted with hardened effluent. His black toenails resembled claws.

"Where the fuck do you think you are?" Ben was honestly offended. "This is Port Royal Battle Station, not Calabar! We never let hands straight off a Guinea man inside. You can drink on the porch if you must. The potboy will bring it to you. Those be the rules at The Mariners. Now, take your African plagues out of here!"

Tom continued up the narrowing stairs to the top room of the house. A lumpy mattress, broad enough for five, sagged to the floorboards on its ropes. It occupied most of the space under the oppressively low roof beams. A printed calico rag, with the same floral pattern as the one on Theodora's cot, quivered over the open window in the salty air. The scrape of Jupiter's whetstone rang out below, mingled with the cries of the seagulls and stallholders in the fish market directly in front of the inn. Matchlock fuzees, powder flasks, bandoliers, and hunting bags packed the corners of the attic. The big-boned, freckled frame of Joseph Connolly sprawled naked across the bed. It always surprised Tom that such a great hulk could have come from poorly fed parents. Perhaps there really had once been giants in parts of Ireland. Tom was five-foot-five, and his Sussex people had rarely starved. The ways of God were mysterious. Joseph snored gently, his sparse blond whiskers vibrating. There was no sign of Malcolm, the third messmate.

Tom pulled a clay pipe from his hatband and stuffed it with moist Hispaniola tobacco. He soon had it burning with the aid of his tinderbox and a short piece of gun fuse. The place being a fire trap, he took care to drop the smoldering cord into the piss pot beside the bed, before leaning over the sleeper and blowing a cloud of blue smoke into his face. The young Irishman moved instantly. His fingers clawed across the mattress and grasped the neck of an empty wine bottle before he opened his eyes. A letter "F," for Fugitive, flamed red on the back of his right hand, a reminder of a failed attempt to escape from servitude in the cane fields of Barbados. He blinked, saw Tom, and waved the bottle at him.

"By Christ," he spluttered, "are you tired of life? Jesus, Tom, I was dreaming a darling dream of mermaids and the Cuban Keys."

"Where's Mal?"

"Mal got itchy feet—or itchy cock, more like. The wee poltroon will be roving the streets chasing skirts, I shouldn't wonder. You look younger yourself, so you do. Been visiting your private Chocoletta Hole again, you old goat? Or have you tried a white woman for a change?"

"A woman's a woman," said Tom. "I don't pass judgement on the horny-handed heifers you consort with. Come on, get up and greet the day. Help me shift the hides to Arkwright's. He shuts at noon. I'm damned if I'm hauling them over to the mainland on Christmas Eve. Then we'll take the shells to the Jew. He tends to vanish on Fridays, as I recall."

Joseph donned his baggy breeches, fisherman's smock, and boots. He carefully concealed the "F" brand beneath a fingerless pigskin glove. Tom extracted a leather pouch from under the mattress and poured out a dozen pearls. They gleamed in the palm of his hand.

"Some of these big pear-shaped ones will fetch a hundred pesos," he muttered. "You can rely on it. They love them for earrings. I reckon we can fit ourselves out handsomely and stay here till the Twelfth Night or longer."

"You don't want to be leaving those in the room again, Tom," said Joseph. "That miserable gossoon, the pot boy, Squeaker, is in the habit of wandering through the building when the guests are out. It doesn't surprise me at all that he has a black eye."

Nobody gave a poor buccaneer hawking hides and tortoise shells a second glance in Port Royal, but if word got out, a single pearl could earn you a knife between the ribs. That was why the Jew, Abraham Henriquez, whose profits came from shipping jewels to Amsterdam, hung a hawksbill turtle carapace over his shop in Queen Street. Shells filled his cavernous storeroom, but he struck the real bargains for precious stones in a locked office. Kobby, a big Ashanti slave with a spiked quarterstaff, stood guard in the dark passage before the office door. To a visitor refocusing from the bright dusty street, he was virtually invisible. Whenever Abraham slid back the peephole, the slave nodded, the key turned in the lock, and trusted customers could enter.

Abraham treated the Ashanti well. He had purchased Kobby cheaply. His original owner had been about to skin the man alive. Kobby had caused more trouble on the plantation than he was worth since his tongue had been cut out for openly speaking his African language. A deep gouge in his lower lip, resulting from the violent amputation, made him drool. This menacing guard, who could only utter vowels and make slurping noises, suited Abraham perfectly. Kobby developed a taste for Geneva spirits, so the Jew made sure there was always a stoneware bottle in the cool storeroom where he slept. It did not make the big African aggressive, but rather had the opposite effect. He simply swayed, crooning gentle melodies with a faraway look in his eyes. Apparently, he had never been so happy.

When Tom and Joseph appeared in the passage, Kobby shook

his head and waved his hand dismissively, shooting glances at the closed door.

"What's the slobbering bollav trying to say?" asked Joseph.

"There's somebody in there with Abraham," said Tom. "Come, get busy. We may as well stack the shells. Kobby can count them as we go by."

"Oh, he can count, can he?"

"He can multiply. He has an abacus."

Joseph tried to peer around the slave. The steel point of the quarterstaff suddenly hovered an inch from his nose. Joseph smiled, stepped back, and followed Tom out to the cart.

"You'll get me killed with your dozy drivel one of these days, Thomas."

"By Cromwell's rotting head," said Tom, "I thought I had enough on my hands with that joker Malcolm. You see that cowry necklace Kobby wears?"

"What of it?" Joseph trundled the cart into the passage.

"That's what the man counts on, like one of your Papist rosaries."

"So how does he multiply?"

"Like everybody else. They didn't cut his balls off."

"Bedad, Tom," said Joseph, heading past Kobby with an armful of shells, "she must have been good this morning. I never thought the day would dawn when I missed Malcolm's wit."

The office key rattling in the lock interrupted their banter. Heavy footsteps echoed on the flagstones. Before he knew it, Tom felt himself being lifted up from behind. His shells clattered to the floor.

"Gott verdammet!" a deep Dutch voice thundered in his ear. Tom spun around like a doll in the strong grip. A gleaming set of white teeth grinned at him from beneath a red walrus moustache, a giant periwig, apple cheeks, and twinkling blue eyes, "Gott verdammet! I thought so! Tom Sheppard!"

Tom was being crushed against a stout belly covered in lace and blue satin. A sickly oriental perfume filled his nostrils.

"It is you!" boomed the man. "I'd know that voice anywhere! Down, Moritz, down!"

Tom had yet to notice the spider monkey, secured to a silver chain round the Dutchman's wrist, clambering onto his hat. It tore out the feathers and flung them at the ceiling. Joseph dropped all but one of his shells and tried to swat the animal with it, but only succeeded in hitting Tom's ear. Kobby emerged from the shadows, grasping his staff with both hands, uncertain whom to attack. Tom glimpsed the white hairs of Abraham Henriquez over the drooling slave's shoulder, like an Old Testament prophet wielding a pistol. The monkey clawed frantically, dodging Joseph's blows.

Tom shouted, "Avast! I know this man! He's a friend! No trouble here! Get that fucking animal off me, Arnout, before it blinds me!"

The Dutchman yanked the chain. The monkey fell away without releasing the hat. Thomas collapsed in a heap of shells and flying feathers. He looked up at the Dutchman's grinning face, with Kobby and the Jew standing behind him, and burst out laughing. They all began to laugh. They had no idea why. Kobby's spluttering roar frightened the monkey. It tried to hide under Tom's hat. This set them off again. Tears ran down their cheeks. Abraham lowered his pistol, but his hand shook. He fired into the floor. The deafening report sobered them a little, but they were still cackling as they ducked and scampered to avoid the ricochet. Luckily, the ball bounced into the warehouse, splintering a tortoise shell.

"Kobby, lock the gates and tidy up," yelled Abraham, the first to recover his composure. "We will continue this discussion in my office. I am curious to know what happened here."

"Arnout," gasped Tom, "Arnout Van Tonder, you old dog. God's wounds, man, give me my hat. And you, you Irish oaf, you can pick up those feathers, now you've finished trying to knock my brains out."

They dusted themselves off and followed Abraham Henriquez to his inner sanctum. Light poured in from a tightly barred window onto a square table loaded with charts, navigation instruments, quills, and inkpots. A mahogany cupboard with drawers of various sizes stretched across the back wall. It would have been unbearably hot without the small vents let into the bricks over the paneling, allowing air to circulate from the cool warehouse and passageway. Abraham locked the door, reached for a decanter, and filled four goblets with French brandy. Joseph leaned against the cupboard and began to reposition the feathers in Tom's hatband. The others sat down in leather-backed Spanish chairs.

"So, gentlemen, I take it that commotion was some kind of reunion," said Abraham. "To what shall we drink?"

Arnout Van Tonder spoke first. "Since I haven't laid eyes on Tom, who is like a brother to me, for...it must be almost ten years…I will drink to friendship."

"Friendship!" they yelled in unison and knocked back the brandy. The monkey strained to lick Arnout's goblet.

"Moritz will give us no peace." Arnout flicked a peso into the air. "He is tired and thirsty. I need him healthy. A gift for a lady. Will your man take him to The Dolphin, Tom? I have rooms above The Pineapple Chamber. My valet can take care of him there."

"This is Mr. Joseph Connolly, Arnout," explained Thomas. "A partner in my business. Would you mind terribly transporting Moritz to The Dolphin, Mr. Connolly? Two streets on the left, by the Exchange?"

"I know The Dolphin." Joseph doffed his battered straw hat with a flourish, took the struggling monkey in his arms, chained it to his wrist and waited for Abraham to let him out. "I'll see you back at The Mariners, Mr. Sheppard. Don't worry, I'll take the cart with me as well."

Abraham refilled the goblets in the silence that followed. The Englishman and the Dutchman stared at each other. Abraham cleared his throat. "I had no idea you two were acquainted."

"Since the Great June Fight of 1666," said Tom. "I was on the flagship, The Royal Prince, stuck fast on Galoper Sands with the Dutch fleet closing in like a pack of dogs. I'd only been pressed into the Navy the month before. By Christ, Arnie, I still dream about those blasted fireships."

"We made it hot for you, ya? You were wise to ignore that screaming admiral of yours and surrender before we burned you to the waterline," said Arnout. "Abraham, I'm sure I mentioned the English prisoner I rescued from the hulks, the one who became a good comrade and part of my family in Holland? This is the man himself. Thomas Sheppard. I finally released him in Tortuga, on the way to New Amsterdam—forgive me, New York—in '69."

"Sure, you spoke of him more than once, but never by name," said the Jew. "I had no idea it was Tom. He's been selling me tortoise shells and quality pearls these last five years. You must have slipped in and out of Port Royal while he hunted on the Keys."

"Well, this is Providence. It is a resurrection, a fond memory brought back to life," Arnout smiled. "I can barely believe it. Let me look at you, Tom. A little worn and discolored, but still the same. Like a well-thumbed book rediscovered in a forgotten corner. I thought you lost, but now you are found. To think that you have been in this very office, which contains so many of my things, for five years; maybe drinking from the same cup. Gott, man," he pointed at a row of pearls on his cuff, "you probably raised some of these from the sea bed yourself."

"Don't remind me," said Tom. "They lie deeper every year, and we have three mouths to feed."

Arnout raised an eyebrow. He turned to Abraham expectantly. The old Jew stroked his beard. Emeralds, set in gold, flashed on his fingers. Despite his joy at seeing Arnout, Tom felt uneasy in front of the two older, more powerful men. What was he compared to them? His friendship with the Dutch officer had never been one of equals. First, he had been his prisoner, then a kind of glorified valet, and finally, with increasing liberty, he had come to depend on Arnout as a father figure. Tom's mother had died in childbirth when he was only two. After they buried her with his stillborn sister, Tom's father abandoned his life as a Sussex fisherman in despair, leaving his son in the care of his brother's family while he joined Colonel Nathaniel Rich's regiment against King Charles I. Within a year, he died of the bloody flux besieging Deal Castle.

Among his noisy, numerous cousins, Tom stood out as a loner, always treated kindly, but with an element of pity. He hated being the object of compassion or charity. He had leapt at the chance of leaving Arnout in 1669 to strike out on his own with The Brethren of the Coast in Tortuga, seeking treasure and adventure. The treasure had eluded him, but he had hung on to his pride. Arnout sat before him, sleek, prosperous, and exuding more confidence than ever. Tom resisted the role of the prodigal son. He resolved not to lose his remaining dignity by begging for any favors.

The Dutchman spoke, "We have great plans for the new decade, Thomas. Things are looking up at last. We aim to make the 1680s as glorious as the '70s were miserable."

"Who's 'we,' Arnout?" asked Tom. "The Dutch West India Company?"

"Pah!" Arnout snorted. "The Company is struggling to survive. You English saw to that. The big investors equip fleets for the East Indian Ocean these days. Abraham and I make our own arrangements here in the Antilles. We are Atlantic men. The Van Tonders have been partners with the Cohen Henriquez family since the days of William the Silent. Abraham's associates are everywhere from Brazil to the Baltic. Mine go back to the wars of the Sea Beggars against the Duke of Parma, remember? Your deputy governor, Sir Henry Morgan himself, has been in our employ from the start. We have tried and trusted captains in these waters, sailing under every flag you'd care to mention, even the bloody Hapsburg cross. We are invisible; we are everywhere, from Hamburg to Havana, from Genoa to Curacao. We play a tight game. Trust; that is all that matters in the end."

Thomas couldn't help laughing. "Everywhere and invisible, Arnout? You mean, like God?"

It was Abraham's turn. "No. God can take care of Himself. The reason we defeat the Spanish and their Pope is because we take life as it comes, not as we think it should be. We don't fit into their picture. We are invisible because they cannot see us, or choose not to, sometimes when we are under their very noses. They are taught from childhood that we are devils. They expect horns, hooked noses, a tail and the smell of sulfur, fiendish Jews and their heretical accomplices, when we are simple, ordinary men. We know that we are mere instruments of the Father, tiny specks in a vast scheme, swept along by a mighty wind. They honestly believe that they can bargain with such a power and represent it on earth. They cling to this absurdly inflated idea of their own importance, and that makes them stupid, cruel, and blind."

"More to the point," said Arnout, "the Turks are mauling them from the east and along the Barbary Coast. The sultan's armies rampage into the heart of the empire. His fleets swarm out of the Mediterranean into the Atlantic. Here in the Indies, they sit under a tree twanging their guitars while everybody else tends to their needs. Silver runs through their fingers like sand. They own half the world, yet in Spain they starve. Only their damned bishops get fat and their churches glitter with gold, as if they can hope to bedazzle their own Creator. Well, my friend, if they don't know how to use their wealth profitably, we'll relieve them of it, just as they stole it from the Indians."

"Good to see you haven't changed, Arnie," said Tom. "I'm all ears, but, I tell you, I have no more stomach for piracy. I sailed with Morgan, damn him, in 1671, all the way to Panama, and returned penniless. Those days are over for me."

"There's no piracy involved," smiled the Dutchman. "What do you take us for? Tell him, Abraham."

"A new player has approached the card table," said Abraham. "A player with a bulging purse. It's all legal, with unimpeachable letters of marque from a sovereign Protestant prince. We can enlist anybody." Abraham fixed Tom with a pointed stare. "Anybody we choose. Here in Port Royal, Sir Henry will hang a few French corsairs at Gallows Point for show. That way, we soothe the Dons and remove competitors at the same time. Meanwhile, we are building a Navy for Fritz William, the Elector of Brandenburg, in his royal docks at Emden."

"Prince Fritz will declare war on Spain at the next opportunity," said Arnout. "The Spanish treasury owes him a fortune and is in no position to repay. King Carlos is a pitiful imbecile who can't chew his food, piss straight, or tie his shoe ribbons. By Gott, he is so inbred even his crown has hairs on it. His old mother spends her days praying and having him exorcised. She couldn't find Brandenburg on a map. Meanwhile, courtiers write verses about raping nuns and stab each other for copper coins in the gutters of Madrid. All the American silver goes straight to the Crown's creditors in Milan, or to pay the Hapsburg troops in Flanders."

"Which," Abraham chuckled, "happens to be a few short miles down the coast from Emden."

Tom sipped the brandy and lit his pipe. The politics escaped him, but Europe! Eiderdowns, cold beer, hot sausages, Flanders lace, chessboard floors, and logs crackling in blue-tiled fireplaces beckoned him back over the ten years. Maybe he'd retire in comfort, married to a blonde merchant's daughter instead of staggering from a leaky skiff to a slave shack in the tropical heat.

"Look, old friend," said Arnout, "I'm expecting the *Eenhoorn* from Curacao. She is due in the North Docks any day. I will sail to the King of Denmark's fortress on St. Thomas, and then we head for Emden with a hold full of sugar and tobacco. Come with me. You don't have to answer today, but at least give it some serious thought. Sleep on it. Then come for Christmas dinner at The Dolphin tomorrow. We'll wash down a side of roast beef with the best Schiedam Geneva, whatever you decide."

Tom swallowed his remaining brandy and thought hard. He suddenly realized there was nothing to think about. The prospect of another season in sweltering swamps among crocodiles and Spanish patrols made him shudder. He rose and grasped Arnout's hand.

"I'm in," he said. "No need to sleep on anything. No need for Dutch courage or roast beef to convince me. From where I stand, I would deserve to be chained up as a raving lunatic if I refused."

Abraham refilled their goblets and said, "You have always been straight with me, Thomas. Never called me Shylock, even when prices were low. Fortune has placed you on the right side of the counter at last. Welcome to the firm of Cohen and Van Tonder, Mr. Sheppard. You will not find our names linked on any register in The Amsterdam Exchange, nor, I hope, in the archives of the Holy

Inquisition, but believe me, we are well established. In the New Year we will emerge under the Red Eagle of Brandenburg, as Prussian officers. We'll give De Graff and Van Hoorn a run for their money. Arnout, our unofficial company motto will serve as a toast."

The Dutchman and the Jew solemnly intoned it; "Take the best and fuck the rest!"

As the three men downed the brandy and settled in their chairs, Arnout reached for the decanter again, "So, Tom, what happened after we parted? You say you sailed with Sir Henry in 1671? To Panama? Abraham, pass me that new book I was showing you; *De Americaensche Zee-Roovers.*"

The Jew rummaged under a pile of papers and handed Arnout two pristine Moroccan calfskin volumes. He opened the title page of the first edition. Tom examined the finely engraved frontispiece showing scenes of pillage and torture above Jan Ten Hoorn's Amsterdam imprimatur.

"It's like a Bible, a devil's Bible," he said, thumbing through the pages, seeing his former life marching invisibly beneath the columns of print. Villainous faces glowered from the portraits illustrating each chapter. He lingered over an apelike rogue brandishing a cutlass. "My Dutch is becoming as poor as my eyesight, but I can make out the capital letters. Here, this Frenchie, L'Ollonais. On the march to Panama, I met an Indian chief who claimed to have eaten his liver. Raw."

"I translated the passages about the sack of Panama to Sir Henry in The Dolphin last week," said Arnout. "He went wild. Called it all a pack of lies. He almost forgot himself completely and wanted to challenge me to a duel. I had to remind him that I didn't write it. For a minute, I thought he was having a heart attack."

"Pity he didn't." Tom thumped the table. He felt the brandy. "I'll never let another bastard like Morgan rob me of my share."

"Easy, Tom," said Arnout. "I guarantee you won't be swindled in our company, may Gott strike me dead. Come for dinner tomorrow. I'll sign you up properly in the Brandenburg Navy, on the Savior's birthday. You can move into my chambers in The Dolphin as my lieutenant, but you must look the part. No more hauling canvas in the yards for you, old friend. Get some decent clothes. Have a shave. Buy a full-bottomed periwig, a beaver hat with ostrich plumes, and an ebony stick. Abraham, I'm sure we could advance Tom some pesos from the war chest, just to make himself respectable, ya?"

"Maybe a little pomade for his cheek too," said the Jew.

"No, no, no, Abraham," laughed Arnout. "Don't be offensive. That blue mark adds character, makes him look fiercer. How did you acquire it, Tom? Storming Panama?"

"Oh, that," Tom ran his fingers down his cheek. "No, that is fresh. A few months back, we almost got ourselves captured by Spanish lancers. I thought I could reload at leisure, but the lay of the land deceived me. A big bastard on a fast horse, helmeted and armored as if he was galloping against the Moors, suddenly appeared on the slope right in front of me, screaming, "Santiago!"—aiming to stick me like a pig. I didn't have time to measure my powder properly. Scorched myself from the eyelid to the chin. He went down, thank God, but I couldn't see out of one eye for a week."

Arnout chuckled and sprang to his feet. He grabbed the key and unlocked the door. "Back in a minute!" They heard him going into the warehouse and rummaging among the shells. He returned with a bundle wrapped in canvas, which he laid on the table before Tom. "Here," he announced. "This will help you avoid further mishaps. You'll never burn your face again. Regard it as a Christmas gift."

Tom unwrapped the cloth. A leather scabbard containing a heavy object, and a fringed buckskin bag decorated with Mohawk beadwork lay inside.

"What have we here?" he said, extracting a peculiar musket with a gleaming octagonal barrel from the scabbard, "Some kind of fowling piece?"

"Not exactly," said Arnout. "The ball is heavy enough to stop a bear, but it is astonishingly accurate, being rifled with a spiral groove to spin the bullet inside the barrel. It is a foot shorter than your average fuzee. However, if you align the breech with the little pimple on the front, you can hit a target 200 yards away. The steel was, I believe, forged in Freiburg. That is an Ulrich Hirsch mark here." He tapped the top of the barrel. "I've seen the same stamp on the Prince of Orange's horse pistols."

"The dog lock is fit for a king," whispered Tom, easing the hammer back and stroking the shard of flint clamped in its jaws. "The tiniest pinch of powder in the vent would set it off. I am overwhelmed. Where did you find this marvel?"

"It found me," said Arnout, "in the shape of a ship's master of the Hudson Bay Company who ran out of pesos during a card game in The Pineapple Chamber. I got it for three Queens and an Ace."

Tom hardly heard him. He was entranced, impatient to fire this ultimate hunter's weapon, turning it lovingly in his hands, examining it from every angle. He picked up a rod with a short corkscrew tip.

"That must be a miniature worm," said Arnout, "to clear the groove after a few shots, like the big ones on siege guns. I'm afraid it will take ages to load."

"It more than makes up for that with its reach," said Tom.

Abraham was about to pour more brandy, but Tom's head was spinning. He declined, picked up his parcel, and prepared to leave.

"Till tomorrow, my friend," said Arnout, turning the key. "Don't be late. We have much to discuss."

Tom was too elated to speak. Tears welled up in the corners of his eyes, threatening to spill down his cheeks. He had completely forgotten the pearls in his pocket. He grunted awkwardly and brushed past Kobby in the passage on his way out. The liquor sloshed like bilge water in his empty stomach. He stopped at the nearby produce market and wolfed down three bananas in swift succession. Then, holding his gift like a newborn baby, he walked through the noisy town, hardly able to digest either the bananas or his abrupt change of fortune. By the time he reached the end of York Street, behind The Three Mariners, he had calmed down a little. He decided not to tell Joseph or Malcolm anything yet. He put on a casual air as he rounded the corner and approached the inn.

"My, my, what have we here? Don Crocodillo and his Irish wolfhound?" Tom saw the pair lounging on benches in the shade

16

of the porch. They nursed leather blackjacks full of wine. Malcolm looked resplendent in a crimson taffeta waistcoat covered in gilt buttons. A brace of dragoon pistols poked out of his red silk waistband and a vicious Turkish sabre trailed from his embroidered baldric. To top it all, the thick dark hair framing his handsome face had been crimped with tongs, to imitate an expensive wig. The points of his thin moustache stood upright, rigid with beeswax.

"Wait till you see his new hat," said Joseph. "It's like a palm tree with all the feathers, so it is. He'll be saving that for tonight, to keep the moonbeams off."

"At least it is a hat," said Malcolm, "and not a tussock of strangled hay. How d'ye hope to get a woman looking like a gormless farm boy? Och, yer a lost cause, Joe Connolly."

Joseph did not react. He had his own circle of friends at The Seven Stars and an arrangement with a buxom Cumbrian fishwife in the market. The chafing of her rough red hands brought him off in half a minute. If he wanted more, she raised her skirts and took it from behind, without removing the stump of a clay pipe from her mouth. Betty the Bloater made herself available whenever the urge took him, for scarcely more than the price of a pint of unshelled prawns. Joseph liked to keep such things simple.

The lanky young Irishman carried a blunderbuss that he could load with nails and gravel if necessary, in his belt. His boarding axe nestled beside it. He had nothing to prove. He was no flashy, dueling fop like Malcolm. It took a lot of strong drink to make him loose his temper. Then he became truly frightening. For Joseph, the Scotsman's efforts to play the rakish cavalier provided free entertainment. As for Tom's penchant for slave women, Joseph found it incomprehensible. It was unheard of among the indentured convicts of Barbados. Their white skin was their last ray of hope. They could hide their brands, but their own bodies doomed those Africans. It hardly seemed necessary to scorch their skin with hot irons, when God Himself had marked them out for slavery. Here, nobody batted an eyelid. Black whores were cheaper, that was all. Many of the sailors had given up women altogether, jerking each other off and buggering servant boys, as they did on board. Some copulated with barnyard animals and hollowed-out fruit. They could withstand hurricanes and cannon fire, but the sight of a moist cunt made them flinch, as if it reminded them of an open wound. Everybody made their own rules in Port Royal, and changed them according to the fall of the dice. Even so, Joseph relished the freedom. There was something for every taste, rich or poor. The unrestrained debauchery distracted him from memories of his starving parents, being flogged as they hauled a plow through the rocky Barbados soil. By Holy Mother Mary, he'd gladly guide a Spanish squadron to Bridgetown and burn that entire island to ashes from end to end.

"I'll be stravaging round the market for a wee while, Tom," he announced. Betty the Bloater always wanted a drink after work. He stepped over an unconscious drunk to vanish in the crowd. It was the dirty sailor from the Guinea man, now covered in a layer of fine dust. Unless somebody moved his dehydrated body into the shade, he would die of sunstroke within the hour. The hot afternoon attracted clouds of flies to the rotting fish guts. The stallholders began to dismantle their booths. Slaves filled the empty barrels that had contained fresh water with stockfish. They rolled them onto ox carts and slowly dragged them towards the Palisades Road and the plantations. There would be no work in the fields next day. African drums had recently been forbidden as instruments of rebellion, but the empty barrels thundered out in the slave quarters at Christmas.

Port Royal braced itself for the 1679 festivities. A blind fiddler placed his hat on the bench and took up position on the porch of The Three Mariners. The signal gun boomed from Fort Charles at the harbor mouth. A ship answered the salute, coming in on the tide. The crew cheered from the yards like madmen, delighted to be back in the wickedest city in Christendom.

Tom considered telling Malcolm about Arnout's offer, but the Scotsman burst out with news of his own. "Word has it a fleet is skulking in Morant Bay, preparing to attack the main."

2
THE COCK FIGHT

"If 'word' has it, Morgan knows it too, as does half the town." Tom looked at Malcolm, unimpressed. Rumors of impending attacks on the main were commonplace. "Morant Bay, eh? Did word tell you who is in command of this so-called fleet?"

"Some of yer old shipmates; the likes of John Coxon and Bartholomew Sharp," said Malcolm. "Joe and I, we thought ye'd jump at the chance to join them. We are resolved to depart willy-nilly, at first light tomorrow."

"I've told you a hundred times, I'm done with all that." Tom felt a certain relief. No need for lengthy explanations. He could simply let the lads go their way, without mentioning Arnout or the *Eenhoorn.* He clutched the bundle containing the hunting rifle. Better to make a clean break. "Trust me, Mal, I'd be a hindrance. I could not abide the long cruises in packed vessels, let alone the battles. I saw too much of them when I was your age, but you go. It's a young man's game. Make your fortunes while you can."

The blind fiddler began to retune his instrument a few feet away. The piercing squeals drove Tom and Malcolm indoors. Friendly shadows and the smell of stale drink embraced them. The bar was empty. They sat down near the open window. Squeaker, the slovenly

boy with the black eye, limped towards them through the tables
and chairs. He had been well thrashed for resisting the landlord's
advances over the flour sacks in the storeroom earlier in the week.
Tom ordered two rounds of wine with fried chicken legs and yams,
which duly arrived. Malcolm ignored Squeaker completely, as if
any contact was beneath his station. His mask of disdain concealed
painful memories of his own childhood. Malcolm's drunken whore
of a mother had sold him to a Glaswegian ship's captain back in
1665. He had been seven years old.

"Joe and I will miss yer fatherly presence," he said, stripping the
meat off a drumstick. "We'll be naked babes among the wolves."

"After three years with you on the islands, I've taught you all I
know," said Tom. "You can look out for each other. Joe's handy in
a tight spot. So are you, if you keep your temper and don't get into
quarrels over trifles. It'll be like Port Royal, except afloat. Just tell
Joe to keep his voice down. That Papist bastard Fitzgerald is making
Irishmen more hated than they already are. He sailed into Havana
with eight Jamaica privateers hanging from his yards last month."

The more they talked and chewed their food, the less Tom felt
inclined to discuss his departure to Emden. He was saying goodbye
to the climate and way of life that had molded him for ten years.
Compared to London, Amsterdam, or even Canterbury, which were
the only European cities he had seen, Port Royal was a shabby
commercial district, surrounded by five forts, bristling with guns,
on a thin strip of sand. At any given time, half the inhabitants were
mortally ill. Everything and everybody had to be imported. The
only cheap goods came from piracy. The thin neck of the Palisades
Road attached the forts to the steaming bulk of Jamaica to the North.
There, the old Spanish ranches were overgrown and the cattle ran
wild. Escaped slaves lived in the mountains. Without the Port Royal
Battle Station, it could all be snatched away from England at any
moment. That, Tom realized, was what he would miss most; the
constant anxiety of surviving on the edge of destruction in the middle
of a hostile sea. He could do without that. His nostrils twitched.
Slaves swept up the last of the fish market rubbish. The smell of

roasting Christmas beef, spreading from scores of little yards and tavern kitchens, saturated the heavy air. Cockroaches the size of dates crawled out of the brickwork to spread their wings.

"Christ's Thorns! Look yonder!" Malcolm pointed a chicken bone through the window at a spectacular whore in an open carriage. "It must be that Belle Beaumont everybody's yapping about."

Malcolm swung a leg over the sill to get a better view. Belle floated down the street, reclining between two solemn black pageboys. They wore scarlet livery. One held a parasol over her head while the other fanned her neck. Belle modelled herself after Louise de Kerouaille, King Charles' French mistress. Auburn ringlets framed her baby face. Her flowing crimson dress revealed perfect white breasts, down to the nipples, with a silk rose in the cleavage. The coachman, in an officer's jacket, handled the magnificent pair of black geldings through the crowd at a leisurely pace. A musketeer from Fort Carlisle acted as footman. Sunbeams flashed off the gilded carriage work. Belle proceeded into Lime Street. A throng of young blades trailed behind her, shouting cheerful obscenities.

"You don't see one like that every day," said Tom. "A beautiful picture! Burn it into your mind. The memory will sustain you on your travels."

"I want more than a bloody picture," muttered Malcolm. "I'd be glad to die for one night with yon bitch. She saw me. By Christ, I swear she winked at me." He climbed down from the window into the market place to catch a last glimpse.

The harlot's progress, the festive spirit, and a jaunty tune from the fiddler had helped to fill the hat of an old beggar known as Dancing Danny. The ragged apparition hobbled into the bar. He collapsed, twitching, into a seat near the door, scattering coins onto the table. Tom shuddered. There was something familiar about the wretch.

Squeaker drained a mug of raw cane spirit from a cask and slammed it down on the beggar's table. He stepped back, folded his arms, and waited. Dancing Danny's right knee pumped up and down. It had a life of its own, out of time with the fiddle music. When he reached for the mug, his wrinkled claw trembled with increasing violence. At that rate, the liquid would never reach his shrunken lips. A sly smirk spread across Squeaker's face. By the fifth attempt, Danny's entire body jerked like a fish on a hook. Squeaker's face compressed, holding in the laughter. His shoulders shook almost as much as the beggar's.

Tom walked over and smashed a fist into the boy's unblemished eye. "There," he spat, sending Squeaker onto the bricks in a cloud of sawdust. "Now you have a perfect pair of matching peepers."

Beneath the wild beard, torn shirt, and blotchy features, Tom had recognized Dancing Danny as his old captain, Daniel Searles from Morgan's 1671 expedition. While Panama burned, a Spanish galleon escaped with the port's dignitaries and the bulk of their gold, silver, and jewelry. The *Santisima Trinidad,* commanded by the wily Don Francisco de Peralta, vanished among the islands in the Gulf. Morgan ordered Searles to speed ahead in a fast sloop and wait for this treasure ship on Taboga Island, with its high lookout point. He was confident that Searles could outstrip the galleon before she reached the sea-lane to Lima.

Peralta bided his time. The vessel was packed with nuns and short of water. He sent boats to fill barrels in the jungle streams. The *Santisima Trinidad,* invisible behind the tree line of the forest along the west coast of the same island, waited for a strong breeze. Meanwhile, on the north side, Searles' crew went ashore. Their sloop rode at anchor before the fishing village. They listened for their man with the spyglass, under the big wooden cross on the peak, to fire his musket as soon as he spotted the Spaniard's sail. Then, they fell into the arms of the local whores and drank themselves into a stupor.

Tom had been that lookout man. When his musket shot cracked over the dawn chorus of the next day, the pirate crew slept on. Tom fired again. He swung the glass towards the beach. A small group staggered in the mud at low tide. They could not see the galleon since it was obscured by the high ground. One discharged a pistol at the sky and fell over. The others looked about groggily, shrugged, and returned to the village. Tom reloaded and fired five times, to no avail. The *Santisima Trinidad* slipped slowly over the western horizon. Soon the tiny dot in the circle of the eyepiece vanished altogether. The lost treasure amounted to four times the quantity captured during the entire cruise. Each man in the fleet could have been set up for life. Searles lay snoring, flat on his face, under a table. That set the pattern for the rest of his sorry existence. Morgan never spoke to him again.

Tom forced a mouthful of firewater between Dancing Danny's toothless gums, whispering, "Steady, Cap'n. Steady as she goes. Down the hatch. Swallow it down. All the way down."

The convulsions subsided with each gulp. Daniel Searles no longer bounced. He drank unassisted. Squeaker raised himself on all fours. Tom aimed a boot at the boy's backside, propelling him onto the porch. The brat ran off to find the doorman, howling. A minute later, Long Ben dragged Squeaker back into the bar by the ear. "This lad has a complaint against you, Tom."

Tom pointed at Dancing Danny. The doorman tut-tutted and gave Squeaker's ear a savage twist. "You've been told before, you indentured idiot: no fun and games with Dancing Danny. Now fetch more red-eye for Captain Searles and be quick about it."

Ben hurled the prankster towards the barrels. He almost collided with Malcolm, back from ogling Belle Beaumont. The Scotsman had found an object worthy of his affections. He planned to do something about it. He sat down next to Tom with a sigh. "It's all or nothing. They'll be fighting three brace of gamecocks at The Mermaid later. I'll wager all my blunt. I'll track the Beaumont bitch down and ram her cross-eyed. I will not be needing money in Morant Bay anyway."

"How do you intend to get there?" asked Tom.

"Some of Joe's mates from The Seven Stars are leaving in a boat tomorrow. There's room for two more. Three if need be."

"Forget it. I told you already, I'm staying here."

A group of Christmas revelers entered the taproom. Tom watched Long Ben haul the barely-conscious Dancing Danny outside. The old beggar had drunk himself stupid in less than five minutes. His bare heels left parallel lines in the sawdust. A damp smear remained on his chair. It was better to die of a musket ball than end up like that, thought Tom...or in a Dutch feather bed. He imagined himself in expensive clothes swanning around Hamburg, pausing to take snuff from a golden box.

Malcolm cut into his reverie, "What have ye got in the bundle, Tom?"

"That? A bargain from a Massachusetts Bay merchant," he lied quickly. "Come upstairs, I'll show you."

They were examining the hunting rifle when Joseph returned from his tryst with the fishwife.

He stared at the contents of the beaded shot pouch spread on the mattress.

"I see it comes with its own wee surgeon's bag." He picked up a spare spring. The heap included a turn screw, pin punch, Dutch flints, a lead ladle, and a ball mound.

Tom added his pride and joy—a powder flask he had crafted from the shell of a giant sea snail—to the collection. Having measured a charge with the little bullhorn cylinder hung round his neck, he rammed a ball down the barrel, with a leather patch to secure the shot.

"There," Tom smiled. "Ready for action! You can have my old matchlock, Joe. Coxon won't allow you on board without one. The Brethren fire volleys, like the New Model Army."

"Don't mention those New Model bastards," said the Irishman. "My father told me all about them."

"You'd better keep such opinions to yourself, Joe," said Tom. "And don't cross yourself in public. Where you are going, not everybody is as tolerant as Malcolm and myself."

"Huh?" Joseph was offended.

"Look," said Tom, "you know I don't care if you worship a pig's turd, but it's different on the main. If you are captured, the Dons will let you, as a Papist, live. They'll hang your shipmates, or hand them to the Inquisition. That causes resentment. The likes of Philip Fitzgerald, attacking us from Cuba, make it worse. All I'm saying is, be careful."

"Dinna fret, Tom," said Malcolm, adjusting his profusely

feathered hat, "I'll watch the Hibernian oaf's back."

"They'll be too distracted by the palm tree on your noggin to pay me any mind," said Joseph, pointing to the Scotsman's hat.

"When are they fighting the cocks?" asked Tom.

"At sunset, behind The Mermaid," said Malcolm. "After that, with a bit of luck, Bonny Belle will be fighting my cock."

"The lads with the fishing boat are in The Seven Stars now," said Joseph. "Will you come and share a jar of scalteen with us, Tom? A farewell drink?

"Not now," said Tom. "I'll catch up with you at The Mermaid."

"No later than six bells," said Malcolm, "or ye will never find us in the crush. Lead the way to the punchbowl, Joe. Old Tom won't rest until he's tested that new musket on some innocent water fowl."

Malcolm was right. Thomas descended to the empty mud flat west of Fort Morgan. He knelt and primed the touchhole. The hammer engaged the spring with a satisfying click. The front sight appeared as a little button between two ridges on the breech. He saw these with less clarity, but well enough to do the job. The button settled under the belly of a sandpiper, fifty yards away on the waterline. Better to aim low, to allow for the kick. A movement on the shining sand to the right distracted him. A pie-billed grebe waddled into view and looked straight at him. He swung the sight until it trembled slightly beneath the new target. The explosion drove the butt into his shoulder. The heavy ball went down the grebe's throat and flew out of its backside in a shower of bloody feathers. It completely dismembered the bird. Tom had never seen such accuracy. He hummed to himself as he reloaded the weapon, slid it into the scabbard, and slung it over his shoulder. He had stuffed his pearls into the bottom of the shot pouch. Squeaker would be looking for revenge. It would be stupid to leave temptation in his path, especially on Tom's last night at The Three Mariners.

The inn, with Thea close at hand, was the nearest thing to a home for Tom. Now, he had lost his taste for the place. Dancing Danny's appearance had shaken him. God forbid that he should end his days like that! Well, God had given him an opportunity. He would wait for the lads to depart for Morant Bay and then decamp to Arnout's chambers in The Dolphin. There, the drunks were helped up to their rooms by valets, not tossed into the gutter like sacks of rubbish. He wondered what shade of satin suited him best. Should he opt for a dazzling crimson display? Cloth of silver, like a Don? He cackled as he imagined himself as a fop. He might have to learn how to dance properly, instead of scampering around the room like an ape with a knife between his teeth. Tom laughed out loud at the thought.

The sinking sun threw the battlements of Fort James, with the tall masts beyond, into relief against the blue and red of the western sky. The bells of Port Royal's two churches peeled in the liquid air. Tom leaned his back against the wall of Fort Morgan's battery. It had been an eventful day. Now, an orange glow suffused everything. The tide swept away the remains of the grebe. He lit his pipe and gazed out to sea, where the *Eenhoorn* would appear any day now. The tobacco gave him a sweet sensation of peace. His pipe fell into the sand. He was fast asleep.

He awoke to find the sea lapping at his feet. The cannon on Fort Charles boomed out a salute to the east. It was almost dark. Tom picked up his pipe, adjusted the rifle on his shoulder and skirted along the wall. He hurried along the battlements towards The Old Church. On the corner opposite the graveyard, pitch torches burned in the street. The overspill of customers from The Mermaid sat on chairs pulled out of the tavern. A group of New Englanders, in black clothes, tall hats, and starched collars, stared in horror at Port Royal's emerging nightlife. One stout Boston trader swatted away a prostitute with his old Geneva Bible, cursing her for daring to lay her polluted hands on The Lord's Elect. She told him to wipe his ass with the Book of Exodus.

A section of the crowd was in high spirits, chanting 'Old King Cole' and adding bawdy lyrics. The landlord, a retired sea rover called Muddy Morris, walked among the revelers singing the praises of his stable of whores. He was particularly proud of Agnes and Esmeralda, 'The Egyptian Sisters,' part of a vagrant family transported to the Indies from Putney Heath. Morris advertised them as "real white heathens, who will serve you as a pair, with all the fiery passion of their nation, if you be man enough."

"If ye be mad enough," said Malcolm, ladling punch into Joseph's leather mug. "After emptying yer pockets, they'll leave ye with a double dose of Royal Egyptian Pox."

"Leave off blathering about those poor girls," said Joseph. "I knew their mother before she hung herself for shame, in this very place." He spotted Tom approaching from the churchyard and waved his straw hat. "Ahoy, Tom! Here's a chair for you! Come on, have a drink, we're down to the strippens."

Tom sat down beside them. Sensing their intention to get him drunk, he sipped slowly. The syrupy mixture at the bottom of the bowl was deceptively strong. The crowd roared boisterously all around. Dice rattled on the barrelheads. He thought it wise to keep his head in such a volatile atmosphere. Malcolm made another effort to convince Tom to join them in Morant Bay. "A quick raid on Vera Cruz or Portobello, and we'll be back before ye know it. What in blazes will you do here in the meantime? Grow mushrooms in yer beard?"

Tom improvised rapidly, "You've heard of the Columbus gold mine?"

Malcolm snorted. "That old wives' tale!"

"Old Abraham Henriquez says he can find it," said Tom, embroidering his story. "He has documents written in ancient Hebrew by Columbus himself, when Jamaica was his private family estate. Maps and bearings. The Jews are privy to many secrets. Columbus shielded them from the Inquisition. Abraham needs hunters to accompany his search party, to keep them in fresh meat. I'll get paid well, whatever happens. Maybe in golden nuggets. I won't be growing mushrooms. Don't be surprised if I'm a rich man when you see me again."

"I heard that Columbus story in The Seven Stars," said Joseph. "The Duke of York sent men to investigate. Nothing. It's fairy dust. If there was any gold, the Jews would have bagged it long ago."

"Jings! Ye'll be seeing us in The Mariners loaded with Spanish silver, Tom," said Malcolm,

"In a few weeks, ye'll be begging us for the price of a drink before ye see a speck of any gold. I hope the Israelite pays ye well for yer trouble."

"Go on, laugh," said Tom, "but I'd rather look for something right under my nose than try and claw it from the Dons hundreds of miles away."

"Aye, if ye say so," said Malcolm resignedly. "Perhaps ye can ask one of yer circumcised wizards to prophesy the winners of this cock fight too. Come, they are opening the pit."

Tom had half a mind to tell them the truth, but it seemed pointless now. The crowd surged towards the gate.

The Mermaid's cockpit occupied an enclosed yard behind the tavern. Being a serious event, it cost an entire Spanish real to enter. Torches, flickering on the low barrier round the sandy circle, gave the spectators a demonic appearance. Disheveled whores and their clients lounged on the overlooking balconies. A crude painting of a gamecock with outspread wings and enormous spurs dominated the rear wall, like the coat of arms on a Hapsburg galleon's mainsail.

The brawny pit master examined the first pair of roosters. He ran his hands over their feathers, checking that they were free of grease. Satisfied, he roared above the din, "On my right, I give you The Red Avenger; on my left, Lucky Lucifer!"

The handlers faced each other, crouching. The cock's plucked heads strained forward, beak to beak. In his eagerness, Lucky Lucifer nearly wriggled out of his mulatto handler's grasp. The spectators began to place bets. Malcolm noticed a fat, well-dressed merchant offering five pesos on Lucifer, so he shook hands and matched him, backing The Red Avenger. Tom nudged Joseph and jerked his chin in the merchant's direction. The man had two big ruffians, their eyes half-closed, at his shoulders. They carried clubs with knobbly ends.

Tom whispered, "Slide round behind those dogs, Joe. If Mal wins, they might need restraining."

The pit master raised his hand. In the hush that followed, he yelled, "Set to!" His slave blew a deep blast through a conch shell. Lucifer drew first blood and pursued The Avenger to the edge. The whores on the balconies shrieked. The crowd became uproarious, urging the birds on to the kill. They did not have long to wait. The Red Avenger tired of being chased. He flapped up into the air and sliced out one of his assailant's eyes with his spur. After that, it was quickly over for Lucifer, who staggered round in a bloody arc before collapsing under a merciless barrage of pecks. The Red Avenger went for the eye wound again and again, until the point of his beak pricked the brain and sent Lucifer into his death spasms.

"Five pieces of eight, if ye please, sir," Malcolm grinned. His dream of bedding Belle Beaumont had taken a step towards becoming reality. He imagined nuzzling her long white neck, tracing her perfume down to her breasts. The fat gentleman's bullies shifted their weight from foot to foot as Malcolm took the coins. They raised the stakes for the second fight. The merchant's bird hacked away for a quarter of an hour, wearing his opponent down until he bled to death. Malcolm watched his hopes drip into the sand. He handed his money over before the damned creature had stopped twitching. He had one more chance, but his purse was almost empty.

"Come," he said, turning to Tom, "it's our last night. Help me with the third wager, Tom. We cannot leave it like this."

They counted a mixture of pesos, pistoles, and florins into Tom's hat. The merchant introduced himself as Sir Digby Townsend, a director of the Royal Africa Company, appointed by the Duke of York himself. He insisted on knowing their names, which Malcolm quickly blurted out as Mr. Munro and Mr. Sheppard. Tom glowered, but there was no stopping Malcolm in such a mood. Discretion had never been his strong point. Tom relaxed, consoling himself with the thought that he would be bound for Europe within a few days. Sir Digby's stake included a shiny new Louis d'Or, a rarity even in Port Royal. He quickly calculated the exchange rates. The Louis, he reckoned, was worth eight pesos. The entire pot came to over five guineas. Sir Digby gripped one edge of the hat brim, Tom the other. They tried to look nonchalant about the small fortune in their hands, but their fingernails dug deep into the felt.

Gambling fever spread through the crowd. Apart from coins, the shouting mob brandished watches, hats, wigs, swords, gold chains, snuff boxes, rings, silver-topped canes—anything to stay in the game. The whores joined in, lifting up their skirts and offering odds for what lay beneath. The noise could be heard from The Turtle Crawls to Gallows Point. Meanwhile, the handlers prepared Harry Hotspur and Don Carlos The Spanish Slasher for the fray, strapping on their spurs. The pit master orchestrated the atmosphere to the point of hysteria. He sent the handlers round the ring with the birds raised above their heads. They completed three circuits amid shrieking pandemonium.

Joseph stood silently behind Sir Digby's bodyguards. He suspected they were his countrymen, perhaps from Dublin itself. They refrained from shouting, but he heard the pockmarked oaf utter something like "tare an ages." Joseph's father had often used that very expression, referring to the tears and aches of Christ, as he slaved in the cane fields.

The conch boomed again. Malcolm backed the black rooster, Don Carlos, against Sir Digby's choice, Harry Hotspur. The well-matched cocks flapped, hacked, and pecked in the torchlight. They had stamina. After ten minutes, feathers and gouts of blood covered the ground, but they showed no sign of tiring. After fifteen, red streaks shone on the cheeks of the spectators straining over the barrier. Tom tightened his grip on the hat. Sir Digby was beside himself. His double chin wobbled as he bawled, "Kill him! Kill him, Harry! Murder the black bastard!" Saliva sprayed from his mouth. Not to be outdone, Malcolm roared, "Give him yer spur, Carlos! Tear out his guts!"

The birds began to move more slowly. Don Carlos soared upwards with a final burst of energy. Harry Hotspur sank his beak into his enemy's exposed neck as it came down, but received a spur in the thigh. It went in deep, cutting the tendon. Blood squirted from the wound in regular bursts. Harry could barely hop away. Sir Digby covered his eyes with his free hand. The two ruffians shuffled uneasily. Malcolm raised his extravagantly plumed hat on the point of his sword in a heroic pose. "Finish it, Carlos, ye bonny fechter!" he yelled. "He limps! He's scuttled!"

Harry Hotspur could no longer defend himself. He tried to flee, clawing at the sand with one foot, but it was hopeless. The punishment continued. Soon he was a bundle of twitching feathers. The pit master declared Don Carlos the winner. The handlers gathered up the stricken birds and swaddled them in cloth. Loud arguments broke out at once. Angry losers invaded the cockpit. A toothless old man snatched Don Carlos from his handler and held the bird aloft. "Look!" he yelled, harp strings of spittle stretching between his rotten gums. "The bloody thing is bled to death! How can it be the winner?" It was true, Don Carlos hung limp above the crowd. The neck wound had drained the life out of him. Others ran towards Harry. His feet jerked and trembled. "Look," they screamed, "Harry is still moving!" They were witnessing the death spasms. "Harry is the winner!"

The pit master, a bearded giant, stood his ground. He gathered the handlers and the slave with the conch around him, drew his pistol, and fired a shot in the air. The crowd fell silent. He cleared his throat and growled, "It was a fair fight. Don Carlos clearly won. That is the end of it! The law says, if the public takes the birds, anyone can break their necks, and it means nothing! My decision stands! Don Carlos!"

That might have been the end of it, but while the pit master spoke, a drunkard sneaked up behind him with a torch. He succeeded in setting fire to the slave's shirt. The slave smashed the drunk's skull with the heavy conch, and then rolled in the sand to extinguish the flames. A group of the drunk's friends snatched up more torches and advanced on the slave, shouting, "Burn him! He struck a white man!"

At this point, a man on a whore's balcony aimed a jet of piss at the burning slave, but he could not make the distance. He sprayed a section of the crowd instead, including the torchbearers, who turned their attention to the wooden balcony. Somebody screamed, "Fire!"

31

The pit master disappeared under a heaving mass of bodies. They trampled the smoldering slave into the dirt. The contents of tankards and chamber pots splashed down onto the torches, followed by a whore's Turkish carpet. A coconut shattered her window. Everybody began to exchange blows indiscriminately. The losing gamblers seized the opportunity to avoid paying. With most of the torches extinguished, the brawlers flailed at each other in near darkness.

When he heard the pistol shot, Sir Digby momentarily lost his grip on the hat with the money. Tom did not wait. The merchant had lost, and that was that. Tom hugged the hat to his chest, bent low, and shoved hard towards the gate. He felt Sir Digby's hand tighten on the strap of his rifle sling, turned his head and sank his teeth into the fat fingers, to the bone. Sir Digby squealed and Tom broke free. The two ruffians, advancing with their clubs raised, never saw Joseph tearing off their caps and cracking their skulls together from behind. As they slid to the ground, Joseph noticed Malcolm sheathing his sabre and bending low to pick up his precious feathered beaver. Their eyes met before the crush of bodies pushed Malcolm back into the cockpit. His hat vanished. He shouted above the din, "Run, Joe! Look after Tom and the money! I'll see ye back at The Mariners!" Sir Digby nursed his bitten fingers, staring at his fallen henchmen and at Malcolm. Had that loud Scottish bastard murdered them? He turned helplessly, trying to catch a glimpse of Tom among the swirling shadows.

Tom felt Joseph thrust him through the tangle of spectators blocking the gate. Once clear, they hurried into the graveyard behind The Old Church. Crouching in the shadows of the tombstones, they had a clear view of the throng outside The Mermaid. Disheveled figures staggered into the hazy light of a lantern. Eventually, Malcolm's long black curls appeared. He tried to look nonchalant and began to wander past The Old Church. Tom pursed his lips to give the low hoot of a burrowing owl, a signal the friends often used in Hispaniola. It did the trick. Malcolm came and squatted beside them.

"Oons," he panted. "Fine entertainment. I lost my hat in that stramash. Ye still have the money?"

"Hush," said Tom. He studied the faces emerging from the cockpit. "There's the fat son of a bitch now, with his two bullies."

On the corner, Sir Digby tore a strip of lace off his sleeve to bind his bleeding fingers and berated the ruffians. They rubbed their heads and shrugged their shoulders. The Mermaid's doorman joined them, engaged in a heated discussion, and vanished. He returned with half a dozen others brandishing torches, staves, and swords. Without glancing at the graveyard, they marched off along the sea front towards Fort Morgan with Sir Digby in the lead.

"Off they go with a flea in their ear," said Malcolm. "Let's see the winnings."

"Not now," said Tom. "We'll share it out in peace at The Mariners. You can go a-whoring as much as you want afterwards."

They crept round the church and came out onto the bustling High Street, giving The Mermaid a wide berth. Tom, still pressing the hat to his body, thought he saw Arnout's blue satin suit through the window of The Pineapple Chambers, but decided not to stop. Sir Digby was bound to have friends at the card tables. They approached the western jetties without incident and arrived at the fish market.

A boy's voice rang out, "There they are, Sir Digby! That's them!"

In The Mariners' porch, Squeaker plucked the fat merchant's sleeve and pointed directly at Tom and Malcolm. Joseph had ducked back into an alleyway. Eight ruffians surged across the market place. Sir Digby waddled behind, egging them on, "A guinea for the man who rescues my winnings! There! The bearded bastard with the blue cheek has 'em in his hat!"

"I'll be damned," said Malcolm. "They knew where to go."

Tom hissed, "Your big mouth, Mal. You gave our names and shouted about The Mariners, remember?"

They followed Joseph into the dark passage.

"I'll put it right then," said Malcolm. He knelt behind a barrel and cocked his pistols. Tom pushed Joseph towards the wharf. "The boat," he urged. "Make for the boat, Joe!"

A doorman from The Mermaid loomed in the mouth of the alley.

Malcolm's shot knocked him down. A hoarse roar came from the market. Sir Digby's scream trilled above it, "Murder! Thieves! Get them! Two guineas!"

The wounded man squirmed on the ground, his legs thrashing. "I'm gut shot! Oh, mercy, I'm gut shot!"

Malcolm tipped the barrel onto its side and kicked it at the five men rushing towards him. He fired his second shot at the leader. The man collapsed, wedged between the barrel and the wall, blocking the way. Malcolm hurled one empty pistol after the other into his pursuers' faces and drew his Turkish sabre. The razor-sharp Damascus blade sliced off the fingers of a hand trying to shift the barrel. With the mutilated man's screams ringing in his ears, Malcolm took to his heels.

A large mob gathered in the fish market, some to watch, some to join in the chase. Sir Digby raised the reward to three guineas. It had become a matter of prestige. The validity of his claim to the winnings was irrelevant. He was after murderers. He represented the law. Shadowy figures poured out of the alleys between the Turtle Crawls and Fort Charles, heading towards the Chocoletta Hole jetty.

Joseph sat at the oars. Tom pointed his new rifle inland from behind the tiller, the hat at his feet. He saw Malcolm racing along the wharf side, sabre drawn, pursued by the screaming crowd. Sir Digby's two henchmen led the pack. Tom picked up the hat. Only one thing could save Malcolm now. Tom took out the gleaming Louis d'Or, clamped it between his teeth, and threw the rest of the money at the advancing horde. Everybody stopped to scramble and fight over the last peso and florin. Only Sir Digby's two ruffians kept coming. Tom let them approach. He could barely align the sights in the gloom.

The leading ruffian tripped Malcolm, kicked his sabre aside, planted a foot on his chest, and raised his club for a deathblow. For a moment, he was outlined against the dim radiance of Port Royal. His pockmarked comrade panted a few yards behind. Tom could not afford to miss. This was no waterfowl. He held his breath, aiming low for a chest shot. The recoil jarred against his shoulder. It moved the boat forward, which brought the muzzle up higher. The ball carried away the man's lower jaw. The pockmarked oaf stood still, transfixed by the sight of his mate's tongue flapping over his mangled throat. Malcolm sprang to his feet, retrieved the sabre, and hacked into the man's gurgling wound. The head came clean away, thudding to the ground a few seconds before the body. Malcolm covered the remaining distance in a flash and leapt into the skiff. Tom pushed the boat off with his rifle butt. Joseph rowed into the pool with mighty strokes. In all their years escaping from Spanish patrols, they had never moved so fast.

The pockmarked henchman splashed into the water. With a roar, he clawed his upper body over the stern, strong as a madman. The gold coin fell from Tom's lips. "Quick, Joe! The blunderbuss!"

Joseph, rowing hard, spat out, "Not loaded!" Malcolm raised his blade, but was unable to use it for fear of cutting into the wrong man. By now, the ruffian had a hold on Tom's neck. The skiff rocked from side to side. Tom found a broken clay pipe in his hatband beneath the tiller. He drove the jagged stem firmly through one of his attacker's staring eyes, into the brain. The man gave a compressed groan, blowing foul odors. His mouth smelled like a plague pit. The hand round Tom's throat tightened, even in death. It took considerable strength to wrench it off. Tom waggled the tiller to and fro to dislodge the body, which slid into the water.

"Jesus," said Malcolm, "those hell hounds were hard to kill!"

"The main thing," said Tom, "is the bastards are dead. Now, let's get out of here."

The skiff's shallow keel scraped over the sand bar guarding Chocoletta Hole. They entered the harbor mouth behind Fort Walker. Sir Digby's fat figure wobbled above the turtle cages on the waterfront opposite the battlements, waving his bandaged fist. The mob stood around him in a long line. A few leveled firearms, hoping to gain favor with such a grand Royal Africa Company officer, but most cheered lustily, which made him more furious. He shrieked, "Shoot them! Somebody shoot them!"

The pockmarked ruffian's corpse rolled onto its back, drifting towards the snapping turtles. The clay pipe bowl protruded from his eye socket like an egg. Raucous laughter broke out when somebody imitated Sir Digby's high-pitched voice and yelled, "Shoot them! Somebody shoot them!" Pistols and muskets flashed, sending up spouts around the boat. Tom swung the tiller, taking them into the open sea. The Turtle Crawls vanished behind the fort. The last thing they saw was a sentry peering down at them, wondering what all the commotion was about.

A warm land breeze filled the sail. They swept into the stream past Drunken Man's Key. Joseph stowed the oars. Malcolm lowered the leeboards into the swell. Tom concentrated on finding the Louis d'Or in the stern. Having found it, he ran his thumbnail over the milled edge and finely engraved curls of the Sun King's full-bottomed wig. All was quiet except for the waves chopping against the side. The moon silvered the edge of a great black cloud to the south.

Joseph broke the silence, "That was a beautiful decapitation, so it was. The finest I've ever seen."

"Does this mean…?" began Malcolm.

"Yes. Damn you. We are fugitives," said Thomas. He could scarcely believe that they had only made harbor on the day before. Had he dreamt it? "Damn you and be thankful it is night, or we'd die of thirst. We have nothing to drink and long hours to Morant Bay." In a low voice, he added, "Merry Christmas."

3
MORANT BAY

Thirst tormented them all night as they sailed east. They did not stop. The breeze sped them along. Eventually, a glow on the bow heralded Christmas Day, 1679. Three merchant ships and a pair of sloops stood outlined against the rising ball of the sun. All was quiet in Morant Bay. Tom steered towards the shacks and canvas awnings under the palms. Steep mountains formed a dark wall to the north. Boats and canoes nestled on the sand. Cicada song seemed to come from all directions at once. At this cool hour, it was muted and strangely comforting.

"Water," rasped Tom, angling the stern to receive the force of the breakers. He did not need to tell the lads to raise the leeboards, jump into the waves, and steady the skiff. He leapt out last, up to his waist in surf, pushing from behind.

A lone cock crowed. None of the figures under the awnings stirred, not even the slaves. They lay in contorted positions like corpses. Smoldering remains of barbecue pits, surrounded by chewed animal bones and empty jars, dotted the shore. Malcolm stumbled to the nearest shelter to fetch a gourd full of water from a butt.

"Jesus," gasped Joseph. "Another minute and I would have drunk my own piss, so I would."

They slaked their thirst and slumped against the hull, surveying the scene through half-closed eyes. Tom climbed into the skiff, pulled down the sail, and rolled it into a big cushion. He tugged off his shoes and soaking breeches, tipped his hat over his face, and was soon snoring. Malcolm and Joseph slept where they sat, gradually keeling over onto the sand.

Tom had no idea where he was when he awoke. He vaguely remembered an appointment for lunch with Arnout Van Tonder in The Dolphin. Then he heard shouts, the cries of seagulls, and splashing breakers. The cicada chorus drilled into his ears. His skin prickled in the heat under his coarse linen shirt. He lifted his hat and blinked in the sudden glare. A pair of watery grey pupils, swimming in yellow malarial eyeballs, stared back at him. The thin lips, sunk in a bleached, wispy beard, displayed a row of rotten teeth and said, "Well, well, well, what have we here? If it ain't me old dicing mate from The Three Mariners. Merry Christmas, Mr. Sheppard. Not too grand for us now, eh?"

Tom recognized the wheedling cockney voice. "Captain Sharp," he began, "I must…"

"Stow it, Tom," said Bartholomew Sharp. "Your Scottish friend told me all about last night in Port Royal."

Tom spotted Malcolm cooling his feet in the surf. Joseph squatted under a nearby awning, in deep conversation with a short, curly-headed fellow. All around, the beach teemed with seamen and slaves, digging pits above the tide line and setting up tables with planks and barrels. They rolled hogsheads of Canary wine into place, ready for the main Christmas feast at sunset. Sharp swung his lean, tall frame over the side and sat down. His knees almost touched his chin. He passed a lighted pipe to Tom, who puffed at it gratefully.

"Keep it," said Sharp. "I hear you left yours in somebody's head." He tipped his hat back. Tufts of hair stood out from his temples like wet straw. "So, you're hiding from Sir Digby Townsend, no less. I can't say I blame you. The fat pig has the whole garrison under his thumb. By now, half of Port Royal will be hoping to earn twenty guineas for delivering you and your mates to the hangman."

Tom pointed at Joseph. "I don't think anybody got a good look at my Irish friend, but you're right about me and Malcolm. We are marked men. Maybe Harry Morgan can protect us?"

"Forget Morgan," said Sharp. "He can barely protect himself. Sir Digby is the Duke of York's man. The Duke's a damned Papist, in love with Spain and France. The king ain't much better. He's sending a new governor from London to take Morgan's place. Why d'you think we're fitting up in this wilderness instead of the North Docks? Face it, Tom, you can't show yourself on the Turtle Crawls again until Sir Digby dies or leaves Jamaica. Could be years."

"We'll come with you, Barty," said Tom. "We'll step ashore somewhere else on the way back, hopefully with a few pieces of eight in our pockets."

"Glad to have you aboard," Sharp's lips twisted into a lop-sided smile. "I can always use a brother who's seen Panama on fire. Half these green lubbers have only dreamt about the Camino Real. You and me, matey, we've fought up and down every inch of it. Remember Fort San Lorenzo? That was real fighting, that was. We're the captains and masters now. No more clawing canvas on the yards for the likes of us." Sharp swept his arm across the bay. "Look. We're filling up the water casks, plugging holes and tarring the ratlines. More men are arriving from Port Royal every day. You'll be the talk of the town with a price on your heads. Make yourself and that Scotsman scarce for a couple of weeks."

"What will we do? Hide in the bilges?"

"Do what you always do. Have a good Christmas drink tonight. Then, go inland. There's wild pigs and goats in the hills, even a few cattle. I've got hunters upriver bagging fresh meat. Join 'em. Meantime, your Irishman can help with loading the ship. He's a fine, strong fellow. Reminds me of meself ten years back. I've got a mind to make him my standard bearer when we attack the main." Sharp thumped the side of the skiff. "Sturdy little boat you have here, complete with leeboards. We'll tie her to the stern of my ship, as my personal barge."

Tom stuck the extinguished pipe into his hatband and pointed at the ridges wreathed in blue mist. "So we'll go a-hunting, eh? Makes sense, but I only know the country as far as the Yallahs Saltpans. I hear the hills beyond are crawling with black marooners who still speak Spanish."

"Don't worry about them. They only have bows and arrows and they won't bother you unless you chase them over the mountains all the way to the Plantain River. This side is safe as far as Point Morant. Look, see that blacksmith's tent back there? Captain Mackett will tell you what to do. Your Scotsman says he has no musket. Mackett will give him an old Spanish fuzee for now. He'll let you have powder and bullets too. Don't mention the Irishman to Mackett. He hates Taigs more than Spaniards. I'll see you when we weigh anchor. Now, make yourself less obvious. Be gone by tomorrow, if you know what's good for you."

Sharp winked at Tom, heaved himself out of the skiff, and strode off chuckling to himself. His tall figure, leaning on a half-pike, was soon lost in the crowd. Slaves, clad in ragged breeches, had strung up a dozen prize cows by the hind legs. They kept the guts, heads, hooves and tails for their own use. The bulky carcasses were impaled on spits over slow fires for the crewmen. The air became heavy. Swarms of flies descended. Roast beef smells mixed with the aroma of baked dough and lard. Circular 'doughboy' loaves, oven-fresh from the ships' galleys, arrived by the boatload, to be stacked on the tables. By general agreement, the wine was to be left alone until sunset. It would be a feast as grand as anything in Port Royal, courtesy of the King of Spain's captured provisions and the offspring of Spanish cattle running wild in the overgrown meadows.

The slaves, too, had been taken from the enemy. Thomas Mackett, with Captain Robert Alliston commanding the other sloop, had boarded a Portuguese trader off Santiago de Cuba. As a result, the pirates acquired sixty Angolan males and twenty females. All had been forcibly baptized in Cape Verde and branded with a cross and an 'S,' for the merchant Da Silva. Additionally, the men's right ears had been clipped with shears, so they were known as 'the silver sheep.' Smaller than the Guinea Coast tribesmen usually imported to

Jamaica, they had barely picked up a few words of Portuguese, and were now learning to respond to orders barked at them in English. Four of the 'sheep' pumped the bellows of the clay furnace in a sweltering tent, their bodies shiny with sweat, turning their old chains into nails and bullets under the watchful eye of the blacksmith.

Mackett, called 'The Old Maggot' by his men, was a strict puritan who did not believe in Sunday, let alone such pagan feasts as Easter or Christmas. As commander of the shore party, he abstained from wine and spirits, dressing like the meanest swab. He quoted passages from the Geneva Bible, as if the end of the world was at hand. In The Old Maggot's opinion, the best way to prepare for the second coming of Christ was to stay sober and slaughter as many Roman Catholics as possible. For that, he needed bullets; many bullets. In 1661, he had fled from London to Jamaica, fearing for his life after Thomas Venner's uprising against the restored House of Stuart.

Bartholomew Sharp, only eleven years old, witnessed the bloody spectacle of Venner being hung, drawn, and quartered in Smithfield. The experience changed him. He stood and stared for a full hour at the rebel's butchered hindquarters impaled on spikes over St. John's Gate while dogs fought over the guts and genitals in the January snow. The following spring, Sharp ran away from his father's house in Stepney to join a gang of fierce street children, robbers, and male prostitutes on the Wapping waterfront. Three years later, when wagons began to carry plague victims to London's burial pits, nine of these Thames mudlarks signed on as deckhands on a West Indies merchantman. By then, Sharp had become their leader. They did not hesitate to support a mutiny and turn pirate. In 1671, they formed part of Morgan's great expedition against Panama. Now, many years and adventures later, six of that original cockney gang remained with Sharp, forming the nucleus of his crew.

When Sharp departed, Tom flapped his breeches in the breeze and pulled them on. Malcolm approached the skiff sheepishly, saying, "Sharp wouldn't stop asking questions. I had to tell him about the cockfight…"

"No harm done this time," said Tom. "Sharp'll look after us, but don't be so free with your tongue in future. There's bastards here who'd gladly knock us on the head and drag us back to Sir Digby in chains. One of these days, your big mouth will have us all dancing at the rope's end. Anyway, you and me will be in the hills by tomorrow. We're to hunt inland until we set sail. Captain's orders."

Malcolm shrugged. "Suits me. I don't see any women here."

Joseph came over with his small friend in tow. "Thomas, Malcolm," he smiled, "meet me old friend Scarrett, late of The Mermaid Tavern. He's a good man, best knife-thrower in Jamaica, and he has some powerful potcheen with him, distilled by the very devil. We can do a lot worse for a messmate, so we can."

The truth was, the Irishman had known Scarrett for years and had kept a brotherly eye on him since the diminutive Gipsy's mother, Esmeralda, had committed suicide. Poor Scarrett had been forced to work as a servant in The Mermaid's brothel, mopping up vomit and emptying the whores' piss pots, including those of Muddy Morris' famous 'Egyptian Sisters,' who comprised Scarrett's only surviving family. Scarrett had often thought of slitting his sisters' throats, and then his own, to avoid further misery, but he could not bring himself to do it. As the Christmas season progressed, Scarrett decided to escape to Morant Bay, driving a mule laden with stolen kegs of overproof rum along the coastal road, hiding by day and traveling by night. He presented one keg to Sharp.

The buccaneer captain took him on instantly, appreciating the ferocious kick of the oily white spirit as well as the nimble little man's potential, both as a thief and as an acrobat in the rigging. As for Tom, he saw a perfect partnership of agility and strength in the pairing of Scarrett with Joseph. With Malcolm and himself, the four of them would make up a well-balanced mess, the basic unit of a ship's crew. With their various talents, they were a force to be reckoned with, as long as they did not fall out. Being the most senior and experienced hand, Tom's job was to make sure that did not happen. Their lives depended on it. When external threats diminished, the sea-robbers tended to turn on each other, usually in arguments over sharing the loot, but sometimes out of simple boredom and frustration. Tom reluctantly began to think of the future, since an immediate return to Arnout in Port Royal was impossible. He reckoned he had the raw material to forge a tight group of messmates, but he would only be sure when they had been tested. For now, Joseph was happy to stay with Scarrett and the boat. Tom and Malcolm sought out Mackett.

They found The Old Maggot hunched over a steaming kettle in the shade beside the forge. Wearing only a pair of wide breeches with a sailor's knife stuck into the waistband and a threadbare Montero cap, the wrinkled puritan was stirring sugar-cane juice into a dark brew of cocoa. He lifted the ladle to his toothless mouth. After swilling it from cheek to cheek, he muttered and added a pinch of pimento. Thick drops ran down his white beard. He was absorbed in his task like a Walloon *chocolatier*, ignoring the flies that sat on his brow.

"Captain Mackett?" asked Tom.

"Aye, that be me. Take a sip," the captain spluttered, proffering the ladle. "Tell me that ain't the best cocoa soup in the world. Slowly, it's hot."

Tom blew on it before tasting. Rich, earthy fumes rose into his nasal cavity, followed by a sweet, spicy sensation as it slid down his throat. He purred like a cat, "Hmmm, that, sir, is perfection. Fit for a king."

"A pox on all kings," growled Mackett. "No royal house, excepting the heathen Emperor of Old Mexico, ever had it so fresh. I think I have the balance almost right. Maybe a twig of vanilla and a wedge of lard would give it sufficient body and bring it to its peak, but it will do. Here, sit and help me finish it. It'll set us up for the day like nothing else."

The three men made short work of the kettle, mopping it clean with strips torn from a doughboy. "Now," said Mackett, "what else do you want?"

Tom explained their situation and requirements, without mentioning the danger from Sir Digby. The Old Maggot used a nail to scratch a crude map into the dirt, outlining the ragged coastline from Cow Bay in the west to Point Morant at the eastern tip of

Jamaica. He marked a rectangle, twenty miles long and ten miles deep between the Crane and Morant rivers, the Blue Mountains and the sea.

"That," he said, "is where we hunt. There are new sugar plantations along the coast. They will offer you hospitality. In return, we will give anybody who helps us some earmarked Portuguee niggers, the ones we call our silver sheep, when we leave. The planters won't get such a bargain again, so you can expect civil treatment. The sheep will haul the carcasses to the beach from Ezra Cribben's landing, four miles up the Morant River. You can't miss it. His compound has a pair of Maroon skulls, painted and feathered like wild demons, above the gate. It is circled with thorn bushes. Ezra's boys make sure there's no pilfering. They may be mulattos, but he raised them as honest Christians."

"We'll need bullets and powder. I have special molds for my Jaeger flintlock with me." Tom pulled his hunting rifle out of its sheath. Mackett gave a low whistle through his toothless lips. "My, she's a beauty. Reminds me of a piece we found in a cavalier's baggage after Naseby. Harkee, my smith can make rounds for this barrel, and grooved swan shot bullets too, for smaller game, if you wish. You'll take a goat's eye out at a hundred yards."

"D'ye have a musket for me?" asked Malcolm.

The Old Maggot smiled when he heard the Scotsman's accent. His father's family had come to London from Edinburgh with James Stuart at the start of the century. He sprang to his feet with surprising speed and ushered them into the blacksmith's tent. Malcolm received a heavy Spanish matchlock, complete with its forked barrel-rest. Mackett soon had the slaves pumping the bellows vigorously. The smith, a brawny giant known as Iron Ned, stopped hammering out nails and began to produce ammunition from melted lumps of lead and broken chains, assisted by a young mate who was learning the trade.

"We might be gone for weeks. Forty bullets should be plenty, including the swan shot," said Tom, who had no intention of returning to the beach before the fleet departed. When Iron Ned took this to mean forty rounds each, Tom did not correct him. Each shot meant another meal or a dead enemy. Despite the weight, Tom thought he might have enough for the entire campaign by the end of the day.

Mackett kept the powder for the shore party in a separate hut, on stilts under a thick tarpaulin roof, overlayed with palm fronds in the shadow of a large rock. A slave funneled the fine black grains into flasks through a rolled leaf. He crumbled any caked lumps between his fingers. The hunters were given an extra supply in sackcloth bags, which they impregnated with tar to keep out water. After that, it was up to each man to measure the powder into a dozen wooden tubes dangling from their 'twelve apostles' shoulder straps. Many preferred to twist the powder into paper or rag cartridges, kept in varnished shot pouches. For quick loading, they tore the container open with their teeth and spat the bullet down the barrel before ramming it home. This could be dangerous, with dangling fuses and clogged vents, but surprisingly few musketeers blew their own heads off. When it came to firing volleys, English buccaneers could drive off any cavalry and out-perform the best infantry in the world. They were fine sharpshooters, too. They were so skilled at 'birding' helmsmen from canoes that few Spaniards were willing to steer a galleon in a fight. Years of experience enabled them to bend at the waist instinctively, absorbing the rocking motion of the waves, while keeping the barrel straight in a rigid grip. When hair's-breadth accuracy was required, the best marksmen fired continuously, their mates passing them loaded weapons as quickly as possible.

Tom and Malcolm spent the rest of the afternoon in hammocks behind the smithy. At sunset, Joseph and Scarrett joined them, wet and tired from the sea. Captain Sharp had insisted on touring the bay in his new "barge," as he called Tom's skiff, with the Irishman and the Gipsy as crew. They searched for turtles in the company of a Moskito Indian spearman known as William. Bartholomew Sharp loved to display his skill at 'turtle striking,' plunging the harpoon through the animal's shell with a crack, to the delighted whoops of his savage instructor.

The clanging from Iron Ned's anvil finally stopped. The furnace was left to cool. The hunters measured and packed their ammunition. Scarrett uncorked a fresh keg of his kill-devil rum. They could see the beach, bathed in a pink glow, through the undergrowth, while they remained invisible in the shadows. Flames leapt from the roasting pits. Repetitive tunes from fifes, fiddles, and Northumbrian bagpipes filtered through the palm groves. Mosquitoes whined about their ears. Soon, the waterside was as crowded as Port Royal High Street. White shirts and red sashes flickered in the dancing light. Hundreds of buccaneers gathered around the wine casks, waiting for the arrival of the commander-in-chief from his flagship and the signal to begin the feast.

John Coxon knew how to make a theatrical entrance. His jolly boat, with four oarsmen on each side and two braying trumpeters in the prow, suddenly loomed out of the waves and sped towards the beach. It crashed, fully laden, onto the sand, to be hauled clear by scores of eager hands. The rowers raised their oars vertically as he stepped out, resplendent in his plumed beaver, officer's coat, and top boots. His face, menacing under heavy black eyebrows that met in the middle, shone as red as his silk waistband. Gold braid and buttons flashed like fireflies from his sleeves and lapels. With a flourish, he fired a pistol over his head, tossed it into the air, caught the barrel, and smashed the neck off a bottle of French brandy with the butt, screaming, "Merry Christmas, you dogs!" Pouring a good measure down his throat and the rest over the bystanders, he roared, "Who'll drink to Neptune, the devil and the Admiral of the Black?"

He was answered by a great shout, "The Brethren of the Coast!" followed by a volley of shots from twenty muskets. The festivities began in earnest. Tom remembered similar gatherings in 1670, the year of the peace treaty with Spain, which Morgan had broken in such a spectacular fashion. Was there any difference between the young men now broaching the wine casks and his erstwhile comrades? They were fewer in number, for a start. Morgan had sailed with thousands. Was it his imagination, or did this mob act more like sneaking criminals than the previous generation? Tom could not tell. Maybe he was simply getting old. He spotted Scarrett coming towards their refuge in the hollow, furtively carrying a rump of roast beef. The Gipsy's hat was crammed low over his face.

"For the love of Christ, Scarrett," said Joseph, "what's eating you? The meat is free for the taking, so it is."

"Back there," Scarrett pointed towards a fire in the middle of the beach, "I saw a gang of customers from The Mermaid with Coxon's crew. They must have arrived today. One is a doorman, and two are guards from Fort James, out of uniform. There are five in all, armed to the teeth. I swear they are not here to go to the main. The bastards are after me. I'll warrant Muddy Morris sent them."

"Did they see you?" asked Tom.

"I don't think so," said Scarrett. "They were too busy drinking and talking to some cabin boy."

"Five with a cabin boy, is it? All after one Gipsy runaway?" Joseph rose to his feet. "Come, show me this cabin boy. I think I might know him."

"Take a good look but keep your heads down," said Tom. "Don't say a word. Come straight back."

When Joseph and Scarrett had gone, Tom placed the beef on a plank and began to carve it up slowly. He divided a doughboy into strips. Malcolm sighed, "We might be in for another lively night. I feel it in my water. Yon Egyptian is more trouble than he's worth."

"Be quiet and eat," said Tom. "Scarrett may have saved our skins, or that gang may simply be on the account against Spain. With luck, it will all amount to nothing."

Tom knew the Scotsman was capable of storming off and assaulting the new arrivals in the middle of the feast. He hoped the food would absorb some of the rum they had been sipping. If his worst fears proved true, clear heads would be an advantage. When they had eaten half the beef, the two men loaded their weapons, rested them against rocks within reach, sat back in their hammocks, and lit their pipes. By now the noise from the beach was considerably louder, with side drums rattling, conch shells booming, Coxon's trumpets blaring, and the occasional celebratory shot. Behind the smithy, the hammock ropes barely creaked against the tree bark.

Almost half an hour later, the bushes rustled. Scarrett led the way. Joseph pushed a small, struggling figure, pinioned at the arms. The boy's terrified eyes stared out from blackened sockets. A rag tied between his teeth reduced his shouts to muffled grunts. Snot and tears hung from his chin.

"We waited till he went for a piss in the trees," said Joseph. "Nobody noticed. They're getting drunker by the minute, so they are."

Malcolm stepped down from his hammock, knife at the ready, hissing, "What a surprise! Squeaker! I'll make ye piss and shit for the very last time, ye treacherous wee nyaff!"

"Wait," said Tom, grasping Malcolm's wrist. "There's only one way to do this properly. First, are we all agreed that this boy means death to us, and that there is no other way to silence him? I say he is irredeemable. He'd say anything now to save himself, but we all know he'd bring those bloodhounds straight to us if we let him go. That means more killing, whatever happens."

There was a pause. They looked down at their feet and nodded. Squeaker twisted in Joseph's grip. He only succeeded in making a noise that sounded like "A woo! A woo!"

"Right," said Tom, peering into the shadows to make sure they were alone, "let's get this over with. We do it together or not at all. Make it looked like he drowned. Scarrett, you're part of it too. Grab his legs. Quickly now."

They carried the boy, upside down, to the half-empty water butt behind the forge. Joseph pushed the neck down and Tom prised the fingers from the side of the barrel while Malcolm and Scarrett held up the ankles. It took an eternity for the jerking movements to reach a climax and stop. Scarrett received a final kick that bloodied his nose. When it was over, the four men sprawled hatless in the wet dirt, looking up at Squeaker's motionless legs. One foot had lost its shoe.

"Jesus, Tom," groaned Joseph. "What in God's Name have we done?"

"What we had to," said Malcolm, "The brat was the only one

who knew the three of us by sight. Don't get soft, Joe."

"It was him or us," panted Tom. "Now let's get his carcass away. I know a cliff above Yallahs, where Mount Morant meets the sea. If they ever find him, it'll look like he slipped and fell off the edge."

"That's more than two miles west," protested Malcolm, "over broken ground, in the dark."

"Very well," said Tom, "we'll bury him here. For Christ's sake, at least push his feet down."

Malcolm folded Squeaker's legs under the rim. Joseph made straight for one of the remaining kegs of rum, opened the brass tap, lifted it to his lips, and took a shuddering gulp. He shook his hair like a wet dog and belched. "I meant to tell you, the boy was not alone. Long Ben from The Mariners was with him, along with the four other bastards."

Scarrett muttered a Gipsy oath. He leaned back to stop his nosebleed. The rest were speechless. Tom rose wearily and rummaged inside the blacksmith's tent. He emerged holding a spade and a shovel. "Come on," he said, throwing the shovel at Joseph, "first things first. There, under the big rock."

They dug down three feet, while Malcolm crashed about in the bushes looking for the missing shoe. He threw it onto Squeaker's chest in the shallow grave. Joseph swore, slotted it onto Squeaker's foot, and tenderly removed the gag. He dug in his pockets for two coins to place on the staring eyes. "There now," he said, "Pay the ferryman and don't be coming back to haunt us."

Tom lowered his head wearily, "Amen to that. You're better off out of it, you little bugger."

After covering the corpse with earth, they piled a big boulder and loose stones on top. Malcolm swept the area with a palm leaf to obliterate their footprints. Scarrett passed the keg round. It was soon empty. They should have been roaring drunk, but they did not feel it.

"Right," said Tom, "we'll get away from this accursed place. Not a word of this to anyone. The boy was never here. Pick up your things, all of them. We're going to find Sharp."

The four messmates picked up their belongings and hurried

away from the gloomy hollow as if pursued by a phantom. Scarrett shouldered his final keg of rum. Malcolm went ahead, cutting through the undergrowth. They did not stop until they passed the last group of revelers at the eastern end of the beach, where the glow from the fires gave way to thick tropical night. Waves thumped steadily onto the sand, overwhelming the shouts and music. The moon was a misty stain reflected in the water.

"Where did you see 'em?" Tom asked. "How far along the shore?"

"Past the mid-point," said Joseph. "A good way from here, so it was. Coxon's flag marks the spot, a red sheet on a pole, with tassels and ribbons. There's a lively crowd around it, but you can't miss it."

"No sense in wasting time," said Tom. "We'll walk down together. That way, if they decide to search in this direction, we can hit them with all our force. As soon as you see 'em, point 'em out, so we don't shoot the wrong men. Prime your pieces. Leave Long Ben to me."

"I'll blast 'em and chop 'em into dog meat," spat Malcolm. "This has gone on long enough, by God's Gristle."

"Don't go off half-cocked, Mal," said Tom. "Hopefully, we'll find Sharp first. Now, look carefree, but keep your peepers open."

They began to walk slowly towards the festivities. They tipped their hats low over their eyes, except for Malcolm, whose hair streamed loose over his shoulders.

Half a mile to the west, Long Ben ignored his comrades under the admiral's red banner. The Three Mariners' doorman did not want to be there. It had taken Sir Digby's threats of having him flogged through the streets and locked up in Fort James to make him join the manhunt. He hated the bruisers from The Mermaid and the soldiers almost as much as he despised the wretched Squeaker. The brat's eagerness to please Sir Digby had led to the present situation. Long Ben had sailed with Morgan. This mission was beneath him. He was happy to drown his sorrows among the sea rovers and put Port Royal out of his mind completely. He refilled his mug of Canary wine often, pausing to puff fiercely on his pipe.

Roderick Hughes, the ginger-headed doorman known as Red

Rod at The Mermaid, thrust his freckled face at Ben and hissed, "The boy is taking an awful long time pissing."

Ben shrugged. "He's probably fallen asleep somewhere, away from those bloody trumpets. It's past his bedtime. Why don't you go and find him and tuck him in?"

The other doorman, a balding ruffian with warts called Sully, plucked Ben's sleeve. "He's in your charge. God help you if we lose him."

Long Ben shook the man's hand off. "Don't discuss our business here and don't touch me, if you know what's good for you. Look, you've spilled my drink. Get me another."

Sully opened his mouth and looked into Ben's eyes. He saw such a mixture of menace and bored contempt that he took the mug and went to the wine cask without another word. He avoided stepping on the soldiers, Carter and Merrins, who had fallen into a drunken stupor in each other's arms. They lay in a heap of tangled bandoliers, muskets, and scraps of food, attracting swarms of mosquitoes.

Meanwhile, after passing through the contingents of Captains Alliston and Cornelius Essex, Tom's group reached Bartholomew Sharp's large, boisterous crew. A pig and an ox rotated on spits, dripping hissing fat into glowing ashes. Some men danced in pairs to the tune of a fiddle and the clop-clop of hollow coconut shells. Others scampered about individually, energized with drink, jerking their arms and weaving patterns in the air with their crimson sashes. Mulatto boys passed mugs of wine around. Sharp sat on a sea chest near the tree line, surrounded by his inner circle, engrossed in a game of dice on a barrelhead. Sweating in a tar-stained greatcoat, he rose and greeted Tom.

"Come out to sniff the air, Thomas?" The captain's tone was mocking. "You look like you're going to war. Enjoy Christmas, for God's sake. Cut yerself a slice of beef, shipmate. It's delicious."

"Not now, thanking you, Barty," said Tom. "I fear you were right about Digby Townsend's bloodhounds. They are here, sitting under Coxon's flag. Five of 'em, including two soldiers."

"Are they, by Christ? Let's have a good look at the dogs then."

Sharp spotted Scarrett with the rum keg. "While we're at it, we'll pay our respects to the good admiral with a toast of yon Egyptian's firewater." He slapped the back of a pale, effeminate youth beside him. "My quartermaster, Mr. Cox, will accompany us, won't you, Johnny? You must be tired of losing your money by now."

The youth scowled. "Aye, Bart, if you say so. Are we expecting a bloodbath? Must I first arm myself to the teeth like your friends?"

"No, Johnny," said Sharp. "Your gloomy countenance will suffice. It is a social call, no more than that. It won't take long."

Sharp led the way, prodding the sand with the shaft of his turtle harpoon. Cox walked behind him and the others skulked a few yards to the rear. Coxon's flag duly appeared above the crowd. Sharp stopped and handed the harpoon to Cox, saying, "Avast. I have an idea." He fumbled in a coat pocket and extracted his telescope. "Here," he passed it to Tom. "Tell me where the dogs are sitting."

"How should I know? I might recognize Long Ben, but the others…" He handed it on to Joseph. "You saw 'em. You look."

"Scarrett knows 'em better, so he does," said Joseph.

The Gipsy had never used such an instrument before. He put down the rum and examined the brass tube. After squinting through it the wrong way, he had great difficulty twisting the lens into focus. The faces that suddenly loomed at him were blurred in the hazy light. He turned it again. Everything went murky. Eventually, he aimed it at the moon, which had emerged from the clouds, edging them with silver. He saw the ridges and craters on the surface for the first time.

"Well, I never," he said. "Can that be the moon? All pitted and scarred like a poxy whore's ass. Solid. Looks heavy; very heavy. Must be over a hundred miles away. Why doesn't it smash down on us like a giant stone cannonball?"

The captain snatched the telescope from his grasp, collapsed it, and put it back in his pocket. He kicked the little rum barrel, saying, "Johnny, pick that up." Quartermaster Cox cradled the keg. Sharp turned and whipped off the Gipsy's hat. He tugged Scarrett's head cloth over his nose and mouth. Then he crammed the hat back over

Scarrett's ears, until the brim almost covered his eyes.

"Right, my moonstruck Egyptian monkey," said Sharp, "enough pissing about. We'll try a different way. Imagine you have been tending a fire and shielding your nozzle from the smoke. Now, no one can see your poxy whoreson's face. We'll walk straight to the flag, just you and me. Show me who the fuckers are, all five of 'em, and don't be too bleeding obvious about it. Whisper into my ear. Then go and climb a tree, at the farthest end of the bay."

The commander-in-chief, John Coxon, sat enthroned on an upturned canoe. He gnawed at a rack of ribs. Above his plumed hat, his tasseled red banner stirred in the sea breeze. His crew gave the usual toasts to the "Admiral of the Black," the "Successor to Mansfield and Morgan," "The New Francis Drake," and the "Terror of Santa Marta." The trumpeters blew an ear-splitting blast. Then, having rapidly drained three mugs of wine, the men launched into their version of a seasonal song:

> *"Old King Cole loved a tight little hole*
> *And a tight little hole loved he!*
> *He called for his pipe,*
> *And stuck it up his bum,*
> *And he buggered his fiddlers three!*
> *Fiddle-dee bum-bum,*
> *Fiddle-dee bum-bum, bum-bum, fiddle-dee-dee!"*

At this, a trio of fiddlers came forward, bending and swaying as they worked their bows, while their comrades poked their backsides and made rude gestures. A fife trilled. Coxon's drummer thumped the goatskin with his fist to coincide with the word 'bum.' The music settled into a repetitive reel with an increasingly ragged chorus, larded with obscenities. Coxon roared at the musicians, "Play, you bastards! Earn your keep, or I'll have you flogged up and down the shore! Make merry, by the Holy Afterbirth! Play till your fingers fall off!" He meant it. As non-combatants, musicians were required to perform tirelessly at festivities, as well as boosting morale in battle.

It was the least they could do, since they were otherwise useless mouths to feed.

Tom, Malcolm, and Joseph retired into the shadows under the trees. They saw Captain Sharp, followed by John Cox with the rum, and the masked Scarrett, bearing a steaming platter of meat, shouldering their way through the singing crowd. Coxon enjoyed three mugs of Scarrett's firewater. His cheeks grew almost as red as his flag. However, when he tried to shoot his pistol into the air again, it failed to fire. He was too drunk to prime it properly. Sharp made light of the bad omen, sharing out more rum. Meanwhile, Scarrett hissed into Sharp's ear through the cloth, indicating Long Ben, Red Rod, Sully, and the two unconscious soldiers at their feet. Then, the Gipsy vanished into the crowd, making for the trees.

Sharp took his leave of the swaying admiral. Accompanied by Master Cox with the keg, he strode casually up to Long Ben. Tom saw Long Ben smile sheepishly before introducing the doormen from The Mermaid. Sharp prodded the recumbent soldiers with his harpoon, but they remained motionless. Red Rod Hughes stared hard at the keg, as if he recognized it. The captain did not offer any rum. Instead, he gave a little speech, slapped Long Ben on the back, and retraced his steps in the direction of his own crew. The Port Royal doormen were left looking distinctly uncomfortable. They fell to arguing amongst themselves. Long Ben threw down his mug, picked up his musket, and began pushing his way to the back of the crowd.

"He's coming over here," said Tom. "Probably searching for Squeaker. Let's be on our way."

They caught up with Sharp and Cox further along the beach, where the crowd was thinner. Scarrett joined them, removing his mask.

"Well, I braced 'em," said Sharp. "Welcomed them to the fleet. Long Ben remembered our games of dice at The Mariners, Tom. I think he got my drift."

"Your drift?" said Malcolm.

"A friendly reminder that we are almost four hundred strong here, and well able to deal with any trouble from Port Royal, even if they send a regiment. I enquired about the health of the two on the ground."

"You think he got the message?" asked Tom.

"Long Ben knows the score," said Cox, "but I'll wager the red ape and his mate are shitting their britches."

Sharp chuckled. "I reckon so. 'You're in safe hands,' says I. Then, I tells 'em about The Brethrens' punishment for traitors and informers, about feeding the filth to the filth. How it works. That'll give 'em something to ponder on, eh, Tom?"

"No doubt about it," said Tom. Among the buccaneers, disputes were normally settled by individual duels. However, when an entire crew was threatened by thievery, the culprits could expect to be marooned on a desert island or a wild shore. For outright treachery, the penalty was more hideous. 'Feeding the filth to the filth' acted as the ultimate deterrent. The condemned men were forced to run between two ranks of seamen who stabbed them with needles used for sewing sails. They ran towards an empty sugar barrel filled with rats and cockroaches. Once the victim had been thrust into the barrel, the lid was nailed shut. Death came slowly, in a cramped, dark nightmare, crawling with vermin. If the crew was particularly angry, the barrel might be rolled about for hours before being thrown into the sea.

"They'll have plenty food for thought, Captain," said Tom. "I'm obliged. Let's hope they take the hint."

"If they don't," said Sharp, "you'll have to sort 'em out, Tom. You go hunting with the Scotsman tomorrow. Get lost in the hills. The dozy lubbers will never find you. I'll make sure nothing happens to Joe and the Gipsy. Now, forget those weasels, man, and let us finish Scarrett's devilish distillation. A few more swigs and we'll sleep like babies."

They settled down by Sharp's fire, in the midst of his crew, passing the keg around. Soon, peace descended on the beach. The ashes glowed and went out. The moon vanished behind the clouds. It was black as tar, except for the ships' stern lanterns glimmering out in the bay. A lone figure inched along the shoreline, peering down at the huddled shapes. Long Ben quickly realized the futility of his search. He was in danger of stepping on somebody and could barely distinguish one inert bundle from another, let alone recognize an individual face. He would try to find the potboy next day. When he made it back to Coxon's flag, he found he could not sleep. He consoled himself by finishing the dregs of a wine cask until the dark clouds began to spin in the sky. Shortly before dawn, weariness overcame his urge to vomit, and he curled up beneath the barrel. He dreamed of cockroaches bathing their feelers in puddles of blood.

Long Ben had not descended into his insect-infested nightmares for more than an hour when Tom awoke at the other end of the beach. The eastern horizon gradually brightened. It took Tom a few minutes to clear his head. He breathed deeply, aware of a dull pain behind his left eyeball. He roused Malcolm, whispering, "Come, lad, I've had enough of this place. Let's go while all is calm."

They slung their guns and ammunition over their shoulders, crammed their haversacks with leftovers from the feast, and helped themselves to a full water skin. All around them the sleeping shapes lay like the victims of a massacre. Red sashes resembled streaks of blood among the bodies. Discarded weapons glinted, catching the first rays of daylight. Some drunks had rolled uncomfortably close to the tide line. The incoming surf would awaken them at any moment. Malcolm bent towards Joseph, to say farewell, but Tom pulled him away. "Leave it. We'll slip away quietly; it's better."

4
THE CAERNARVON ESTATE

Before Tom and Malcolm reached the coastal road, they crossed a wooded area behind the dunes. Flies crawled over piles of feces. The undergrowth reeked of stale piss. A little further on, a dozen bruised and bloodied Angolan women were huddled together in a clearing. A young girl, completely naked, lay to one side. Her dead eyes stared up at the treetops. A lone silver sheep leaned against a trunk, his head in his hands, barely covering his cropped ears.

Tom shuddered. "Some fools think a black woman can cure the pox."

Malcolm was about to make a rejoinder about Theodora, but thought the better of it. They hurried on, turning right along the road. It was little more than a dirt track, with deep grooves gouged by the wheels of ox carts. Whenever a stream trickled through, it became a quagmire. A barrier of lush vegetation, speckled with bright flowers, rioted on either side. The two heavily laden hunters plodded along steadily.

Finally Malcolm spoke. "D'ye have the faintest notion of where in hell we are going, Mr. Sheppard?"

"I haven't been in this neck of the woods for a while," said Tom, "but the land will be the same. Mackett says they've planted sugar recently, over the old hemp fields. We might have to cross an estate or two before we head north along the Morant River. We can't go astray with the sea at our back and the mountains in front. There's no hurry. The idea is to keep out of harm's way. I don't intend to strain myself to feed those bastards in the bay."

"Ah," Malcolm smiled. "His Lordship merely fancies taking some country air, is that it?"

"You have it. A gentle stroll from house to house, with some hunting and fishing, if I feel so inclined. We have credit with the planters. They covet our Negroes. I mean to take advantage. Dangle the prospect of some silver sheep before them. That'll be worth a soft bed and good cooking. Then, we'll enjoy the fresh breezes on the high ground. We'll shoot goats and make a hearty stew. I need a rest after the nonsense of the last two days; time to think. Maybe I'll like it here. It is not graven in stone that I will sail to the main, not by any means."

"Ye'll have to live in the backwoods, like a hermit, if ye want to remain in Jamaica," said Malcolm. "The swine Townsend will make it too hot for ye in port, and he'll have friends among the planters. Ye'll have to change yer name, at least, and walk in constant fear of the noose."

"There are other ports, Mal." Tom was on the point of mentioning Arnout, but added, "Other ships."

"Aye," muttered Malcolm, "and other nooses."

The sun climbed over the bushes. Malcolm knotted a square of black silk over his head. After an hour, Tom paused beside a gatepost. "This is new," he said. "It must have cost a fortune." He indicated a long driveway, sprinkled with seashells, lined by trees sprouting blue flowers, which led to a two-story mansion on a hill. A red-nosed man stood in the portico. Under a broad hat, his wig cascaded over his shoulders. He carried a coiled bullwhip. A black groom was adjusting the bridle on a chestnut mare. The man brushed the groom aside, hauled himself into the saddle, and trotted towards them.

"Hah! More of Coxon's rascals, I'll warrant," he said.

"Aye, sir, that we are, rascals and rapscallions," answered Tom, "and thirsty too."

"Good. Very good. Welcome to the Caernarvon Estate. I'll attend to you presently. No time now. Ajax, take 'em to the kitchen."

With that, he thumped his heels against the mare's ribs and rode down the valley towards a group of stone buildings clustered around a smoking chimney. Cane fields, alive with half-naked black figures, rolled towards the hills beyond, partially hidden by a line of palms. The groom led them to rear of the house. A young Irishwoman in a cap and apron fanned herself on the kitchen step. She gave Malcolm a gap-toothed smile.

"Go in," she said, shifting to let them pass. "Martha will see to you."

They were soon sitting at a table in a great kitchen, eating eggs with their reheated slices of beef and freshly fried onions. Copper pans gleamed all around. The pantry shelves were strung on tarred ropes and the table legs stood in clay cups of water to keep the ants at bay. Martha King, a plump cockney who had a livid scar over one eye, boiled them a kettle of chocolate to wash the food down. In spite of her bruised appearance, she had clearly been beautiful once. A mulatto woman swept the tiled floor.

"Has the old bastard Craddock gone to the fields yet?" Martha wanted to know.

"If you mean the bottle-nosed cavalier with the whip," said Tom, filling his pipe, "he has. He seemed to be in a hurry."

"It's too hot near this chimney," said Malcolm. "I'll smoke in the fresh air." He introduced himself to the Irish girl. Their voices grew fainter as they moved a short distance along the wall outside. Martha raked over the ashes in the grate. She took a generous pinch of Tom's tobacco and stuck a short clay pipe into her mouth. Bands of red skin surrounded her wrists.

"Yes, go on, look," she sighed. "I'm no stranger to the bilboes. The pigs kept me in irons all the way over from Wapping."

"How long did you get? Seven years?"

"Five and a good floggin', for nothing but tryin' to earn me livin'. As from last night, I done three years, two months, and twelve days."

"You're over halfway. You've broken the back of it."

"Yeah, but it's broken the back of me too, it 'as. Even if I survive this hellhole, I'll still be stuck on the wrong side of the ocean, won't I? I've 'ad a gutful, I 'ave. All fever, flies, and scorchin' sun. And the air! Like livin' in a wet blanket." She puffed on her stubby pipe and coughed, "Things was more civilized with young Sir Leonard 'ere. He built this place up, but then he made so much money last year, he sailed back to live in England, and we're stuck with Mr. Martin Bloody Craddock, commandin' a gang of Papist bogtrotters and a couple of loony bookkeepers, all surrounded by hundreds of black heathens with dirty great knives in their paws. It don't bear thinkin' about, it don't. One day, they'll chop us up in our beds. At least with you sailors roaming about, ready to shoot an' all, we feel a bit safer. If it was down to me, you could stay forever, the more the merrier. Does your fleet ever visit London, or Bristol, or Plymouth? I'd even settle for Dublin."

"Not our fleet, my darling," said Tom. "We'll be lucky to reach Portobello in our worm-eaten tubs. Anyway, there's no room for women. We are fighters, not merchants. You wouldn't want to sail with us, believe me."

"I'd sail with the Old Nick and every fiend in damnation to get away from here, mister. Craddock forced nearly all the house slaves outdoors for the harvest."

Riding boots crunched on the gravel outside. Craddock greeted Malcolm and barked at the Irish girl, "Be about your business, you swooning slut, before I take the skin off your ass. Look, the sheets are gathering dust on the washing line. I'll attend to our guests."

The chief overseer's red nose poked round the door. "Martha, make sure we get a bottle of claret in my office. After that, see if Mr. Wilmot requires attention upstairs."

Tom and Malcolm, still carrying their gear, followed Craddock into the depths of the mansion. They crossed an airy dining room. Silver candlesticks stood on the gleaming table. In the hall, above the chequerboard tiles, a small black boy polished the carved acanthus scroll on the balustrade leading to the upstairs chambers. Here, everything smelled of tar oil and vinegar, to discourage insects. They entered the office. Its long, leaded windows opened onto a distant view of the sugar works beyond a lawn and a pineapple patch. Craddock settled in an armchair, beside a desk strewn with bills and letters. He motioned them to occupy a pair of seats. They set their weapons down on the floor.

"Forgive the haste," said the overseer, throwing his hat and whip onto the papers. "We are in the middle of harvesting, burning, planting, crushing, boiling, and curing, all at the same time. You catch us at the height of our busiest season. I am Martin Craddock, controlling the estate for my partner, Sir Leonard Paulet of Bristol and Bath. You men are with Captain Coxon, I take it, presently anchored in the bay?"

"Yes," said Tom, "I am Thomas Sheppard from near Bright Helmstone in Sussex, and this is Mr. Munro of Glasgow. We sail with Captain Bartholomew Sharp, under the overall command of Admiral Coxon. We have come to hunt for provisions while the fleet takes on water."

"Sharp? Oh, yes, the one who stuffed the warehouses with cocoa and logwood last month, am I right? Glutted the exchange for months." Craddock frowned. "Well, that's all the same to me. My only concern is sugar, more sugar, and nothing but sugar. I aim to clear and plant a further five hundred acres next year, maybe more. For that I need Negroes, more Negroes, and nothing but Negroes, in short order, by the shipload, and fit for hard labor. They are so much better than the damned Irish. The freckled Hibernian scum need to be pampered, whereas, I swear, the Lord specifically created Africans to cut cane. They even sing of their own accord, in time to the work.

"Music to the ears, sugar in the barrel, and silver in the chest. All good, if you know how to keep 'em tame. I give 'em raw rum on Saturdays, strong enough to penetrate their woolly skulls till Sunday night, but allow no other liberties. They thrive on loblolly with salt cod during the week, and we are blessed with fresh streams from the mountains. You must see our water mill. She's a beauty, with

61

three copper-clad rollers. She grinds the fraggots quicker than the Duchess of Portsmouth's thighs grind the spunk out of the king's cock. Ah, at last, the wine! God's bones, a man could die of thirst in this house!"

The mulatto woman hovered over the desk, uncertain where to place the tray.

"There, on the table by the window, you yellow lizard," cried Craddock. "Help me off with these boots, since you're here. Pull, bitch, pull! Now, fetch some more of the Porto we had last night. This will hardly wet our throats."

Craddock was suddenly silent, intent on pouring. In his eagerness to wet his throat, he emptied two glasses in swift succession before offering any to his guests. He loosened his neck cloth, then tore off his sweaty wig, wiggled his toes in his stockings, and sank back into his seat, taking his third drink in more measured swallows. His face gradually turned the same ruby color as his nose, up to his white shaven scalp. Tom thought the overseer's head resembled a shining egg in a red cup. Malcolm spluttered into his wine to stifle a laugh. Craddock's eyes misted over, no longer darting from side to side.

"There," he groaned, emptying out the last drops of claret. "That's better. We can start on the Porto. Not on parade anymore. Thank Christ for small mercies. This game is mainly about appearances, but I don't have to tell you that. I'm sure you know the value of a brave front in your line of business, with your sashes and mustachios. It'll take more than the crack of a whip to frighten the Spaniards, eh? I saw the embassy Dons slaughter King Louis' delegation in the streets of London, once. Made mincemeat of the French fops. T'was a pleasure to watch 'em."

"Aye," said Malcolm. "The Dons usually put up a better fight than the Frogs, but we make all the priest-buggered, garlic-breathing mollies scream for their maithers just the same. For all their preening, few of them know one end of a musket from another, never mind a ship."

"The Dutch are a different matter. Thank God their main thrust is to the east these days," said Tom, helping himself to the port.

"Hopefully, we won't need to fend off the likes of Tromp and De Ruyter again. At least we retain the best tobacco fields in the Americas. May I light my pipe, sir?"

"Please do," said Craddock. "I prefer snuff, but your fumes will help drive those blasted merrywings away from the window. By God, if I close it, I stifle to death. If I open it, they swarm in to sting me. You suffocate or you scratch yourself raw. This country is pretty enough to look at, if you like mountains, but the plain is little more than a pestilent gnats' nest, fanned by ill winds and hot vapors. There's poor Wilmot upstairs, gnashing his teeth in a desperate ague. I doubt if he will be with us in the morning. He had to fall sick at crop time, when every man is needed. At this rate, I'll have to find another replacement; the third bookkeeper since August. If they don't run off screaming, they drown in their beds, soaked, blathering like babies, pissing blood and puking black bile. We exist in a charnel house. Only the Porto has preserved me these five years, I am sure of it."

They drank in silence for a while. Tom studied a framed map of Jamaica on the wall. In the bottom corner, a pair of plumed cavaliers dueled with rapiers. Compass bearings and vessels leaning in the wind crisscrossed the seas around the island. At the top, the head of Charles II, with crown, lion's wig, big nose, and square jaw, smiled among clouds blown by cherubs. There was a hesitant cough in the doorway. The little boy from the hall stared at his feet, murmuring.

"What is it?" snapped Craddock. "Louder, you monkey, or I'll make your screams deafen God!"

"Coco, Massa. Dem say Coco do cacka," came the high-pitched reply.

"Coco? Cacka? You see what I have to endure!" The boy retreated, raising his hand as if expecting a blow to the head. Craddock violently pulled his boots on and snatched up his wig. Papers fluttered to the floor. "Luckily, like Saint Francis, I have learned to converse with the birds and animals. Come, gentlemen, I would appreciate your presence at the boiling house. Leave your bags here, but hold your weapons up. As I said, this game is all about appearances. Let us

63

overawe the brutes."

He screwed his hat onto the top of his wig and slapped his boot with his whip, pausing to take another swig of port before stomping from the room. Tom and Malcolm picked up their muskets and followed him outside through the hall. In the porch, a ragged Irish servant joined the group. Within five minutes, they entered a yard in the middle of a complex of outbuildings, Craddock leading the way on his horse.

A whipping post and a gallows tree stood near the wall of the boiling house. Out in the dusty yard, under the blazing sun, a black man's head and hands poked out of a pillory. The day before, during one of his rides round the plantation, Craddock had spotted the slave, Coco, chewing on a cane stalk as he cut the crop. This was pilfering. When Craddock's bullwhip snaked through the air and cracked across his back, Coco hurled the soggy stalk, hitting the horse's head. Craddock almost fell from the saddle as he struggled to control the rearing animal. Other cane cutters, including women, paused to observe the scene, shading their eyes. Although nobody moved, the overseer felt the menace of their sullen stares and curved blades. He charged at Coco, whipping him from the field towards the sugar works. Coco's impulsive reaction could have sparked a massacre of every white on the property. This rugged frontier was not Barbados.

Fortunately for Craddock, Coco ran blindly into the yard, where two alert Irishmen swiftly clamped him into the stocks. After administering a sound thrashing, Craddock retired to his office to let the situation, and his pulse rate, calm down. Outside, all remained peaceful. The watermill clanked steadily. No screams or flames erupted from the outbuildings. Two bottles of claret, followed by a few glasses of port, helped him to devise an appropriate punishment. Hanging, although tempting, was out of the question. So was amputation. The field gang was overstretched as it was. The trick was to find a deterrent that fitted the crime, without losing the offender's productivity.

This morning, with news of Coco's bowel movement, the time

had come. The unexpected presence of two well-armed buccaneers would lend the occasion extra gravitas. There would be enough witnesses for word to get around. Crouched in the stocks, between the mill, the boiling house, and the curing shed, Coco was the center of a scene of bustling activity. A steady stream of harvesters passed the entrance to the mill's rumbling crushers to deposit their bundles. Mr. Denby, the junior bookkeeper, leaned on a silver-topped cane, sweating. His wig lay on a windowsill. He fanned himself with his hat. The gleam of copper cauldrons, tended by naked blacks with skimmers and ladles, emanated from the smoky interior. The heat on the roof slates made the air dance. A staccato sound of coopers, hammering hogsheads into shape, came from beyond the curing shed, along with the lowing of draught oxen. Upstream, the chimney of the distillery let out a thin line of white wood smoke against the backdrop of the mountains.

The shadow of the chief overseer and his horse fell over the stocks. The slave was either dead or unconscious. On closer inspection, Coco shuddered slightly when he breathed. The morning dew had given him a chill. Craddock summoned an Irishman. "Here, James! I trust you are ready."

James wore linen, unlike the dirty sackcloth of the other white servants. His cheeks were shaved and his shoes almost new. He nodded, calling, "All right, lads!"

Two poorly shod, bearded ragamuffins approached the pillory from behind. They carried sponges and a calabash of lime juice laced with hot peppers. James brandished a short length of sugar cane, which he dunked in the fresh excrement lying under Coco's bench.

"Now!" shouted Craddock.

As soon as the sponges applied the juice to his raw back, Coco's mouth opened to scream, and was immediately filled by the filthy end of the cane stalk. While he choked and spat, Craddock gave him a short lecture about pilfering and how fortunate he was not to lose his life, or at least one hand, for daring to raise it against his master. All around, the work continued in a mechanical rhythm. It was impossible to tell whether the other slaves noticed the proceedings. They shuffled about their tasks like sleepwalkers. Coco was released. The cramped position in the frame overnight had left him unable to stand. Nobody assisted him as, hawking and spitting, he inched forward on all fours, out of the yard, towards the stream.

"Right," said Craddock to the ragged servants, "handsomely done. I think he has learned his lesson. Back to work! It is not yet lunchtime!"

Tom and Malcolm stared at the man crawling, with difficulty, through the harvesters' legs.

"It would be a mercy to shoot him," said Malcolm.

"Not only him," said Tom quietly, and spat.

"Come, sirs," said Craddock, "everything seems to be in order here. We'll finish the Porto. Then, you will be shown to your quarters."

This time, Craddock fell asleep over his documents after one glass, a trail of pink spittle staining the paper, his wig on the floor under his stockings. Martha King entered and shook her head wearily. She placed a full bottle on the side table and a chamber pot beside the armchair.

"There. That'll keep 'im quiet. In one end and out the other. I reckon, if they bled 'im, they could sell it as wine." She flicked the smooth, white head with her forefinger. "Dead to the world. Come on then, you two." Tom and Malcolm followed her to the storeroom beside the kitchen.

"We ain't got no more 'ammocks," she said, "so these'll 'ave to do you." She pointed at a pile of rope mats, rolled up against the wall. "Make sure you give 'em a good shake when you spread 'em out. I saw a spider the size of me 'and in 'ere the other day. The water in the butt won't give you bellyache. It's fresh from the stream. Anything else you need," she winked, "we're just round the corner. Don't worry about Craddock. I 'ear 'im prowling about in 'is room all night, talkin' to thin air. The bastard can't sleep in the dark, so 'e'll be dozing for most of the day now. We serve the main meal at sunset, like proper gentry, in the dining room. Then the fun starts.

We got the mill workin' twenty-four hours at present, so anyfink can 'appen. Wait and see!"

When she had gone, they made themselves at home. They doubled the mats to make thicker beds, then lay down and blew smoke rings at the ceiling, as if they were in their garret at The Three Mariners.

"The whole house reeks of tar," said Malcolm. "Reminds me of a ship."

"Without the tang of the bilges, thank God," said Tom. He rose to scoop a mug of water from the butt. "Ah! Cool and clean, like the woman said." He refilled the mug, placing it beside his mattress. "Right, I'm going to have a rest. I suggest you do likewise."

"Sweet dreams, yer Lordship," said Malcolm. "I'm off for a stroll."

Tom closed his eyes. "Foolish puppy! Take your musket. Don't forget; appearances."

"Ach, no," said Malcolm, adjusting his sabre. "The sword is ample. I'm not in Mr. Craddock's militia. I don't need a matchlock for what I have in mind. I'll borrow yer hat, though. It's fair scorching out there."

When Malcolm had gone, Tom found himself alone with his thoughts. He still struggled to come to terms with the events of the last two days. It had all happened too fast. His mind spun in circles, running up against the impossibility of contacting Arnout. He thought of stealing some of Martha King's clothes, draping a cloak over his head, and sneaking up the Pallisadoes road, disguised as an old woman. That might work in the fogs of London or Amsterdam, but few women got old in Port Royal, and they certainly didn't walk with a sailor's gait, concealing a hunting rifle, swaddled in shawls in the heat of the sun. Forget it, there'd be no room to hide anywhere, unless he crawled into a sea chest. Supposing the *Eenhoorn* was delayed indefinitely, or Arnout had already sailed? How long would he last with a price on his head, in such a buzzing hive of gossip? Could he skulk for months, with only the drooling slave in the Jew's dark warehouse for company? No, he had to stop thinking like that. Squeaker's death was a sign from God, the devil, or whatever powers guided the stars, to cut his ties with Jamaica, once and for all.

A small blue lizard on the wall took him back to Theodora's hut. His plan to buy her and open a shoemaker's shop near the tanneries resurfaced in his mind. One could make more money producing footwear in Port Royal than in Boston or London. Shoes were essential to avoid chiggers and other nasty worms that drilled into the feet. The poorest servants scraped their coins together to buy them, and they wore out quickly. There was a fortune in it, with careful saving, and he'd be his own master. Ah, well, that pipedream was a dead end, too. He'd soon have to cut down his own boots into marching shoes and use the surplus leather to make a pair of light sandals for work on board. On the coming voyage, the decks would become hot enough to melt tar.

He took a sip of water. The sooner Coxon sailed south, the better. The fleet might encounter salt or logwood merchants bound for Holland. Failing that, Tom's best bet was the island of Curacao, that ghostly reminder of the Dutch West India Company. He formed the word slowly, whispering, "Coo-raa-saa-ow." It soothed him. Tin trays clattered in the kitchen next door. Homely sounds and comforting smells; Martha was baking. Who was she speaking to, the Irish girl or the yellow woman? Yawning, Tom stretched out his limbs.

Birdsong and cicadas came through the slats in the high window. In the distance, the watermill clanked, accompanying the repetitive chants of the harvesting gang in the fields. A nasal, rasping voice sang an African phrase to which the weary chorus replied, again and again. Soon, Tom was breathing in time to the cadence, fast asleep. He did not notice Malcolm come in with the Irish girl or hear their grunts and giggles as they tussled on the other mattress. When he awoke, he was alone. The chanting had stopped. Outside, judging by the angle of the sun, three hours had passed since Coco's punishment. Tom followed the scent of fresh bread into the kitchen.

"Smells good," he said. A basket of orange-brown buns sat on the table. The mulatto woman turned chickens on a long spit in the fireplace. The tops of her breasts glistened over her shift.

"Stop gapin' at Maria," said Martha, sitting in a rocking chair, chewing her pipe. "Go on, 'elp yourself to bread."

Tom took a bun and sank his teeth through the warm crust. Cornmeal mixed with buttermilk and sweet potato flour. His mouth filled with the rich flavor. When he was able to speak, he said, "Very good. Fit for a king."

"I should fink so," said Martha. "It's called 'yam bulla,' like potato bread, 'alf Irish, 'alf niggerish, like Maria 'erself. She grinds up Jamaica peppers with the dough, don'tcha, my love? Little allspice berries, taste like nutmeg and cloves. They can't get enough of the stuff round 'ere. You wait. I'll sprinkle a little bit into the big bowl of bumbo tonight. That'll put lead in your pencil. With 'er buns and my bumbo, you can keep it up all night."

Maria shook her head and smiled. Mr. Denby, sweaty from the boiling house, suddenly appeared in the doorway. Maria's expression became stony. The junior bookkeeper was in a temper. His wig hung off the back of his head and one stocking had slipped round his ankle. He nodded curtly at Tom and speared a bun on the point of his cane. Then, grinding his thin jaws, with a wild look in his eyes, he seized Maria by the wrist. Within seconds, his shoes thumped up the main staircase as he dragged her to his bedroom. They heard a muffled shriek, a slammed door, then silence.

"Charmin'," said Martha. "That's 'ow it is 'ere lately. The place runs itself, while the gentlemen are all in the 'ouse, ill, drunk, or molestin' women. That Mr. Denby's the worst. 'E'd be locked up in Bedlam back 'ome. Such a quiet boy when 'e first arrived. Wouldn't say 'boo' to a goose. Now look at 'im; barely 'uman, foamin' at the mouth. Belongs in a cage."

"So, nobody is in control at the moment," said Tom. "The place could go up in flames without warning. A mutinous ship would be safer."

"Our Irishmen keep a lid on things here," said Martha. "They'd never join with the niggers, not like those fools in Virginia. They may be servants, but they've got enough sense to remember what color they are."

"Virginia? Three years ago, wasn't it?" said Tom. "I heard the rebels were Roundheads, Fanatics, Quakers and such, not Irish."

Martha snorted, "Still fools. All got strung up, didn't they? The best any of us can hope for 'ere is to stay alive long enough to get as far away from fuckin' Jamaica as possible. The rest can go to hell, Roundheads, Cavaliers, Quakers, Jews, masters, servants, slaves, black, white, brown, yellow, purple, whoever they are. All idiots. Get out and leave the place to the Maroons and the cannibals, I say."

Tom laughed, "Don't forget the buccaneers! We need to eat as well."

"I know your sort," said Martha. "You wouldn't think it to look at me today, but I've entertained some of the boldest knights of the road before their last dance at Tyburn. One of 'em, Monsieur Claude, 'ad more style than all you sea dogs put together. I'll never forget my Claudie. 'E used to be the Duke of Richmond's footman."

"Not Claude du Val, who danced with duchesses by the roadside while he stole their jewels? They sing about him in the Port Royal ale shops to this day." Tom was stunned. "Are you speaking of *the* Claude du Val?"

"I am. I wore some of those jewels. People said it was an honor to be robbed by 'im. 'E knew 'ow to treat a lady too, trust me. Proper manners, 'e 'ad, never raised 'is 'and to a woman. Pigs who do that ain't much good at raisin' nuffin' else, in my book. My Claudie still looked gallant after they cut 'im down. We sat the body in the Tangier Tavern, in his best silk suit and curly wig, like 'e was 'olding court, with a glass of brandy on the table, pipe in 'is fist, beaver hat on 'is 'ead, huge white feather, kid gloves, everthing. One or two drops of belladonna, and 'is eyes sparkled like 'e was lookin' at you. We made a tidy profit that day, even after the landlord took 'is share. There was no smell. It was January, freezin' cold, and we didn't light the fire, to keep 'im fresh. All London wanted to see 'im. Watchmen, officers, everybody. 'Alf the cradles from Highgate to Holborn were full of 'is babies. A few of the mothers, with four- and five-year-old children, were able to give the nippers a last good look at their father, to remember 'im in all 'is glory. Oh, those were the days! I was the toast of Drury Lane. Too good to last, it was."

She paused, wiping a tear from her eye, and drew in her breath. "Talkin' of gallants, don't think I ain't noticed what your Scottish friend is doing with our Katie. Better watch 'is step. She's spoken for. Mr. Wilmot wants to pay off her indenture and marry 'er."

"How is Mr. Wilmot?"

"Burnin' up. 'Is face is yellow and 'e groans all the time. We 'ad the surgeon ride over from Spanish Town on Christmas Eve. Charged five guineas, no less, to bleed the poor bugger with twenty leeches. Left 'im worse than ever. Craddock reckons it's mortal. 'E's searchin' for a replacement already. It's a shame. Wilmot's the only one with a shred of decency in 'im."

"I'll take a look at him, if you like," said Tom. "I've seen all kinds of fevers in my time."

"Can't do any harm, I suppose," said Martha. "But I wouldn't bleed 'im again. Them leeches was fat as sausages, fit to burst, by the time they rolled off."

They went upstairs, ignoring the muffled thumps and cries coming from Mr. Denby's room across the landing. Mr. Wilmot lay high on the four-poster, shaking in a tangle of vomit-stained bedclothes. Martha straightened him out, placing the pillow back under his head.

"I'll tell Katie to fetch clean sheets," she said, "when she honors us with 'er presence again."

"So, this has been going on for days, has it?" said Tom. "Wilmot! Can you hear me?"

The sufferer's skin was as yellow as his greasy fair hair. He answered through chattering teeth, "Y-y-yes. Are you anoth-other d-doctor?"

To save argument, Tom nodded. "I am. I will do what I can for you. No more leeches, I promise. Have you been able to piss lately?"

"A few d-drops. Hurt like he-hell, it did." Veins pulsated on his temples. He groaned, "The be-belly ache is bad, b-but the he-headache is worse."

Tom scrutinized the meager contents of the chamber pot, swilling them round and sniffing. "No time to lose," he said. "We might save him yet. He can still see and talk sense, but he is squeezing out drops of stenching piss like a blood orange. A fierce flushing is needed, before it turns darker. Come, woman, let's see what you have in the larder."

Back in the kitchen, Tom took a copper pan from a hook. "Stoke up the fire," he said. "If we do nothing, he is scuppered. I will cook up a witch's brew that might pull him back from the brink. Do you have ginger root? Grate a goodly amount into a pint pot and mash it into a paste with your strongest rum. I must fetch something from outside."

Borrowing an axe from the storeroom, Tom hurried past the front of the house, into the driveway, and chopped deep into the trunk of the nearest tree with blue flowers. He came back with a thin wedge, complete with the heartwood, which began to turn green in the moist air. While Martha prepared the ginger, he reduced most of the wood, including the bark, to small chips. He stewed these in another pan, producing an oily tea. This was stirred into Martha's paste.

"Good," he said. "Now heat a bottle of Craddock's Porto, but don't bring it to the boil. That would kill its power."

Finally, they strained all the steaming sludge into a punchbowl, adding a cupful of molasses.

"Pity we have no honey. Now, go," said Tom. "Make him drink it all down, to the last drop. Don't take 'no' for an answer. Force it into him, as if he was a baby. I'll be up presently."

"I 'ope you know what you're doin'," she said, using a cloth to pick up the bowl. "Chopped trees! Well, I never!"

"Tricks I learned from the cannibals," he said. "I've seen them perform miracles when our surgeons stood helpless. Now shift yourself. As soon as he has it inside his guts, we must drive out the ague with heat. Fight fire with fire."

She had hardly gone when Malcolm and Katie appeared in the kitchen. They tried to make their flushed faces appear serious, but smiles played at the corners of their mouths.

"What are ye doing, Mr. Sheppard?" asked Malcolm. "Raiding

the pantry with an axe?"

The Irish girl stifled her giggles with her hand to her lips.

"While you lovebirds are cooing in the meadows, a man is dying of marsh fever upstairs," said Tom. "You, Katie, get us clean sheets. Malcolm, take the carpet from the table in the hall and follow me."

Tom grabbed his tinderbox and a frying pan full of yellow splinters, leading the way to the sickroom. He opened the widow, closed the curtains, and ignited the sapwood. The same Palo Santo smoke that Theodora used in her cabin started to perfume the darkened room. Katie spread fresh sheets and tucked Wilmot in. Martha spoon-fed the patient. He resisted at first, but gradually slurped the brew, between little belches. When he finished and sank back onto the pillow, Tom spread the carpet over the bedclothes.

"There," he said, "with luck, he won't spew. He must sweat it out. We should take turns to watch him and make sure he does not throw off the carpet. Only remove it to let him piss. Have a jar of water handy for when he wakes; he'll be damned thirsty. The rest is in God's hands. He'll either be cured or dead in the morning."

"I'll sit with him," said Katie, easing herself into a rocking chair, "for as long as it takes."

They left her to it. Silence descended on the upper floor. The noises from Mr. Denby's bedchamber had subsided. Back in the kitchen, Martha said, "That Katie knows which side 'er bread is buttered. She'll take good care of 'im. Why does it always 'appen to the good ones, when the bastards, who should burn in hell, lead a charmed life?"

"Och, woman, it was ever thus," said Malcolm. "I often wonder why brave young souls are snatched away while horrible, white-haired buzzards feast on their entrails."

"Careful, Pastor Munro," said Tom. "Judge not, lest ye be judged."

"Hearken to the Bishop of Bollocks!" Malcolm chuckled grimly, thinking of Squeaker. "Remind me to attend yer next baptism!"

Tom stepped outside, beckoning Malcolm to follow him. He walked towards the storeroom, swung round, and grabbed the

Scotsman's shirtsleeve. "You are steering close to the wind again," he hissed. "You and your loose tongue! Don't look innocent. Another minute, and you would have given that blabbering bunter enough rope to hang us. When I say, 'Never speak of it,' I mean *never*, not even in jest."

Malcolm stood corrected. He looked at the ground, shaking his head. "Aye, yer right. I was distracted."

Tom was unconvinced. "Do not take it lightly. By Christ's bones, do I have to worry about what you are warbling into the Irish doxy's ear too? Tread carefully. I hope you know she is engaged to poor Wilmot up there. If he dies, she will fasten on you like a limpet. We have enough entanglements. We leave in the morning, before this estate becomes a death trap. Craddock and Denby are desperate, and more than a little mad. They would love to keep us, under any pretext, to work in their fucking boiling house. We'd have to fight 'em to get away. Can you guess what would happen then? The Negroes are near the end of their tether, with the mountains beckoning. I've seen it in their eyes. Those Irish beggars would be overrun in three seconds. Think on it."

"Calm yourself, Thomas," said Malcolm. "There's no harm done. I'll be quiet and humble as a church mouse."

"Good," Tom released his sleeve, "for I am tired of leaving blood and ashes in our wake to cover your careless words. Give these people no excuse to get their hooks into us. We have enough troubles. At any moment, I expect to see Long Ben and his soldiers come marching up the drive. Now, let us be as blithe as bumpkins, friendly and helpful, until we shake the dust of this place from our feet. Eat, drink, sleep, and smoke your pipe. Make commonplace remarks. Keep your gear in order for a swift departure. Nothing else."

The afternoon passed in relative peace. Malcolm took Tom's advice, ate his fill and lay down for a long siesta. Denby, his lust temporarily sated and fortified with rum, took over from James in the all-important boiling house. The simmering copper vats required constant vigilance. Two Ibos, called Gog and Magog, took turns supervising the skimming and ladling. They had become experts, taking care not to let the brown syrup congeal or splash terrible burns onto the workforce. For this, they were allowed to select helpers from among their tribesmen, give basic orders in their Ibo language, and receive extra offal from the kitchen. Still, a white man needed to be present in the murderous heat, complete with pocket watch and notepaper, for the precise timings. He also kept a loaded pistol and stout cane handy.

Irish servants worked close by. A close-knit team of trained slaves often formed the nucleus of a rebellion, but, in this case, teamwork was a priority. If the watermill broke down, an old ox-driven grinder could be brought back into service, but if the boiling process was interrupted, the entire production chain snapped. Luckily for the overseers, the Ibos, from the Bight of Bonny, considered themselves superior to the great gang in the fields, who were mainly from the Gold Coast. Gog and Magog's group had distinct crossed brands with Portuguese letters from Sao Thome. Unlike the Angolans, their ears were intact. The field hands simply had DY, for James, the Duke of York and principal shareholder of the Royal Africa Company, scorched into their chests.

Each tribe stuck to its own huts, with separate Saturday night dances and rituals. On the Caernarvon Estate, they were allowed small percussion instruments, but not the long drums, which could be used for signaling across the fields. Due to the scarcity of clerics, as well as any interest in spiritual matters, no attempt was made to evangelize the slaves. Somewhere, buried among the ancient laws of England, an awkward clause prohibited the enslavement of fellow Christians. Very well: let the blacks remain devil-worshippers and idolaters. It suited everybody. The alternative was unthinkable. The gospel weakened the efficiency of the Papist colonies. Apart from wasting time and giving the Africans ideas above their station, what good could it do to introduce Jesus and His girlish ideas? That nonsense suited the Quakers and Puritan fanatics in Massachusetts. See how long they would last, trying to manage hordes of savages wielding billhooks on isolated islands in a hostile sea. There was room for only One Unholy Trinity in Jamaica: God the Father— Hard Cash, God the Son—Hard Work, and God the Holy Spirit— Hard Liquor.

The chief overseer emerged from his office, demanding claret and a basin of hot water. Martha informed him of Tom's efforts to save Wilmot. He would see about that later. Once his hands stopped shaking, Craddock shaved himself, scalp and all, up in his room. He never allowed a valet, black or white, to come near him with a razor. A few self-inflicted nicks were preferable to the risk of a cut throat. The little boy polished his riding boots in the hall. Spruced up, the chief overseer rode off to inspect his domain, to see and be seen. He had entrusted a recently imported bloodhound to Old Carney, the toothless, hatchet-faced dog handler, who already cared for two bull mastiffs. The kennels adjoined the distillery yard. Dogs kept the servants away from the rum, but it also meant that Carney was often blind drunk. If anything happened to those dogs, Craddock had sworn to double the handler's indenture, after a good flogging. Today, with the tension following the Coco incident in the air, it was a relief to see Carney only mildly tipsy. Thurloe, the bloodhound named after Cromwell's old spymaster, suffered in the heat, panting with his tongue out.

Craddock reminded the handler to replenish the hound's water bowl and proceeded to circle the cane fields. The labors of Hercules seemed easy compared to managing a sugar plantation. There was so much detail to worry about. Denby's increasingly erratic behavior did not bode well. If Wilmot succumbed to his fever, that blue-faced buffoon, Sheppard, would have to pay for it. Nobody had given the rogue permission to experiment on the sick bookkeeper with heathen poisons. It should not be too difficult to surprise the pair of pirates, disarm them, and chain them to the boiling house wall, at least until the end of the harvest. No one would care, certainly not the Jamaican planters' assembly. The landowners were heartily sick of Sir Henry Morgan and his ilk. The Spaniards were bankrupt and tired of endless war. Their king was a gibbering imbecile. The buccaneers had served their purpose.

Now, the sea dogs only made the harbors unsafe, destabilized the Port Royal Exchange, and fraternized with French outlaws in the sea-lanes. They had become more trouble than they were worth. Hopefully, the new governor from London would arrive soon with more Royal Navy firepower. A modern version of the Cromwellian general-at-sea, another Robert Blake, able to enforce the 1670 peace treaty, was needed. But no, King Charles was merrily gambling and fornicating in Newmarket, content to leave the defense of the islands to thieving scum. It was no way to protect such a lucrative industry. Why didn't the royal goat, however blinded by lust, understand that sugar was becoming as precious as silver? A child could see it.

Craddock rested in the stirrups. What was he thinking? Holding the pirates against their will was pointless. They'd never knuckle under. The effect of the wine was wearing off. A feeling of loneliness threatened to overwhelm him. Seeking temporary relief between a black girl's legs was no longer an option. Unlike the rampant Denby, Craddock had recently become impotent. Nothing he could do, or imagine, helped. Further efforts between the sheets would invite mockery from the slave women, and he could not risk that. He observed the harvesting gang, resuming its labors after the midday meal of corn mush and salt fish. The work song recommenced, punctuated by chopping noises. The sound steadied his resolve. Each chop brought him closer to his goal. It promised to be a bumper harvest. He just had to stick it out and keep the wagonloads trundling towards the North Docks. One day, he too would earn enough to leave all this behind. He envisaged riding through his own deer park under English oaks, past swans afloat in dark green ponds. Perhaps the old feeling would return to his loins in his native climate. It couldn't happen too soon.

In the storeroom, Malcolm awoke to find Tom sitting beside him. "Sweet dreams on a full belly?"

Malcolm blinked. "Pass the water." He gulped greedily. "This place takes me back to the Guinea Coast. It must be the singing. I dreamt I was on a rocking deck over a stinking cargo, but the captain had Craddock's face. Then, suddenly, I was in the shrouds, slicing the lanyard of a deadeye block and letting it fall to spill his brains like an egg yolk. The brains fried on the planks, and I ate them up, straight from his cracked skull."

"I saw your teeth gnashing," Tom said. "It must have tasted good."

"Och, that wasn't the end of it. 'Tis fresh in my mind. Ye know how dreams can be. Fifty red-eyed blackies, clanking in chains, crawled out of the hold. They heaved us both overboard, me with the egg dribbling down my chin. When we hit the water, I became a shark, one of those hammer-headed beasties that follow slavers. Craddock turned into a big, slimy medusa. He kept stinging me, until I gnawed off all his feelers. His head floated to the surface. His ruddy face melted away. The sun shone clear through the jelly, beating like a heart above me. I swam up for a bite. Crivvens, it was too sweet. Awful. Then the sea salt made me sick. Thank God for this water, Tom, or I might have spewed for real."

"Your belly is not accustomed to the rich fare in Martha's kitchen," said Tom. "Don't wolf it down so fast. Chew properly."

"Och, away and boil yer brains! I have cast-iron bowels. When I was a bairn, on Sundays in Glasgow we feasted on blood, lungs, livers, and peppered oats stuffed into a cow's stomach, all washed down with usquebaugh. In Guinea, I thrived on fried bats' wings, baked bilge rats, and devilled lizards' kidneys. They swam in sauces that would scald yer Saxon guts till they wriggled out of yer backside. I was the only man dropping solid stools into the waves from the chains while the rest of the crew wallowed in bloody fluxations. I can digest anything that grows or crawls on the face of the earth or swims in the deepest oceans. The speed of my chewing is neither here nor there."

Tom chuckled. "You and I, young man, we'll have a wager when we reach the main. The Indians have diablo peppers that will make you dance screaming over a cliff top with volcano smoke puffing out of your scorched asshole. Your jaws will lock tighter than a bear trap before you empty half your bowl. I'll lick mine clean, and ask for a second helping, with your pesos in my purse. Wait and see.

Meanwhile, prepare yourself for a heavy dinner this evening. Make the most of it. Tomorrow, with luck, we'll be far to the east of this madhouse by sunset."

The meal began formally, with toasts to His Majesty's health. Martha and Maria brought the dishes to the dining room door. O'Hanlon, an old servant wearing a blue jacket, distributed plates, napkins, and silver cutlery. The little black boy topped up the wine glasses. The four diners occupied one side of the long table, facing the window and a view of the last rays of the sun caressing the misty mountaintops. They sat in a row, first Malcolm, then Craddock, then Denby, and, finally, Tom, beside Wilmot's vacant seat. For a while, the orange light in the sky blended with the red leather wall covers and the candlelight. The room seemed to be stained in blood. Ten minutes later, it was pitch black outside.

Thanks to his years in Arnout's household, Tom manipulated the cutlery without difficulty. Malcolm had never used a fork in his life, and did not try now. Forks were effeminate French inventions; even officers scorned them on English ships. He spooned up sweet potatoes, rice and a variety of meat and fish, sometimes grabbing with his fingers, or hacking with his knife, as the fancy took him. It made no difference whether meatballs fried in suet, pork plastered with oysters, hashed capons, or olio stew appeared—everything was jumbled together on his plate and shoved into his mouth willy-nilly.

Beside him, Craddock pecked at his food decorously, using it to accompany his drinking rather than the other way round. Denby ate with furious concentration, sweat on his brow, as if each dish were a personal enemy, to be impaled with deadly precision. His jaws worked incessantly, like the watermill's crushers, his right hand darting forward to seize his glass at regular intervals. After the royal toast, few words interrupted the serious business of keeping body and soul together. Gradually, the main course was demolished. They dabbed their chins.

"Mrs. King has promised us," announced Craddock, "her famous cheesecake, containing slices of pineapple from our own garden, glazed with our own sugar. We can also expect rum from our own distillery in a spicy bumbo, along with the Porto and cherry brandy."

Denby, who had only grunted hungrily so far, spoke for the first time. He sneered, "No doubt, our own spicy mares, Martha and Maria, will bring it to our own table too, so that we can congratulate them with a well-earned slap on their very own cherry rumps." He addressed nobody in particular, staring at the candlestick in front of his plate.

"My word," said Craddock, "we are in an impertinent mood this evening. Perhaps you need an early night after today's exertions, Mr. Denby? I would never deny a gentleman his amusement, but I must ask you to refrain from tearing Maria's clothes and bruising her arms. She belongs to the estate that employs you. If you damage the property, I am within my rights to dock your wages."

Denby swung round with the look of a rabid dog. His mouth twisted, as if to yell an obscenity, but he bit his tongue. Instead, he assumed a cavalier attitude. "Ah, Craddock, you are trying to needle me. Look, here comes the cake and bumbo. Perhaps O'Hanlon can regale us with a soothing tune on his lute?"

The old servant produced the instrument from behind a corner chair, sat down, and began to pick laboriously at a repetitive descending scale. The women entered, carrying the cake and a brimming punchbowl. Denby made a great show of standing, bowing, and drinking to their health. Maria took care to keep her distance, sidling towards the door. Martha stood with her hands on her hips. She had shaped the pineapple slices on the sides of the cake into waves. A chocolate frigate, complete with paper sails, rode on a sea of cream. The masts were sticks of vanilla.

"There," she said. "You won't get better in Paris."

Tom was touched. "Ah, you done us proud, Mrs. King. I pray a full-sized version of such a vessel carries you home one day."

"Aye," said Malcolm, "'tis a shame to damage it."

They made short work of the cake, but left the ship standing on the silver tray to admire it. When the punchbowl was almost empty, Craddock called for a decanter of cherry brandy. The little boy removed the stopper and walked up and down, serving them with hardly a pause. Tom asked O'Hanlon to accompany Malcolm's tenor voice.

"What is it you wish for?" asked the musician.

"Ye ken 'Henry Martin' from the time of the king's grandsire? It is a favorite in Port Royal, with a slight change in the name. I recall a verse or two, I think," said Malcolm. "No need for fancy finger work. Pluck the main chords and I'll supply the melody."

He intoned the old Scottish air tunefully, clinking his knife against the bowl in time. O'Hanlon became animated and embroidered the rhythm with Celtic frills. Craddock's great wig nodded appreciatively. Malcolm's voice soared triumphantly.

> *"Come lower your topsail and brail up your mizzen*
> *And bring your ship under my lee,*
> *Or I will give you a full flowing ball,*
> *Flowing ball, flowing ball,*
> *And your dear bodies drown in the salt sea.*
>
> *"With broadside and broadside and at it they went*
> *For fully two hours or three,*
> *Till Henry Morgan gave her the death shot,*
> *The death shot, the death shot,*
> *And straight to the bottom went she."*

Initially, Denby drummed his fingers. By the end, he was smashing his fist on the table until the glasses rattled. His wig slipped down over his eyebrows, making him resemble an angry monkey. He attempted to follow Malcolm by howling garbled lines from a penny gallows ballad.

> *"Aaaargh, I'll die in a rope*
> *Without any hope*
> *My own dear loving brother*
> *And we'll all be hanged together!"*

O'Hanlon lost the tempo and stopped in a discordant jangle. Denby splashed brandy on him, shrieking, "Come on and keep up, you Irish idiot, before I shatter that twiddle box over your thick skull!"

Craddock seized Denby's arm. "Enough! Enough, I say! You are out of order, sir!"

"Enough? Unhand me, sir! I am the one who has had enough!" Denby wrenched himself free and sprang to his feet. His chair crashed to the floor. "I've had more than enough, slaving in that boiling house night and day! I envy Wilmot. At least he sweats peacefully in his bed, untroubled by flies, the stink of niggers, or the fear of a knife in the ribs. By God, it's all right for you to go riding about like the king of France, inspecting your domain and giving yourself airs. Look, you entertain thieving vagrants as if they were lords of the realm you had summoned to complete your mad illusion. I, sir, do the work of ten men. At midnight, I will be out there again, taking care of business until dawn, because you cannot pay anybody enough to perform such tasks. Without me, this whole bloody shambles would collapse about your ears. You, sir, are the one who is out of order!"

The color of Craddock's face deepened into a frighteningly intense purple. His nose seemed ready to explode. His shaking hand grasped a fork as if it were a weapon. His tongue flapped, but no words came out. Tom brushed past Denby, who fell against the wall, and loosened the lace round Craddock's throat.

"Hurry," he said, "get water before he has a fit."

Denby lurched forward and clawed his way along the table. On his way, he picked up the chocolate ship, crammed it into his mouth, and seized the brandy decanter from the boy. A candlestick fell. Malcolm set it upright before it caused a fire. While Martha assisted Tom, Denby swayed in the doorway, spat out the paper sails and launched into a final tirade. Chocolate dribbled down his chin.

"There!" he screamed. "If that cockless eunuch wants to dictate how a real man behaves, let him try it! Look, he swoons like an old duchess! One foot inside my chamber, and I'll blast his beetroot chops to kingdom come. I have a brace of pistols primed for the occasion. That goes for the rest of you assholes as well."

With that, Denby lunged at Maria in the hallway, but this time she escaped in the dark, leaving her torn sleeve in his fist. The decanter lay broken at his feet. Martha went to investigate, found him sprawled at the bottom of the stairs, and kicked him in the balls. She sarcastically begged his pardon, pretending she hadn't seen him. After vomiting, he heaved himself up one stair at a time, whimpering, "I'll kill you for that, you fat cunt! By God, you'll get another seven years!"

"Go on, try it," she rejoined. "So I can plug yer noisy gob with yer own little pizzle. I might as well be hung for a sheep, or in your case, a pig. Now go to your bed, or, by Christ, I'll get my carving knife and do it right away!"

She came into the dining room. "That's been brewing for some time," she shook her head wearily, "'E ain't had one of 'is rages lately. The bastard never remembers a thing in the morning. 'E goes quiet for a few days, and then it all builds up again, and—bang!"

"Aye, it gets some of 'em like that," said Malcolm. "I've seen it aplenty. That's normal behavior for most merchant sea captains."

Tom had removed Craddock's wig. Martha mopped his bald white head with a wet napkin. "Like polishing a billiard ball, ain't it? Let's get 'im upstairs."

Once the chief overseer had recovered, Tom and O'Hanlon helped him from the table and slowly out of the dining room. Malcolm and Martha led the way, holding candlesticks, guiding them round the broken glass, spilled brandy, and vomit. The little boy followed with the wig. Loud snores came from Denby's open door. Soon Craddock was also asleep. Before they descended again, Tom peered into the gloom of Wilmot's bedchamber. He heard steady breathing from two dark shapes in the bed.

"Well?" Martha whispered at his elbow.

Tom held his finger to his lips. "Shhh. The worst is over. I think Katie completed the cure."

She sighed. "I could do with some curin' meself, if you know what I mean."

Later, when Malcolm was asleep, Tom stole out of the storeroom. By the light of a single candle, panting beneath his thrusts, Martha miraculously shed her years. Surprisingly agile, she became an eighteen-year-old beauty in the throes of passion. Tom found it easy to imagine himself as the gallant heartbreaker, Claude du Val. Tomorrow, Martha King would be a plump, worn-out servant. Thomas Sheppard would be a crusty old sea dog again, but tonight all that was forgotten.

5
THE BLUE MOUNTAINS

The following morning, Tom and Malcolm skirted the edge of the thick forest that covered the foothills of the Blue Mountains. Martha had given them two rolled-up sleeping mats. The Caernarvon Estate lay behind them near the coast. Tom followed Captain Mackett's instructions. He headed for an outpost on the western bank of the Morant River, above the immense territory belonging to Colonel Freeman. Tom remembered smallholdings, animal pens, cocoa walks, and indigo works in this area. A sea of sugar cane had swallowed them all up, spreading south, down to the great Freeman mansion at Belvedere, overlooking the Bay. The massed green stalks, over twelve feet high, rippled in the breeze as far as the eye could see, interspersed with kitchen gardens and slave provision grounds. Many smallholders had accepted the Colonel's offers and sailed away to the Carolinas. Windmills turning the fraggot crushers dotted the landscape. It was all sugar. Colonel Freeman was lord of all he surveyed. The big planter imported everything else he needed. He owned a private jetty at Freeman's Bay, where ships could land their cargoes without paying customs duties.

Tom gazed across the cane fields. Lines of harvesters appeared as black specks in the distance. "It makes Caernarvon look like a widow's cabbage patch. I wonder how many Craddocks, Wilmots, and Denbys are strutting through those acres every day."

"And Cocos. They must eat up armies of Negroes," said Malcolm. "No wonder they want our silver sheep."

"A drop in the ocean," said Tom. "They need a constant procession of ships from Africa to keep the numbers rising. Canny men could make their fortunes here."

"If they owned the ships or the land," said Malcolm. "The likes of us only see pennies. I've had a gutful of the slaving business. Privateering suits me better. I'll go straight to the top of the accursed pyramid, take the Spanish silver, and to hell with the rest. When I have collected enough, I'll make sure I never have to see a sugar works again. Those slave gangs make me gloomy. They are walking corpses, damned souls, chanting dirges at their own funerals. Did God make Negroes for that? Why do they put up with it? Eating raw shite, by God! They all have sharp sickles in their hands and there are enough of them to defeat an army."

"Why does anybody put up with anything? Why are we hiding in the wilderness? While there's life, there's hope, even in the life of a beast of burden. Ask Joseph about Barbados. Think of the King of Spain's galleys. White men submit as readily when the other choice is a sound thrashing or worse. Fear not, we'll steer clear of them," said Tom. "Crabbe's place lies beyond the plantations. Look there. See where the land dips into the valley? I reckon that's the spot, among the trees, where the rough country begins."

Ezra Crabbe's compound occupied a rocky outcrop overlooking the Morant River. Later in the year, it would become a raging torrent, but now, in December, the thin stream snaked through a ditch of dry stones. A mulatto youth goaded a pair of oxen, pulling a tree trunk towards a shaded sawpit. Two slaves, one above and one below, sawed vertically through great red logs. Behind them, a stout fence enclosed a meadow full of cattle.

"Mahogany, thick, and hard as rock," said Tom. "They'll be lucky to cut up one tree a day." He hailed the mulatto. "Ahoy there, laddie, where can I find Mr. Crabbe?"

"My name is Jonathan Crabbe," said the boy in a surprisingly refined accent, "but if you want my father, Ezra, he's in the house. Who are you?"

"Sailors, hunting for Coxon's fleet. I believe your father has some of our Angolans carrying meat downriver."

"Go in that gate. You'll find him there."

A palisade rose above the boulders on the bank. At its base, thorn bushes formed a spiky barrier. Two gateposts, each bearing a human skull, flanked the only entrance.

"Who lives here?" wondered Malcolm. "Cannibals?"

An old man with a long white beard came out to greet them. He pointed a stout stick at the skulls. "Don't mind them. There's worse on London Bridge. Anyhow, these be not Christian bones but those of heathen runaways. They make the Maroon savages think twice before entering. I employ Satan's own tricks against his offspring."

"So I see, Mr. Crabbe," said Tom, extending his hand. "I am Thomas Sheppard. My friend is Malcolm Munro."

The shaggy hermit's grip crushed his fingers. "Call me Ezra. You must come from the privateers in the bay, yes? Looking for game? Dozens of your shipmates have passed through already. You won't find any wild herds this side of the Plantain Valley now. They've been frightened by the shooting, gone to higher pastures. I fear Coxon has had all the fresh meat he's going to get. We need all our beasts to supply the plantations."

"And the Angolan Negroes Coxon sent you?"

"Angolans? You mean the crop-eared wretches? Pah! I returned them the day before yesterday. I kept two for myself, as agreed, but they will need months of good feeding before I can find a use for them. The poor wraiths can barely lift a rack of ribs between 'em. Come inside. We'll talk in the shade."

They encountered another skull, festooned with parrot feathers, above the door to the main hall. Thick bamboo pillars supported a palm-thatched roof, high above mahogany floorboards. Lattice walls allowed a breeze to circulate. Clothes, bags, weapons, ropes, and tools hung from nails in every corner. The furniture had been fashioned from roughly hewn tree trunks.

"Plenty room to spread your mats," said Ezra. "Nobody steals in this place. You can put down your gear in safety."

They walked through the hall into an enclosed yard, surrounded by huts, within the palisade. A clay water cistern sat to one side. In the middle, a sturdy Cuban Bark tree blocked the sunlight. Hammocks swung from the roof posts. A toothless black woman with breasts as flat as pancakes pushed cornmeal dough into an earth oven. An Angolan listlessly swept the leaves under the tree. Chickens pecked at fallen crumbs. Ezra chopped open three coconuts.

"You've had a wasted journey, Mr. Sheppard," he said.

"Oh, I don't know," said Tom. He raised the coconut to his lips and drank greedily. "I like it here. Last night we stayed at a plantation that was pure Bedlam. We are in no hurry to return to the beach either, Ezra. Perhaps we can be of service. How do you like the idea of fried ram's liver on your table? I want to test my new hunting piece on the mountain goats. They will be much easier to carry than cows."

"A good thought. Try to bring some back alive," said Ezra. "A mating pair if possible. We ate our last goats at Christmas. I miss their bleating. Take my son, Jonathan, and a hound with you. He knows the high ridges. Atop the peaks, you can sometimes glimpse the mountains near Saint Jago in Cuba, far across the sea. Only make sure you don't run into a Maroon war party. They have been raiding to the edge of the cane fields lately, trying to get their hands on food, tools, and stray women. They generally scatter at the first shot, but they become bolder up in the mist."

"Will they attack us on sight?" asked Malcolm.

"If you leave them alone," said Ezra, "they usually leave you alone, but it pays to be careful. They cannot abide hunting dogs. Our mastiffs scare them off."

"Sound like Indians," said Tom.

"Nowhere near as dangerous," said Ezra. "The Maroon spears and arrows are puny twigs compared to Indian weapons. They don't feast on people either. Most of all, they want to be allowed to live in peace. Of course, there are always hotheads, like the previous owners of those skulls. Three runaways got into the yard. We killed the buggers. One came screaming into my bedchamber with an axe in his hand and a set of dog's teeth tearing his ass. Luckily, I keep a loaded pistol within reach when I sleep. Take a look over the front door, the one with the feathers. There's a round hole in the middle of the forehead. A miracle. It was too dark to aim properly. The pistol lies next to my Holy Scriptures. God guided the bullet."

"When did this happen?" asked Tom.

"Over three years ago, back in '76. This place ain't been bothered since. The Lord watches over the righteous. Make yourselves at home for today. The rules of the house are simple and easy to remember. No stealing, fornicating, or drunkenness. Up to now, I have only been forced to banish two of your comrades from the premises. If they return, they won't get off so lightly. You can count on it."

"What rules did they break?" asked Malcolm.

"All of 'em," growled Ezra, "adding the abomination of swinish sodomy to their other sins."

"Sodomites! I'd have hanged the pigs," said Malcolm, "facing each other, with both necks in one noose. That way, they could enjoy a last dance together. By letting them live, ye have created enemies who may yet lurk in the bushes."

"What were their names?" asked Tom.

"I'd rather not remember them. To me, they do not exist as men," Ezra's voice hardened with contempt. "But, since you ask, the old rogue calls himself Godfrey Stone. His nose is flattened, from a blow or, more likely, the grand pox. He calls his pussy boy Little Walter, a plump, greasy pup, half Indian, by the look of him. You are right. I should have killed 'em. I have read Isaiah. It would have been the godly thing to do, but I feared a vengeful visit from their shipmates. Are they known to you, by any chance?"

"No," said Tom, "the combined crews are at least three hundred strong. More arrive every day, from all points of the compass. To be honest, Ezra, I have not been on a privateer's account for many a year. Among that crowd, I barely recognize a handful of faces from the old days, when Morgan was at sea."

"Ah, well," said Ezra, "the chances are, the buggers have left for the coast with their shitty tails between their legs. Good riddance. They were not keen to enter the forest. You, Tom and Malcolm, you'll bring us back something larger than a couple of land crabs, I hope?"

Hunting in the mountains required greater preparation than simply walking out with a musket. The next day, Ezra's son Jonathan appeared at the gate with a mule and a slave holding a big dog on a leash. The mule carried cloaks, ropes, blankets, axes, and dry meat, wrapped in tarred canvas. Everybody had slept well in the airy wooden buildings. Ezra insisted on early nights, after a Bible reading, and nothing stronger than hot chocolate to drink. The party followed the river upstream with clear heads and refreshed muscles.

Their eyes soon adjusted to the relative darkness beneath the high canopy. Jonathan was familiar with the steep forest tracks. On previous visits, he had cut notches into the barks of certain trees. He pulled the mule along with one hand and chopped away new growth with his cutlass in the other. After a while, he gave the reins to Malcolm. The slave, a squat Ibo called Addy, took the lead, dragged along by the eager hound. They climbed for hours, refreshing themselves at streams. Tom held his hunting rifle at the ready.

"There don't seem to be any of yer famous Maroons about," said Malcolm. "Only birds and butterflies."

"We've walked past a lookout, for sure, hiding up a tree," said Tom. "This forest is their first line of defense. They don't let you see 'em till they're on top of you. I hope your musket is primed and your tinderbox handy. You've got to be quick with these monkeys, not so, Jonathan?"

"Oh, yes," Jonathan smiled. "Fast as lightning."

"Och, to hell with ye both!" Malcolm frowned. He tugged at the mule's bridle. The kerchief round his head darkened with sweat. Eventually they reached the edge of a wide clearing above a ridge and rested beneath the last tall pines. The trees became shorter after that, interspersed with ferns. Overhead, dense mists hid the peaks.

Looking back, they could see the windmills from Freeman's sugar works, and the coastline, all the way to the Yallahs Saltpans. The ships in Morant Bay appeared no bigger than pond insects. Jonathan produced a spyglass to survey the scene in detail.

"Your shipmates are busy taking on water," he said. "There they are, clear as day, hauling barrels on deck from the boats."

"Here, let me take a look, boy," said Tom. He tried to identify Joseph, Scarrett, or Sharp among the moving figures, but it was impossible. Was that the flash of Coxon's jacket near the flagship's mizzen? The red smear might equally be a buccaneer's sash, spilt wine, or turtle's blood. Tom twisted the lens, scanning the rolling country around the Caernarvon Estate. A column of smoke rose from the boiler house. The watermill lay concealed in a wooded hollow, but he thought he could recognize the eastern wall of the mansion, with the white frame of Craddock's bedroom window against the brickwork. He began to examine the nearby woods.

Suddenly, he glimpsed a flashing pinpoint, eight hundred yards away, at the green edge of the clearing. Tom sharpened the focus on the tree line. Nothing. Perhaps a bird taking to the air. Wait! There it was again, bouncing in the scrub, attached to a low, dark shape, moving fast. A big dog raced forward and paused on a rock. The sunlight caught the gleaming spikes on its war collar. Now, Tom spotted another dog behind it, leading a scattered handful of men out of the bushes. He slowly moved the glass to the right, to see what they were chasing. Well ahead, there appeared to be a bloodhound, pulling its handler towards an isolated Blue Mahoe. The ancient tree spread its thick branches over a stony elevation halfway across the field, closer to Tom's position.

Tom hissed, "I'll be damned!"

"What is it?" asked Malcolm.

"Get down. Keep the mule out of sight. Restrain the dog," said Tom, still peering through the glass. "I fear we have unwelcome visitors."

"Let me see," said Jonathan. "I might know them."

"Wait. I recognize three of 'em, coming up to that tree," said

Tom. "Yes, by Christ, that's Long Ben and the two bastards from The Mermaid. There are five in all. I've never laid eyes on the rogues with the dogs before."

Malcolm lit his musket fuse. He growled softly, "No soldiers with them, eh? Right. This time. This time we end it, once and for all."

Tom heard the flint clicking in the tinderbox and hissed, "Don't shoot yet, whatever you do, Mal. You'll alert them to our presence."

Jonathan became impatient. "Soldiers? What are you talking about? Here, let me see!" He snatched the telescope from Tom and aimed it. "There's Old Carney with the bloodhound, and his mate with the big dogs. They catch runaways from Caernarvon. The others are new. Somebody is hiding up that tree."

Luckily, Addy had trained his own dog well. The big beast lay flat, panting rhythmically. Malcolm tied the mule to a trunk deeper in the shadows. Tom settled the hunting party down. They passed the telescope round, chewed strips of dried meat, and drank from a water skin, observing the activity round the Blue Mahoe. A black man, wearing only sackcloth breeches, clambered among the dry russet leaves near the top. At such a distance, they could barely hear his shouts, answered by the barks and jeers of his pursuers, who had gathered beneath the branches.

Malcolm squinted through the glass, giving a commentary. "Hah! The ginger bastard from The Mermaid, the one they call Red Rod, is throwing stones at yon nigger in the tree. Looks like he hit him. The others are joining in. He's getting a good pelting."

Tom heard another sound over the distant racket. At first, he paid no attention to the plaintive meowing of a turkey buzzard. When it was repeated, he turned to Jonathan. "Strange," he said, "when the crows call like that, you always see them, protecting a nest, wheeling about in the sky. I see nothing."

Jonathan looked into Tom's eyes. They whispered in unison, "Maroons."

Tom grabbed Malcolm's shoulder and whispered, "Keep your noise down. Maroons hate nothing more than runaway catchers. If they are here, they won't stand idly by."

"Wait," Malcolm shrugged him off, chuckling. "Long Ben is climbing into the branches with his cutlass between his teeth. Damn, I can't see for the leaves. There. He's chopping and prodding. My God, the nigger's on his back. They're…they're falling together… the dogs…the dogs are all over them. Ben is bitten in the ass. The nigger is banging Ben's head against the tree. The nigger…it's Coco! Coco with the cacka! Och, now Red Rod is kicking Coco's balls! The bloodhound wants to join the fun. Crivvens, he's off the leash! The others are dancing about, shrieking like fishwives in a fit. This is fine sport, Tom. See for yerself, man."

"Shut your hatch. Remember where you are," Tom growled, taking the spyglass. "This ain't a Southwark bear pit. Get back and look to your weapons. Stay hidden."

When he had focused on the writhing figures, Tom had to smile too. The escaped bloodhound had caught a fresh scent. It was sniffing towards the edge of the meadow to the right, with Old Carney in pursuit, screaming, loud enough for all to hear, "Here! Thurloe! Here, boy! Thurloe! Stop, you son of a bitch!"

Addy's dog stood up, drooling spittle and wagging its tail. The Ibo stuffed a piece of dried meat into its mouth, rubbed its neck and hauled the beast past the mule, further back into the woods. The buzzard's call hung in the air again. Crouching beside Tom, Jonathan sprinkled a pinch of powder into the pan of his matchlock and lit the fuse.

"That's right, son," Tom told him. "We may be forced to defend ourselves. That was no bird."

By now, Carney's mate had restrained the attack dogs and tethered them to the Blue Mahoe. Long Ben tried to stand, but fell, clutching his ankle. Red Rod twisted Coco's arms behind his back while his pockmarked mate, Sully, punched the runaway slave repeatedly in the belly. Coco spat a mixture of bloody teeth and saliva into Sully's face, for which he received another kick in the crotch. He slid to the ground, took a boot to the jaw, and lay motionless. Fifty yards across the field, Thurloe nosed around a bush. Old Carney bent down, seeking the trailing leash.

The bush quivered. The bloodhound gave a piercing yelp. He turned to face Old Carney, howling and pawing at an arrow, which stuck out from the folds of skin above his collar. A second later, Carney stared at a second arrow sprouting from his own stomach. Tom thought he saw a dark shape flitting among the trees behind the bush, but it was gone in a blink. Carney's hat fell off. He sank to his knees and pulled out the arrow. Thurloe circled around the kneeling man, still pawing, until a massive spurt of blood cut short his howls and he collapsed. With great presence of mind, Old Carney took out his knife, cut the sleeves off his jacket, and used them to bandage his wounded belly.

Tom swept the lens to the left. The rest of the slave-catchers remained unaware of the fate of the bloodhound and its master. They scarcely glanced at Old Carney. He had his back to them and appeared to be settling Thurloe under the bush. The spreading puddle of Thurloe's blood was invisible to them. Carney's antics with the sleeves went unnoticed. The attack dogs, straining at their tethers, made such a din that any other yelps and howls were inaudible. By the time five ragged, half-naked black men, carrying bundles of bamboo spears, burst from the forest, there was little time to react. An emaciated, white-bearded Negro crouched behind a rock, to aim an antique Spanish crossbow. His comrades sprinted towards the group under the lone tree.

Long Ben saw them first. His shout of, "Maroons!" rang out across the clearing. The mastiffs were silent for a second, and then continued their barking with renewed vigor. Ben crawled towards a bundle of gear and pulled a pistol from its sling. Old Carney's mate fumbled frantically with the knot on the first dog's leash, cursing himself for making it so tight. The animal did not help by tugging at it fiercely.

"Cut it, you fucking idiot!" yelled Red Rod. "Use your knife!" The man did not hear him. He continued to work at the knot with shaking fingers, piss staining his breeches, while his hunting knife hung unused from his belt. Rod slapped the man's cheek, extracted the knife and hacked at the leather. The mastiff sprang free, straight at the advancing spearmen. The last thing Red Rod felt, before he could reach the second dog, was a crossbow bolt slamming into his skull through his woolen cap. He was dead before he fell across Coco's unconscious body. The slap brought the handler out of his panic. He prised the knife out of Rod's fist and cut the other beast loose. It bounded forward like a cannon shot.

Tom grinned, passing the glass to Jonathan. "Better and better! Take a peep. God willing, they'll all slaughter each other."

"My God!" said Jonathan. "Those dogs can fight! I don't believe it! Look! Old Carney's made it back to the tree. He's loading up a musket."

The crack of Long Ben's pistol coincided with a blast from Sully's musket. Carney fired shortly after, immediately beginning to reload. One spearman tumbled into the grass, another wrestled with the first mastiff that tore his throat and ripped the skin off his chest with its war collar, in spite of the spear planted in its ribs. When a second pair of jaws sank into his wrist, the Maroon stopped twitching, but the dogs continued to worry at his corpse, ignoring the rest of the action.

Malcolm crawled forward. "Will ye gimme the glass? I'm missing the fun… Jesus! Is that Red Rod on the ground yonder? I think the son of a bitch is dead. One less devil to send to hell. What's with Long Ben? He is barely crawling."

"Must have snapped his ankle in the fall," reckoned Tom. "He won't be chasing anybody for a while, even if he gets out of this pickle. I hope he does. I always liked Ben."

"Shouldn't we help?" asked Jonathan.

"Not on your life," said Tom. "I'll explain later. Trust me, lad, those men are not our friends."

Seeing two of their number dead, the remaining Maroons hurled a shower of spears, one of which pinned Sully's foot to the earth. Then they turned and ran. The war hounds started after them, leaving their victim's ripped remains. Old Carney fired a final shot in their direction. The speared dog quickly tired. He sat down, staring mournfully, the shaft stuck between his ribs, and his long tongue gradually turned red. The other hound plunged into the forest after the fleeing Maroons. It never re-emerged.

Sully screamed and yanked the spear out of his boot. He hopped over to Red Rod's body, using his musket as a prop. The ginger-haired doorman seemed to be alive, feebly pushing himself up. It took Sully a moment to realize that Coco had regained his senses and was stirring under the weight of the corpse. Coco pulled free, groaning and clasping his broken jaw. Sully raised his musket by the barrel, to club the runaway's brains out.

"No!" Sully cried. "You will not live, you black turd! This is all because of you!"

Long Ben, leaning against the tree, ramming a ball into his pistol and shouted, "Avast, you fool! He's worth at least twelve guineas! Leave him be!"

It was too late. The butt of the weapon smashed Coco's head like a pumpkin. Brains splattered Red Rod's dead face. Sully propped himself up with the musket again, tears streaming down his pitted cheeks. "There," he gasped. "That's for poor Roderick."

Long Ben muttered, "For all the good it did him. You've made it all pointless, you moon-faced sot."

Sully swung round, his eyes blazing, but the words stuck in his throat, from which a final crossbow bolt protruded, squirting blood. Long Ben turned to see the wizened Maroon rise from a rock pile, twenty yards away. The old marksman's grin formed a toothless black crescent in his white beard. Sully crashed, face down, beside the other bodies. The ancient black warrior yelled, "Santiago!" in Spanish, followed by a vulture's call. He raised his weapon above his head in triumph, like a crucifix. Then he vanished, as if folded into the earth. The entire business had taken no more than five minutes. Now, real buzzards rose in the thermal currents and echoed the old Maroon's cry. A big bird landed. Its beak tore Thurloe's wrinkled skin. Others followed. The sun disappeared in the mist. A rumble of thunder announced a shower of cooling rain.

Malcolm prepared to advance towards the scene of the action, but Tom restrained him. "No, not yet, lad. God knows how many

Maroons are still lurking in the bushes. Let's see if they want to finish what they started."

Jonathan added, "Well said. Whatever happens, the Maroons will want to remove their dead. They need the bones for their ceremonies, to send the souls back to Africa."

Tom marveled at the mulatto's perspicacity and fluent speech. Ezra Crabbe had instructed Jonathan in good English, to improve his prospects. With his handsome looks and manners, the youth would never rise to the top of West Indian society, but he could hope for a more comfortable life than the average free man of color. Perhaps, in time, his descendants would even pass for white.

"So, the sneaky buggers will be here for a good while yet, watching the field. In that case," said Tom. "We should continue north-east without drawing attention to ourselves." He patted Malcolm's shoulder, giving him a warning look. "Slave-catchers mean nothing to us, unless Jonathan feels a neighborly obligation to the Caernarvon Estate."

"God rot Caernarvon," said Jonathan. "Since Craddock took charge, there has been nothing but trouble, with runaways and Maroons breaking into the cow pens. Payments in barrels of rum. All sorts of malarkey. My father prefers to deal with Colonel Freeman. But look, Old Carney is no fool. See, he's making ready now, to get clear of the woods afore nightfall."

After calming their nerves with tobacco, the three survivors under the Blue Mahoe paid scant attention to the corpses, except to remove Red Rod and Sully's purses. The assistant handler scattered the vultures to retrieve the dog collars, strapping them to his belt. Old Carney gathered the water skins and muskets. Long Ben trimmed a forked branch into a serviceable crutch. Then, with apprehensive looks and weapons at the ready, they retraced their steps to the west. Long Ben hopped downhill, brandishing a cocked pistol. Old Carney seemed unaffected by his tightly bandaged arrow wound. He occasionally walked backwards, crouching to aim along the tree line. Soon, they had vanished. More vultures fought over the carrion in tussling mobs. As the shadows lengthened, Maroons emerged silently to scour the area for abandoned knives and clothing. They shooed away the birds and carried off their dead friends. They also took Coco's body. As a runaway, he was treated as an honorary Maroon. Unable to liberate him alive, they would chant and drum his spirit back over the ocean from the security of their mountain stronghold.

Tom's hunting party had long departed. Jonathan chose a camping site among the stunted trees and dripping ferns of the higher eastern slopes, four miles away. He advised against lighting a fire. The Maroons could follow the tang of wood smoke over great distances. The hunters huddled together in their blankets and settled down to sleep. A dark, clammy, velvet fog enveloped them.

"So," said Jonathan, "the strangers with Old Carney were shipmates of yours?"

Tom had anticipated the question. He tried to divert Jonathan's curiosity. "Yes. From another ship, but we are well rid of them."

"Why, pray?"

Tom spat, "Sodomites."

"Aye," said Malcolm, catching Tom's drift. "Sodomites of the foulest sort. The Maroons did the world a great service. The two that died, Red Rod and Sully, were the worst in the fleet, devils to the cabin boys. Thrashed the wee bairns naked at the mast every morning and comforted 'em at night with rum and swinish caresses. Those two would have made a meal of a bonnie laddie like yerself in the bat of an eye, no matter how ye struggled and squealed in their hairy embraces."

Jonathan winced, but persisted, "And the tall one who hurt his foot? You called him Long Ben, no? Is he one too? We had more than enough of such filth with Mr. Stone and Little Walter. My father swore he'd hang the next sodomite that crossed his path, drunk or sober."

"Yes, so I heard. Disgraceful," said Tom. "But Ben? He's harmless on his own, without the others to egg him on. More so, now that he can hardly walk. What do you care about the old molly anyway?"

"Nothing," said Jonathan. "Only, he is certain to go to my

father's house. Old Carney knows it is the nearest place of safety. Hereabouts, my father is held in high esteem for his skill in healing wounds and setting bones, but…"

Tom pulled his blanket up to his chin and drew his knees in, "…but he cannot abide sodomites. I don't blame him. Put your mind at rest, for pity's sake. Long Ben won't give any trouble in your father's house, and his abominations ain't branded on his forehead. Ben could pass for a Quaker. Don't lose sleep over it, boy. I am more concerned about the Maroons. Will they turn their attention to us?"

"I doubt it," said Jonathan. "Since the governor's treaty, we are officially at peace with them in these parts. After today, they will go back to their village, lick their wounds and tell tall tales round the fire. They have their funeral rites for the fallen to attend to. Of course, Craddock will make a mighty fuss, but Colonel Freeman would never call out the dragoons to start a war over dead dogs and a brace of slain sodomites."

"A paltry matter indeed," said Tom. "Good. Tomorrow we'll find us some goat meat and go home. Enough now. God bless and good night."

Before he closed his eyes, Tom glanced over at Malcolm. The Scotsman's shoulders were shaking with suppressed laughter. Luckily, Jonathan, tucked beneath his blanket, noticed nothing. Addy already snored, curled around the mastiff. The mule stretched its neck almost to the ground, breathing heavily, a rope of spittle hanging from its slack mouth. Tom found himself wondering whether he could engender a fine son like Jonathan with Theodora. Then, the thought of his dashed dreams in Port Royal overcame him. He plunged into a dreamless sleep.

Despite Jonathan's protests, Tom insisted on climbing further east in the morning. He had noticed fresh goat droppings among the rocks in that direction. By midday, they agreed it was safe to light a fire and brew a pan of chocolate. At this altitude, they looked down on the lowest clouds, swirling beneath them, partially hiding the lowlands.

"I left Scotland without scaling the mountains," said Malcolm, "but they kinna be more magnificent than this. We float in the heavens, like wizards."

"We are also lost," announced Jonathan. "I've never been this high, or so far to windward."

"How can we be lost?" said Tom. "The peaks are before us, to the north, the coast to the south. This gives us east and west, without even considering the path of the sun."

"Ah, but wait," said Jonathan. "Wait until you are caught in the folds of yonder ridges towards the Plantain River. They say that the valleys in between curl back upon themselves like snakes. When the sky is overcast, men have wandered round in circles, trapped in a devilish maze."

Nevertheless, they continued through an unearthly landscape in which tall trees became stunted dwarves and smaller herbs grew into giants. They found sheltered wallows, where the goats had bedded down, among droppings, scraps of chewed ferns, and moss. Suddenly, the ground dipped sharply at their feet. The mule splayed its legs and refused to go further.

Tom sniffed the air. "I smell sulfur and brimstone rising from below. A hot spring, without a doubt. More than likely, there'll be a salt lick nearby. That's what the goats must be after."

"Good," said Malcolm. "We can bag a few and be on our way back. This place is too uncanny for my taste. It reeks like the mouth of hell."

"Take care," said Jonathan, "or we'll be sliding down on our asses."

It took them half an hour to make the mule descend the slope, back through the mist, into a forest valley. A cold stream sped over boulders between walls of lush greenery. They splashed along the bank towards steaming hot water, which cascaded above their heads.

Jonathan saw the goats first. He stopped and made a downward movement with the palm of his hand. A little herd had gathered round a mineral pool, deep within a cleft in the mountainside. They were licking salt from the wet stones. Tom signaled for Jonathan to keep still among the leaves. He carefully retraced his steps to confer with Malcolm and the slave.

"We're in luck," he whispered, taking a coil of rope from the mule's back. "The goats are trapped. Mal, prime your piece and follow me."

"Why the rope?"

Tom cut it to make nooses. "Let's see if we can catch a couple live for old Ezra."

It was like shooting crabs in a barrel. The hunters blocked the only exit. After the first volley, three goats lay dead. Another fell to Malcolm's pistol. In desperation, the remainder charged, led by a big, bearded ram with wicked horns. Tom stopped him with the butt of his rifle, stunning the beast. Jonathan and Addy pounced on two females, quickly slipping nooses over their heads. The survivors fled, pursued into the stream by the mastiff. The hungry hound dragged a kid onto the bank and proceeded to devour it.

"We'll return the way we came," Tom announced, "to avoid losing our way." Then, to Jonathan and Addy's amazement, he began stripping off his clothes.

"Ah," said Malcolm, "now I suppose ye expect us to gut and skin the carcasses, while ye enjoy one of yer washes."

"You are all welcome to do the same," said Tom. Naked, he found a pool among the rocks, where the steaming water hit the stream, and lowered his body into the warm bubbles with a groan of pleasure. Nobody joined him. Malcolm explained, "Old Tom kinna pass by a hot spring without bathing. It revives his very marrow. Gather leaves; we may as well smoke the meat now."

"I could stay here all day," said Tom. "The king of France does not possess such a luxury in his finest palace. You don't know what you're missing."

The others lit a fire within the cavern, to roast the livers and kidneys of the slain goats. They cut bamboo for a smoking frame to cure the rest of the meat.

Tom was vaguely aware of their movements, the dog's jaws noisily crunching bones, and the occasional piercing birdcall. He looked up. The swirling mists made the treetops appear to move.

For a moment, it was as though he was peering downwards, ready to fall off the earth's surface. He closed his eyes to stop the dizzy sensation. The knot of tension spreading from the base of his skull into his brain slowly unwound. Soon, he was half asleep, imagining himself back in Theodora's hut, feeling a stirring in his loins. He lost track of time. Sweat trickled down his forehead. The channels in the back of his nose unblocked with tiny crackles. He barely noticed the sulfurous fumes. The prickly, gaseous stew allowed him to float effortlessly, scarcely touching the bed of stones. His pulse pounded steadily in his ears. He no longer felt his sore feet. This, he reflected, would be a pleasant death: to drift into the afterlife, painlessly dissolving, and relaxing one's grip on existence.

A poke in the scrotum snapped him back into the present. Malcolm stood above him, holding a sharpened twig. "Wake up, Mr. Sheppard! Come and eat yer share of the delicacies ere yer skin boils off. And, afore ye emerge," he laughed quietly, "I'd allow the stiffness to drain out of yer pizzle. Young Jonathan might take ye for a rampant sodomite and feel obliged to slay ye in the name of the Lord."

Tom cursed and splashed water at him, but swam into the cool stream to let his erection subside. He dried himself with a blanket, pulled on his breeches, and sat at the mouth of the cavern to chew the juicy titbits skewered on pointed sticks. He relished the taste of the liver with crumbled rock salt sprinkled on top.

Within two hours, they were traversing the strange highlands above the clouds again. The big bearded goat, recovered from his blow to the head, tugged at his rope, leading the procession into the fitful rays of the western sun. A thin drizzle descended. Tom was anxious to return to Ezra Crabbe's compound, to confront Long Ben and find out what, if anything, he had been saying. With Squeaker, Red Rod, and Sully dead, the tall doorman of The Three Mariners was the last link to Port Royal and the gallows. If a man like Craddock became aware of the situation, no good would come of it. The overseer was just the type to ingratiate himself with Sir Digby by raising the alarm again. Malcolm was right. It had to stop.

As he stepped into the light along the crest of a ridge, a terrified whimper made Tom look back. He recoiled at an appalling sight. In the shadows below, the slave cringed on the ground, the dog howled, the mule's eyes bulged, Jonathan folded his hands in prayer, and Malcolm aimed his musket at the sky. Framed in a circular rainbow astride the eastern peaks, a monstrous dark giant, fifty feet tall, towered over them in the mist. For a few seconds, they were rooted to the spot. Tom raised his arms in supplication. The giant did the same, looking more menacing, as if he wanted to grab them. Malcolm fired, the sun slid behind a thick cloud, and the giant vanished. Addy gibbered, "Amadiora magbukwa gi!"

Unnerved, they all rushed downhill, the dog barking, the mule braying, and the goats bleating. They did not stop, crashing through the undergrowth, until they found themselves on the edge of the field with the Blue Mahoe. By now, the sun had vanished completely and night was closing in, but the tree, with the two doormen's rotting corpses beneath its branches, was unmistakable. Vultures had stripped the flesh from their faces, giving them the appearance of grinning puppets.

Tom was the first to regain his composure. He shouted hoarsely, "Follow me!" and led them away from the tree, to the rocky outcrop where the old Maroon with the crossbow had hidden. "Here's as good a place as any. Fetch wood. Maroons or no Maroons, we need a fire tonight."

Hot cocoa, blankets, sheltering stones, and a crackling fire brought a semblance of normality to their campsite. Jonathan tried to console Addy, who was still shaking and muttering. Eventually, he tucked the slave up, with a blanket over his head, and turned to Tom. "The poor wretch is convinced that we have offended an African mountain giant by taking the goats. He expects this vengeful demon, Amadiora, to hurl a thunderbolt at any minute, to blast us off the face of the earth."

Malcolm prepared to reheat some half-cured goat meat, spitted on the point of his sabre. "We offended something. If we had a few jugs of rum from the Caernarvon distillery, I'd drink myself so stupid that I wouldn't mind being struck by lightning. By the Staring Eyes of Satan, this place makes the hairs behind my bollocks bristle."

Tom puffed on his pipe, slowly shaking his head. "I've been thinking," he said, "that monster must have been a trick of the light. Remember the shapes of animal heads you can make on a wall with your hands and a candle? They appear much bigger on the far side of the room. Over a mile, they would be huge. When the sun hit me on the hilltop, it cast my form onto a distant cloud, magnifying it into the figure of a giant. I am sure of it. The creature raised its arms when I did. It was my shadow, thrown across the ridges, reflected in the heavy mist."

"Aye," said Malcolm, "I can see the sense in that. By God, who would have thought it possible? Tom Sheppard, the phantom colossus of the highlands!"

Jonathan held his hand up to the flames and looked at its flickering outline on the rocks. "Yes, I remember you, caught in the sunbeams above us, Tom. That must be the answer. I've been hearing about giants in the mountains for years. I thought they were stories spread by the Maroons to scare people away, until I saw that thing just now."

Tom said, "I've heard yarns telling of all kinds of sea monsters, hungry whirlpools, sky-high waterspouts, and ghost ships that sail through the air upside down, but that vision almost stopped my heart. I had to think it through, or I would not have been able to sleep here tonight, frightened witless by my own shadow."

At noon the next day, they were back at Ezra Crabbe's palisade beside the Morant River. The slave, Addy, had developed a vacant stare and continued to babble about angry gods, but everybody else had calmed down. Ezra shouted with delight when he saw the goats. He gave the half-cured meat to the old woman, who took it to the back yard and began to stew it with salt, hot peppers, and onions in a great cauldron. An Angolan lit the clay oven and kneaded cassava dough into flat circles.

"I am glad to see you hale and hearty," said Ezra. "Jonathan, did you come across any Maroons? It seems they have forgotten the peace treaty again. Some survivors of their savage attacks came here late on Sunday night, the same day you went into the hills. One poor soul with a broken foot is still here."

Tom pretended to stumble and fell against Jonathan, giving the young man's elbow a sharp squeeze, and said, "Woah! I must be more exhausted than I thought! What's that? Maroons? No, Ezra, nary a whisper of any Maroons. Your son is a good guide. Knows the mountain trails like the back of his hand. He kept us out of danger."

Malcolm chimed in, "'Tis a pity, but we saw neither hide nor hair of them. I was looking forward to shooting at least one of the heathen monkeys."

Tom patted Jonathan's shoulder. For a second, the lad hesitated, but feeling Tom's grip tightening on the back of his neck, he mumbled, "No, Father, we were lucky. No Maroons at all."

"Very good," said Ezra, gazing at his son with pride. "I was afraid I'd never see you again. Now, come inside. Clean yourselves up. You can tell me all about your hunting party while we eat your prey."

They found Long Ben, smoking with his feet up in a hammock, watching the old woman as she stirred the stew. Bandages swathed his ankle and held a splint on his shin. His eyes darted at Tom and Malcolm, although he tried to affect a jovial manner. For the benefit of their hosts, the former occupants of The Three Mariners behaved as if they had not seen each other since the day of the cockfight, which was not mentioned at all. The tall doorman was passing himself off as a simple adventurer in Coxon's fleet. He described the pursuit of Coco, and the fight with the Maroons, exactly as they had witnessed it.

"And your dead shipmates?" asked Jonathan. "That must have been a heavy blow."

Long Ben looked straight into Tom's eyes when he answered, "Those two? In truth, they were no great friends of mine. I didn't know them from Adam, until last week, and the little I came to know about the slimy rogues was not to my liking. No, son, I will not miss Red Rod or Sully. I am only thankful to have been in the company of a brave soul like Old Carney and to have met such a skilled bonesetter as your father, God bless him."

"Carney was very lucky," said Ezra. "The point did not penetrate beyond his belly muscles. The wound was clean, no broken pieces or bits of cloth inside. He'll be good as new. An Indian battle arrow, barbed and smeared with venom, would have been a different proposition. I reckon those Maroons were hunting for wild pigs. The sight of the runaway enraged them, so they attacked in the heat of the moment. I don't think it will cause a new war. Only Craddock's nigger and the dogs were killed, and, to be honest, the other two dead men don't count. Colonel Freeman regards pirates, privateers, buccaneers, and freebooters—whatever you like to call yourselves—as vermin. The planters tolerate you in these parts because of your numbers and the captured slaves you sprinkle about. In their hearts, the planters would like to see you all hanged and live in peace with Spain."

"Aye," said Malcolm, "things get tighter all the time. Last year we would have sailed out of Port Royal Harbor, saluted by cannons. Now, Navy frigates would blow us out of the water. Even so, everybody knows we are here, a few miles along the coast. They also know we can fight better than any other force in the Indies. Can ye imagine what a mess we would make of a gaggle of prancing buffoons like Colonel Freeman's regiment? The planters should thank God that we have a soft spot for our own countrymen and confine ourselves to attacking Spaniards, or this parish would burn to the last stick."

"Now, now, Malcolm," said Tom, "anyone would think you were a bloodthirsty sea wolf who had torched Santa Marta instead of a glorified turtle fisher. Nobody, certainly not Coxon or Sharp, is going to shit on his own doorstep in Jamaica. They may sail under French letters of marque, but our captains know they must be wary of the Papists in Petit Gouave. King Louis is quite capable of dispatching them to the galleys. It's no use taking a holdful of silver if you have nowhere to spend it, among gibbets and burnt buildings. Let Colonel Freeman parade his buffoons unmolested, and save your strength for the Dons. Believe me, you will need it. You'll see flames, death, and explosions till you're sick of them. Why don't you tell Ezra and Ben about the hot spring, the goats, and the giant?"

"First," announced Ezra, "we will give thanks to the Lord for your safe return and ask Him to bless the food you have brought from His munificent bounty, especially the Billy Goat and his two concubines. May they be fruitful and multiply."

They all murmured, "Amen." Malcolm prattled on while the stew was served in wooden bowls, mopped up with sticky, flat cassava cakes. Ezra was fascinated, asking Jonathan to scratch a rough map of their route into the dust. The wild mountain country north of the palisade was a place of magic and mystery to the old man. Malcolm's weird tale did not disappoint him. The Scotsman omitted any mention of the fight over Coco. Meanwhile, Tom approached Long Ben, under the pretext of refilling his bowl.

"Put your mind at rest, Ben," he said. "I can guess who sent you, but you have nothing to fear from me."

The doorman nodded. "It was against my will, Thomas. Anyhow, without the others, and in this condition, I can do you no harm. My foot will not mend for weeks. I kept my mouth shut at Caernarvon, as did the others. I haven't said a word about Sir Digby to anyone here either, but I might be able to do you some good. Do not return to Port Royal for any reason. Half the town would knife you for the reward. Ah yes, another thing; before we came after you, that Dutchman with the monkey offered me a considerable sum to let you go. I was to give you this letter, if I had the opportunity."

Long Ben carefully extracted a sealed envelope from his jacket. Tom slipped it into the pocket of his jerkin and took Ben's bowl to the cauldron. When he returned, he patted Ben's arm and spoke louder, "Get well soon, shipmate. Malcolm and I will rejoin the fleet tomorrow. Maybe next time you'll come with us and fill your chest with silver too, eh?"

That night, in the comfort of their quarters, Tom waited until Ben and Malcolm were fast asleep. He lit a candle to read the letter. Arnout Van Tonder's personal signet ring had pressed three zigzags, symbolizing lightning bolts, into the wax seal. He found a paper note and an elaborate certificate inside. Tom narrowed his eyes with the effort of distinguishing the words. Luckily, Arnout wrote in a clear, flowing hand.

> *"Thomas, my friend, in haste.*
>
> *I heard about your trouble. I was to give you this at our Christmas feast, remember? It is your commission as a Leutnant in the Elector of Brandenburg's Army. Keep it safe. It will stand up in any court of law, better than a pirate's false letter of marque. Stay out of Jamaica. Make for the port of Charlotte Amalie on the Danish island of Saint Thomas, if you can, and ask for Hendricks at the sugar works. May fortune smile on you until we meet again.*
>
> *Yours, as ever, Arnout."*

The certificate was a work of art. A fearsome portrait of the double-chinned Prussian Elector, Friederich Wilhelm, wearing armor and an enormous wig, glowered at the top of the page. The words 'Leutnant Tomas Schepphardt' stood out from the Latin script, with a heraldic eagle in red ink underneath. The eagle wore a coronet and held a sword and a scepter in its claws. A ribbon, bearing another Van Tonder seal, completed the effect. It looked regal and menacing. He was a Prussian officer! Even an illiterate would be impressed. Tom decided to make a waterproof container to protect the roll of parchment during the uncertain days ahead. A small bamboo tube, stopped with a cork, would do the trick. Only God knew if the certificate would serve any purpose, but it was a comfort to possess it. Before retiring, Tom stepped silently into the yard, memorized the contents of Arnout's note about the island of Saint Thomas, and burned it in the embers of the fire.

Fresh proof of his links to the Dutch captain made Tom feel less alone. Before he fell asleep, he recalled the horrors of his great adventure with Morgan, and felt lonelier than ever. It had involved constant sailing, marching, and fighting, often on the verge of starvation. He'd soon be living in a different world entirely. The day after tomorrow, January 1st, 1680, heralded a new decade. Tom remained as penniless as he had been back in 1671. He prayed the fleet would strike it lucky, in a lightning raid, leaving him with the means to reach Saint Thomas quickly. He feared that the rigors of a long campaign might overwhelm him. On the bright side, Bartholomew Sharp had a reputation for avoiding unnecessary risks. The presence of Malcolm and Joseph helped allay his anxiety a little more.

The image of the mountain giant loomed in his mind's eye. He shivered. It seemed to symbolize his hunted existence, always running from the long shadow of his past, trying to escape into a hazardous future. The misty vision pursued him into his dreams. Before he knew it, the cocks crowed loudly to welcome the sunrise. Why did Jamaican chickens seem to make more noise than any others on earth?

The birds roused Ezra Crabbe from his slumbers. His advanced years caused him to take afternoon siestas and sleep little at night. Over boiled eggs in the yard, he entreated Tom and Malcolm to forget the buccaneering cruise, proposing a partnership in the timber business. Tom politely declined. Finally, seeing they were determined to leave for the coast that very morning, Ezra presented them with a cow from the pen, saying, "May God bless your endeavors. If you capture a good share of Papist silver, don't spend it all in Port Royal like fools. If I'm here, my offer still stands. In case I have gone to my Maker, Jonathan will honor it."

They said farewell and walked downriver, leading the cow along the bank, like a couple of heavily armed looters on the road in wartime.

"D'ye think the lad will keep his mouth shut?" asked Malcolm.

Tom shrugged. "Who cares? It appears he has so far. Now, it hardly matters. Jamaica no longer matters."

"Aye, but I'll miss that Caernarvon lassie, Katie. She jumped into bed with the sick bookkeeper faster than a scalded cat, in case I'd filled her with a bairn. Who knows? In nine months, I might have a wee son being raised as a gentleman and be none the wiser. Tell me, Tom, how did you like having a white woman for a change?"

"Any port in a storm," said Tom. "You know the way it is."

6
THE TEMPEST

At first glance, it was as if the Christmas festivities had never ceased. Sailors who hailed from the Scottish islands made a point of celebrating January the first. They forced Admiral Coxon's trumpeters to blow until their lips were raw. To Malcolm's delight, they screamed, "Hogmanay! Trollalay! Ram it up Auld Clootie's airse today!" before drinking themselves stupid. The idea was to clear the air of 1679's evil spirits by making as much noise as possible. The English joined them, although their New Year did not officially begin until Lady Day, in March. The sporadic orgy of eating, drinking, and cannon fire known as "The Daft Days" was set to continue until Twelfth Night. Work was almost an afterthought. On closer examination, piles of rubbish and the fierce stench of offal, vomit, and excrement in the undergrowth had rendered the area squalid. Black ash pits pockmarked the beach. Further back, ants had reduced the dead Angolan women to skeletons. They lay under a growing pile of turtle shells, thrown on top of them, as if to keep their ghosts from wandering at night. It was unadvisable to walk barefoot on the sand, due to the buccaneers' habit of hacking through the necks of bottles with their cutlasses. Rusty nails and splintered planks, lying beneath discarded rags, added to the hazards.

During the remaining weeks in Morant Bay, everyone preferred to spend longer periods aboard, to escape the swarming flies. Luckily, there was plenty of manpower. The sea-robbers always relied on overwhelming strength of numbers. Individual messes only needed to ferry supplies from the shore infrequently.

Word came through that a crew had been detained in Port Royal after a drunken disturbance on a plantation. Nobody wanted to wait for them. By the first weekend in the January, all the captains were ready to sail except old Cornelius Essex. The others threatened to leave him behind. The timbers of his vessel barely held together. In desperation, Essex ordered the framework to be 'wolded,' or strengthened by strapping cables tightly round the hull. Somehow, he would reach the main. Twelfth Night fell on the Monday. Thanks to the lucky capture of a Spanish merchantman, full of wine barrels, by a bored Captain Alliston, there was more than enough to drink. The assembled crews held a final council of war at the eastern end of the beach. The commanders were confirmed in their positions, with Coxon as admiral, to universal acclaim. He had spread the rumor that the target would be Portobello, and he now announced it officially. It was a popular choice. The great silver depot was overdue for another visit. According to the latest reports from French corsairs, tropical diseases had decimated the garrison. A quick in-and-out raid should produce instant success.

Coxon was enough of an orator to rise to the occasion. He had his speech down pat. Standing on the lid of a barrel, he bellowed to be heard by everyone. "Tomorrow, we leave these landlocked lubbers to their drudgery," he roared. "For them, every day is the same. For us, every day brings new adventures. When work is sport, it ceases to be work, and we are the greatest sportsmen of them all. What is a month at Royal Newmarket, with all its excitement, compared to our races across the sea, in the teeth of the elements and our implacable foes, with the promise of great treasures before us? Kings envy us. They rule over little piles of earth, while our ocean empire swirls all about them, ready to devour them at any moment. We are all equal, all kings, beholden to nobody. We are the Sons of the Wind, the

Riders of the Storm, free to come and go as we please, to stuff our pipes with rolls of tobacco, fill our bellies with hogsheads of wine and spray the tavern walls with pesos and piss. If the easterly breeze holds, we sail for Portobello tomorrow. Let us make it another Santa Marta!" Those who had not been there were, by now, heartily sick of the subject, but Coxon's crew shouted, "Santa Marta!" so loudly that everybody, drunk or sober, joined in again. The drums rolled and stopped abruptly when Coxon raised his pistol. Silence fell. The admiral allowed the seconds to pass slowly. This time he had primed the weapon as carefully as he had memorized his speech. He knew that captains lived off their legends as much as their luck. He wanted to engrave the moment onto their memories, to make them talk about it in quayside alehouses around the world, for years to come. With a sly grin, he let the tension rise. Then he cried, "To the ships! Happy hunting! Sound the horns!" and fired. His weary trumpeters brayed a fanfare on cue. The Brethren of the Coast rose as one, cheering and feeling invincible.

Coxon set sail on Tuesday morning, the seventh day of January. The omens were excellent. Superstitious sailors pointed out that seven was the luckiest number, especially following the religious holidays. A freshening east wind confirmed their optimism. The capstan teams sang as they wound in the anchors. The men in the shrouds dropped the sails into position. Even diehard Commonwealth veterans, who had no time for Christmas, Twelfth Night, maypoles, or any other pagan nonsense, felt elated as the five ships glided out of the bay. With the flagship in the lead, the larger vessels discharged their cannons.

Bartholomew Sharp's merchant ship, originally the *Rosario*, had been renamed the *Rose*. Sharp had his personal ritual for the departure. For luck, he dipped into his pocket and sprinkled a fistful of salt from the Yallahs Pans into the waves. Then he spat into his palm and rubbed saliva onto the whip staff. The captain was back in his element. He felt the mighty push of the current against the rudder tremble through the wood into his hand. She was *his* now. The *Rose* responded well, pitching forward eagerly, her sails bellying out and towing Tom's skiff in her wake. She followed the flagship, second in line. A crimson streamer snaked forward from the main top, circled by shrieking gulls.

Tom grasped the taff rail. The Blue Mountains, with the memory of the misty apparition, stood proud in the sunshine. His little skiff, empty except for memories, danced over the waves, separating the stern from the shore, as if being dragged to school by a bigger brother. Sharp welcomed Tom, as a 1671 veteran, into the captain's circle on the afterdeck. Joseph, who had become familiar with Sharp's cockney cronies, attended him. Malcolm and Scarrett had been sent into the bows, to man the spritsail. Since the crew was so numerous, the men expected to luxuriate in eight-hour gaps between watches instead of the usual four. They could slake their thirst, at any time, from a barrel of wine lashed to the main mast.

The mountains dwindled to a speck on the horizon behind them. A sail appeared to port. The colors of a corsair from Petit Gouave soon identified the vessel. After firing a salute, the Frenchman joined the rear of the fleet, which was heading due south, in a straight line to the San Blas Archipelago. The Isle of Pines served as a rendezvous with the friendly Kuna Indians. Sharp realized that the *Rose* made better headway than Coxon's ship. Muttering, "No point in upsetting the prickly cunt," he began to zigzag, to avoid overtaking the admiral. He even slackened the mainsails. The ships behind were in danger of falling out of sight. Essex's wretched tub was barely visible. But, within an hour, all of Sharp's delicate maneuvers would appear ridiculous. A mighty weather system spiraled towards them from the east.

"What d'you make of that?" Sharp asked nobody in particular. He pointed to a lurid yellow stripe in the heavens, with groups of wispy black clouds hurrying across it. In the distance, a pair of waterspouts lurched towards each other drunkenly before collapsing. For a few minutes, the storm seemed to duck back behind the horizon. Then, suddenly, the black clouds were back, sweeping over half the sky to swallow the sun. A roll of thunder ended with a mighty bang. Rain pelted down. The yards swarmed with sailors. They did not wait to be told. They eased the foreyard down towards the deck and left the spritsail in position. Every other scrap of canvas was tightly furled. "That's it, lads, leave me a little wind to steer with," Sharp braced himself, calling Joseph to help him hold the tiller against the surge. "Come, boy, let's see if yer as strong as you think. Hold her steady with me. Remember, the current wants to pull us northwest to Campeche, away from our course, which is due south. We'll compensate, whichever way the wind blows. Always leave enough water to larboard."

"It's gusting from the north, so it is," said Joseph. "Just as we want."

"For now," said Sharp, "and it's strengthening. The current is streaming into the teeth of the wind. We are in for a lively time, lad. Above all, help me keep her stern to the building waves. I don't have to tell you what might happen if a big rogue hits her side."

The ship reared and plunged down the slope of a huge roller like a galloping carthorse. Joseph swallowed hard, imagining the ship sinking at the bottom of the trough. Sharp yelled at the few remaining men on deck, "Get below! Fasten the hatches behind you! I'll let her run before the wind!"

Below decks, Tom marveled at the chaos. He did not bother trying to find Malcolm or Scarrett among the writhing mass of damp clothes, knees, and elbows. They were probably well forward, near the galley. Swaying lanterns added to the confusion, casting shadows in all directions over the crewmen packed between the shuddering planks. Here and there, a man vomited, to the disgust of his neighbors. The noise from the crashing waves, howling gusts, and creaking timbers made talking impossible. Dim figures huddled together silently. The unsteady light caught flashes of clenched teeth and anxious eyes. Tom could hear the ballast stones churning in the bilge water below. He sat on a sea chest, stemming his feet against the main wale, struggling to light his pipe from a taper that was passed around like a sacred flame. Soon, clouds of tobacco smoke curled up towards the heaving deck. It felt as if the entire ship was praying.

The rest of the fleet had vanished behind curtains of driving rain. Thunder crackled on the northern horizon. Sharp detected a subtle change in the wind. "It's not so fierce now, boy. Shifting round, coming from the west."

The deck tilted alarmingly. Joseph adjusted his balance, still firmly gripping the whip staff. "Is that good or bad, Captain?"

"You think you're a sailor because you can hunt turtles in the bay?" Sharp grinned, water dripping from the hat crammed tightly onto his head, spikes of hair sprouting like straw from the sides. The pearl at his ear caught the reflection of a distant lightning flash. "Well, Joe, you'll soon learn that nothing is ever entirely good or entirely bad out at sea. I like the westerly wind because it keeps us off the lee shore in a storm. I don't like the westerly wind because it drives us away from our destination in the Samballoes. I reproach the westerly wind for blowing so rudely out of season. Having said that, I hate THIS westerly wind, because it's turning into a fucking sou'wester, and a horrible strong one. THIS sow's cunt of a wind is going to try and drown us."

Sharp grasped the edge of the binnacle box and stared down at the compass, then forward to the patch of white canvas straining in the bows. He punched the side of the box and returned to take the whip staff.

"Right, Joe, we're getting out of this before it sweeps us all the way onto the reefs in the Florida Keys. I'm going straight down its throat, and I mean STRAIGHT. I want her ass down and her nose in the air, face into the wind at all times. Run and see if that skiff's still hanging from the stern."

Joseph tottered over to the taff rail. Tom's little boat was barely visible in the wash.

"Aye, Captain," he yelled, "she's swamped. Only the wood is holding her up. Shall I cut her loose?"

"No, you Irish fool! Put that knife away! Didn't you hear me say I want her ass down? That skiff can be our sea anchor. Now, hard to starboard. We're breaking out. On my word, one, two, three—now!"

Joseph had no time to think clearly. A great wave swept across the quarterdeck, sending him sprawling towards the rail. He turned, just in time to see Sharp hanging on to the whip staff with water breaking over his back, hatless and on his knees. Joe grabbed the lanyard on the nearest piece of rigging with both hands. He lost his footing, but hung on until the wave had passed, taking his own hat with it. He lurched back, accelerating with the dropping deck, and collided with the captain, throwing the staff back to port. Both Sharp's fist and another wave hit him at the same time. Joseph held on when the tiller returned to starboard.

"By Christ, Joe, what are you at? Are you trying to sink us, you bloody bogtrotter?" Sharp spat salt water. "Now hold this course with me and stay on your feet, even if a whale lands on your head."

"How much longer, Captain? Should I get help?"

"No time. Hold the rudder steady with me. Nothing else, got it? Look, the waves are coming at us head on. That's what we want. Straight down its screaming throat. See the sunshine yonder, past the edge of the clouds?"

Joseph looked up. The bowsprit pointed at a thin line of light blue between the dark sea and swirling clouds. The waters boiled, with high waves advancing like armies, hammering the hull and tearing the unfurled canvas from the foremast in strips. Gleaming serpents of water spat foam to the sky, which seemed to be full of writhing dragons, spinning in the center. The wine barrel had been reduced to splinters, but the binnacle box held firm. Sharp and Joseph could do no more than crouch on either side of the whip staff, soaked and glistening beneath the torrent.

The final wave almost killed them. The *Rose* had taken a beating but only lost a few yards of cloth, a barrel, and a couple of hats. They were near the edge of the storm and the calmer seas beyond. Some choppy water remained, rolling up from the south. Heads were beginning to pop out of the hatches when Joseph looked over Sharp's shoulder and shouted, "For the love of God, will you look at that!"

Sharp swung round and screamed, "Shut those hatches!"

The heads disappeared. The hatches slammed. He grabbed

Joseph and dragged him to the mizzen. They hugged the mast and held their breath. The rogue wave came in from the west, thirty feet high. They felt the ship being lifted in a slow, powerful grip and wobble on the crest. Their stomachs jumped as the *Rose* skidded down, finally crashing into a wall of water. As luck would have it, her bows took the full impact. It had nothing to do with seamanship. The rudder was swinging free, Sharp and Joseph having abandoned their post. Below, few escaped without bruises, but the *Rose* floated, her bowsprit shattered, the spritsail trailing in the water, into the light of a peaceful evening. Soon, she was alone on a flat sea, drifting towards the setting sun. The carpenter's mate supervised the fastening of the snapped forestay to the beak head, to restore tension to the masts. Sharp sent men aloft to set all the available sails.

The entire crew crowded onto the deck, with a barrel of wine to replace the one broken in the storm. They brought blankets and dry clothes for Captain Sharp and Joseph, who were toasted as the heroes of the hour. Before he became too drunk, Sharp instructed his young friend, the quartermaster from New England, John Cox, to sail southwest during the coming night. He was to approach the Spanish Main. A quadrant reading could be taken the following noon. If the coast appeared in daylight, Sharp was confident he could identify any familiar landmarks from Vera Cruz down to Cartagena. The watchman in the crow's nest was given a telescope to search for other members of the scattered pirate fleet. He saw nothing.

Tom returned to the taff rail and looked back. Malcolm joined him with a mug of wine in his hand. They stared at their shattered boat, still trailing on her cable.

"She must have crashed against the stern," said Tom. He cut the rope, leaving the knot on the rail. Malcolm poured wine into the wash. "Fare thee well, auld faithful! At least we're all in one piece, Thomas. The Irishman has done us proud. I have no further duties but to get drunk, since we have no bowsprit. As for Scarrett, he hasn't a care in the world. He's taken to smoking dried hemp with his tobacco. The mad Egyptian gathered a bagful of leaves from the fields with one of the Angolan niggers. He swears by its calming effect." Malcolm paused as the effeminate figure of Quartermaster Cox appeared on the quarterdeck.

"What d'ye make of our quartermaster, Tom? He's a strange one, that John Cox, neither fish nor fowl."

"Oh, definitely fowl, I'd say. A weird bird, if ever I saw one. Also foul in the other sense. Perhaps some kind of a eunuch. Even his name seems half-finished, like an incomplete version of the admiral's."

"Incomplete?" said Malcolm. "Castrated, more like. Yon wee man makes my skin crawl."

Tom spat over the edge. He searched for Scarrett among the crowd of drinkers. At length, he spied the little Gipsy smoking alone with his back against the foremast, in the orange light of sunset. When darkness came, half the men chose to sleep in the warm air on deck. Sharp went below, leaving John Cox in control. A mulatto cabin boy helped the captain to his berth.

Four days later, the captain recognized the shape of an elevated point on the green coast to starboard as *El Manzanillo.* From there, it was a few miles east to the agreed rendezvous on the Isle of Pines in the San Blas Archipelago.

They sailed among hundreds of islands, some barely large enough to support a palm grove, others boasting mountains, rivers, and Indian villages on stilts. Sharp took the whip staff. "Run up the white ensign with the cross of Saint George," he ordered. "The natives will welcome us as enemies of Spain... and take in the topsails. Slowly does it through these reefs. We'll have quite an escort by the time we get there."

At first glance, they seemed to have entered paradise. White sand shone through the turquoise shallows. Palms, laden with coconuts, swayed in a gentle breeze. Beautiful naked women, their bodies painted with vivid red designs, flashed smiles and waved from tidy bamboo huts. Fishermen paddled up to the ship displaying the best of their catch. Tom looked over the side. Tears formed in the corners of his eyes. He had forgotten how lovely the place could be, especially along this chain of coral islands. His heart welled up with pity for his former carefree self. As the captain steered carefully towards a big island near the shore, Tom remembered the jagged dangers under this gentle vision of Eden: hull-tearing reefs, the vicious spikes of the thorn bushes, deadly insects among the mangrove roots, barracudas' teeth, and the poison arrows of the Kuna Indians. Life was like a fast-ripening fruit here, glorious and sweet, but quickly ripped apart by sharp spikes. The place was constantly making a meal of itself. Then, on top of these memories, came the roar of Spanish guns, the barking of war mastiffs, neighing, trampling horses and the screaming war cry, "Santiago!" All this lay ahead of him again, just when he had hoped to be free of it.

Beside him, Joseph and Malcolm marveled at the scenery, especially the women. Tom sighed. This was definitely a young man's game. What was he doing here? He knew of a few buccaneers, mainly French, who had married into the tribe and settled in the jungle. The idea was tempting. During the 1671 invasion, Tom had befriended a war chief called Andreas and enjoyed his hospitality. The native houses, built with hardwood, bamboo and palm thatch, were sturdier, cleaner and airier than anything in Jamaica, the women pretty and vivacious. Food and fresh water abounded. Tom shook his head. No, it wasn't for him. It struck him that such a life would be utterly meaningless, like the existence of a parrot. He wanted to be remembered in English, Dutch, French, or Spanish— not some obscure forest language spoken by a handful of savages. Although, thinking about it further, what difference did it make who remembered him and in what language? In the great scheme of things, a king, eaten by worms in London, was as indifferent to his fate as any dead monkey, eaten by centipedes under rotting leaves in the wilderness of Darien. Why should he, the long-forgotten son of a dead Sussex fisherman, care? Tom realized what lay behind such thoughts. He was afraid that he no longer possessed the vigor for such a place. The well of courage in his soul had nearly emptied over the years.

By the time the *Rose* anchored in the narrow channel between the Isle of Pines and the mainland, log canoes full of painted warriors surrounded her. Sharp beckoned three of the leaders onboard. As they came up the entry steps, Tom recognized his old friend. Slightly more wrinkled, the face under the four-feathered hat belonged to Captain Andreas, the Kuna war chief responsible for liaising with the English. Andreas pointed to Tom's blue cheekbone with a questioning look, as if wondering why anybody would decorate himself in such a slapdash fashion. Tom squeezed an imaginary trigger, made an exploding sound, and held the right side of his head as if in pain. The chief said, "Ah," and embraced him. Sharp ordered the spanker yard to be lowered down the mizzen, so that the sail shaded the quarterdeck. They sat cross-legged. Mugs of wine appeared, which the two other chiefs neglected to drink after a first polite sip. Only Andreas appeared to enjoy the taste. The conference began in broken Spanish and sign language. It quickly emerged that Tom and Captain Andreas communicated most effectively, each man interpreting for his side.

"Captain Sharp is delighted to reaffirm his alliance with the Emperor of Darien," said Tom, "and make war on Spain, to the mutual benefit of his English soldiers and your good selves, the rightful and original rulers of this land. We are the first of many ships."

Captain Andreas reciprocated, "I speak for the Emperor, and he is pleased to welcome you." He pointed to the humpbacked outline of the Isle of Pines. "You can stay there with fresh water and gardens of fruit and vegetables. As you know, the sea is full of fish and turtles."

As they talked, with pauses to translate, the buccaneers crowded round, jostling and commenting. Many of the sailors had never seen such Indians before. The Kuna were well-built little men with long, thick hair. The warrior chiefs painted themselves with red and black stripes of varying thickness and carried ornate, ceremonial stabbing spears. Apart from parrot feather headdresses, each man wore a golden crescent, which dangled from his nostrils over his top lip, and a golden plug through his lower lip. The conical, silver sheathes strapped over their penises caused astonishment and hilarity among the crew.

Bartholomew Sharp held up his hand to address the crowd. "We are having an important meeting here; important for everybody. I can't make half of it out because I am hemmed in by a mob of cackling geese." He drew a pistol from his waistband. "Do I have to shoot somebody to clear this deck? Go on, give us some room! You'll be seeing more than your fill of the Indians soon enough!"

The crew gradually dispersed. Tom understood the Kuna point of view, especially that of Captain Andreas. Even after ten years' absence, he was able to gauge how things stood in Darien with some accuracy. After the chiefs' departure, each with the gift of a boarding axe and a handful of glass beads, Tom said, "They were not over-friendly, Captain."

"I can't tell what they're thinking at the best of times, Tom. It's like talking to a bunch of stone-faced tortoises. Even your mate, Andreas, hardly smiled. Why d'you reckon that is?"

"They only half believed me when I said we were part of a larger fleet. I think they hope for a grand enterprise against Panama, something like Morgan again, to hit the Dons hard. These war chiefs dream of driving all the Spaniards into the sea and getting rid of them forever. Instead, the Spaniards are advancing, attacking villages that used to be safe. The chiefs are disappointed that we are so few."

"But they won't give us any trouble?"

"They will let us anchor behind the island, safely out of sight, until more ships arrive. The longer that takes, the less helpful they will become, because they will begin to doubt our intentions. As usual, they will wait for their wizards to consult their demons about the best course of action. Meanwhile, the island is ours. I saw them moving the young women to the mainland, so there will be no sport with them on this occasion."

"Just as well," Sharp turned to his cronies, "we've got work to do. Send ashore for food and water. We'll pump her out, plug the leaks, and make her a new bowsprit. When Coxon arrives, I want us ready."

It transpired that there was no need to hurry. The carpenters found a stout piece of pinewood for the bowsprit. The ship was restocked and repaired, but the weeks dragged by, with no sign of Coxon or anyone else. Boredom caused squabbles. The men cleaned their weapons till they shone. There was no prize money to gamble. The Indians continued to keep their women out of sight. Sharp organized turtle-spearing competitions and rolled out barrel after barrel of wine. The ship's self-appointed scribes and mapmakers, a pair of bright young clerks called William Dampier and Basil Ringrose, never complained of the tedium, constantly sketching, scribbling, and measuring. John Cox was prompted to ask Sharp, "What are those two doing? They behave like a pair of bloody spies."

"Calm yourself, John," said Sharp. "There's profit in more than pieces of eight these days. Tom Sheppard told me of a Dutch book about the old days in Panama with Morgan. Apparently, such sea stories sell like hot cakes. If they succeed in Amsterdam, you can be sure they'll catch on in London soon after. Enjoy your 'Adventures on the Spanish Main,' in your taverns, coffee houses, and stately mansions, matey! As for coastal charts, everybody needs 'em."

"Maybe," Cox frowned. "I'd still like to see what those two are up to. If we are captured, their scribbles might get us hanged."

"I doubt it. Dampier loves strange beasts and savages. He draws 'em and describes 'em. There's no harm in that; just the thing for the Royal Society. As for young Basil Ringrose, I want his maps myself. His lines, distances, and bearings are perfect. They'd be valuable to the Admiralty."

"Maybe," muttered Cox, not entirely convinced.

"Be sure of one thing, Johnny," said Sharp, "if the Dons ever take us, it won't matter a rat's fart what papers we carry, whether they're French commissions, logging permits, pictures of monkeys, or homemade maps. They'll hang us anyway."

One hot morning in mid-February, Sharp decided to wait no longer. The men had become too restless. He overheard some of them planning drunken forays to rape Kuna women. He couldn't risk anything like that. As it was, the Indians doubted the existence of Coxon's ships. Sharp wondered if he'd seen the last of the flotilla too. Perhaps the storm had driven Coxon and the others onto the rocks. He contented himself by leaving a scrap of parchment nailed to a tree on the beach. It said, "Capn Bart Sharpe. 18 Feb. Gone to Springer's Careening Key." At any rate, the buccaneers were outstaying their welcome. Crucially for the captain, the wine was almost finished. Supplying generous quantities of wine was his favorite way of keeping the crew happy. Sharp announced the *Rose's* imminent departure. He had enough water, turtle meat, and half a dozen dugouts strapped to the deck. The sails picked up a westerly breeze shortly before noon. Tom recognized Captain Andreas in one of the canoes that suddenly appeared. He yelled to him, in Spanish, that they were going to find the fleet, and would return shortly. Andreas sat behind the curved prow of the dugout, watching the ship disappear behind the palm trees on the headland without expression. Tom saw the gold flash on the chief's upper lip before he vanished from sight.

Sharp ordered Dick Chappell, the big bosun at the whipstaff, to swing out to starboard. "I don't want to be trapped against the lee shore, Dick, not in this tub. She's sluggish; bearded with weed and barnacles. We'll give her bottom a good scrape at Springer's Key."

Beyond the reefs, a school of porpoises sped ahead of their bows, which everybody took as a good omen. Within a few hours, the Keys appeared to port and Sharp took back the whipstaff. He eased the *Rose* into the channel between the sandy islands and the shore, out of sight of any passing Spanish merchantmen sailing to and fro between Portobello and Cartagena. The crystal-clear water rendered the lead line unnecessary. Through a gap in the coral, Sharp was able to anchor within pistol shot of a gently sloping beach, lined with stout palm trees ideal for careening. This involved tying cables round the trunks and winching the ship ashore with the capstan drum. Then the seaweed and shells could be scraped off below the waterline. It would be heavy work, and nobody was keen to make a start. In fact, nothing was done for three days, except finishing the remaining wine, grilling fish on the beach, and relaxing in the shade of the palms.

This laziness was fortunate because, on the fourth day, the channel suddenly swarmed with canoes and pirogues. Sharp climbed into the rigging for a better view. At first it seemed as if the entire Kuna tribe was on the move, but as the leading pirogue drew nearer, they recognized Captain Mackett from Coxon's fleet, clearly outlined against its sail. About two hundred and fifty buccaneers sped along in his wake.

"Bartholomew Sharp! We'd given you up for drowned." Mackett pointed eastwards. "We're on our way to Portobello. Wait for our ships. They are following behind, with five-man crews to anchor beside you."

Malcolm turned to Tom. "I'm damned if I'm stewing in this tub while The Maggot and his rascals have all the fun. Ask the captain if we can take a canoe and join the attack."

Sharp had overheard him. He announced, "Anyone who wants can grab a canoe and go for Portobello, but it will be equal shares amongst all the crews in the fleet, whether you go or not."

"The more of us," said Malcolm, "the more to share."

The four messmates, Tom, Malcolm, Joseph, and Scarrett, fetched their weapons and joined a further eight men in a long dugout. As they struggled to catch up with the attacking force, they saw the first of Coxon's ships approaching the Key behind them. The fleet was finally reunited after the storm. The business of raiding the main could begin.

7
PORTOBELLO

Five dugouts departed from the *Rose,* leaving Sharp and Cox behind with twenty men. Tom and his messmates sped forward. They strained to keep the main body of raiders in sight. As the sun began to set, the assault force stopped to drag the pirogues and canoes onto a beach near the overgrown ruins of an abandoned harbor. Eighty hungry-looking Frenchmen, whose ship had been hiding in the mangrove swamps of an easterly key, joined them en masse. All the captains except Sharp were present, which caused murmurs about his commitment. That night, they slept between the crumbling battlements and rotting sheds, with shrieks and growls from the jungle and the whine of mosquitoes in their ears.

In the morning, Coxon clambered onto the remains of a wall. He struck a theatrical pose, raising his sword, to deliver another of his harangues. "Here we are at last, my merry lads, twenty leagues short of Portobello. We cannot risk proceeding by sea. There are no more reefs or islands before the Portobello Bastimentos. Their bloody Armada might sally forth to pin us against the shore, so we will march up the coast, slipping behind their watchtowers. We'll catch 'em with their britches round their ankles, take 'em from behind, blast 'em to hell, and strip 'em to the bare bones. All their batteries will be pointing in the wrong direction. With luck, the stores will be packed with silver, fresh from the Camino Real. I hear that the Dons are so afflicted with agues and fevers, they are scared stiff that their own niggers will overrun 'em. Captain Alliston has offered to lead the way. He knows the lay of the land. We also welcome the gallant Capitaine Lessonne's crew from Sainte Domingue. Remember Santa Marta! It is time to become as rich as lords, boys!"

"By Christ," Malcolm hissed in Tom's ear, "if he mentions Santa Marta again, I swear I'll shove that sword up his airse. Santa Marta! We heard of nothing but Santa Marta, in every whorehouse and taproom, for over three years. The French took the lion's share of the treasure at Santa Marta. Coxon merely held their coats. Then he thrust his paw out for the leftovers. Hark at him, drooling over the gallant Capitaine from Sainte Domingue. Nobody's heard of the bugger."

"At least," said Tom, "he has not brought his trumpeters along, and, whatever you say about Coxon, he captured the Archbishop at Santa Marta and held him to ransom."

"Pure luck. He found that prize Papist idiot wandering in the street after the battle," muttered Malcolm. "He's a chicken-hearted, bragging bag o' shite. Ye'll see that I'm right. Coxon knows the ground as well as Alliston, yet he will skulk in the rear, coming in like a vulture when the fighting's over. I'm damned if I'll die to fill his pockets."

"And our own good Captain Sharp is safely back on the ship, with his feet up, if you please," said Joseph.

"That's the way to prosper in this game. You don't gain experience by throwing your life away," said Tom, strapping his precious hunting rifle over his shoulder. He turned to Scarrett. "Don't forget your water there. Wake up. We're on the move."

The first day's march was relatively easy, along sandy beaches under palm trees, with a brief diversion into the thick forest to avoid a lookout platform. Peering through his spyglass, Coxon thought of killing the watchman, but changed his mind when a cluster of huts and canoes came into focus. Someone was bound to escape and raise the alarm in Portobello. The column slipped into the shadows of the tall trees. On the second day, sharp rocks, coming down to the water from a series of hills, took their toll. The column grew longer. Stragglers, whose footwear had fallen apart, hobbled into camp many hours after the vanguard. After the third day, only those wearing stout shoes could keep pace with Robert Alliston. Tired of stumbling through the undergrowth in a slow, cursing procession, Tom's little group found itself among the 'forlorn hope,' spearheading the raid.

During the night, they lay in the forest and were bitten by clouds of mosquitoes. Joseph wondered, "Now why d'you think it is that some men get stung almost to death, while others wake up with scarcely a mark on 'em?"

Red sores covered the Irishman's freckled skin while Scarrett was virtually unscathed. Tom and Malcolm had a few more bites on their wrists and ankles than usual, but nothing that bothered them unduly.

"I've noticed," said Tom, "That women suffer more than men, no doubt because their blood is sweeter and their skin smoother. Also, in general, large people are bitten more than small ones."

"You mean," said Joseph, "being taller, their skin has more surface to cover, and is therefore stretched thinner, and easier to penetrate?"

"No," said Malcolm, "he means yer naught but a big, sweet, delicate molly, Joe."

"Carry on like that," said Joseph, "and I'll be ramming your grinning Scottish face into the next wasps' nest we come across, so I will. Then we'll see who's delicate."

"I know I'm the smallest," Scarrett broke in, "but I also reckon these dried hemp leaves keep the flies at bay better than tobacco on its own. The Africans in Morant Bay were no fools. I find the stuff makes me merry and takes away unpleasant memories. Try some in your pipe, Joe."

"That only proves you're the maddest Gipsy that ever played a fiddle," Joseph snorted. "You won't catch me smoking that. It stinks poisonous."

"Our brave leader could do with some comforting," Malcolm pointed at Alliston. "Offer it to him."

The captain was sweaty, feverish, and covered in bites. Like everybody else, he had eaten nothing and scarcely slept for three days. He scratched his neck distractedly before urging them all to be as silent as possible. They were only two or three miles from the Camino Real, the Royal Highway from Panama that led to the undefended, inland side of Portobello. Alliston looked around nervously, counting roughly fifty men. The bulk of the force, starving and footsore, was catching up in dribs and drabs. Admiral Coxon trudged wearily in their midst, half a mile back through the trees.

"Prime your muskets," Alliston ordered. "We're going in."

The buccaneers saw the entire harbor, its seaward battlements nestling in an elongated horseshoe bay, from the top of a ridge. Forts bristled with cannon at either end of the horseshoe. A powerful battery of field guns lined the esplanade in between, protected by crenelated stone embrasures. They did not see the Indian quarter in a hollow directly below them until they had entered it. Dogs barked and women hustled their children into hovels. The men stopped to stare impassively at the dirty, unshaven, white intruders. These natives lived in peace with the Spaniards. Unlike the Kuna, they wore Spanish cast-offs and boasted no body paint, feathers, or golden jewelry. One young man shouted, "Ladrones! Thieves!" He turned and sprinted downhill towards Portobello, with the tired raiders hot on his heels.

Tom raised the rifle to his shoulder. This was the perfect test of its accuracy against a moving target. He would aim slightly ahead of the chest, to allow for the runner's forward motion. He saw his chance when the boy was about to vanish behind a mud wall. Suddenly Mackett's angry face blocked his view.

"Don't you dare," the captain snarled, grasping the barrel and raising it skywards. "That would warn 'em for sure. Hurry along, now. The faster we all get down there, the better."

The inhabitants of the port reacted slowly to the boy's shouts. At ten o' clock on a lazy Saturday morning, most of the people in the streets were slaves who didn't care much about the fate of the place, one way or the other. They went about their errands with a casual lack of enthusiasm. Only the free blacks and mulattos showed any interest in working. They hammered and sawed in their artisans' shops, making every minute count. Many of the whites were indeed sick. The very air of the place seemed to make Europeans languish indoors, wasting away on sweaty mattresses. The few who strolled about, the men under big hats, the ladies swathed in veils, paid scant attention to the screaming boy. They assumed he was mad, playing a prank, or pursuing a petty thief from a market stall. The Indian grabbed a stylish gentleman's sleeve to get his full attention. The foppish Spaniard only stopped beating him with the flat of his rapier when the first Englishmen appeared, discharging their muskets down the street. Both the boy and the fop tumbled into the dust, entangled like lovers in a puddle of blood. Heads popped out of windows and quickly popped back, slamming the shutters tight. Loud altercations and the sound of crashing furniture came from within the thick adobe walls.

Alliston's vanguard headed for the fabled silver vaults that lined the sea front behind the fortified battery. At the end of a cobbled street, they ran into a double line of mulatto militiamen with cutlasses and half-pikes. A few of these part-time soldiers had managed to strap on breastplates but the majority wore everyday linen clothes and straw hats. They were free men, the illegitimate sons of Spanish masters and slave women. A fat, white sergeant, wearing a crimson sash, bellowed at them to straighten their ranks. A little drummer boy tapped out the call to arms. The morning sun sparkled off the silver thread woven into his jacket. His chin jutted out and his eyes gleamed with pride. Behind the militia, the edge of a tower cast a long shadow, like an old crusaders' keep. Waves glittered through a slit between the granite bastion of Santiago de la Gloria and the nearest house. Church bells clanged. Regular Spanish infantrymen hastily loaded their old muskets by the gate, fumbling with flints to light their match cords. Cannon fire from the other side of La Gloria was answered by signal shots from the Fuerte de San Felipe, built on hard coral, guarding the eastern half of the bay. The sound of barked orders, screaming women, running men, and horses came from every direction.

"The Dons are coming into the day, shipmates," said Alliston. "Wake 'em up properly. Give 'em a volley."

Seeing that they were about to be shot where they stood, the mulattos milled about, bumping into each other, some trying to charge forward, the rest attempting to escape. When the smoke cleared, the sergeant lay dying beside a dozen groaning men and corpses. The militia had vanished. A single figure remained. The little boy's sticks fell onto the pavement. Tears began to roll down his cheeks. He suddenly plunged through the musketeers, back into the fortress, one knee thudding against his drum.

The Spanish musketeers stepped aside to allow a troop of lancers to come trotting out of the gateway. The riders spurred their steeds towards the buccaneers before they could reload. A row of pikes and plumed helmets appeared behind the horsemen, advancing steadily, with musketeers on both flanks, blocking the end of the street. These soldiers looked like the brutal Tercios who terrorized the Netherlands, with their scarred faces and bristling black moustaches. Groups of citizens, clutching infants, jewelry boxes, hatfuls of coins, and bundles of expensive cloth, seized the opportunity to run into the gateway. On the beach beneath the ramparts, families piled their belongings into small boats. Domestic slaves rowed them to safety under a raised portcullis on La Gloria's seaward side.

The main body of the buccaneers descended into town as the lancers charged. The horsemen were either pistoled and clubbed from their saddles by Alliston's men or shot by the new arrivals. Two riders disappeared into a side street and were later spotted in the distance, galloping up the Camino Real, no doubt to call in reinforcements from Panama. One pirate had caught a spear point through the middle of his chest. He spewed red froth like a harpooned porpoise. Sliding down a wall, he choked in his own blood. Another sat looking at his teeth, scattered on the pavement, kicked out by a rearing horse. With a howl of rage, the buccaneers stormed forward.

Their speed and fury astonished the Spaniards, who fired a ragged and inaccurate volley, dropped most of their pikes, and retired into the castle. They closed the massive, studded gates behind them. Now, Coxon came into view, surveying the scene with a look of grim determination.

"We can't waste time taking that place," he announced. "We'll keep the buggers bottled up inside." Coxon turned to the sweating Alliston, adding in a lower voice, "That will be a task for the gallant Capitaine Lessonne."

The French contingent settled in opposite La Gloria, shooting, from neighboring houses, rooftops, and hastily erected barricades, at anything that moved on the battlements. They prised the iron grills off windows, using them to roast fallen horses in the shade of the narrow side streets. Wounded Spanish cavaliers lost their rings, gold chains, and fancy swords before their throats were cut. Their broken spears made good kindling. The men from Sainte Domingue nursed bitter grudges against all mounted lancers. Ransoming these particular gentlemen never occurred to them. The corpses were left to rot in a heap at the end of a deserted alleyway. Barrels of wine, rolled out of the bodegas, appeared on every corner. Slaves were forced to light the bakery ovens and carry fresh bread to the firing line round the clock.

Coxon dispatched patrols to pin down the San Felipe garrison overlooking the eastern entrance to the harbor. The admiral installed himself with his principal officers in the cathedral facing the main square. It became the collection point for loot, as groups of buccaneers fanned out through the storehouses and residential districts.

Tom led his friends into a quiet area between the plaza and the southern slopes. "If memory serves," he said, "this is where the rich merchants live. Somewhat decayed since I saw it last."

Terraces of two-story houses lined cobbled streets, with niches containing shrines to holy saints and virgins on the corners. Here and there, the roots of great trees, growing in gardens enclosed by the houses, cracked through the pavement. Green and yellow lichen stained the masonry. Weeds sprouted everywhere, even on the roof tiles. Overhead, rusty bars protected balconies resting on stout timbers. The heavy doors and shutters had been tightly locked. Distant sounds came from the shooting at the waterfront. Here, the boots of Tom's party made the only noise, but the men sensed that they were being watched. Something lurked behind the silent shutters and seemed to be holding its breath in the midday heat.

"It's massy. Tight as a clam," said Malcolm, examining a door. "A shot would bounce off the lock. We might blast through with a keg of powder, or spend hours hacking at the frame. We have nothing fit for the purpose but Joe's wee axe."

"I can get inside," said Scarrett. "Pick any house you fancy. I'll run along the rooftops from one end of the street to the other. It'll be easy to break in from above."

"Easy?" Tom scratched his beard.

Scarrett explained. He asked them to knot the ends of their red sashes together, making a strong silk rope. Then, squatting on Joe's shoulders, he tied the handle of his throwing knife to one end and threw it neatly between the bars of the nearest balcony. Grasping both ends, he hauled himself up. Within a minute, he had scrambled onto the roof. He stood up, untied his knife, took a bow, and flung back the sashes. They floated down in artistic spirals.

"Our Gipsy friend swarms over buildings as if he was on the topsail yards," said Tom, retying the silk round his waist.

"He thinks he's at a fairground, so he does," said Joseph. "His mother brought him up on tales of daring feats in the days of the king's sainted father. Now that weed he smokes has given him wings."

"There's a fine courtyard down there," said Scarrett, pointing over the ridge of tiles. "Like a palace. Looks like nothing from the outside, but these people are worth a fortune, or I'm a Dutchman. Let's see if they've left anything worth taking. I'll come down and open the front door."

"Wait," said Tom, "what if they're still at home? Don't get yourself killed, man!"

The Gipsy had already vanished. Tom examined the door,

picking at the iron studs and the keyhole in the giant lock. Joseph and Malcolm looked up and down the street. It remained deserted. Shots sounded sporadically from La Gloria. Snatches of drunken singing drifted from the plaza, punctuated by shouts and cheers, but nobody else had thought of searching this outlying district yet.

"The Egyptian's been hit on the head, for sure," said Malcolm. "He'll be lying in there somewhere with his brains smashed out."

"Don't be so damn cheerful, Mal," said Tom. "Anyway, they are hardly likely to have left a key behind. No way in, unless we clamber up after him like monkeys."

Suddenly, the barred peephole in the center of the door snapped open. Scarrett's voice hissed, "Joe? Tom? I reckon there's nobody here, but this lock is an impossible bastard. I think there's some sort of stable back there, round the corner. Maybe easier to open."

"Wait," said Tom, "back where?"

"To my right, behind me, leading to the next street. Look for high double gates, big enough to drive a wagon through. With luck, they're only bolted from within."

"Seen anything worth having?" asked Joseph.

"You won't believe it, Joe. There's nothing like it in Jamaica."

Once the Gipsy had let them in, they found themselves staring at a coat of baronial arms chiseled into the back wall of a roofed coach hall. At ground level, a bright garden beckoned through the arches of a stone gallery. More doors were set into the sides. Above, two staircases led in opposite directions to the upper story. Pieces of clothing and a dented silver cup lay on the flagstones, as if dropped in a hurry.

"First things first," Tom slotted the bolts back into place and replaced the heavy iron bar across the center. "It's only a matter of time before the others start sniffing around this street. I think we'll be happier on our own for a while."

The cavernous space embraced them. Their sweat felt clammy under their shirts in the darkness. Virtually no noise penetrated from the outside. Inside, it was easy to imagine that nothing unusual was happening in Portobello that Saturday. They decided to explore the labyrinth in a group, ready for unwelcome surprises. Suddenly, a series of high-pitched screams startled them. Joseph's blunderbuss crashed to the floor. Fortunately, it did not go off.

"That came from the garden," said Tom. Emerging from the gallery, weapons at the ready, they came slowly into the glare of a tropical Eden. Pink paths of crushed coral formed a symmetrical pattern through brilliant flowerbeds enclosing a giant mango tree, heavy with fruit. A child's swing dangled from a branch. A peacock advanced towards them, its tail feathers fanning out, shrieking petulantly.

"Will you look at that," said Tom. "Beautiful."

"I've a good mind to blow the spangled banshee to hell," said Joseph, while the others recovered. "It fair froze my blood, so it did."

"Och, did ye think the fairy folk had come to chase yer freckled airse all the way back to Connaught?" hooted Malcolm. "Careful, Joe, those things'll nip yer bollocks off!"

Scarrett pointed a finger at the bird and shouted, "Bang!" The peacock stared at him with one eye, then the other, folded its tail and stalked away, as if deliberately ignoring the intruders. Even Joseph shook his head and laughed. They turned back into the gallery, gasping with relief. Joseph's axe and a few good kicks got them into the private quarters to the right of the staircase. Soon, they were barging through the upper chambers, rummaging in chests, overturning mattresses, taking down mirrors, looking behind tapestries, and opening cupboards stacked with porcelain.

"Fine work. Thin as an eggshell. I haven't set eyes on the like since Holland," said Tom, examining a bowl with delicate blue Chinese designs. "It must have come in the Acapulco galleon all the way from Manila, but it's too fragile for us. Look for small, precious things that don't break."

"Ye mean, the kind they would not leave behind," sighed Malcolm, "like coins. I doubt we'll find a single peso here... or a decent pearl."

"In a blind rush," said Tom, "people forget things. Keep

looking." He replaced the bowl and began to rip the stuffing out of an embroidered cushion.

"No, wait," said Malcolm, "who's in a blind rush now? Before ye tear everything apart, we must sit and think how best to proceed. Calmly. There's a fortune here somewhere, I feel it in my water."

Tom sank into a leather-backed armchair, lit his pipe and gazed at a painting of Jesus being scourged by Roman soldiers. "Good God," he groaned. "Here's me trying to be calm. What a sight to wake up to every day! More blood than in a slaughterhouse! These Papists would flay Christ all over again, if he were daft enough to return."

"Reminds me of Barbados," said Joseph, lifting bolts of cloth out of a chest. "It wasn't your Papists doing the flogging there, as I recall." He paused. "Look, cloth of silver, with gold thread too, right at the bottom, under the cheap stuff. With a good tailor, we could dress as kings, so we could."

"Put it to one side," said Tom, "and any wigs and silk. The tapestry in the first room, with the boar-hunting scene, take that as well. Roll it all up together."

"We could wrap it round the Chinese crockery, as it is so precious," said Joseph.

"Do what you like," sighed Tom, "but you'll be hauling broken shards to no avail tomorrow."

"I want food," announced Scarrett. "I'll look below. There must be a kitchen somewhere."

Joseph threw the cloth down. "I'll go with you. My guts are growling like a pack of wolves."

"Careful," said Tom, "they sometimes poison their provisions for the likes of us. Especially the wine." When they had gone, he turned to Malcolm. "Come, we might be luckier up the other stairs. Remember, small and portable."

"Ye've no intention of returning to Jamaica, am I right?" said Malcolm. "That's what 'small and portable' means; squirrel some choice pieces away and jump ship at the first opportunity. Beware, Mr. Sheppard: holding back shares means death in this fleet."

"So does a loose tongue," Tom tapped out his pipe. "Let's go."

"Ye don't need to be coy with me, Thomas," said Malcolm, as they clattered downstairs. "I'll not talk."

"As Saint Peter discovered when the third cock crowed," said Tom, "you'll be surprised what trusted friends do when their lives hang in the balance."

"Play it close to yer chest," said Malcolm, "that is all I ask. They'll lump all us messmates together. I'll not be marooned for something I have no stake in. Understand?"

"Don't fret," said Tom. They stood on the landing. "We'll see that you have a little nest egg too. Now, what's behind this door? Whatever it is, it stinks to high heaven. Smoky. Something's burning in there."

They struggled with the door handle. It refused to open. A brass shield, engraved with the same coat of arms, held the lock in place. Tom removed his hat and tried to peep through the hole, but the key was inside, blocking his view. The dry, acrid smell grew stronger, mixed with olive oil and garlic. He put his ear to the wood. He thought he heard the creak of floorboards, or a mattress straining on its ropes. After replacing his hat, he cocked two pistols and motioned for Malcolm to do likewise, whispering, "Somebody is creeping about in there. I'll blow the lock off. When I kick it open, you fire both barrels at waist height."

It took three hard kicks to free the lock from its splintered frame. Malcolm's pistols blazed into the dark opening. They heard a pot shatter, a splash of liquid, and a woman's scream. Then, they stepped forward through the gun smoke, into the chamber. It was even darker inside, with all the shutters closed. Smoldering sagebrush, in a small brazier, caused a choking fog to hang in the air. A buxom slave woman, heavily pregnant, cowered in a corner. She held a knife, but immediately dropped it when Malcolm advanced.

"Aqui nada," she wailed, pointing to a huddled figure lying on a cot in the opposite corner. "Solo fiebre amarilla!"

Tom bent over the man on the bed and quickly recoiled. The young Spaniard's skin was yellower than the medallion of the Virgin round his neck. Tom could not bring himself to get any closer, although it was pure gold. The sufferer's breath came in bubbling gasps. Dried scabs rimmed his eyes and black vomit stained the sheets. Septic flux congealed further down. The slave woman had tried to cover the stink by sprinkling oil and crushing garlic into the floorboards.

"She's right," Tom said. "He's boiling up with the Yellow Jack, much worse than Wilmot. The end stages…"

The woman's sudden rush for the door interrupted him. Tom hurried to the landing. He saw Malcolm grab her wrist. She wrenched it free, but lost her balance, shrieked and toppled down the stairs, cracking her skull on the flagstones below. Joseph and Scarrett came out from the kitchen and stared at the blood pooling around her head. The Gipsy turned her over and saw her belly. "Gone," he said, "like her baby, unless somebody fancies cutting it out. I don't. We are cursed enough."

Joseph crossed himself. "Holy Mary, Mother of God…"

"Get her out of here," shouted Tom, "into the garden! Now! Come, Malcolm, we'll see who's cursed!"

They returned to the sick bed. The young man, unaware of his surroundings, seemed to be in hell already, raving at invisible devils. Judging by the well-manicured fingers clawing at the sheets, he'd never done a day's work in his life. Probably, thought Tom, a son and heir. The family must have considered him too ill for the flight into the forest. It was a reasonable risk. The house was strong and the slave woman, like many Africans, was probably immune to the disease. She would have remained safe if she had not panicked. The young grandee, however, was doomed.

"It will be a mercy to put his lordship out of his misery," said Tom. "I'll not soil myself with a pillow over his mouth, but this should do the trick." He pulled the foot of the cot away from the wall. "Take the other end, Mal. Tip it over completely. On its head."

With the mattress and bed frame pressing down on him, the sick man gave a final series of stifled moans. The upturned bed shook violently. When all was quiet, Malcolm said, "That's enough for me. By the Living Christ, he reeks worse than a dead dog in a ditch. I'll see what the others are doing."

Tom heard Malcolm's boots clomping downstairs. Focusing his eyes on the dark corner behind the overturned bed, he reached down and pulled out a small, flat box. He carried it to the far end of the chamber, overlooking the garden, and opened the shutters. Light and air streamed in. The lid came off easily. At first glance, the box appeared to contain a handful of cloudy pebbles, slightly green, black, and purple in color. Tom knew what they were immediately. He had seen uncut emeralds and amethysts years ago, in the workshops of Amsterdam's Jews. These appeared to be of the finest quality, large and free of blemishes. He stuffed them deep into the fringed ammunition bag. With his pearls and the gems, he now possessed a small fortune. He'd have to keep the bag close by at all times. Just as well Malcolm had seen nothing. The lad could never keep a secret for long.

Peering down into the garden, Tom saw a corner of the dead slave woman's apron and her naked foot sticking out of a woodpile by the wall. He looked for the peacock, but it had vanished. After a fruitless inspection of the rest of the sick room, he descended to the kitchen. As he suspected, Scarrett had plucked the bird, stuffed it with peppers, and was roasting it on a spit in the fireplace. He twisted it over the heat like a medium-sized turkey. Joseph collected stale bread in a silver filigree basket. A bowl of olives, a jug, and cups of wine completed the preparations. After a while, Scarrett declared the meat ready.

"There," he said, "it'll be nice and tender now."

Malcolm unsheathed his knife, poised to cut into the bird's back. The Gipsy grabbed his wrist. "Avast!" he cried. "Leave it for a while! If you break its skin before it cools, all the juice will steam out. Then it'll be dry as a bone."

"As ye wish, Yer Highness," said Malcolm. "I apologize, but we seldom dined on peacocks in Glasgow or even on the Guinea Coast. Ye'll have no objection to me wetting my whistle, I hope. I take it nobody has been poisoned." He raised a wine cup to his lips. "Tom, did ye find anything of interest upstairs?"

Tom shook his head. "I had a quick look but the stink overcame me. I let some air in." He examined the peacock's tail that lay on the windowsill. "We'll keep these feathers. The Indians like nothing better. They make perfect gifts for the chiefs."

An hour later, the peacock had been reduced to bones. A few crumbs remained in the basket. The messmates lit their pipes and filled the wine jug from a barrel in the corner. It was their fifth jug. Soon, they were sprawled back in their chairs, dropping off to sleep. Shadows spread over the garden. The mango tree caught the orange light of the setting sun. Mosquitoes whined under the table, feeding on the exposed skin above the men's rolled-down stockings. They were woken up by a series of crashes resounding through the building.

Joseph sprang to his feet. "Mother of God! The Dons are back!"

Tom rolled off the chair and pulled himself up slowly, gripping the edge of the table. "The Dons will have a key to their own house. That'll be our boys, more likely. Light a candle! It's black as Satan's ass in here!"

Four buccaneers were heaving a short log against the front door. Four more held torches near a laden donkey cart. Tom hailed them from the balcony, "Ahoy there! Go to the next entrance. We'll let you in."

Tom held up a candle. He recognized the 'Old Maggot,' Captain Mackett, leading the drunken gang into the hall. The captain was not pleased. "Ah, Tom Sheppard. We've been ramming that door for some time. What the fuck were you sons of bitches doing? Hoping we'd go away?"

Mackett's men rampaged through the chambers without further ado. One ruffian raised the sodden mattress in the sick room and tore the gold medallion from the corpse's neck. In the street, the bolts of cloth and tapestry were loaded into the cart with the silverware from the kitchen table. The cart groaned under the weight of plunder from other houses.

"We were resting," Tom told Mackett. "Tired after all the marching. We lost track of time."

"Sharp's crew again, eh?" growled Mackett. Blood and sweat

stained his shirt. His nose seemed to have been recently broken. He spat orange saliva. "Lazier than your bloody captain, who isn't even here. For your information, it is six bells in the late dogwatch. The sun has been down for a good hour. We'll shift this stuff to the cathedral. You beauties can go back to sleep now, unless you take a fancy to fighting Spaniards for a change."

The Old Maggot turned to go, but suddenly changed his mind. "Ah, yes! Sheppard, you understand the Spanish lingo, do you not? The admiral needs you to read some letters for him. Come along with me!"

Leaving his friends in the mansion, Tom followed the torchbearers and the donkey cart. He soon found himself under the barreled vault of the cathedral roof. All the candles blazed, none brighter than those in a magnificent silver chandelier. It dangled from the roof, big as a cartwheel. A handful of wounded pirates lay near the font attended by a surgeon. All around, Coxon's crew sorted through piles of loot. A sailor climbed over the altar to gingerly remove the forked golden rays from a halo behind the head of a life-sized statue of Christ carrying the cross. Normally, the man would have simply toppled the Papist idol onto the floor, but this statue was different. He took care to avoid touching the carved wooden surface.

The effigy was famous throughout the West Indies. The face, with its melancholy expression, seemed to be alive, ready to move and speak. The wood shone beneath a dark patina, worn smooth by seawater and scorched by the sun. It was a 'Jonah Christ,' washed ashore after a storm, credited with curing plagues and bringing terrible misfortunes to heretics. As if that wasn't enough, as a 'Criminals' Christ,' it had the power to pardon penitent robbers and murderers. Any buccaneer who touched it would be damned thrice, for being an impious Protestant, a shameless felon, and a likely candidate for drowning. The man gripped the golden prongs by their tips and wrenched them away quickly before descending. He did not dare to finger the equally valuable crown of thorns embedded in the blackened head. He threw the pieces into a chest full of other fragments and poured himself a cup of communion wine. The Black

Christ of Portobello kept his embroidered purple cloak about his weathered shoulders. Less important statues of local saints and virgins lay abandoned under the benches, faces down, stripped of their adornments.

Tom saw that Coxon had turned the sacristy behind the altar into his headquarters. He heard the admiral barking out questions in pig Spanish and pounding the table. An elderly priest sat, strapped to a chair, while Coxon's bosun tightened a cord around his temples, forcing the eyeballs to protrude from their sockets. Coxon waved a document in front of the terrified old man. The priest only made squealing noises. Alliston, unsteady with drink or fever, prodded him with a rapier. At another desk an illuminated Bible served as a paperweight, resting on a pile of unsealed letters. Basil Ringrose busied himself, opening and scanning each piece of correspondence from a taller stack, before slipping anything of interest under the Bible. He swept the rest to the floor. When he saw Tom, Ringrose beckoned him over. "Mr. Sheppard, come and help me with this correspondence. I can understand the legal documents and church accounts in Latin, but some of the Castilian handwriting eludes me."

Tom pulled up a chair, keeping his rifle close at hand and the fringed pouch tight over one shoulder. He picked up a letter. "Yes, I can get the sense of it, I think, if you lend me your magnifying glass. Bring the candle closer. My eyesight is not what it was."

Coxon thundered, "Can you read it, man? You're not too blind for that? It might contain information concerning our enterprise, the silver transports and the enemy's dispositions. I trust you have the brains to know what is important and not to bother me with trifles."

"Aye, Captain," Tom nodded, "this is not too difficult. Nothing in code and all in a fair hand."

"Good," said Coxon, "we won't need this Papist turd any more, then." He cut the goggle-eyed priest loose and drove him out of the sacristy with a series of kicks in the backside. Once the priest had crawled away, the admiral lit his pipe and looked around thoughtfully. Tom observed him moving towards the far end of the room with a deliberately casual air, throwing some vestments behind a stone basin. Then Coxon summoned Alliston and the bosun to follow him into the main body of the cathedral. "Come, we can't risk a ship under the harbor guns. We need to gather a goodly supply of little boats, to slip below their angle of fire, or we'll never get all the stuff back to the fleet. Slaves or no slaves, I'm damned if I'll struggle through that bloody forest with the added weight."

When he had gone, Tom sidled over to the basin to wash his hands. He lifted a vestment and saw a wine jar brimming with doubloons. The gold gleamed like Sir Digby's Louis d'Or, but was engraved with King Carlos' misshapen profile. No less than a king's ransom. It took all his self-control not to reach down and pocket a handful. Then Tom remembered that the gemstones in his pouch were risky enough, and that Coxon might have counted the coins. He dried his fingers and dropped the cloth over the jar before returning to his task beside Ringrose.

A letter from the Viceroy of Peru bewailed tensions between Dominicans and Jesuits. A monk was on trial for stabbing a priest in Lima. A freed African had killed a Spaniard for raping his wife and would be flayed alive in public. The Panama Assembly apologized for a further drop in the quantity of silver arriving from the Potosi mine. The Inquisition at Cartagena announced a campaign against clerics who fornicated with their housekeepers, recommending public flogging, defrocking, confiscation of goods, and exile to Chile. Another inquisitor argued that a simple flogging would suffice. The main demand was for more African slaves, since the Indian population was dwindling at an alarming rate. A mine owner suggested breeding more half-black, half-Indian 'lobos.' He hoped to combine the muscles and lung capacity of both races, to work above the snow line in the Andes. The costly installation of artillery and new stone defenses at Panama and Callao was the only subject of any interest to the buccaneers, apart from constant references to problems caused by smugglers and a chronic shortage of firearms on the Araucanian frontier, in the deep south near Valdivia. Harbormasters were urged to look out for secret Jews hiding among Portuguese crews, trying to infiltrate the Spanish

Indies. A circular from King Carlos, composed by his informants in Brussels, warned of increased pirate activity since the end of the Anglo-French alliance against the Dutch. Protestant pirates were to be enslaved if they converted to Catholicism or garroted if they did not. Slowly, Tom and Ringrose fought their way to the bottom of the pile. They had just finished when Coxon returned. Tom summarized the dispatches for him.

"Nothing of much consequence," said Coxon, "apart from the dearth of silver. God's Blisters, you should have seen the bars stacked up in the strong rooms when we were here with Morgan."

"I did, they came up to my chin," said Tom, immediately wishing he had not spoken. The admiral began to take more interest in him. "We were a mighty host. Whose ship did you sail in?"

"I was with Captain Searles all the way to Taboga in the South Sea."

Coxon stroked his whiskers. "Ah, yes, Dancing Danny, who now shits himself in public. A sorry business. You'll have better luck with us, Mr. Sheppard, I guarantee it." The admiral paused to admire Tom's rifle. "What on earth is that? An eight-sided barrel? I've seen some flintlocks in my time, but this beats the devil himself."

Tom explained, "It's a hunter's rifle, Captain. The grooves in the barrel spin the bullet. Three times as accurate as your common musket."

"A rifle? Never seen one like this." He turned it over in his hands. "I thought only princes and kings owned them, but do not fear, I will not enquire as to where you found it. Instead I insist that you bring it here tomorrow morning, climb to the top of the bell tower, and shoot some of those Dons off the walls of La Gloria. I'll give you four pesos for every one of the fuckers you put out of action. Amos here," he pointed to the bosun, "will keep score with a spyglass. What d'ye think of that, eh? Are your eyes up to it?"

"I have no trouble at long range. I'll give it a try, Captain, but they are likely to keep their heads down after they realize what is happening, when the first two of three have been hit."

"That's what I want. Prevent 'em from moving about freely. Give 'em a good peppering if they try to point their cannon over the water or launch a boat. Anything that moves—shoot it! Lessonne has 'em bottled up tight on land, but you have the instrument to make life miserable for the bastards to seaward. Their muskets won't reach you in the tower. They'll be at your mercy. So get plenty of sleep. You look bleary, Sheppard. Lay off the wine. Tomorrow will be a long day for you."

Tom retraced his steps to the baronial mansion through streets alive with shouts, torches, and rushing shadows. That night, the four friends slept in different chambers. Tom had the great matrimonial four-poster all to himself. For a while, he rolled about and extended his arms and legs in all directions. It was a shame to waste such luxury. Maybe he could find a slave girl somewhere. He remembered the pregnant woman falling downstairs. She lay in the garden, maggots popping her skin, her baby dead inside. His mood darkened. He recalled Squealer's death struggles in Morant Bay. How that ugly brat had kicked! The misty giant in the Blue Mountains stalked his dreams. The phantom had acquired the penetrating gaze of the Black Christ of Portobello. Eventually the nightmares stopped and he slept like a rock at the bottom of the ocean. The bed was so comfortable that the sun was high in the sky before he awoke.

Amos, Coxon's bosun, waited on the cathedral steps. "There you are at last, Mr. Sheppard! Don't worry. The admiral was up all night. He's snoring in the priest's room, dead to the world and all its doings. We can climb up to the bell tower in our own sweet time."

The Hapsburg flag flapped defiantly in the salty breeze above La Gloria. Under it, the defenders on the roof of the square castle had a commanding view of the town, from the hills behind to the sweep of the foreshore and the indistinct line between the sea and the sky to the north. Since they had been driven into the fort, the Spaniards kept up a series of fusillades on the streets below, making it difficult for Lessonne's contingent to move about. More importantly, two field guns on the roof could be wheeled into position to bombard the anchorage when the time came for the buccaneers to withdraw.

Half a mile away, the cathedral tower was the only structure that looked down on La Gloria. The Spanish musketeers manning the battlements, barely glanced at the cathedral. They assumed nobody could shoot at them over such a distance with any accuracy. The Spaniards missed the bells ringing out the hours, or calling the faithful to mass, but that was all. They moved about on their platform without a care in the world, taking pot shots over the side whenever they felt like it. Tom's first bullet spun their commander around with a wound in his liver. The officer writhed on the stones while his men backed off in amazement.

"Got him!" laughed Amos, sitting beside Tom, beneath the bells. "The ants are scuttling round the nest! Look! They think it was one of their own men misfiring!"

He offered the telescope to Tom who brushed it aside. "Let me reload. With luck, I can bird another before they realize what's happening."

Tom's second shot shattered a Spaniard's elbow. Amos whooped. This time, the wounded man screamed and pointed directly at the bell tower with his good arm. A wisp of smoke from Tom's rifle was curling into the air. The musketeers crouched behind the parapet facing the cathedral and let off a volley. The balls rattled harmlessly off the surrounding roof tiles.

"Now it becomes interesting," muttered Tom, slipping into a corner of the arch. "It'll be like shooting coconuts. I hope you are keeping count." He measured half a finger of powder from his seashell flask into a thimble and poured it down the barrel. The bullet fitted in tight once the scrap of leather had been rammed over it. When all was ready, Tom aimed beneath his target's plumed hat. He fired into the Spaniard's smoke.

Amos twisted the telescope into his eye and said, "Missed. You took a bite out of the wall, about four inches too low. Look out, here comes their answer!"

One ball clanged off the bell above their heads. It fell and rolled at their feet. The rest flew wide again. "Looks like we're in for a long day," said Tom. "I'll have to worm out the burnt powder after seven shots. Give me some wine."

During the next hour, Tom blasted off one man's hat and blew out another's brains. Amos kept score until he became bored and amused himself by pretending to be wounded when the Spaniards fired, splashing red wine over his face and lolling against the arch. His antics fooled one musketeer who cheered and waved his hat. Tom was able to hit him in the shoulder. After that things quietened down. The day grew hotter. Sporadic shots from both sides produced no further results. Tom sighed. "I make that five in all, Amos. Coxon owes me twenty pieces of eight."

"I'll vouch for that, mate," nodded the bosun.

Meanwhile, the French buccaneers in the houses near the fort took advantage of the Spaniards' discomfort. They packed round-bellied wine bottles with gunpowder and fuses. Safe from enemy fire, they stepped out onto the balconies and lobbed the glass grenades over La Gloria's battlements. The fort's gun platform swiftly emptied, leaving nothing but a pile of smoldering bodies and a cannon sagging on a broken wheel. With no more to do, Tom and Amos descended the spiral stone stairway.

Sitting in a grandee's pew near the altar, Coxon listened to Amos' account of the morning's events while a slave cleaned his boots. He gave Tom his twenty-peso reward and said, "So, your fancy musket is more than just a conversation piece. Good work, Thomas. Don't be surprised if we require your services again." He turned to Amos. "Get Mackett. At the last count, we had twenty-eight boats and canoes. We need forty, at the very least. Even then, some will have to make two trips to the Bastimentos. I want everything that can float over a shoal to be ready in the harbor tonight. Take every last fishing boat and Indian pirogue you can find. Tie 'em all up to the jetty with the others."

"Beg pardon, Captain Coxon, sir," said Amos, "but why don't we load up one of the merchantmen and have done with it?"

"Have you seen the state of those tubs?" snapped the admiral. "They're so worm-eaten, if I stamped my foot, I'd go right through. Apart from that, they'd soon run aground where we are heading. Stop mithering, man. Just tell Mackett and Alliston to collect the boats."

Tom walked out of the cathedral, past the wounded buccaneers, onto the steps. Although he did not look, he felt the staring eyes of the Black Christ following him, reproaching him for shooting defenseless men in exchange for a few coins. It was small comfort knowing that, given the chance, the Spaniards would have done the same to him. Five pesos for a life! The cash was an insult to both the killer and his victims. He would not have felt so cheap if he had done it for nothing. Now, he realized, Arnout's gift had made him a long-range angel of death on the battlefield. He'd have to get used to that idea of himself.

"Why so gloomy, auld man?" He felt Malcolm's hand patting his shoulder. "I hear ye've been knocking Dons down like skittles. Come, it's time for a rest and I've found just the place!"

"Everything in order back at the house? No more visitors?"

"Aye, all under control," said Malcolm. "Wait till ye see this fine Spanish bordello behind the docks. It makes the Port Royal taverns look like dog kennels. Our lads have kicked the pimps out, taken over, and set the prices. The women are delightful if ye like 'em brown, and they serve proper French brandy in glass cups."

"You go," said Tom. "I may have become a murdering thief, but I haven't turned into a glutton for whores. In fact, you'd be doing me a favor if you spent these bloody pesos for me."

Malcolm counted the reward money. "Are you sure? This is far too much for a bottle and a fuck. What's ailing ye, Thomas?"

"Never mind what's ailing me. Drink a few bottles. Get as soused as a Dutch herring. Fuck three or four at a time. Play dice with what remains. Do it on my behalf. I will see you later."

He turned on his heel and strode across the plaza. "As ye wish," said Malcolm. He had grown accustomed to Tom's moods over the years. The young Scotsman looked at the coins in his hand, shook his head, and made for the docks. Peacock feathers graced his black Spanish hat. His sabre hung in a dazzling gold-threaded baldric. Both had been taken from the baronial house. If there had been a horse with silver shoes in the stable, he would have ridden it. He had every intention of acting the grandee while he had the chance.

Tom did not feel grand at all. He could not put his finger on the reason for his bleak frame of mind. If it had been possible, he would have walked straight out of town to brood on a lonely beach. The bell tower shootings had not pleased him, but it went deeper than that. Everything about this adventure was wrong. He took an aimless detour through the streets and found himself drifting into a meaner district. The smell of wood smoke and effluent grew stronger. The underlying stink of a tannery and rotting fish reminded him of Port Royal. Thin yellow dogs searched for scraps in the shadows. There were mainly black and brown faces here, crowded together in small houses that had not been considered worth looting. The handful of white men all seemed to be drunks or beggars, rags barely covering their dirty skins.

He paused in front of a leather worker's shop. A wrinkled mulatto gripped a big curved needle, the type used for sailcloth, to sew the edges of a decorative Spanish jerkin. Shoes waited to be repaired on shelves behind him. Tom studied the man's technique. Swirling patterns on the sides and old-fashioned slashes at the shoulders turned the jerkin into a reminder of a bygone age.

"Trabajas Domingo?" Tom found himself asking. "You work on a Sunday?"

The old artisan looked at him as if he was mad and answered in educated Castilian, "Yes, the church is closed. Now why would that be, I wonder, Englishman?"

Tom had to laugh. The deft action of the needle had made him forget that he was a pirate raiding a foreign town. For a minute, he had spoken as one craftsman to another. The man glanced up and down the narrow street. A group of young mulattos, similar to the militiamen who had run from La Gloria the day before, emerged from an alley. Their eyes narrowed. Tom found himself walking faster and looking over his shoulder with his musket at the ready. If they rushed him, he was prepared to make at least one them pay for their little victory. Before reaching the corner of a broad avenue, he noticed a thrown pebble kicking up dust in front of his boots. A small black child scampered away. Tom rounded the corner and was relieved to see a gang of French looters pulling a cart. The young mulattos melted into the shadows.

"By the Scourged Rump of Christ," he hissed to himself. "Straying about like the village idiot! I must be tired of life!"

Back at their borrowed house, the atmosphere was relaxed. After letting Tom in through the front door, Scarrett returned to chopping vegetables on the kitchen table. He indicated the wine barrel in the corner. "Help yourself. There's plenty left."

The Gipsy wore a bloodstained leather apron. A cured pig's haunch hung by its trotter from a ceiling hook. A butchered goat simmered in the cauldron over the fire. Joseph sat in a tub of warm salty water to soothe his insect bites. The Gipsy had finally convinced him to puff a pipe of Angolan weed. At first, Joe coughed and spluttered. Now, after a fit of laughter, the big Irishman felt carefree and comfortable. He forgot the grim scene when they had hauled the stinking bed linen, containing the young hidalgo's corpse, to the woodpile in the garden, flung it onto the dead slave woman, placed the mattress on top, and burned the lot. The bones now lay under smoldering ash. A sooty stain ran up the boundary wall. They had scrubbed the filthy floorboards in the sickroom with vinegar as if they were slave shelves, getting rid of the smell and the blowflies. All the windows overlooking the garden were wide open, those facing the street firmly shuttered. The long afternoon promised to make the streets quiver in the heat.

Tom sat down and tapped his pipe out onto the floor. He gave a brief account of his sharpshooting exploits in the bell tower. Joe said, "Add a little of the Angolan hemp to thy next smoke, thou mighty hunter. It's sweet after a few puffs. I take back everything I said. Brightens the day, so it does. At any rate, it's cheaper than scampering around town like Malcolm, looking like a popinjay and acquiring a fresh dose of the Royal Spanish Pox."

"The scabs on your body would make the ugliest whore tremble, Joe. I agree. You're better off where you are." He suddenly rose to his feet. "I need to use your sail-making needles and some strong thread. Where's your bag, laddie?"

"Upstairs, in the first chamber, hanging from the chair. I rolled the needles and two bobbins of good twine in a grey cloth. Should be near the bottom. There's no thimble, but look here," he pointed to his fingerless glove on the tiles beside the tub, "that will shield your palm if you slip a coin inside. You'll be fixing your boots, eh?"

"Something like that," said Tom, picking up the glove. "I'll want that apron too, if you don't mind, Scarrett."

The Gipsy handed it over. "Here you are, Mister Sheppard. I've done all my chopping. I'll call for you when the food is ready. It'll be a proper Sunday feast today, fit for the Sovereign of the Seven Seas, if Joe gets out of that tub and fetches bread from the Frenchies."

Tom went upstairs to his quarters. The old Spanish leather worker had given him an idea. He spread the apron out on the floorboards, cut away the strings, squared the ends and sliced two generous armholes out of the soft hide with his knife. Then he folded the edge down around the collar, tapering it off to a point halfway across the chest. Yes, this would make a durable little waistcoat, ideal for protecting his shoulders from his chafing ammunition bag, bandolier, and musket strap. More importantly, he could sew his collection of uncut gems and pearls tight under the collar fold. The leather was stained and ugly. It would not arouse curiosity. The waistcoat would serve as his secret emergency fund. Nobody would give it a second glance. At any rate, it was safer than leaving such valuables rolling in the bottom of his Indian pouch, which was unusual enough to attract attention. His Prussian officer's certificate in its small bamboo sheath could remain where it was. The Brethren had no law against personal papers.

After various attempts to thread the needle, Tom went downstairs to seek help. In the evening gloom, even with three candles blazing nearby, his near vision was not up to the task. Joe had gone for bread, so the Gipsy did it for him. Back in his room, sitting on the four-poster, Tom got down to work. It wouldn't be a precise job, but it would be tight and firm. The waxed twine was made to resist wind and weather. He criss-crossed the stitches over the little bumps made by the gems until they formed a crude pattern round the back of the neck. Joe's voice called him to supper when he was starting on the first lapel. He stuffed everything under the bed and descended to the kitchen.

He asked, "No sign of Malcolm?"

The others shook their heads. The three men slurped and chewed until they were sated. Joseph belched. He had been very hungry. Tom rose to his feet. "I'll go up and finish my sewing."

"Give me back the needle and thread in the morning," said Joseph.

Tom tied off the final stitch around midnight. His head ached from narrowing his eyes to focus. He banged the waistcoat against the wall and ground it under his heel. No problem, it was tough as nails. Soon, he was asleep. He did not hear Malcolm knocking on the coach gate an hour later or cavorting with a giggling Portobello whore in an adjoining chamber. Joseph and Scarrett settled down further along the corridor. This would be their last night in a comfortable bed for a very long time.

Mike Hawthorne

8
THE LION'S SHARE

Early on Monday, Coxon's small boats began to transport the loot under the guns of Fort San Felipe. They rounded the eastern headland towards the Bastimentos, a pair of keys once used as supply depots by Columbus. One long canoe was overloaded with valuable fabrics, including the tapestry and cloth of gold from the mansion. It overturned, leaving the crew clinging to its sides. The heavier material sank to the bottom of the deep harbor. Bolts of gossamer-thin Chinese chiffon unfurled and spread out on the surface before slowly submerging.

The silky gauze settled over the 74-year-old wrecks of Sir Francis Drake's ships, rotting in the shifting sands among the remains of a burned Spanish fleet. The great Elizabethan navigator lay down there, in full armor, sealed within a lead coffin. Portobello had exploded in flames as they dropped his sarcophagus overboard, to haunt those waters forever.

At ten in the morning, Malcolm's whore helped herself to a bundle of dresses she had found in a closet. The Scotsman agreed to escort her back to the eastern district behind the docks. Passing the bullion vaults, they saw Coxon, Ringrose, and Amos arguing with a group of wealthy Spanish prisoners. The grandees' black garments dazzled Malcolm when sunbeams flashed off their silver embroidery beneath the colonnade. Before his whore guided him out of the plaza, Malcolm noticed most of the dignitaries, including senior churchmen, being marched towards the jetties and hustled into canoes. A select few were simply allowed to melt away. Of these, one still wore his sword. These were no ordinary captives.

"Ah," Malcolm muttered, "so that's the game." The admiral appeared to be conducting personal business with certain *hidalgos* on his own account, barely bothering to conceal the fact. Malcolm remembered that Coxon's crew were a law unto themselves. Alliston, Mackett, and Lessonne were not to be seen, and a lone straggler with his moll would ring no alarm bells. Nobody gave the couple a second glance. Malcolm noticed that the supply of dugouts was dwindling. Commanders like Coxon had been known to abandon involuntary rearguards on the shore to fend for themselves. It would be a good idea to keep a boat in reserve. He turned to the whore. "Maria, canoes? Canoes?" He made a paddling motion.

"Ah, canoas! Si!" She took him beyond the docks to a swampy inland lagoon linked to the harbor by a narrow channel. The stagnant water hummed with dragonflies. Small fishing craft dotted the surface. On the far bank, a path snaked through a banana plantation, cutting behind Fort San Felipe towards the Bastimentos. Malcolm gave Maria a final lingering kiss, slapped the curve of her rump, and marched purposefully back to the town house. He walked against a swelling stream of pirates carting loot in the opposite direction. One pair supported Mackett, shivering with fever. Alliston stumbled behind a laden donkey wagon. They were followed by a dozen walking wounded with bandages round their heads or their arms in slings. Jamaican mulatto boys carried chests and sacks for the surgeons. Casualties had been surprisingly light. Just six corpses were dropped onto Drake's wrecks, stitched into sailcloth shrouds with cannonballs at their ankles. It was better than burying them ashore. The Spaniards were sure to dig up the bodies and feed them to the dogs. This way, their bones rested appropriately, among English ships' guns and timbers, slowly turning to coral in Drake's underwater graveyard.

The four friends left their comfortable chambers for the last time. Without looking back, Malcolm led them to the lagoon. They found a skiff similar to Tom's old boat. With Joseph rowing, they headed into the narrow channel that led out to sea. At one point, they scraped along the bottom. Everybody leapt out to push, soaking their plundered Spanish boots and breeches. After a few heaves, they skirted the edge of the bay on the eastern flank of Coxon's escaping canoes. Above, from the right, San Felipe's guns fired occasional shots. Almost all splashed harmlessly between the boats. Only one ball found its target, splintering a dugout and maiming a buccaneer, throwing his guts over the captured grandee beside him. None of the remaining fifteen occupants could swim. The broken halves of the canoe sank beneath their weight. They all drowned within sight of land.

"Nary a pearl diver among 'em, that's for sure," said Tom, as the last thrashing figure disappeared. The wind of another shot passed close to the skiff's sail.

"Don't be tempting fate," said Joseph, ducking his head and crossing himself. "You wouldn't want to be snatched away like that without the time to make your peace, would you now?"

"Spoken like a true Papist," said Malcolm. "Surely ye know, we can commend our own souls to God, or Auld Clootie, whenever we choose, man, even with bubbles coming from our mouths. By Christ, would ye have us sail with black Jesuit crows in cassocks wailing a death mass on the quarterdeck?"

"That would attract a storm for certain," said Tom. "A good lesson in swimming is worth a thousand masses, or, for that matter, any number of old wives' tales about walking on water."

"Begorrah, but you're a tribe of heathens," said Joseph. "Worse than the man-eating savages. I'll pray for your poor damned souls, so I will."

"You do that," Tom pointed ahead. "Look, there's Drake's island, if I remember rightly. We'll keep to larboard."

A hot land breeze sped them along. They carried no loot other than their new clothes and the items secretly stitched into Tom's homemade jerkin. Scarrett had brought the leg of cured ham, a full wineskin, and the remnants of last night's bread. The skiff entered the channel between the point and Drake's deserted island from which they saw Portobello's buildings standing in a long crescent. Although Lessonne's crew was withdrawing, the defenders inside La Gloria stayed put. The inhabitants would be glad that the entire port had not been torched. Tom took a final look at the cathedral's bell tower as it vanished behind the palm trees. Behind him, San Felipe's guns seemed to salute the pirates' departure.

A grey fin advanced towards them from the island. It was followed by two more. Reef sharks, hiding under coral overhangs, had caught the tang of blood and guts in the current coming out of the bay. They came close, almost scraping the hull. A pirogue, making the return trip to the jetty for more loot, appeared behind the sharks, as if being pulled along by the big fish.

"Go back, you dogs," yelled one of the men on board. "You're sailing empty!"

Tom turned to Scarrett. "Smile at 'em and give 'em some of your Gipsy gibberish."

Scarrett let fly a torrent of Romany abuse with an angelic grin on his face, accompanied by dramatic gestures. The sailors in the pirogue flashed by, open-mouthed.

"I heard 'bongo' and 'chee-chee' among all yer twiddle-twaddle," said Malcolm. "Sure ye weren't regaling them with nigger talk?"

"If you'd listened more carefully," said Scarrett, "you might have also picked out the word 'cunt.'"

"Children, children," said Tom. He steered towards a couple of larger coral islands barely a quarter mile down the coast. "The Bastimentos!"

Men were dragging canoes and pirogues onto a crescent-shaped strip of white sand. Some hauled the plunder into a coconut grove. Others dumped bags, rolls, and chests on the beach, relaunched their boats and headed back to Portobello for more. Tom abruptly swung the tiller, turning the bow in the opposite direction. The sail went slack.

"Aren't we landing, Tom?" asked Joseph.

"Not yet. I don't want to get in among that crowd so soon. I'd not relish having any of 'em visiting us either, and I'm buggered if I want to be pressed into returning to port. Mackett took our plunder. We're not a haulage service. We'll keep our distance. Dive down, Mal, see if you can find a rock and secure the anchor."

"Are ye mad?" said Malcolm. "I'll not do it, Tom. Those sharks were hungry. I swear there's more hereabouts, sniffing for a kill."

"You're right," said Joseph. He pointed to a tangled mass of mangroves on the nearby mainland. "Why, for the love of Christ, don't we grapple her to a branch over that side? We can go in a wee bit, out of sight, cozy as clams."

"Do as you please, if you prefer crocodiles and spiders to sharks." Tom settled his shoulders against the hull and pulled down the brim of his hat. "Only, get on with it."

Once they had moored, they untied the sail and stretched it above the boat for shade. Scarrett carved slices of ham and passed round the stale bread. Then, it was time for wine, tobacco, and sleep. Tom cast his eyes over his snoring comrades. He toyed with the idea of slipping away, but quickly thought the better of it. Judging by their submissive demeanor, the local Indians would gladly sell him to the Spaniards. The mangroves did not look inviting. The boat stirred lazily on the ebb tide.

Heavy with wine, Tom dropped off. In a dream, he was enslaved to the old Portobello leather worker, chained to a bench, stitching jerkins until his fingers bled. He heard the babble of the street market. Sweat ran down his neck. The old man was never satisfied, continually telling him to unpick the yarn and start again. He was forced to conceal his gemstones in his hatband. Eventually, he could stand it no longer and stuck the needle into the old man's backside, making him scream and swing around. Tom found himself peering up at the face of the Black Christ, who fixed him with his mournful stare and whispered, "Why?" He heard the cathedral bell toll. Again, "Why?" Another bell, another whisper, and he sank into dreamless oblivion. When he woke up some hours later, yet another bell rang, this time accompanied by Malcolm's curses.

"Christ on a crusty cunt!" Malcolm shouted. "We're bogged down, like rats in treacle!"

The receding tide had left the little boat stuck in the thick brown ooze among the exposed roots, which became a meeting place for insects from above and crabs from below. Bright blue butterflies fluttered over the scene in festive mockery. Tom blinked and said, "Was that a bell?"

"There," Joseph pointed to seaward, above the tops of the furthest mangroves, "two mastheads in the channel. It came from that sloop."

"Aye," said Malcolm, "looks like Alliston's tub. He flies an old sheet with Saint George's cross from his topmast, with the red tail of the pennant all frayed to ribbons, just like that one."

"Somebody must have got word back to Springer's Key," said Tom. "The ships will be coming to fetch us off."

"And we are stuck fast," Malcolm thumped the hull. "We'll die here, eaten by bog crabs and hairy spiders, while the others share out the loot and depart. Crivvens, are we brainless lubbers, or what? Whose idea was this? It had to be an Irishman!"

Joseph was about to rise from his seat, but Tom restrained him and said, "We were all tired. If anything, it was my fault for not insisting that we anchor off the beach. Now, we'll simply wait for the tide to flow in. Look, it's nearly sunset. Whatever happens, they won't navigate in the dark among the reefs."

Malcolm would not let it rest. "How long have we been sleeping? Ye dinna know! That might have been the last of them sailing away! I've a mind to climb through the branches and make sure they're still here."

"Go then, you Glasgow fartgullet," said Joseph, shrugging off Tom's hand. "I've a mind to throw you into the mud myself, so I have. Go with God, but go! Swing through the bracken like the wee furry monkey you are!"

"Och, to hell wi' ye!" Malcom leapt over the edge and sank into the slime, deeper with every pace. He reached for a root, grasped a higher branch, and impaled his hand on a thorn. Letting go, he fell on his side with a dull smack. Crabs scuttled in all directions.

His friends roared with laughter. They watched him turn and attempt to crawl back to the boat. Soon, he was spitting mud out with his curses. His body had disappeared and only one arm was free. He tried in vain to reach the mooring rope, but missed it by inches. When they finally hauled Malcolm aboard, on the end of a sash, the sun's last rays were painting the sky red. He was reduced to a glistening blob of silent misery. The mud had swallowed both his boots and pistols. His hat, with its peacock feathers, remained out there too, lying somewhere in the shadows. Stranded, he could not even clean himself with seawater.

"Look on the bright side," said Tom, "you still have your sword."

Malcolm grunted. He reached for the almost-empty wineskin, rinsed his mouth, and spat over the side.

"How long till we float again?" asked Scarrett.

"With luck, we'll be on our way before midnight," said Tom. "I reckon that big island will cause double tides, like the Isle of Wight."

"Where, in the name of Christ, are we, Tom?" asked Joseph. "I've fair lost my bearings, so I have. We've been here how long? Three or four days? I swear, it feels like weeks. All these islands look the same. Rocks on the outer side, sand and palm trees on the other, with the sea in between. There are hundreds of them."

Tom sighed. "God preserve us." He laid an oar across his knees ceremoniously, catching the fading light, with the blade pointing back towards the red glow above the trees. "Say the oar is the shoreline. Here, where my left hand is, that's Portobello, in the West. My right hand, down here, is Springer's Key, where we left the ships last week." His right hand slowly crawled along the shaft towards his left. "Now, we're marching from the Samballoes' Gulf, up from the east, through the forest, remember? Now, we're passing this point, where we're sitting now, about half a mile inland. And NOW," he yelled, grabbing Joseph by the throat, "we're attacking the town!" He rocked Joseph's head sideways, to the rhythm of each separate word, "Do-you-know-where-we-are-now?"

"Yes! Enough," said the Irishman, rubbing his neck. "Don't

forget, you're the only one who knows this coast."

"As for the islands," Tom continued, regardless, "they are all different shapes and sizes, with sands that can be anything from snow white to charcoal, and every shade in between. Some are big, with hills and streams, others barely support three trees and a clutch of crabs. Here, east of Manzanillo Point, they're not so numerous, but we still have the Bastimentos, Bald Island, Deaf Island, and the Isle of Goats, followed by Snake Rock and The Maggots, down near Puerto Escondido and the Rio Quango."

"Now, wait," said Joseph, "you're making all this bald, deaf goats' bollocks up. We sailed into Puerto Escondido last year, and that was in Cuba."

"God save us from imbeciles," said Tom. "Don't you know that Puerto Escondido simply means 'Hidden Port'? That's where the Dons buy African cargoes from heretics, outside the law, like ourselves and the Dutch. There are hundreds of secret ports all over the Spanish Indies, man, including the one a few miles from here. Of course, they are not really secret. The same grandees who are paid to enforce the laws buy their own slaves in such places."

Tom continued to pass the time by lecturing Joseph in this vein. They paused to smoke, chew the remaining hardened breadcrumbs, drain the last drops of wine, and gnaw the cured ham to the bone. When Tom had talked himself hoarse, they slapped at the mosquitoes that whined through the swamp and watched the moon climb in a misty haze. Malcolm gradually came back to life. He stripped and beat the caked mud off his clothes against the side of the boat. Having dressed again, he sat quietly, dirty and barefoot, thumbing the blade of his sabre. Joseph knew better than to tease him. The last hour, before a low gurgle under the keel announced the incoming tide, passed very slowly.

Scarrett tossed the hambone into the deepening water. It made a bigger splash than he expected. "I saw its thorny tail," he cried. "A crocodile, I swear!"

Malcolm broke his silence; "This country is like a million pairs of hungry jaws with pointed teeth, dying to take a lump out of us."

"It should suit your humor then," said Tom, glad that the Scotsman was talking again, "for, surely, you are here to take a few lumps out of it."

"Wait and see!" Malcolm snapped his sword into the scabbard.

Back on the island, the loot had been stacked and surrounded by heavily armed guards. Alliston's sloop had indeed arrived, only to be sent back to fetch the whole fleet from Springer's Key. Tom and his mates located the water butts. They rested around their new skiff, as they had for years around Tom's old boat. It was as if they always returned to the same stretch of sand, but with constantly changing vistas of rocks and trees. All became quiet except for the crackling fires, which illuminated the great pile of booty on the hill. The heavens seemed very close.

Tom traced the familiar outline of Orion the Hunter. The constellation blazed so fiercely in the black void that he felt he could reach out and touch it, grasping the stars like handfuls of diamonds. The unmistakable glow of the Pleiades attracted his gaze. He felt sure that, if there was life after death, this mysteriously welcoming cluster was the gateway to an enchanted paradise. Perhaps the mother he had never known awaited him there. In Sussex, his native chalk cliffs carried the stars' name, the Seven Sisters. He had often stared at that very glow from his bed in a haystack on warm English nights. Lonely nocturnal rambles had made him feel intensely alive as a boy, out hunting rabbits with an impossible love for some farmer's daughter pounding in his heart. He remembered the sweet smell of the late summer woodbine. Those stars could only be female. The moon, with its misty halo, now inched slowly over the sea, towards Springer's Key, the lands of the Kuna Indians and, still further, Cartagena. Unable to sleep after his afternoon siesta among the mangroves, Tom's mind circled around his predicament. It would be wise to escape after the division of the spoils. If Coxon decided to assault the walls of Cartagena, perhaps in league with the French, Tom was determined to desert the buccaneer fleet and make for nearby Curacao and the safety of the Dutch garrison. He would ask Captain Sharp to tie this new skiff to the stern of the ship, as he had the old one, just in case. Whether he could persuade Malcolm, Joseph, or even the Gipsy to join him was another matter. If necessary, he would go it alone.

Eventually, he gave up trying to sleep, leaned back against the hull, and lit a pipe. The awnings, beneath which the wounded lay in a makeshift hospital, rippled in the sea breeze under the swaying palms. New guards replaced the men watching the loot after four hours. By now his thoughts trudged wearily round like convicts in a prison yard, ready to drop, but too anxious to rest. Tom went through all the possible variations of escape plans, from Mexico to the shoulder of Brazil, depending on where he imagined Coxon might go next. For once, he wished he had drunk himself senseless. Something deeper bothered him. The buzzing in his head merely distracted him from what was eating him inside. Everything and nothing! He felt the symptoms, but could not identify the cause. Sleep finally claimed him shortly before dawn. The noise of his mates preparing cocoa for breakfast did not wake him. It was almost ten in the morning when he heard the cannon shot of the first approaching pirate vessel from Springer's Key.

The best navigator in the fleet had fired the gun. Bartholomew Sharp led the other ships into the channel between the Bastimentos, invisible from the mainland. The anchorage quickly sprouted a grove of masts belonging to Sharp, Coxon, Alliston, and Mackett. Cornelius Essex's rotten tub was the last ship to arrive, floundering along behind the French vessel. It was a miracle old Essex was still afloat. Everybody wanted to be present while the loot was shared out, and it was vital that this should happen in public. At noon, a final contingent of French buccaneers emerged from the forest beside the mangrove swamp. They had followed the path from the inner lagoon that Malcolm had observed on the previous day. When the last man had been safely ferried across, the entire force sat in a great semi-circle to divide the spoils. A small group of Spanish prisoners watched grimly. The pirate captains, quartermasters, mates, and surgeons stepped forward to receive their larger slices of the pie. Then, suddenly, a pistol shot and a desperate scream brought the proceedings to a halt.

"Get down! The Dons are here, aiming at us!" a sailor who had turned to relieve himself among the bushes raised the alarm. He saw ranks of Spanish soldiers lining the leeward shore, pointing their weapons across the water. Troops of lancers trotted up behind the musketeers in a bristling mass. At least seven hundred strong, these reinforcements from Panama vastly outnumbered the buccaneers. Had they arrived a few hours earlier, it would have spelt disaster. The sun gleamed off spear points and breastplates. Musket muzzles flashed. The shoreline vanished in clouds of smoke. Lead balls snapped through the palm fronds above the pirates' heads. The Spaniards had misjudged the distance and angled their barrels too high. A mad scramble ensued, to drag the plunder, the prisoners, and the wounded over the brow of the hill, before the enemy could reload.

"Keep moving," Coxon shouted, and pointed at the small craft on the outer beach. "Take everything to the next island. The bastards can't reach us there."

Three hours later, the semi-circle of pirates gathered before the same pile of loot on the windward key, well out of reach of their pursuers. By now, everybody was tired and thirsty. Barrels and cooking fires in the enemy line of fire had been abandoned on the first island. The men were nervous. Luckily, the ships were stocked with fresh water from the San Blas rivers. It was decided to postpone the division of shares until the following day, with guards, selected from each crew, taking turns to watch the plunder like hawks. Others climbed up the mastheads to scan the horizon for Spanish sails. A few boys remained, perched up in the crows' nests, peering into the night.

Bartholomew Sharp disembarked briefly to cast an eye over the takings. He did not like the way some of Coxon's crew stared at him, as if reproaching him for not participating in the attack. Coxon himself only acknowledged Sharp's presence with a curt nod. Tom, Malcolm, Joseph, and Scarrett accompanied the captain back to the ship. Tom wanted to attach his new skiff to the stern.

"You can tie her on for now," said Sharp, "but she stays here when we make for the open sea. Your last boat seemed to carry angry ghosts and attract tempests, Tom."

"You may be right, there," muttered Tom. The Jamaican skiff had contained recent memories of Sir Digby Townsend's hirelings, the wretched boy Squealer, poor Coco, and the Mountain Apparition, while the new one was freighted with specters like the pregnant slave, her diseased master, the victims of Tom's rifle, and that fearful Black Christ. The last phantom alone could summon up the mother of all hurricanes.

Captain Sharp was in fine sprits. If Admiral Coxon's surly behavior had offended him, he did not show it. While the assault force sweated in Portobello's fever-ridden alleys, Sharp had feasted on tropical fruits and enjoyed fishing with the Kuna tribesmen in the balmy breezes off Springer's Key. His pale eyes almost sparkled. The insect bites around his nose had cleared up. Even his straw-like hair appeared to shine and bounce a little. In general, the fleet's sailing crews, sleeping on open decks away from the steaming jungle, enjoyed rude health. Most of the Portobello raiders, by contrast, suffered from alternate bouts of hot flushes and shivers. The Spaniards had been mad to establish their main silver depot in such a place. It was a death trap, fit only for Africans inured to equatorial plagues. Feeling the salty air in his nostrils and the currents under the ship's keel, Tom felt instantly better.

Next morning, the Gipsy delighted in climbing up to the main yard, leaning back against the mast and surveying the broad expanse of ocean to the north. He saw the dark edge of a storm spiraling away on the western skyline. Shortly after that, a triangular sail cut across the horizon from the east. It appeared to be tacking leeward towards Portobello harbor. He yelled, "Ship ahoy, on the port bow!"

Sharp strode towards the main rail with a telescope in his hand. He focused on the distant triangle as it quivered in the contrary wind. "A Cartagena bark," he said, snapping the spyglass shut and heading back to the tiller. "Make sail! She's wallowing in the road like a Dutch lugger. I'll take the helm!" Tom untied the skiff as the canvas opened out on the yards.

The land breeze caused difficulties, but Sharp made the approach look effortless. By hugging the coast, keeping an eye on the leeward reefs, he was able to pounce on the Spanish vessel as it struggled at the entrance to the bay. It looked as if he was about to ram her from behind, but a last-minute adjustment of the whip staff brought the sides together with inches to spare. The crew cheered. Some sailors clapped their hands in glee before leaping onto the prize. Weapons were not required. Unarmed, outnumbered ten to one, the Spanish crew meekly agreed to bring her back to the key under supervision. Tom and his mates took charge. For an hour or so, he savored the experience of captaining his own small ship.

At first sight, she was not much of a catch, laden with nothing but flour and salt. However, at that moment, the members of the expedition needed precisely those staple foods as the best insurance against the bloody flux. The surgeons believed that flour helped feces to solidify and prevented the bowel lining from melting into the foul, dark-red mucous that squirted out of the sufferers' backsides. The baked dough supposedly absorbed such bilious, liquid humors. Also, the salt lost in constant sweating clearly had to be replaced. The men set about baking as much salty bread as possible. They built a crude earth oven on the island and lit up the brick galleys aboard the larger ships. Turtles had been brought in bamboo cages, regularly doused in seawater, from the Gulf of San Blas. They were now butchered. Another day passed. The feasting pirates cast sidelong glances at the pile of treasure. It remained untouched, under guard. Lengths of tarred sailcloth were draped over it, to shield it from the elements.

Captain Sharp became popular for a few hours. His absence during the Portobello assault was temporarily forgotten. He was loudly acclaimed when his men rolled out three wine barrels, which they had concealed until sunset. Sharp's crew kept back two barrels aboard for themselves. They continued to drink through the night, sitting in little groups. Rope mats and blankets staked out their sleeping areas on the deck. Murmurs and subdued laughter made for a peaceful, almost civilized scene in the moonlight. Tom took a leisurely midnight stroll round the ship, as if enjoying a promenade. He paused with his hand on the mizzen mast and looked up at the shrouds.

Sharp called to him from the quarterdeck, "Those ropes are dry as bone, Tom, and sagging like dead men on gibbets. A garden of weeds grows beneath the waterline. Worms are burrowing into the keel as we speak. The whole damn tub needs scraping and refitting. As for Captain Essex, I have laid bets that his rotten pile falls apart within the week."

Tom approached the captain's circle in the stern and asked, "Then why are we lingering here, so close to the enemy? We could make our repairs in a quiet spot among the Indians; on the Moskito Coast or in the Samballoes."

"If it was up to me, we'd do as you say," said Sharp. "We'd be long gone. But Coxon still has hopes of ransoms from Portobello for his prisoners. That's why he's delaying the share-out, I reckon, to keep us within reach of the Dons' relatives."

John Cox cut in, anger distorting his pale face and womanish lips. "Another day and that bastard admiral will have a rebellion on his hands. We should take all the treasure and leave him here, with only his precious prisoners for company. The fool endangers us for no reason. If ransoms were forthcoming, we would have heard from the Dons by now. Suppose the Windward Armadilla comes sniffing out of Cartagena. Do we want a battle to no purpose at all?"

Cox made Tom shudder. He looked like a sicklier, more petulant version of Malcolm. Nevertheless, Cox was Sharp's right-hand man. Tom thought it prudent to agree with him in public. He nodded. "Yes, Mr. Cox, we should share out and ship out. We'll see what tomorrow brings. Good night, one and all."

It was not to be. The following morning provided another reason for delay. The boy sitting under Alliston's ragged pennant spotted the enemy ship first. A fair-sized trading galleon cleared the western point of the key and bore slowly to starboard, aiming for the mouth of Portobello Bay. Soon, the sun caught the full sails of three ships, tilting in the wind. At first glance, they appeared to be moving in line together peacefully. Alliston, with Coxon coming up from behind, was hunting the Spanish vessel. Sharp and Mackett decided to sit this attack out. Essex was in no condition to do anything. The men, anchored at the key, climbed into the rigging and shielded their eyes to observe the action. It occurred near the horizon. Spyglasses passed from hand to hand.

They saw puffs of cannon fire followed, after a pause, by distant thuds. The Spaniards fired their eight guns only once. The buccaneers raked the galleon from stem to stern, with Coxon's six guns, all pulled to starboard, firing relentlessly amid the constant crackle of musketry. Through the glass, the spectacle resembled a Dutch painting of a sea fight. The Spanish ship, flying her huge red Hapsburg X, held the two small English bloodhounds at bay for an hour. By then, her decks streamed with gore and the survivors were hiding from the murderous pirate sharpshooters in the hold. A handful of officers stood defiantly on the poop deck under their giant flag. They finally dropped their swords when Coxon's men swarmed aboard from one side and Alliston's from the other. The attackers loaded and aimed the Spaniards' own swivel guns at the ship's interior until the crew emerged to surrender. Thirty African men in chains climbed out last, blinking in the light. On the island, the spectators cheered and settled down to await the new prize. Armed resistance usually meant treasure.

They were to be disappointed. When he moored, Coxon, in the prow of the galleon, announced that it only contained more flour, wine, and salt, with a few bolts of silk, as well as the slaves. The Africans scrubbed the blood off the decks and prepared to shift the Spanish dead ashore for burial. A priest was found among the prisoners to officiate. By mutual agreement, the bodies were interred before they bloated and stank in the heat. Common sailors ended up in a mass grave. Two officers of nobler birth were buried individually, under temporary wooden crosses, until their families could reclaim their remains for proper entombment on the main. Astonishingly, the English had only suffered a few cuts and bruises.

Coxon called across to Sharp's vessel, "Ahoy there, Barty! Send

Mr. Sheppard over to me! We have a pile of Latin and Spanish correspondence here, addressed to King Carlos. It's too much for Mr. Ringrose on his own."

So, Tom found himself plowing through a stack of letters with Basil Ringrose again, this time in the Spanish captain's quarters. Ringrose resembled the poet John Milton, shuffling his papers, more than ever. He greeted Tom with a roll of his eyes and handed him a magnifying glass. As before, the messages were mostly irrelevant to the pirates' expedition. Eventually, Tom spotted a report from the Cartagena Cabildo, the city's assembly of grandees, which he decided to bring to the admiral's attention. Coxon was roving restlessly around the ship, but regularly popped his curly wig into the cabin.

"Found something yet?"

Tom hoped to convince Coxon to head southeast, nearer to the Dutch in Curacao. He seized his chance. "Aye, Admiral Coxon, sir! Here is a report describing the attacks of Indios Bravos, unconquered savages, who live in the hills east of Cartagena, which are rich in gold and emeralds. The Dons are begging His Catholic Majesty to send Tercio veterans to deal with them. It seems they have formed an alliance with large villages of Cimarrones, runaway slaves, in the forests. The Cabildo also requests significant funds to buy slaves, sorely needed to strengthen the city walls."

"Why should that concern me, Mr. Sheppard?"

"I thought we might join these Indios and Maroons in a combined assault, from land and sea, and take the richest city in the Indies, sir. If they are cowering behind damaged fortifications and screaming for assistance, now is an opportune time. The French would relish the prospect. With the Blacks and Indians, we'd have the numbers. It could be even more magnificent than your Santa Marta victory."

Coxon came towards the translators. "You might have something there, you old dog! Take a look, Basil. If this is true, it is certainly worth considering. I'll put it to the other captains. Before we decide anything, we must share out the treasure, first thing in the morning. Spread the word. You may leave those papers on the table when you finish."

Coxon slammed the cabin door on his way out. They soon heard his heels rapping on the poop deck above their heads. Tom put down the magnifying glass with a sigh. "Suddenly, our commander is in a hurry, after dawdling for days."

Ringrose sorted the papers. He extracted the pages with blank backs and placed them to one side, next to the Spanish captain's quills and inkpot. "These are for me," he said. "I intend to keep a journal of our adventures."

"Ah," said Tom, "I see you wish to imitate the Amsterdam surgeon's account of Morgan's cruises. They say the rascal makes more from his book than he ever saw in prize money. Sir Henry is furious, threatening legal action against anyone bold enough to print it in English."

"It is the talk of Port Royal," said Ringrose. "Morgan cannot stop it. The king himself could not stop it. Hundreds of English scholars in Holland have access to printing presses. Thousands of smugglers bring goods into London all the time, and nothing sells like a forbidden book. You're right, Tom, it could make my fortune if I survive, but I don't go about proclaiming my intentions to all and sundry. Captain Sharp has similar ideas concerning new maps. I can also draw up navigational charts, with the captain's assistance. The Admiralty pays handsomely for those, while my adventures will be read out in every coffee house across the land. It's another string to my bow, but keep it under your hat. There is enough envy in this unlettered mob."

"I will, Basil, as much as anything can be kept quiet at sea. For all we know, there may be a boy with his ear pressed to the cabin door, listening as we speak."

Ringrose crept up to the door and swung it open," Nobody!" he said, and returned to gather the pages and writing materials. He paused, leaning towards Tom, and continued in a low voice, "There are whispers about the admiral too. I think you know what I'm talking about."

"He conducts private business with his rich prisoners, that is obvious. One of my messmates saw him at it, in the Portobello vaults. What is worse, I think I caught him concealing gold coins in the cathedral."

"You noticed that too, did you?" Ringrose smiled. "Well, friend Thomas, rumor has it that this very galleon contained much more than flour, cloth, and a few niggers. Apparently, before Alliston's men were allowed into this cabin, a jar of three hundred gold doubloons was handed over to Coxon, in exchange for the release of all the prisoners on the island."

"Tomorrow's share-out will be the proof of the pudding, Basil. Then we will know for sure."

In the morning, after a breakfast of freshly baked doughboys and kettles of hot chocolate, the crews assembled in front of the loot again. Only the boys and slaves remained aboard the ships. The buccaneers sat cross-legged, quietly smoking their pipes, in the shade of the palms. The prisoners had been herded onto a rocky outcrop beyond their dead comrades' graves. Captains, quartermasters, carpenters, bosuns, and surgeons gathered in a separate group, directly in front of the great pile of bullion chests, sacks, barrels, and bolts of cloth. Coxon himself pulled the canvas covers away with a flourish. One of his trumpeters sounded an alarum. Lessonne stood by, ready to explain the proceedings in French, in case of any confusion. Mackett sweated profusely. Recurring bouts of fever forced him to sit down.

The customs of the Brethren of the Coast, which had been established three generations earlier on the island of Tortuga, required that the most valuable items were divided first, beginning with gold, silver, pearls, gemstones, jade, ivory, and crystal. A large pair of scales weighed any precious artefacts that had not been melted down into coins or ingots. Slaves were allocated to each ship according to its size. Then came weapons, pelts, tapestries, carpets, silks, calicos, pet animals, rare feathers, and other sundries. Woolens, footwear, and ordinary clothes were distributed randomly as slops, to be kept aboard for general use. Lost limbs, fingers, and eyes merited due compensation. The share-out had to be fair in everybody's opinion, or all hell would break loose. This made the process both solemn and slow. Nobody minded. Anticipation of riches produced a fidgety excitement in the crowd. The pile began to diminish, bit by bit, as it was separated and counted. Some crewmen fumbled in their pockets for dice, eager to hazard their shares in bouts of gambling, especially against the French.

Tom sat among his mates at some distance from Ringrose. While the count proceeded, they exchanged meaningful glances. As Admiral of the Black, Coxon was entitled to four times a deckhand's share. He chose to take this mainly in gold and gemstones. The jars full of doubloons did not appear. It was as though they had never existed.

The commander-in chief-was usually permitted a certain amount of leeway. Now, as Coxon's sea chests filled up, low groans emanated from sections of the crowd, but they were uttered in a spirit of mocking humor. Tom realized that only he, Ringrose, and perhaps a few of Coxon's most intimate cronies had any idea of the scale of the admiral's dishonesty. Eventually, after the captains had claimed their double shares, the quartermaster one-and-a-half, and the specialists, like carpenters and surgeons, one-and-a-quarter, each buccaneer pocketed one hundred pesos. Tom made a quick calculation. Coxon's official share amounted to the equivalent of four hundred silver pesos. In fact, he had withheld a further undeclared five or six hundred golden doubloons, at a conservative estimate. Round it down to five hundred. Each doubloon was worth eight gold escudos, or sixteen pesos. Without counting other private deals with prisoners and hush money to his friends, Coxon had secretly boosted his share from four hundred to eight thousand, five hundred pesos. He had stolen a fortune from the fleet.

The admiral presided with a broad grin. It might have signified benevolent complicity with the men. To Tom, it looked like a superior sneer. He gave a low whistle, shook his head and said, "The shameless swine!"

Malcolm, who was having trouble stuffing a heavy load of coins into various pockets, looked up. "Who d'ye mean by that, Tom? Coxon? He's welcome to his ransoms. Surely, this will suffice for now. I can barely carry it all."

"Nothing," said Tom. "Portobello was a poor target."

"We dinna come all this way for one attack. There'll be more. Och, ye kanny fool me, man, I wasn't born this morning. Something else is gnawing at yer vitals. Let it curdle inside. Ye'll let the cat out of the bag in good time."

Tom had no intention of telling Malcolm. The young hothead would stir up a mutiny. More than likely, he would get himself, and his friends, killed. The admiral was doing exactly what he himself was, holding back loot, albeit on a far larger scale. Tom hoped the notion of attacking Cartagena would prove irresistible, bringing him a little closer to the comforts of Europe. He imagined the smell of starched linen bedclothes as he dropped the hundred pesos into his bulging haversack. Tying up his belongings, he settled down in his messmates' corner of Sharp's ship.

Tom remembered the Amsterdam jewelers' shops, in a long row under the arches in the main square. In his mind's eye, an old Jewish refugee carefully examined the pearls and uncut gems, working his toothless gums and peering through his magnifying glass, before screwing the price down. Tom was familiar with all the dealers' tricks, from the grease under the hairs of their straggling beards, for catching stray diamonds, to the silent sand boxes behind the counter. Then there were the footpads, lurking in the alleys. That was the way it went, by all accounts, from Port Royal to Hamburg, from Venice to Constantinople. The way of the world. He'd make sure that business was conducted on a well-lit table, directly beneath a window, with his back to the wall and a primed pistol to hand. Then, he'd return to a clean Dutch inn for beer and sausages, like a real Prussian officer, followed by a roll in snug eiderdown with a chubby, pink whore.

Joseph cut his reverie short. All around, men ordered their belongings, stooping in the dull lantern light. The Irishman crashed a hooped chest onto the planks beside him, saying, "Here, from the Spanish ship. We can stow all our pesos in it together. In separate bags. Look, I even have a key for it. You should take charge of that, Tom. Hang it round your neck."

"Your chest, your key," said Tom, placing his pesos into the box, bundled up in a greasy Monmouth cap from the slops. He held back his reserve of pearls and stones, although he knew that Joseph was trustworthy. Moreover, pirate crews never stole from each other at sea, let alone messmates. If it had been otherwise, no buccaneering voyage would have survived the first raid. Still, thought Thomas, one never knew. It could do no harm to keep most of his little fortune about his person, in case an unforeseen chance to escape presented itself.

Then came the influx of silver-fueled gambling sessions. The dice rattled through the night, from Sharp's quarters in the stern to the fore-chains. It was the same story on every ship, especially that of Lessonne. The favorite dice game, *battaille*, being French, the English were keen to beat them at it. By dawn, the losers only had a few coins left. Malcolm was quickly down to thirty pesos. One reckless man lost everything. He pretended not to care. The sea dogs affected a lordly indifference to the fortunes of the gaming table. It was part of their much-vaunted 'easy-come, easy-go' attitude to life. Deeper down, however, the tensions caused by gambling built up, along with rumors of cheating, ready to surface during future periods of boredom.

Tom was not made that way. As he grew older, his tendency to hoard, in hopes of a comfortable retirement, increased. While the others rolled the dice, laughing and cursing, he sat quietly in the bows. The moon climbed in a clear sky, shedding a line of broken yellow reflections, a golden stairway across treacherous waters. Tom glimpsed the eternal Seven Sisters, pulsing to the beat of his heart. Twinkling Orion chased animal constellations until they dipped beneath the horizon, forever out of reach. He settled down onto his rope mat with his precious hunting bag as a pillow, the rifle by his side. On deck, he could hardly smell the bilges.

Early next day, the pirate captains met aboard the flagship. Given the parlous state of the fleet, another coastal raid was, for the time being, out of the question. Worms gnawed into the planks among the seaweed beneath the waterline. Admiral Coxon suggested heading for the Bocas del Toro islands to the west. He followed the course of Columbus' final 1502 voyage, when the explorer had made his last, hopeless attempt to break through to the Indian Ocean, unaware of the vast continent and open sea to the west. The local natives had been on the warpath ever since, never allowing the *conquistadores* to gain a foothold. These Guaymi Indians welcomed all enemies of the Spanish crown. They regarded Spaniards as voracious, plague-carrying insects, calling them 'sulia,' or cockroaches. Furthermore, the Bocas climate was a touch less torrid, with many types of food, including delicious manatees. The careening beaches were ideal, protected by long, razor-sharp coral reefs. Stout palm trees took the strain of the cables as the ships were hauled ashore. It was, in short, a buccaneer's paradise.

Upon anchoring off the largest island in the archipelago, it became clear that Cornelius Essex's ship was beyond repair. She filled with water and settled into the shallows to windward, shielded from the pounding breakers by an outlying key. Broken up, she became a source of timber, metal, canvas, and cordage for the others. Essex transferred his crew to the captured Spanish flour barque. The old captain, whose nose had erupted into a red blister, pitted like a strawberry, made himself comfortable in the stern. The vessel was clean enough, he said. A couple of new ropes would suffice to tighten her shrouds. His fat, fierce tabby cat would keep the numerous bilge rats under control. He spent most of his time in his cot, showing no interest in anything other than the brandy served by one particular brown-skinned cabin boy. Whenever he sank into one of his deep, long sleeps, his little cabin became the scene of debauchery for the other boys and sailors. The place began to resemble a pigsty. Essex did not care. Upon awakening, he would fire a pistol into the deck above and scream for more brandy. Sometimes he appeared to think he was ashore, in a tavern, back in Wapping, or sprawling like the Grand Turk in his harem.

Coxon refurbished the armed Cartagena merchantman. He ran his old vessel onto the sand at high tide, looped an anchor cable behind a stout palm tree, and whipped a dozen slaves round the capstan to heave her clear of the surf line. With holes cut in the hull and canvas awnings overhead, she served as his wooden headquarters during the following weeks. The well-built Spanish galleon needed few repairs, in spite of her battle scars, and became his new flagship. Lessonne's Frenchmen occupied the key across the channel from the big island. Their ship's keel, bearded with algae, lay exposed on the shore. The crew began to make feeble attempts to scrape her hull.

Thankfully, Mackett and Alliston had it easier manhandling their lighter craft. The captains and deck hands of the sloops needed time to recover from raging fevers. The big island provided ample fresh water. Stiff sea breezes kept the flies and mosquitoes away.

Bartholomew Sharp supervised the landing of the *Rose*. "Take your time, lads," he announced, when she lay on her side in the morning sun. "I don't care if she's pretty, as long as she's seaworthy. Mr. Cox will keep an eye on things. He has plenty of Boston tar, as good as the Stockholm juice, so spread it on thick and dark." He summoned the carpenter and his mate. "When she's afloat again, I want her gaff-rigged from stem to stern, Jamaica fashion, nice and tight to the wind. Get any wood and cordage you need from Captain Essex. He'll hardly notice it's gone. Only bother Coxon if you must."

"Ain't you staying with us, Captain?" asked the carpenter.

"I'm off hunting," said Sharp, brandishing a harpoon, "for manatee. You'll see. Once you've tasted a roast sea cow, you'll want nothing else." He turned to Tom, screwing up his voice into an aristocratic braying sound, like a prince inviting a courtier to chase deer. "I say, do attend me, Mr. Sheppard. Pick a canoe, sirrah. Bring one of your minions. We'll see who can fetch the most meat, shall we?"

"At once, your Haggard Highness, your wish is my command." Tom swept his hat off, bowed and went to find Malcolm, although he knew Sharp probably had Joseph in mind. He thought the young Scotsman needed cheering up. Scraping the hull under Cox, with the Gipsy and a gang of slaves, would do Malcolm no good at all. The manatee hunt promised to be fun. The strongest Moskito spearman, a tall lad called William, accompanied Sharp. William wore ordinary seaman's slops, but stripped to the waist for the trip. The hunters set out in two small dugouts, paddling towards a channel between the main island and a wide estuary to the northwest. Here, sitting low in the swirling green current, they spotted a canoe, manned by a pair of Guaymi Indians. The hunting party was to number six, by prior arrangement with William.

"Ah, there they are!" said Sharp. "Welcome to the Jaws of the Dragon, lads!"

"So that's what they call this neck of the woods," muttered Tom. The Indians looked unlike any he had seen before. Shorter than the Moskito, but taller than the Kuna, the two men were stocky, dark, and well-muscled. The large holes in their earlobes contained black wooden disks with a single crimson spot in the center. The rest of their bodies were decorated with horizontal black zigzags, except for a shark's tooth pattern in red across their foreheads. Their hair hung loose down to their backsides. They wore no golden rings or plugs, and no penis sheaths, only leather breechclouts. Their hardwood paddles were pronged, like huge spears, and their harpoons, tipped with long metal barbs, were tied to coils of twisted liana rope. Finally, they carried heavy, bone-crushing clubs in the bottom of their dugouts. As the buccaneers drew closer, the Indians looked at them impassively.

Malcolm whispered to Tom, "What cursed cannibals have we here? They stare straight through a man."

William communicated with the Guaymi with a mixture of guttural words and hand signals. They nodded gravely and passed Tom a harpoon, a club, and a coiled rope. Sharp, who already had a harpoon, took a club. He showed his stained, broken teeth in a wide grin. There was nothing sly about the captain now. He was happy as a Thames mudlark on a spree. "Follow us, Tom," he said. "Keep quiet as you can. We are to watch the Indians, and learn how they do it. William will interpret for us. These bastards would rather cut out their own tongues than speak Spanish, and they know nothing of English at all."

Tom and Malcolm took long swigs from their water skins. The

hottest time of day approached, settling over the Jaws of the Dragon like a sweat-soaked blanket. The hunters paddled quietly, slipping through the oily stream, past fallen trees full of iguanas, in the wake of their new Indian comrades. In the distance to the west, they heard the breakers crashing on the reefs.

Mike Hawthorne

9
THE JAWS OF THE DRAGON

The hunters pointed their canoes away from the foaming headland, which formed the upper jaw of the Boca Dragon strait, opposite Columbus' large island. They paddled along the swampy mainland coast. Further into Almirante Bay, William, Sharp's Moskito spearman, pointed to a thin column of smoke rising from a clearing between the mouths of two streams. The insistent chirps of insects obliterated all other sounds. The older Guaymi Indian nodded, indicating that they had reached their campsite. The warriors hardly ever spoke, and, when they did, it was in a slow, monotonous rumble. Interspersed with lengthy pauses, one word sounded much like another. Mostly, William had to divine their intentions from their gestures.

"Old one called Ima," said William. "He hunt sea cow here, in water grass."

"We'll watch how he does it, though I warrant he won't have much to teach a Moskito hunter," said Sharp. "Follow him quietly, Tom. No splashing."

Half a mile beyond the camp, the Guaymi paused in a wide river mouth. Old Ima moved his open palm up and down, as if patting the air. The others understood that they were to wait in the middle of the stream, paddling gently to keep their station. Under the western bank, a meadow of eelgrass undulated into the bay. The sun caught the outlines of fat grey bodies, encrusted with aged, brown algae, floating lazily in the shallows. Occasionally, a bewhiskered snout broke the surface and snorted a lungful of air before sinking back down.

"Look," whispered Malcolm, "how could those great turds be mistaken for mermaids? They're more like walruses, but without the teeth. Big as horses. Could they smash a boat?"

"No," Tom answered softly, "sea cattle are gentle. They would not hurt a fly, let alone a rogue like you."

Sharp watched intently while William kept the canoe steady with alternate strokes. The younger Indian stopped his canoe at the riverside by clinging onto the bank. Ima sat motionless in the bow. Covered in horizontal zigzags, he resembled a carved wooden statue. Suddenly, he swung the paddle over his head and brought it down with a smack on something in the water beneath. A glistening fat belly, showing a very human navel, barreled up from the weeds. Above the shoulders, the mournful face of the stunned manatee, with its flabby upper lip, stared at the sky. A split second later, Ima cracked its skull with the heavy club. His companion pushed the dugout forward and reached down to tighten a rope around the broad, flat tail. They pulled the carcass upriver and hauled it ashore, beckoning Sharp and Tom to join them.

"Did you see how he did that, lads?" asked Sharp, leaning over the animal. "Splash, crack, and it's all over! Half a ton of beef and blubber!"

"Like hitting an auld grandfaither in his armchair," said Malcolm. "Not much sport in it."

"He made it look easy, Malcolm," Sharp grinned. "When we've butchered this plump fellow, the next one's yours, my son."

The old warrior made a slicing motion and held out his hand

towards the captain.

"Ima want knife now," said William.

"Why?" said Malcolm. "He has one in his belt."

"Be quiet, lad, this is how we pay 'em. It's impolite to mention it." Sharp took a beautifully engraved Toledo dagger, recently the property of a Portobello grandee, from the bottom of his canoe, and gave it to the old Indian. "They can never get enough cold steel. This one's a chief. He gets the best."

Ima bent the pointed blade to test its temper, grunted his approval, and began to peel off the tough hide, including the thick layer of fat adhering to the underside. The young Indian, called Nicho, hacked down some nearby foliage and deftly wove it into sturdy baskets with shoulder straps. Only the large intestine was thrown into the bushes, where a cloud of flies appeared immediately. Everything else, meat, hide, and bones, ended up in separate baskets, to be carried to the campsite. The Guaymi warriors were so sure of this shoreline that they left the clubs and harpoons beneath their overturned dugouts unguarded. They were the lords of all they surveyed, dominating the Bocas del Toro islands, and vast swathes of the hinterland, with such fierce confidence that their reputation made raids by rival tribes or Spaniards highly unlikely.

At the camp, an old woman with flat breasts and two younger ones shooed away a yellow dog that came out of the shade of a palm-thatched shelter to sniff the baskets. Children stood staring with big, hungry eyes. Ima and Nicho scooped out a shallow pit next to the fire. The old woman placed a pair of calabashes containing maize beer beside them. Most of the meat ended up cut into strips on a bed of smoldering embers, covered with salt, leaves, and a layer of earth. The young women scraped the blubber off the hides. It fell into clay jars, ready for rendering into lamp oil. They pulverized the bones to produce a medicinal powder. The thick skin was stretched over bamboo frames in the sun. It would make tough shield covers, belts, quivers, and shoes. Nothing was wasted. Nicho impaled alternate red lumps of liver and choice cuts of steak, sliced from the manatee's back and belly, on bamboo skewers. A little feast began. The Indians and their guests held the skewers over the flames and passed the beer around. Malcolm tried to conceal his growing fascination with the breasts of the young women, pretending to scan the tree line when his gaze was returned with a shy giggle. A stony look from Ima cooled his ardor.

After a couple of mouthfuls, Sharp said, "Wonderful! The back tastes like the finest roast beef, the front like juicy pork."

"If you can take a few of these sea cows back to the careening beach," said Tom, "the men will never forget it, captain. It'll make 'em strong as lions."

"Aye," said Malcolm, wiping the grease from his chin with his sleeve, "they need cheering up. Portobello delivered much less than it promised."

"Don't despair, lads," said Sharp. "I heard something down in the Samballoes that could, with luck, make each man jack of us worth over a thousand pounds. Coxon is muttering about sailing south, but we are nearer to a great fortune than we know, with far less danger. The Kuna Indians speak of a poorly guarded gold mine, ripe for the picking, over the mountains in the forests of Darien. It's an entire hillside, riddled with tunnels, another Potosi. It's too bloody tempting to ignore, even for Coxon. Better than running up against the Cartagena batteries. Mark my words, we'll all be rich men afore long."

"I'll drink to that," said Malcolm, slurping from the calabash. Tom's smile concealed a growing dread. Was this another in a long line of fabled treasures, like Columbus' hoard in Jamaica, or the great Eldorado, that lured hapless explorers to their deaths? He remembered, from Morgan's raid, that the Indians often told Europeans what they wanted to hear, misleading the white men for their own ends. The Kuna, in particular, after seven generations of resistance, could be very cunning. Their chiefs were sure to downplay the risks and exaggerate the prizes. For them, the buccaneers were useful but expendable reinforcements, pushing the Spaniards back while the tribesmen reoccupied lost territory.

Tom trembled at the three little words, 'over the mountains.' They were significantly more jagged and daunting than the misty heights above Morant Bay. He knew what a formidable barrier they made to his plans of returning to Holland. There was always a chance of a favorable wind or current in the sea-lanes, but to be trapped behind those precipitous ridges in the depths of the Darien jungle was a different prospect altogether. The manatee's beef in his mouth suddenly tasted less delicious. Tom belched, stood up and wandered into the bushes to piss, whistling to hide his disappointment. His dreams, his Prussian officer's commission, and his very existence seemed more pointless than ever.

His mood had not improved by the time the hunters slid silently into the river mouth again. The temptation to raise his rifle and simply shoot the beasts proved hard to resist. He paddled mechanically, his thoughts elsewhere. When Malcolm made a poor job of stunning a manatee, enabling it to turn away, Tom handed him the harpoon instead of the club. Malcolm had no alternative but to throw the barbed spear before his prey swam out of reach. The iron held fast. The Scotsman cursed and tightened his grip on the line. The canoe followed the bleeding animal's tail into the bay at high speed, but this was no whale. The manatee tired rapidly. It began to sink through red bubbles in the deeper water. Luckily, it remained buoyant enough to drag back into the shallows without upsetting the dugout. In the end, Malcolm leapt into the river and manhandled the body onto the bank. Up to his waist in the current, he said nothing, but glared and shook his head.

"What?" said Tom. "We got him, didn't we?"

"I got her," Malcolm spat. "She'd have made ye a fine wife." A neat pair of breasts stuck out above the grey belly.

The Indians landed a heavy male fifteen yards upriver. Sharp returned in triumph too, having employed a combination of paddle, club, and harpoon. His Moskito Indian companion picked up a bonus in the bloody water near the bank. Hearing the squeaks of a cub, probably the offspring of Malcolm's female, William had hauled it aboard and knocked its brains out. This did not please the Guaymi, despite William's protests that the baby would have perished without its mother's milk. Ima shook his head. Another recent mother would have nursed it. Then, he spread his arms over the body. The cub should have been allowed to grow sufficiently to be worth killing. He refused to let anybody cut the little thing while the adult animals were butchered.

William furrowed his brow. "Him say it bad luck. Him talk shit. Want best meat himself. Me keep baby."

After giving Nicho a trading knife and Ima a fistful of nails wrapped in printed calico, the buccaneers waved goodbye. They carried all the innards and meat, folded in banana leaves, in their canoes. The hides and bones remained with the Guaymi, except one length of thick skin, which Sharp wanted for making a bull whip. The dead cub lay at William's feet, its dead eyes staring at him. He prodded it with his foot and laughed. To avoid the ocean swell, they paddled round the bottom of the big island to reach the windward keys. They were back on the careening beach an hour before sunset, impatient to show their shipmates what succulent steaks they had brought for them. The men ashore had made a good start on one side of the hull. They were hungry. Everybody got a taste of the aquatic beef, except the slaves who received the offal. It was agreed not to share information about manatees with the other crews—let them find their own.

During the following weeks, sailors from the other ships made independent hunting arrangements with Guaymi warriors. Inlets and river mouths full of sea cows abounded throughout the archipelago. Coxon began to suspect that his men were working deliberately slowly, in order to prolong the feasting, so he ordered his fellow captains to provide manatee meat purely as a reward for completing specific tasks.

"You'll get no more until this tub is clean as a whistle and tight as a drum!" he shouted. "So, look lively! Scrape those sides and caulk those gaps! Keep the niggers at it too! Why d'ye think I captured them? For fucking French lamp stands?" This gave him an idea. When a feast was finally permitted near the flagship, he organized it after dark. Musicians thumped out crude minuets and

Africans dressed in Spanish finery, complete with powdered wigs, held up torches. Other slaves pounded log drums and rattled chains. Coxon made sure Capitaine Lessonne was invited, accompanied by his officers. Sharp, Alliston, a feverish Mackett, and the half-crazy Essex also attended. A small group of senior Guaymi chiefs could hardly believe their eyes, maintaining their composure with difficulty. The cabin boys wore feathers, necklaces and women's dresses. They pranced about in hilarious mockery of the Sun King's court at Versailles. Ragged, weather-beaten sailors leapt onto the boys, simulating an orgy on the sand. Essex lunged forward to join them. He fell unconscious, face down in the sand. His mates rolled him over before he suffocated. Coxon presided on a high bamboo throne covered in Chinese silk, with a red parrot chained to one arm and a spider monkey on the other. Some tough old pirates had tears of laughter running down their cheeks, bowing and scraping before 'His Majesty' before hacking off portions of manatee or scooping wine from a huge barrel.

Suddenly, a tall sailor waving a sharpened bamboo trident and a conch shell jumped into the glare of the torches. He was covered in strands of seaweed and wore a crown of scallop shells woven into knots of rope. An oil lamp blazed from the top of his headdress like St Elmo's fire. The tanned, drooping jowls of a bewhiskered manatee had been strapped over his nose and mouth. Coxon choreographed the show to perfection. He rose to greet 'Neptune, God of the Oceans.' Neptune speared choice cuts of meat in a bowl and offered them to the chief guests. Finally, Neptune threw the trident over their heads and scampered into the surf, blowing deep blasts on the conch. The apparition vanished under the black waves. The flame on his headdress sputtered out. Nobody saw where he emerged or discovered his identity.

Later, Sharp told Tom, "Say what you like about Johnny Coxon, he knows how to impress the Indians and keep the men's spirits up. That was better than Christmas. I've seen him employ his Neptune dozens of times, but the sea cow's face! It will be hard to forget nights like that. William says the heathens want to put on a big show before we depart. There'll be some strange sights, for sure, Tom, me old mate. The savages will try to outdo the admiral."

Sharp was right. Ima, as the local clan chieftain, fixed a time for a four-day festival on the mainland, starting at the next new moon. By then, the cleaned ships rode at anchor, the leaks were plugged and the tightened rigging was covered in tar oil. The slaves tried to scrub out thousands of lice, fleas, cockroaches, and mushrooms. Hundreds of bilge rats had been killed. They were smoked out of the holds and ran up the beaches. A ring of burning rope slowed them down long enough for men to chop them with cutlasses and axes. This was done out of boredom more than anything else. Many rats survived with missing tails and singed pelts. Since it only took a handful of breeding pairs to produce a booming new rodent generation, their squeaks were soon heard again, not only among the ballast rocks in the ships' bottoms, but all over the islands, as a lasting reminder of the fleet's visit.

In the end, a greatly reduced English delegation accompanied the Guaymi tribesmen into the forest. Coxon had declared the Indian women to be off limits. "These savages are jealous. I will not risk our best refuge on the Spanish Main for a few fucks." It was enough to discourage Malcolm and numerous others. The usual percentage of crewmen suffered from bouts of quartan fever, as did Captains Mackett and Alliston. Cornelius Essex was too mad to understand what was happening. Many more declined because they mistrusted their grim-looking hosts, half-expecting to be lured into a trap and eaten during cannibalistic rites. Tom decided against attending for a different reason. The thought of Coxon, glorying in his role as guest of honor, turned his stomach. Sharp agreed to take Joseph and the Gipsy instead. After weeks of drudgery on the beach, they were jubilant. William Dampier insisted on going along, eager to gather information for his manuscript, accompanied by his fellow scribbler and mapmaker, Basil Ringrose. In the end, thirty buccaneers, including Lessonne and three of his officers, paddled towards the mainland behind Ima's canoe.

"If we're not back in five days," joked Sharp, "come and fetch our bones!"

For a moment, Coxon looked as if he wanted to change his mind. Then, to save face, he laughed and fired a parting salute with his pistol.

With Coxon gone, the Englishmen hunted manatees at will. Their remaining captains lay incapacitated in the shade. Scattered groups paddled and rowed out of their anchorages during all daylight hours. Sea beef accumulated by the hundredweight, as did all manner of fruit, wild vegetables, turtle meat, and shellfish. Big kettles of salmagundy, a mish-mash of any ingredients that came to hand, stood on the quarterdecks. The French, for some reason, stayed close to their ship. Unsupervised, they preferred to buy their supplies or gamble for them. Compared to the English, they were a filthy, undernourished rabble. Tom reckoned Lessonne's crew was in the wrong line of business. He felt the same about himself, but never let it lower his spirits to the miserable level of the Frenchmen.

Whenever he could, Tom roused Malcolm and pointed their little dugout in a new direction to explore Almirante Bay's lower reaches. Sometimes, they forgot about hunting and allowed the canoe to drift lazily in the current. One day, they came upon a bank that supported spindly bushes, bending under the weight of pale green, knobbly fruit. Tom made for the spot and jumped ashore.

"Haha!" he cried. "Grenadillos! Let's see if they're ripe!" He sliced through the hard skin, scooped out the slimy white pulp, sniffed, licked, and finally slurped it down. "By Christ, that's a life-saver!"

Malcolm hauled the boat ashore and joined him. "Aye, that's fit for a king," he spat out the black seeds. "Sweeter than custard."

"Maybe we should save a couple for the captain's cream-faced cousin," mused Tom. "Butter him up a bit. See what he's like."

"Dinna bother yerself. I can tell ye exactly what John Cox is like," said Malcolm. "He not only looks like a woman, he sounds like one when that big bosun, Dick Chappell, is giving him one up the airse. I heard them behind the dunes the other night. When they came back down the beach, there was nobody else around. They thought they were unobserved."

"Well," said Tom, "at least they are discreet. I wouldn't want to be anywhere near the sodomites' sty on Captain Essex's ship. The man has lost all control, like the Grand Turk in a bed full of naked eunuchs. Some youngsters are murmuring about knocking him on the head and leaving him to the crabs under the timbers of his wrecked tub."

"So why don't they? Who's to stop them?"

"Ah, Malcolm, you don't understand these London privateer crews. They go back generations, all from the same parts of Stepney. It would be like killing a father or an old, familiar uncle. Many were pressed, like myself, to fight the Dutch. Then, instead of starving while waiting vainly for the Duke of York to pay 'em, they took the chance of going aboard merchantmen. Whole gangs of them, friends from childhood, signed on together. Been at sea ever since. Some have never glimpsed an unclothed woman, wouldn't know what to do with her. Take Sharp. Barty started as an eight-year-old cutpurse on the Mile End Road, robbing travelers all the way into the city walls. His mother was dead from pestilence and his father in jail for debt. He had to work his way up to lead the pack, after the plague and fire. To show who was in charge, he'd bugger the smaller brats in burnt-out buildings, like a dog. I had to listen to his tales often enough since Morgan's glory days. To think, as lads in Sussex we envied those Cockneys, imagining they lived off the fat of the land in the big city! In truth, no decent woman would look at the hungry, rag-arsed mud larks. Whores were too pricey for 'em. They were little whores themselves. If they weren't thieving, they were tossing off sailors' cocks for pennies on Shoreditch steps. If things got too hot, the ships were waiting to take 'em away. In a trice, they threw the captains and chief mates overboard. They never looked back. The remnants of the original gangs are the backbone of this fleet. You can't simply knock lunatics like Essex on the head. Remember that, if you want to live. They're all expert mutineers themselves, cunning devils, even when they appear mad as baboons."

"So, then, who the devil is John Cox? What is he to Sharp?"

"I believe he's a younger cousin or nephew on the mother's side, also from Stepney. They say he ran things for Sharp in Boston, as a servant and spy in the Bay Company. Someone higher up became suspicious of him, so Cox drummed up a gang of harbor wastrels and made off with a fully laden ship. They sailed for Jamaica. That's why we have so many barrels of tar on board, and enough beaver skins to make a thousand hats."

"...And Dick Chappell?"

"Another rogue from the Wapping docks. Most protective of Sharp and Cox. Over the years in Port Royal, I've known him as Dick Williams, William Richards, Robert Williams, and William Roberts. The Chappell bit is the first time he's shown any originality with his name. Makes me wonder if it might not be his real one. He's as thick as a tree trunk, round the neck and between the ears, but a loyal guard dog to his masters. Steer clear of him, Malcolm. Chappell is strong as a bear and will fuck anything with a suitable hole, whether it's breathing or not."

"And ye want to make a point of giving Cox one of these?" Malcolm cut open another sugar apple. "Why?"

"To see if the miserable bastard ever smiles," said Tom. "John Cox is the gloomiest string of bilge rat's urine I've come across in twenty years of sailing. He has the kind of face you want to throw to the sharks as a Jonah, regardless of tempests or fair winds. But humor me. I want to see if he can bring forth a single smile, or just one tiny word of thanks, out of that cunt he calls a mouth."

"Ah, well," said Malcolm, "that explains it then. Me, I wouldn't waste a flat raisin, combed out of the clinker in a cross-eyed bunter's backside, on the likes of such a squealing molly."

"It's good to see you in fine spirits again, lad." Tom wiped his beard with his shirtsleeve. "Back to your old self. Come, help me load the boat with grenadillos. There's enough here for half the company. We'll have no trouble trading 'em for a few flagons of brandy."

On board the ship, Tom did not present the fruit to Cox. He changed his mind when Chappell helped himself to an armful without asking. The ruffian stared straight into Tom's eyes while he did it, challenging him to protest. Tom humored the brute, "Ah, Dick, you know what's good for you, mate. Sink your choppers into them beauties!"

From his position on the foredeck, Tom caught a glimpse of Cox's pale face under the awning astern. The quartermaster spent most of his time in the shade, issuing instructions and fussing with the captain's treasure chests. His method, Tom soon realized, was to gradually exchange large, unwieldy objects, like plates, communion cups, bejeweled rapiers and crucifixes, for smaller coins and gems. Cox continued Sharp's practice of organizing boozy gambling sessions. If he lost a bulky trophy or two, it did not matter, as long as doubloons, pesos, pearls, rubies, and emeralds drifted back to his end of the table. When the big items had gone, they often reappeared, broken down and bereft of inlaid stones, in humbler games of dice on the quarterdeck. Meanwhile, the concentrated, easily transportable wealth stayed with Sharp, Cox, and their bosom friends from Stepney.

Tom's heart sank. The decision to cross the Darien ridges had clearly been taken. Sharp's henchmen were making ready to carry the best of their treasure about their persons, in leather bags and purses. Hauling heavy chests over the rough terrain ahead would be out of the question. The leadership was unconcerned about the rest of the sailors with their more unwieldy loads. Tom pinched the collar of his jerkin to feel the hard emeralds within. Perhaps, there would still be a chance for him to slip away before the march inland. An escape might be possible from the islands in the Gulf of San Blas, helped by Kuna friends. Or, Coxon might prefer to stay at sea with the French rather than risk a campaign on an unknown shore. After all, the admiral had collected a personal fortune already. Would he let Tom join his crew? It was more than likely, after his display of marksmanship in Portobello.

Tom's thoughts were interrupted by a commotion on the beach. He joined the curious spectators leaning on the landward rail. In the long, late afternoon shadows, they saw a group of slaves depositing a dark shape onto the sand near a launch and shouting. Buccaneers walked towards them from various points on the shoreline. John Cox appeared at Tom's elbow, focusing his spyglass on the disturbance. A smirk spread along the quartermaster's feminine lips. He purred, "What's bothering those jabbering monkeys, I wonder? They were sent to fetch water an hour ago. Where are their barrels?"

Tom indicated the glass. "May I?"

"Here," said Cox. "What d'you make of that hullaballoo, Mr. Sheppard?"

"They've found one of their own. Dead by the look of it, with at least three arrows in him."

"That's what it looks like to me too. Take a canoe, if you please, and find out what happened there. We need that water before sunset. Go with him, Dick. The black bastards are threatening our men."

"Aye," grunted Chappell, "nothing a length of knotted rope won't cure."

Malcolm had gone forward into the bows to avoid Cox. Tom, his rifle over his shoulder, followed Chappell down the wooden slats that led from the ship's waist to the waterline. They hauled in a dugout and paddled it quickly towards the knot of gesticulating figures.

Six loudly arguing slaves stood around the body of a seventh. The corpse had two arrows in his chest, one in his neck, and another in his thigh. A ragged red cut remained where his genitals had been hacked off. Half a dozen sailors peered down at him, adding their opinions to the confusion. More beachcombers approached to see what the fuss was about. Chappell strode into the throng and bellowed, "Shut your traps! All of you! First, where's the water?"

"The niggers left the barrels at the stream," answered a bald, heavily bearded pirate. "They will not go near the place again, Dick. That's where they found their friend here, full of arrows, with his cock and his balls in his mouth. He must have bumped into the wrong Indians."

Although they had picked up a few barked English orders, the Cartagena Africans understood mainly Spanish, so Tom was asked to inform them that they were to fetch the water butts, guarded against further Indian attack by an armed escort. The dead man, apparently a respected leader, would be taken back to the ship and treated with dignity. Shooting fearful glances, the slaves walked slowly back to the tree line. A buccaneer patrol rushed noisily ahead, brandishing muskets and slashing at the undergrowth.

"Hurry!" shouted Chappell. "It'll be night soon!" He grabbed the corpse under the armpits and turned to Tom. "Don't touch the arrows. Take his legs."

They swung him into the bottom of the beached canoe, on his back, and returned to the ship. There, he was displayed, complete with arrows, lying on a rope mat at the foot of the main mast. The vessel's other slaves were given every opportunity to witness the spectacle. Sailors began to mutter about bad luck and throwing him overboard, but Cox made them wait until the slaves came back with the fresh water.

It occurred to Tom that this was all an elaborate piece of theatre when he overheard Cox whisper to Chappell, "Carry on, but don't overdo it." Chappell then strutted about cursing the bloody Indian savages and their heathen ways. Pretending to straighten the dead man's neck, Tom discovered a soggy fracture under the matted hair on the back of the skull. Before anything else, he concluded, the man had probably been knocked on the head. Cox must have ordered it. The Guaymi never showed the slightest hostility towards the Africans. In fact, Sharp's spearman, William, had described how the Indians helped runaways reach Cimarron hideouts throughout their territory, thereby creating more allies against Spain. William's tribe did the same on the Moskito coast. In all the weeks among these islands, there had never been any signs of hostile activity by natives working for the Spaniards.

Eventually, Cox allowed the slaves to remove the arrows, wash the corpse and wrap it in sailcloth. The Africans knelt in prayer and crossed themselves. Cox recited a passage from his Geneva Bible in a solemn nasal voice. A low chorus of "Amens" concluded the ceremony. Chappell made a show of organizing English oarsmen to row the body to the eastern point, nearest Africa, for burial. The slaves were assured of an armed guard whenever they worked ashore in future. Later that night, when the wine flowed, Tom heard that the dead man had simply been tossed into the sea with a stone round his ankles once they had rounded the headland.

He shared his suspicions with Malcolm during the dawn watch. "We've got a sly, devious snake there, Mal. The whole thing was a ruse to stop the slaves running for the hills, while Sharp's away with Coxon. A clever bastard, young Quartermaster Cox. Almost had me fooled too."

Malcolm spat over the rail. "All that fuss to keep a few Spanish niggers! Now the ships are clean and tight, we'd be better off without 'em. They can't trim a sail and they'd likely turn on us in a battle."

Tom nodded. "You're right. It makes little sense. I reckon Cox enjoys the game for its own sake. It's nothing more than his spidery nature. He wouldn't know what to do with himself if he wasn't scheming."

"I wish they'd dangled the bastard from a gibbet in Boston," said Malcolm. "Talk of other things, will ye, old man. I'm trying to forget I'm on the same deck as the slimy cunt."

"Well, you could always transfer your allegiance to old Cornelius Essex," Tom said. He instantly regretted it. "I'm sorry, lad. It was a poor joke. I'm sick of these cockney bastards too. You might consider a way out of the whole mess before we get in too deep."

Malcolm sighed. "I know what yer planning, I've been in yer company long enough to read yer bloody mind, old man. But look, where is it any different? Remember what happened in Port Royal. Even in Bristol or London, we'd get the shitty end of the stick. Get used to the idea, Tom, I'm seeing this through. I want to have a crack at a gold mine or the Acapulco galleon. This life is not so bad with the promise of some pesos in yer pocket. It's nothing compared to a slave run, believe me. Those Guinea captains make Essex look like a saint."

The ship's timbers creaked. A lone parrot screeched among the trees across the channel. Tom stared up at the Morning Star in the black sky and murmured, "So be it." He slapped Malcolm's shoulder. "We'll see what delights tomorrow brings."

The next day brought the returning revelers from the Indian festival on the mainland. They blew little reed whistles. Coxon, Sharp, and Lessonne sported arrays of bright new feathers in their hats and wide seashell collars, stitched into triangular patterns, on their shoulders. The Northumberland bagpiper squeezed out a meandering tune. A fiddler in the adjoining dugout attempted a desperate accompaniment, which drove the gulls mad overhead. Many sailors had lost their caps, jackets, and waistcoats. A few were stripped to the waist, barefoot and painted. They displayed an amazing variety of red, brown, and white skin, spangled with scars and livid rashes. Everybody appeared tired, but cheerful and relaxed. They drained the last drops of maize beer from calabashes in their canoes before clambering into the ships.

The first thing Sharp did when he stepped on board was to insist that all the whistles were thrown into the water. "Get rid of 'em now! You know we don't allow that fucking noise at sea, unless the bosun wants your attention! You'll be pleased to know, we came across Dick Sawkins' galleon in Boca Dragon. He's waiting for our old friend Peter Harris to sail in, and they'll be joining the fleet shortly. A bigger army will guarantee bigger prizes!"

A final trill from the whistles and wild cheering followed.

"Ah, you don't know what you missed, boys," laughed Joseph, when he sat down heavily on the foredeck beside Tom and Malcolm. "That was one hell of a hooley, so it was, strong enough to sweep off every Quaker's hat in Boston!"

Scarrett was happy, clutching a bulging gunnysack full of tow weed mixed with dark tobacco. "Here," he said, "this sweet hemp will keep the devil at bay for a month or two. It comes from the Cimarrons up north. By Black Sara's buns, the heathen wizards know their medicine! They brew potions that can make you hear angelic choirs or take you straight to hell."

"High praise from a son of Egyptian sorcerers," said Malcolm. "But tell me, what, in the name of Christ, happened to yer legs?"

Both Scarrett's and the Irishman's shins were bound with strips of cloth and leaves. Joseph's stretched from his knee to his toes. Tom noticed that certain other returning buccaneers had similar bandages.

"Ach, they're almost healed now," he said. "They were black and blue two days ago. The Indians make this sport, so they do, where they throw staves at each other's feet. It hurts, but when you take more than twenty hits, you are considered a brave man. If the wee savage strikes you over the knee, you can remove the feather from his hair and kick his ass out of the game. I was not nimble enough. They battered me something rotten, but Scarrett here did us proud, didn't you, mate? Almost as good as Moskito Billy. You skipped about like a spring lamb, catching their ankles every time. They gave you a prize of leopard skin, with head and teeth and tail. A real beauty it was, but you had to go and trade it for that sack of shite you like to smoke."

"If I want to see a strange, spotted animal," said the Gipsy, "I only have to look at your fleabites, Joe. This stuff helps me cope with such sights."

"And the women?" asked Malcolm. "Surely to God ye managed the odd fuck?"

"Not a chance," said Joseph. "They danced round the fires, embracing their painted sweethearts' necks, in long lines, stamping their feet for hours. Strictly to admire from afar, they were. You'd be dead on the spot, so you would, if you tried to prise one away for yourself. The chiefs watched us like hawks. We slept on a platform in a big, separate barn, away from any womenfolk. We ate herds of sea cows, land crabs, turtles, piglets, and Christ knows what else. Then, they gave us more than enough beer to knock us down at night. To be sure, we needed it, what with the howling monkeys, worse than a pack of banshees in the treetops all about. Scarrett's right, it was like heaven and hell jumbled together."

"Where did you come across Richard Sawkins?" asked Tom.

"Up near Point Dragon," said Joseph, "standing off a beach with the sand so white it blinds you. Your man Sawkins shouted down to us that he tried to join us in Morant Bay, but the Navy detained him in Port Royal jail with Captain Harris until the New Year. He asked if we had Cornelius Essex with us. Called him a useless, scurvy swine, so he did. Said, 'If Essex is with you, count me out.' Coxon just laughed, told him to sail briskly into the bay when Harris arrived, and not to worry his head, because the devil was taking care of Captain Essex in person."

"I wonder what's behind that bad blood," said Tom. "I never met him, but I hear Sawkins is a young firebrand, keen to make his mark. They say he cut into the Dons like a raging fiend with Coxon at Santa Marta."

"And Harris?" asked Malcolm.

"A stout soldier," said Tom. "Hard as nails. He was with us in '71. Been at sea ever since, mainly among the Cuban keys and in the Florida channel. Swoops down from Tortuga with French commissions. Peter Harris attacks Dutchmen as well as Spaniards, regardless of whether England is fighting Holland. He once said, 'By the time a declaration of war reaches us in the Indies, a new peace treaty might have been signed, or it might not. I assume it hasn't until I hear to the contrary from an unimpeachable source. I don't often come across one of those. What is more, if England isn't fighting the Dutch, the French probably are, and I carry King Louis' warrant.' Harris rarely lands in Port Royal. Prefers to unload elsewhere if possible. Seems he was careless over Christmas. Him and Sawkins! Those two will be a handful, especially if they're acting as partners."

"Good," said Malcolm, "we need fresh blood in this sad stew, or we'll all end up perishing from fevers in some godforsaken swamp without so much as two groats to cover our eyes."

"I told you before," said Tom, "glory hunters get you killed. All that hot ambition ain't worth a pig's turd if you're dead. We're better off with the lazy old vultures. Sharp has a keen eye for rich pickings with little danger, and that's the kind of captain who has my vote. Why are you youngsters, with your whole lives to look forward to, always in a hurry to throw them away?"

"For the same reason," said Malcolm, "that ye mangy old dogs, who'll never get a full cock stand again, are so eager to prolong yer miserable days."

Tom lit his pipe, blew a smoke ring and said, "I see my hard-earned wisdom is wasted."

The following morning, a little galleon sailed into Coxon's anchorage, followed by a larger ship with twenty-five guns. Both flew the four red bars, on a yellow ground, of the Kingdom of Aragon. The admiral recognized Sawkins in the small vessel, and immediately sent word to all the other captains to assemble for a council of war aboard the flagship. Sharp left John Cox in charge, as usual, and took Tom, Basil Ringrose, and Dick Chappell with him. A scabby first mate represented Cornelius Essex, but he said nothing, merely drooling and nodding occasionally with a faraway look in his eyes. All the other commanders were able to attend in person.

Coxon leaned over a table made of planks and barrels on the quarterdeck. It was covered with sea charts, weighed down with pistols, quadrants, and goblets of wine. He cleared his throat. "We are all delighted to see our good friends Richard Sawkins and Peter Harris again. You missed a good storm and a glorious battle, lads, but I know you'll soon make up for that. Are those Cartagena tubs you sail in? With those stripy flags, it's fortunate we met at Point Dragon the other day. Otherwise, we might have exchanged fire."

"We took these ships in the Bay of Honduras," said Harris, "and you'd have been blown out of the water. Mine alone carries twice as many guns as your entire fleet, with near on two hundred experienced fighters, champing at the bit for blood and treasure."

"So she does," Coxon smiled. "As I said, a most welcome addition. Much more than we expected when you failed to meet us in Morant Bay. Rumor has it, you were clapped in the irons at Port Royal over Christmas, but I'll sound you out over that later, in private. For now, we must urgently decide on our next move."

"In private?" Sawkins was on his feet, hatless, his fair hair streaming in the breeze. "Be damned! That pig's ass Essex landed us all in the shit, up to our necks, and I don't care who knows it. See, he hasn't had the guts to show his face today, because he knows I'll cut off his head and piss down his neck!"

"All in good time, Dick," said Coxon. "Don't worry, Cornelius will give no trouble." The admiral stared at Essex's first mate and yelled, "Will he?"

The first mate first shook his head, then nodded and finally took a swig of wine. Sawkins could not bear to look at him, but muttered, "This ain't over."

Coxon slammed his fist on the plank, sending a chart onto the deck. "It's over for now! We are all free men! Free to join whichever command will have us! Free to fuck off if we don't like it! To business!"

The buccaneers discarded all but three possible courses of action. A suggestion to join forces with the French under a Captain Bournano on the mainland collapsed when Lesonne painted a very unflattering picture of his countryman. It seemed Bournano had a reputation for grandiose schemes, which he was never able to accomplish, preferring to settle down with Indians and their women until they grew tired of it. Tom convinced Sharp to make a case for a raid on Cartagena, the biggest prize of all. However, Sharp continued with an enthusiastic description of his Kuna gold mine plan. At the word 'gold,' the atmosphere changed. Even Harris licked his lips. After a unanimous vote in favor, Coxon summed up.

"An invasion of Darien, quite apart from the gold, takes us within striking distance of Panama and the Potosi cargoes. On the other hand, we know Cartagena is heavily fortified, in a maze of lagoons and dead ends. We would need an army of thousands to contemplate such a venture. Furthermore, Cartagena would be seen as a naked act of war, and all nations will hang us for it in peacetime. On top of that, many of us here are Panama veterans. We did it before, and we can do it again. The Dons will never expect an approach from the South Sea coast. Their defenses are concentrated eastwards, along the Camino Real to Portobello, which cost us so many lives in '71. But we'll be smarter than Morgan. We have to be. We can't afford big losses, even with Captain Harris' reinforcements. We'll surprise 'em from the direction they least expect. Then we'll march back through friendly territory to the fleet in the Samballoes and be rich wherever we please. The Darien Indians are always at war. Their country has never been conquered, so we can act on their behalf as legal privateers. I've seen worse arguments stand up in court. It's decided! We sail for Golden Island in the Samballoes, in search of gold!"

The meeting ended with a toast and a roar of, "Gold!" As soon as the goblets had been tossed aside, everybody dispersed to ready their ships. Tom managed to catch Peter Harris' arm before he climbed down the side step.

"Remember me, Pete? I was with Danny Searles."

"Aye, of course, as soon as I saw you with Barty! Tom Sheppard!" Harris grinned. "Turning into a grey old badger with a blue cheek! So, it's Panama again. Who would have thought it, after so many years?"

"Tell me, what went on in Port Royal over Christmas? I had quite a time of it too. Nearly got myself hanged over some stupidity, so I was unaware of anything else."

"Christmas? Don't remind me! Me and Sawkins come in to land a Honduras cargo, quietly, and sail on to meet Coxon. Everything's going smoothly, Morgan's friends in the Exchange agree to a good price; we're waiting for delivery, when suddenly all hell breaks loose. Essex sails into harbor, with two Navy frigates after him. His men get drunk and burn down Jenks' plantation, just west of town. The pilot on *HMS Success* drives her onto the rocks, bilges her on her own anchor. Soldiers race around town throwing privateers into Marshalsea jail until the walls are splitting with the press of bodies. There's Essex in that fucking dungeon, drunk, buggering a poor boy in a private chamber and trading the necks of two of his crew to get Jenks off his back. In the end, our indigo profits are taken as a ransom for our release. Morgan's powerless, because Essex attacked a planter's property, and the assembly overrules him. Luckily, our ships are in Negril Bay the whole time. But Essex goes free and we sweat it out in the bilboes, penniless, among the rats and lice, until after New Year's Day."

"Well, Pete," said Tom, "if it's any comfort to you, Essex won't last the week, let alone enter Darien. His nose is a volcano of pus, his breeches red with flux, and he can't rise from his stinking cot. Whatever was left of his addled wits has deserted him. The man is drowning in his own vomit, rolling in the scuppers, buggered to blazes, and overripe for Satan's griddle."

"Sawkins will be pleased to hear it, for we will not sail or march with such a sack of shit as Essex." Harris paused and then slapped Tom's back. "So, shipmate, we're heading for the Great South Sea again!"

"Yes. Coxon wants his name up there with Drake and Morgan. For all our sakes, I hope this gold mine exists. If it's rich enough, maybe there'll be no need to continue the campaign as far as Panama itself."

"What's wrong with you, Tom?" asked Harris. "Are you losing your nerve with the advancing years?"

10
THE EMPIRE OF DARIEN

Malcolm let out a sigh as a long dark turd uncoiled from his backside. "Oof! That's better!"

"Great God, man," Tom protested. "Do you think we want a full view of your ass in operation at breakfast time?"

Malcolm, squatting twenty feet upwind, reached for a handful of sand. "Concentrate on yer chocolate and allow me to concentrate on mine. Yer only jealous because yer fluxy shite could pass for gravel exploding from a Dane gun. It's a rare pleasure to make such muscular stools. Like smooth baby dolphins they are. They clear the brain."

Joseph glowered beneath the brim of a new palmetto hat and said, "Sure, if the sight does not make us sick, the bluebottles will. Shit the other side of the rocks or I'll rub your Scottish snout in it!"

The sky above the bulging green headland of Cape Tiburon was tinged with glowing orange. Endless ridges glittered on a sea like polished steel to the north, lining up to flop onto the beach in regular gasps. Every fourth wave crashed down with an echoing double thump, driving the teeming surf towards the trio on the black rocks. Malcolm hitched up his breeches and approached the bubbling cocoa pan.

"Stay well away until I've finished my chocolate, Mal," Tom slurped from a calabash. "It will be some time before I will be able to erase the memory of that foul vision."

"That's the spirit," said Malcolm, "let yer mind linger on it, you old rogue. The memory will sustain ye on your travels." He dipped a mug into the steaming pan and sipped, wincing as he scalded his lips. He twirled the points of his moustache and flounced his locks. "Shit, sugar, and sand! The only way to start the day, eh Joey?" He tapped the Irishman's shoulder.

Joseph swatted him away with his straw hat and turned his eyes on Tom. "We are decided then? We continue with Captain Sharp?"

"Yes," nodded Tom, "I am decided. He knows his work. That is what matters. He is the best navigator of them all, drunk or sober. When I was new to the game, I followed blowhard captains like Sawkins. Whatever you think, I saw a lot of men die for nothing. Now I am old, I cling to life. Sharp is a cunning bastard. He is keen to save his skin and make some money. He is no fool."

"Even so..." began Joseph.

"You decide," said Tom. "My joints ache. If it wasn't for your blasted cock fight, I'd be on my way to Emden in comfort. I hope to make this my final cruise. Yes, Bartholomew Sharp is a snake. Give no offence and don't get too drunk with him or his cronies. Avoid John Cox. Act stupid. That should be easy for you. Then we'll all stand a chance of returning with a few bags of gold. Sharp has agreed to lead the column over the mountains. He knows that's the easiest part of the expedition, but it will impress the new hands."

"Since when is scaling mountains easy?" wondered Malcolm.

"The hard bit is fighting Spaniards," said Tom. "On a mountain, it makes no difference if you are the first or the last; you still do the same climbing."

"Sharp drank himself stupid last night," observed Joseph. "Fell down in the scuppers, pole-axed, so he did. A fever boiled him up, sweat everywhere. I threw a cloak over him."

They rose to their feet, slung their equipment over their shoulders, and took a last look at the ships riding at anchor in the cove, manned by skeleton crews who had no stomach for a land campaign. Commanded by the invalids Mackett and Alliston, they were under instructions to assemble in Harris' twenty-five-gun galleon and Coxon's eight-gun flagship, if attacked. If the ships were still in the Golden Island channel when the expedition returned, they would receive their full shares of loot. As Tom had predicted, Cornelius Essex was no longer a problem. His ship had lagged behind since the fleet left Almirante Bay. It was never seen again after the night of March the 24th. The generally accepted view was that the drunken madman had probably smashed into a reef in the dark. Captain Edmund Cook, waiting at the Isle of Pines in a two-gun sloop with forty hands, replaced Essex. Cook had a reputation as bad as that of Essex, but he had never done Sawkins or Harris any harm, so he attached himself to the fleet without trouble. Almost anybody who could swell the numbers was welcome, since the French contingent refused to march inland. They preferred the more familiar waters around Hispaniola.

Scarrett inhaled a mouthful of weed with a sharp sucking noise. Malcolm tightened the buckle on his sabre's baldric. Joseph jammed his straw hat onto the back of his head. Tom threaded his Port Royal Louis d'Or onto a ring through a hole he had made. The coin dangled from his left ear, as if daring somebody to tear it off. Then, the messmates turned as one and made for a grassy meadow surrounded by palm trees. Drum rolls broke through the hubbub of a jostling crowd. Gaudy banners marked the rallying points of the various commanders. The rising sun suddenly cleared the headland and aimed blinding yellow shafts that glinted off hundreds of musket barrels, short pikes, and cutlasses.

Sharp's company was assembling round a hogshead of Portobello wine. His red flag, with white and green streamers, floated in the sea breeze near a banana tree at the top of the field, nearest the jungle. To get there, the four friends had to push through all the other crews. Edmund Cook's rearguard milled about beneath their stolen red-and-gold Spanish ensign, swigging and filling leather bottles from their barrel. Cook had added his personal emblem, a hand waving a Turkish scimitar, to the flag. He sat on the barrel wearing a filthy French wig that cascaded over the shoulders of his blue coat, agleam with golden embroidery.

"Cook looks like Old King Louis himself," said Malcolm, "after a night in a ditch."

"He's bald as a coot," said Tom. "He thinks the wig makes him handsome. Never accept an invitation to his cabin unless you want to gaze at the Man in the Moon through the wrong end of his telescope. Especially you, pussy boy," he nudged Malcolm. "You're just his type."

"Sharp's not like that, is he?" asked Joseph.

"Don't worry, grown men are safe with Sharp. He only likes young cabin boys. Can't abide deep voices and hairy chins, our Bartholomew," grunted Thomas as they jostled through Captain John Coxon's large force, gathering under two scarlet standards.

Coxon had been confirmed as overall commander, in spite of a growing number of Sawkins' supporters. Although he tried, Coxon could not conceal his hatred of both the upstart Sawkins and his friend Peter Harris. The admiral liked to keep them where he could see them, marching directly in front.

Malcolm said, "This is like an Irish fairground. All the cutthroats in the world are here."

He stared at the variety of human types with every conceivable combination of hairstyles, whiskers, hats, and clothes, from tramps' rags and naval slops to ostrich feathers and costly Italian brocades hanging off their hungry frames. Each man carried a long hunting musket, twenty pounds of ammunition, one, two, or even three pistols, a dagger, and a cutlass. A few brandished boarding pikes and had axes stuck in their belts. Bags of jerked meat and freshly baked doughboy loaves added to the weight, along with wine and water skins. In addition to all this, their pockets jingled with the pieces of eight plundered from Portobello. The captains were accompanied by mulatto slave boys, the bastard offspring of the Port Royal brothels, who carried their provisions and the quadrants and compasses of the navigators. These were expected to get their bearings at noon, whenever possible, to check that the Indian guides were leading the army in the right direction. The handful of surgeons jealously guarded balls of opium and little instrument chests. Blacksmiths and carpenters took along the tools of their trade. Each color party had its own drum-and-fife musicians in addition to bagpipers, fiddlers, and trumpet players.

Gnarled veterans of '71, like Tom, were thin on the ground. The majority of the buccaneers sprouted sparse beards, were in their late teens or early twenties, and lean but strong as oxen. Since this was to be an overland march through dense jungle and over mountain ranges, anybody missing more than an eye or a couple of fingers had remained aboard the ships.

"The Dons won't know what hit them; we must number well over three hundred," said Joseph.

"If we can get at them without killing each other first," muttered Thomas, walking steadily through the babbling mob with his back hunched and his chin tucked in.

A few yards away, Bartholomew Sharp leant heavily on a pikestaff, sweating profusely and working his jaw beneath the freshly inflamed insect bite on his nose and his straggling moustache. He looked older than his thirty-two years, with dark patches under grey, misty eyes. Dick Chappell offered him a goblet of wine, but he shook his head and fanned himself feebly with his red-plumed hat.

Joseph produced a jar of rum that he had won in a game of dice. "Try it, Tom."

"I'll rub it into my elbows first," said Tom, remembering Dancing Danny. "Let's pray for fresh water ahead, or you'll be in deeper trouble than the captain, laddie."

The friends positioned themselves at the very front of the vanguard. Drums rattled up and down the columns. The empty barrels were kicked over and the little army lurched towards the trees like a savage carnival procession. Each troop was led by a diminutive Kuna pathfinder, considerably smaller than the Moskito turtle hunters and naked but for wide golden nose ornaments, erect silver penis sheaths, and black streaks of paint on their legs. They carried short bows and quivers full of arrows, some poison-tipped. The leading buccaneers drew their cutlasses to slash through the dense coastal undergrowth. The air was heavy with mound. It was stifling. When they entered the trees, the canopy shielded them from the rapidly ascending sun but trapped the odor of decay and made breathing difficult.

Joseph and Malcolm hacked at creepers and branches while Tom plodded silently behind them, only occasionally taking a swipe. Scarrett looked as if he was sauntering down Lime Street in Port Royal.

Malcolm pointed his blade at the Indian treading swiftly and easily ahead. "I love the way his wee bollocks bounce along. D'ye think those cock funnels would catch on in London?"

"They would quickly become obligatory at court, considering the character of our king," reckoned Tom.

Malcolm said, "At this moment, I'd sooner have my balls dangling free. My breeks are sodden."

"I saw enough of your nether regions this morning, Mal," said Joseph. "The thought of your sweating bollocks is liable to make me miss my stroke and geld you. Then you'll be able to wear your balls as Dutch earrings and give them a proper airing." He sliced through a hanging vine.

The woods echoed with piercing high-pitched screeches. The forest canopy rustled. The Indian guide suddenly stood still and aimed his bow upwards. The small body of a monkey thumped to earth. Resuming his stride, the Indian scooped the animal up, extracted the arrow, bored through its jaw with the point, threaded its tail through the hole and swung it over his shoulder like a bag. He had hardly paused. The buccaneers exchanged meaningful looks.

"This place is like an immense larder to him," said Malcolm.

"He has no musket to advertise his presence and no powder and bullets to lug," added Thomas. "Compared to him we are cart horses."

"How did the Dons ever conquer such people?" wondered Joseph.

"They set tribe against tribe," said Thomas, "but the Kuna are unbeatable. Never conquered. Pray that we don't offend them, or none of us will put to sea again."

The black stripes on the Indian's legs merged with the shadows ahead. At times he appeared to be no more than a floating torso, vanishing and reappearing in the foliage. His name was Kinki, 'Sure Shot,' and he was using the crashing herd of buccaneers as beaters to stir up game as he led them. The noisy procession sent larger animals like peccaries and squealing tapirs off to the east and west, where parallel Kuna hunting parties, secretly flanking the main column, could intercept them.

Fresh meat would compensate the Kuna families along the way for the corn and plantain rations they had been asked to prepare for their English allies by the paramount war chief, Ukkupana, the so-called 'Emperor of Darien.' Kinki felt the monkey's warm fur on his skin and wondered whose bad spirit he had just liberated. A truly vicious man's soul returned as an entire troop of monkeys, so this one was nothing much to worry about; one less screaming voice in the branches. It was comforting to know that the more colonists they killed, the more new animals would be born. Kinki relished the thought of using the ferocious English to kill the Spanish. The column behind him had fallen silent with the effort of marching. The stink of their sweaty clothes, carried on a salty breeze, assailed the Indian's nostrils. Suddenly, the little army stumbled out of the gloom into a sunlit bay.

"The sea again!" groaned Joseph, sheathing his cutlass and pulling down the brim of his hat. "Is he leading us in circles?"

"We have avoided a mangrove swamp," said Thomas. "Surely you've had enough of them."

Bartholomew Sharp strode forward mechanically and announced, "We will stop here for half an hour." He sank onto blazing white sand and beckoned Kinki to his side. The buccaneers poured out of the forest in hundreds, threw down their burdens and stretched their limbs. Coxon and Sawkins joined Sharp. Their flags were tied to boarding pikes as sunshades. Chappell summoned up water, bread, and wine. A pair of Moskito spearmen and a Flemish sailor who spoke Spanish completed the party. They drank, chewed, and talked while Sharp and Kinki drew lines in the wet sand with a sword. Coxon studied his compass. Sharp called for a quadrant and aimed it at the sun. Kinki was dismissed and gutted his monkey, throwing the entrails into the surf. He peeled away the fur, wrenched off the limbs, and gnawed them raw after rinsing them in salty water. The captains extracted clay pipes from their hatbands and enjoyed a smoke of rich Kuna tobacco.

Malcolm cooled his feet, paddling up to his knees, and studied the Indian closely. After a minute he approached Kinki, pointing to his mouth while rubbing his stomach. The Indian grinned with bloody lips and passed him a leg.

"By God's Wounds," shouted Joseph, crouching over the rum with his Gipsy friend, "you are regaling us with some lovely sights today, you heathen dog! The two of you look like a pair of Hebrew midwives devouring a newborn babe!"

"Is it possible to perform any natural function without commentaries worthy of a Carmelite virgin from yer lips, Joseph?" Malcolm paused with a tendon string hanging off his chin. "It is very good. Ye should taste it." He wiped his mouth, tore at the last piece of meat, and tossed the monkey bone over his shoulder. Kinki picked it up and sucked out the marrow.

"Missed the best bit," cackled Tom.

The buccaneers were making themselves comfortable along the length and breadth of the bay when Sharp hauled himself wearily to his feet, giving off a loud belch. Coxon rose and bellowed, "Drummers! Rattle those skins! We have an appointment with the Emperor of Darien! Let us not keep him waiting!"

"Into your columns, Spawn of Satan!" boomed Sawkins. "No prey, no pay!"

The men did not need telling twice and were soon ascending a valley through waist-high razor grass. As the sun finally began to sink in a pink glow to the right, they reached a wide riverbank and gulped down the fresh water like cattle at a trough. When some of them began to curl up and sleep, Kinki and the other Indians became agitated, making hissing sounds. The commanders had another conference and then spread the word that venomous serpents came out at night. It was necessary to construct bamboo frames, called barbacoas, to sleep on. Meanwhile a group of Harris' men claimed to have seen gold glittering in the water and dived into the current, emerging with twinkling rocks which they excitedly smashed to bits.

"Fool's gold, and even bigger fools to soak themselves before sleeping," muttered Tom, and pulled off his shoes. "Malcolm, fetch some wood, boy."

"Ye surely don't intend to build a bed? Why not a house?"

"As you know, I have my own way with snakes. See if you can find kindling and a log that isn't too damp. We'll brew cocoa, like we always do."

"Aye-aye, Captain Sheppard, I'll see if I can dig up some coal too," Malcolm walked towards the tree line in the fading light.

When Joseph returned with Scarrett they agreed to finish the rum between them. The cocoa pan began to bubble. Little fires sprang up everywhere among the dark silhouettes around them. The Indian guides had walled themselves in behind wild sugar canes. They were terrified of snakes. O'Hare, the most gifted musician in Coxon's crew, plucked a slow tune on a mandolin. It blended with the repetitive chanting coming from the Kuna hut and was strangely soothing. Sharp insisted on a barbacoa, complete with a roof of palm fronds and cane walls, which the slave boys fetched and tied together.

Tom gulped a thimble of overproof rum and exhaled fiercely. He scored a shallow circular trench round their patch with the point of his cutlass and sprinkled a fistful of powder into it.

"You think gunpowder will stop the snakes?" asked Joseph.

"Gunpowder and hot pepper. Stops any snakes when they snort it up their nostrils," replied Tom. He walked to the river and washed his hands carefully. "I've had pepper in my eyes too often," he said, unfastening his belt and waistband. "Burns worse than the clap," he added, deliberately urinating on his feet before aiming the stream into his shoes, filling them to the brim.

Joseph protested, "It's like living in a cesspit with you pigs, so it is! First Malcolm's stinking crack at dawn, now this swinish splashing in the evening."

"I recommend you do the same. Let the leather soak overnight. We've got a long march ahead. Here, Scarrett, give me some more of that kill-devil." Instead of drinking it, Thomas rubbed a few drops into the skin on his wrists and ankles. "Keeps away mosquitoes and oils the joints." He laid his head on his knapsack. Within seconds, they heard his snores.

"Sing us a lullaby, Mal," grunted Joseph, swooning with alcohol and exhaustion. Malcolm Munro's melodic tenor rose in the warm breeze over the insistent chirping of the crickets and the rushing flow of the river,

> *"Hush ye, hush ye, dinna fret,*
> *The Black Tinker winna get ye yet..."*

Scarrett sat up and kicked him. "No more rum for you, you Scottish dog."

"Beg pardon, yer Egyptian Majesty," replied Malcolm and farted.

A few miles away, on the coast of the Great South Sea, and from Cadiz to the Philippines, Spanish mothers sang and rocked their babies, telling them to be still or "El Draque," the bogeyman Drake, would get them. Hundreds of dark shapes on the riverbank promised to give the century-old threat a new lease of life.

At sunrise, a pistol shot, flat and muffled in the saturated air, announced the beginning of the second day of the campaign. One of Sawkin's boys found a four-foot snake hiding in his gear and shrieked when it bit him in the shin. Two Kuna guides rushed over. They sat the patient up, twisted a length of rawhide round his thigh and took turns sucking at the little puncture mark and spitting. The expedition's surgeons and a Moskito Indian crowded round to observe and comment in a mixture of hand signs and different languages. Meanwhile, Scarrett speared the snake with a boarding pike and flung it towards the tree line. This was easy since the animal was sluggish and had a large lump in its belly. The viper was digesting a water rat it had caught nibbling at the contents of the man's knapsack during the night.

Scarrett prodded the snake. "That," he said, "is what the Dons call an 'equis.' Look at the X pattern on its back."

"Then, our shipmate doesn't have long to live," reckoned Joseph.

"Nonsense," said Tom, booting the animal's swollen belly like a football. "Serpents have no poison when they are full of food. He'll live. All that sucking and spitting was for show. Go and sprinkle the last of the rum on the bite." He stamped on the snake, breaking its spine. Sure enough, the lad's leg was hardly swollen. He was walking and laughing with relief a few minutes later.

The buccaneer captains sat by the river in the yellow morning light, smoking their pipes and sharing hot cocoa with the Indians. The Kuna had been joined by one of their chiefs, Tom's old friend, Captain Andreas. He wore a linen shirt painted with hooked-cross symbols and a straw crown with three vertical vulture feathers. His Spanish was excellent and he even spoke a little English. Coxon and Sharp traced lines in the earth again. They unrolled a Dutch sea chart. Andreas gave Kinki two little sacks, one filled with corn, the other empty, and sent him to the head of the column. Kinki squatted in front of Tom's group sifting the grains through his fingers and humming.

"What's the wee monkey-man up to now?" asked Joseph.

"Perhaps he wants to feed us like chickens," said Malcolm, tipping the last few drops into his mouth from the rum jar and shuddering.

"He is going to count us as we march past, one grain for each man, like a shepherd," said Tom. "That way the chiefs ahead will know how many mouths to feed when we pass through their villages."

Joseph crammed his straw hat onto his greasy hair and asked, "Did these Kuna Indians help old Harry Morgan, too?"

"Morgan would never have reached Panama without them," said Tom, staring at the captains' conference on the riverbank. "So don't upset them. If the women want to sleep with you, fair enough, but never force yourselves on them, or we'll all be dead. They could easily wipe out a force this size."

"They're not like the Boca Dragon people? With their women?" asked Malcolm.

Tom grinned, showing his stained teeth, as if remembering something. "The men have authority in the forest, at sea, and in the mountains. Once inside a village, and especially within the houses, the women have the final word. If one of them takes a shine to you, it's your lucky day. The man pretends not to notice. Don't go for a walk alone with him in the forest afterwards though."

"Where are all the women? What are they like? I mean, will they really let us…?" asked Malcolm.

"On campaign, they are out of harm's way on the islands and hidden in secure villages. What are they like?" Thomas chuckled. "Wait and see!"

The council of war by the river was over. Drums sounded along the columns. Captain Andreas came up to Tom, placed his hand on his shoulder, and squinted into his eyes. "Ah," he said, "Tomtom! Ai! Como Johnny? Johnny Gret?"

"Johnny bueno," answered Tom, his hand on the chief's shoulder.

Captain Andreas laughed. "A la montania! We inik anmar naoye!" He patted Tom's arm and took Kinki's place as pathfinder.

"What was that gibberish all about? It sounded worse than Scarrett's pig Latin," demanded Joseph.

"I'll tell you later," said Tom, adjusting the strap of his rifle.

Captain Andreas wet his lips and blew a long booming note on a conch shell, waving at the troops to follow him. Parakeets screeched back from the trees. Kinki sat dropping corn grains from one bag into the other as the men lumbered past. If he had been able to remember numbers beyond twenty, he would have counted three hundred and thirty-one heavily laden buccaneers. He hummed a repetitive tune, putting two grains into the pouch at a time. Alone at last, he flung the leftovers of the original bag into the woods and carefully poured six hundred and sixty-two corn grains onto the ground. He then divided them equally between the bags. Kinki had made two counts. He looked up at the sky before trailing the column at a distance. Turkey vultures circled the rearguard before gliding up into the mountains on the thermals.

A hot wind, full of rich tropical scent, blew down into the raiders' gleaming faces from the green slopes rising before them. Four sad figures quietly deserted from Cook's rearguard. Their feet were covered in blisters, so they had decided to limp back to the ships. They passed Kinki without a word. He discarded eight grains. An hour later, a solitary deserter with bloody flux and wrecked feet hobbled by, leaning on his musket to prevent himself from rolling downhill. The Indian crunched two grains, one from each bag, between his teeth before vanishing silently into the dark green shadows to the west.

At the head of the column, Tom's group stepped aside to allow those coming behind to hack at the twisted creepers and branches. The little Gipsy had decided to stay near his friend, Joseph. They fell back until Bartholomew Sharp and his cronies were within earshot, even if they could not see them among the trees. Sharp was feeling much better.

"Don't fret yourself, Johnny," he was saying. "If there ain't enough gold, all the Potosi treasure must come up to Panama from the South Sea. It is a constant stream of pieces of eight."

"We'll see," replied Cox's nasal voice. "I'm concerned we've had no reliable charts since the Isle of Pines. Everything is blank."

"Even more was blank when Drake came by in the *Golden Hind*, John. I have a rough draft of his South Sea map. At least we know the general shape of things now."

"God's Blood, Barty, we are certainly getting to know the general shape of these mountains," whined Cox.

There was a loud crash and a curse as one of the musicians fell onto his drum and slid back into a tree trunk.

"Break that drum, Jonas," laughed Sharp, "and I'll use your skin to make a new one!"

"And your bones for drumsticks!" added Chappell.

A scarlet macaw flashed over Joseph's head.

"Now he'd look handsome on your shoulder, eh, Mal? Squawking in your ear?"

"I'll have to settle for yer blarney in my ear for now, Joe." He continued in a low voice, "What's that whining weasel Cox saying back there?"

"Nothing of any consequence," said Tom softly. "You can bet your life on it. Talking of sodomites, did you get a good view of Edmund Cook this morning, with his curly wig?"

"Oh, the King Louis item!" said Malcolm, heaving his legs over a rotting tree. "Very fetching! We mix in the most elevated society!"

"Be grateful, Mal: you're doing well for a former cabin boy on a Guinea slaver," grunted Thomas.

They fell silent, catching their breath. The path grew steeper. Idle chatter died down. Captain Andreas led them into clouds that sat on the mountaintops like fluffy white smoke rings. Soon they were inching round precipices in a cool mist. Raw rocks plunged down into a green carpet of trees on all sides. King vultures glided overhead. Occasionally, they caught glimpses of water glittering on the far horizon, the legendary Southern Ocean, but quickly concentrated on their feet again to avoid plunging over the edge.

The wind changed direction and now blew cooler through the branches onto their backs. Heavy grey clouds scudded in from the northern sea. Then they were back in thick jungle again. The canopy was lower here. Ferns and crimson flowers brushed their faces. Their shoes crunched over centipedes. The sound of rushing water grew louder. The branches were studded with fungi. A refreshing mist of spray enveloped them. Captain Andreas had decided to lead them up a fast-flowing stream, crossing from bank to bank at intervals. He knew that the heavily laden white men would need plenty of water in the heat. They paused as they filed over the greasy boulders and dipped their hats into the current, pouring it over their heads and down their throats. Meanwhile, Andreas sat on his haunches and sang softly to a yellow frog speckled with black dots. He seemed satisfied when the frog blinked at him, let out a dry belch, and hopped away downstream.

That night they camped by the source of the river. A fast-flying cloud of bats followed a brief shower. The buccaneers gnawed their hardening doughboys and quickly fell asleep from exhaustion. They barely noticed the forest music of birds and insects that surrounded them. The breeze continued to blow from the north, parting the clouds and bathing the scene in moonlight.

Suddenly Joseph was wide awake. He heard the deep growl of a big cat in the blackness of the trees. A leopard? He sat up and peered at the sleeping shapes. It was amazing how much he could see. How many of these snoring souls would make it back to Jamaica? There was old Tom cradling his rifle as if it were a woman. Scarrett lay face down, his arms spread out like a small scarecrow.

God bless the little Gipsy, thought Joseph: at least, even if he dies tomorrow, he's free of that cathouse in Port Royal where he had to watch his mother and sisters be shagged into early graves. Yes, he was better off here, among the monkeys and Indians with a cutlass in his hand, than being kicked in the backside by roaring drunks and emptying piss pots from the window of their bedroom prison at The Mermaid.

Joseph had deserted his Irish family at the earliest opportunity, leaving them chopping sugar cane in rags on Barbados, eating less than the Africans. He'd seen the splinters fly in a cruise against Spain before meeting Thomas. Apart from a long scar down his left side, he was unscathed. To be sure, he'd survive this new jaunt in one piece. He yawned and settled back onto his knapsack. Malcolm lay beside him, curled up like an embryo. He studied the young Scotsman's face with its fashionably pointed moustache and beard.

Joseph noticed something odd about Malcolm's neck. His goatee seemed to be moving curiously in the moonlight. Joseph instinctively crossed himself and blinked, peering closer. Something was sitting under Malcolm's chin, making little slurping noises. He looked closer until he was only a few inches away. The black thing had four legs and was hunched over the paler skin beneath the jaw line, flicking its tongue in and out of a miniature fiend's face with large eyes and pointed ears. Joseph started. The gargoyle glared, suddenly rose up on its long thumbs and shot vertically into the air.

217

It extended a pair of wings and flapped away. Malcolm moaned in his sleep and turned over. Joseph drew his kerchief tightly round his throat, crammed his hat over his eyes, and hugged his knapsack. The cicadas drilled into his ears insistently. It took him a while to get back to sleep. The vision of that tiny hellish face with its gleaming eyes refused to disappear until exhaustion overcame him.

Joseph watched Malcolm carefully at breakfast. The little mark on his neck was less noticeable than a love bite, hardly visible at all. When Malcolm had gone down to the stream Joseph turned to Thomas. "I saw a wee bat on Malcolm's neck last night. It looked like the very devil, so it did. It was drinking his blood."

Tom raised an eyebrow. "Best not tell him. He might think he has acquired a succubus."

"Then we'd have to burn him at the stake!" chuckled Scarrett, stirring the cocoa.

"You wouldn't laugh if you'd seen its face," said Joseph. "This country has a thirsty soul, what with the leeches, mosquitoes, and now the sucking bats. Tell me, Tom, are those wee creatures dangerous?"

"I heard a story that bats bit some Dons near Campeche years ago and they all died of the rabies. The Mexican Inquisition tried to discover the caves to burn the little bastards back into hell, but they never found them," said Thomas, lighting his first pipe of the day.

"Rabies!" shuddered Joseph.

"If Mal comes at you with foam on his lips, shoot him before he can bite," advised Scarrett.

Malcolm returned and stopped in his tracks. "What are ye gawping at? Have I grown a tail?"

At that moment, Sharp's red-plumed hat appeared behind his back. Andreas was with him. The buccaneer captain cleared his throat. "Men! Shipmates! You will be pleased to know that we have almost reached the main settlement of the Darien Indians. The Emperor's son himself awaits us. Admiral Coxon will attend a council of war with him in order to plan our next move. My good amigo, Captain Andreas," he placed a hand on the Indian's elbow, "assures me that there will be feasting and merry-making to celebrate our alliance. There will be oceans of beer and some fine-looking ladies. I have assured him in turn that any man who offends our Indian brothers will be handed over to them for justice. I advise you not to let that happen, because they are experts at keeping a victim alive for weeks while they slowly kill him. They let their children slice the culprit into a thousand pieces with seashell razors, half an inch at a time. You may frolic, but do not fight. You may roister, but do not rob. Save all that for the Dons."

The men answered with a hoarse roar of approval and shouldered their burdens. Andreas raised the conch to his lips and gave a long blast. A troop of howler monkeys answered back. The little army filed into the trees, still following the precious river.

"How in Jesus' name are they going to get oceans of beer up here, Tom?" Joseph wanted to know.

"Same stuff as what you had with the Guaymi. They brew it from corn, bananas, and sugar," replied Tom. "After one or two bowls the taste seems to improve. Anyhow, it has the desired effect. They can make strong liquor too, if they want. I once had a pineapple brandy that almost blinded me, up in San Lorenzo. By the way," he lowered his voice, "if anybody mentions a certain Johnny Gret, be sure to look happy and say he's enjoying life in Jamaica."

"Who is this Johnny Gret?" asked Malcolm.

"The first Kuna warrior to make friends with us," said Tom. "He cruised with Cook and Coxon for a season and introduced them to the Samballoes' tribes. Some of the Indians miss him and expect him to return one day."

"I take it," said Joseph, "that means he is dead."

"Yes, he's dead," said Tom. "Edmund Cook tried to sell him as a slave in Port Royal. Johnny went for Cook with a knife, but Cook's cronies bashed his brains out on the Turtle Crawls. If Andreas learns the truth, things will become very ugly."

"Do any of them understand English?" asked Joseph, stepping warily round a thorn bush.

"A very few of them, like Andreas, know one or two words. Most of them understand Spanish. They sometimes serve the Dons in a native regiment. I picked up a smattering of Kuna last time I was here—'hello,' 'goodbye,' that sort of thing." Tom went on, "Even if I was fluent, they have another secret language in which they commune with the gods and spirits. Andreas was using it with the frog yesterday. Those spotted frogs are considered lucky. They are like little angels, messengers of the gods. I've seen solid gold statues of them near Boca Del Toro. Worth a fortune."

"Perfect witchcraft! Communing with their familiars! The damn wizards would all be reduced to ashes within a week in Scotland." Malcolm continued, "Having said that, we could make a tidy sum harvesting golden statues, nose ornaments, and cock sheaths too."

"Put it out of your mind," said Tom, "unless you want to become the main dish in a cannibal feast after a fortnight of torture."

Deep in thought, Captain Andreas walked easily and silently over the damp carpet of leaves. He traveled at half his usual speed to allow the buccaneers to keep up. They were fit by European standards, used to clambering up rigging in all weathers and winching heavy anchors, but they slogged through the jungle at a snail's pace. Andreas would have to make allowances when timing the assault on the gold depot. He came to the conclusion that a small fleet of dugout canoes was needed. First things first, he thought, detecting a trace of wood smoke in the air.

They emerged into a clearing and saw a village with wooden slatted walls and thick palm thatches stretched out across the valley in the midday sun. A gaggle of naked children shrieked when they spotted the first buccaneers. They raced off ahead. Curious faces appeared in the doorways, dark eyed women among them. Kinki stepped forward with a group of painted warriors carrying bows and bamboo spears. They joined Andreas at the head of the column and led the way, chanting, through the narrow paths between the huts to a large central square of well-trodden red earth. Here, at last, the little army could fling down their weapons and draw breath. Monotonous drumbeats thumped out of a long building on stilts, accompanied by unearthly wailing. The Englishmen swallowed hard and peered around from beneath the brims of their hats. They were completely surrounded by howling warriors pounding the shafts of their spears into the dust.

11

THE CHILDREN OF THE MOON

The Indian settlement was spread over a slope above a green valley. It was laid out like a Spanish town with a large plaza in the center and roads running off in all directions, but the plazas were round and all the paths curved. Where the Spaniards used stone, tiles, and straight lines, these forest Indians built with palm thatch and every conceivable type of wood following the lay of the land. Thin yellow dogs sniffed at the weary buccaneer army as they removed their shoes and lit their pipes, grateful for the clouds descending from the mountains and shielding them from the sun. Women with golden nose rings, shining black hair, and red body paint moved among the crowd offering calabashes of fresh water. Hundreds of eyes observed the assembly from chinks in the surrounding wooden walls. Some of the raiders fell asleep where they sat, oblivious to the women, the drumming, and the chanting, hats over their faces, their clay pipes smoldering on the well-trodden ground near their weapons.

While Tom and Scarrett snored beside them in the red dirt, Malcolm and Joseph stared at the Indian women, especially the younger ones.

"My, my," groaned Malcolm, scratching the hardening scab on

his neck. "I think I've died and been swept into paradise. Tired as I am, I believe I could service half a dozen right now."

"They are a fine sight, no doubt about it. I have rarely seen the like. I'd be more than content with just one. Like that one over there," agreed Joseph, tipping his straw hat at a ripe-breasted girl with a spiral pattern on her belly. She caught his eye and shielded her mouth, although she was virtually naked.

Malcolm pointed at Tom. "Him I can understand, old as he is, but how can the Gipsy boy sleep with such visions of beauty parading before him? Has the spunk curdled to cheese in his sacks?"

"Your spunk would be maggoty if you'd seen what he has in Port Royal," replied Joseph.

Suddenly Bartholomew Sharp strode up to them and barked, "Wake Old Tom up! I know he has passable Spanish. We need him in the parliament house."

More women circulated, distributing roast corn and plantains. While the men chewed and relaxed, the captains and interpreters entered a large barn with a steeply angled roof. Small wooden effigies lined the walls. A medicine man adorned with shimmering quetzal feathers blew tobacco smoke in their faces and waved a rattlesnake's tail at them as they blinked in the darkness. Edmund Cook cursed. He reached for the handle of his pistol, but Coxon restrained him with a fierce look. A muscular young chief sat astride a hammock, wearing an embroidered cape and a crown of beaten gold. The precious metal from his crown, nose ornament, lip pendant, armbands, necklace, and penis sheath caught the beams of light from the gaps in the walls. A painted, double-headed snake curled round his torso. On this special occasion, the Indians diplomatically waived the customary ban on weapons within the council house. Kinki and Captain Andreas straddled hammocks on either side of the chief, smoking cigars and sipping a murky liquid from saucers made from the tops of human skulls.

Each captain handed the Prince of Darien a gift. He ran his thumb along the cutting edge of the axe, swirled the red silk sash in the air, bit the golden Spanish crucifix, and sifted through a box of glass beads. Incense from burning cocoa pods rose out of an upturned conquistador's helmet wedged into the ground by its crest. Finally, Sharp offered the prince an oval mirror with a gilt handle. The prince was enthralled. He gazed at his reflection and then caught a light beam and made it dance around the gloomy interior. Satisfied, he grunted his approval. The medicine man kept on wailing.

Other warriors quickly strung more hammocks for the guests, who swung their legs over them as they had done so often, below decks, letting their swords dangle on the floor in their baldrics. Soon the buccaneer commanders were smoking cigars and sipping cloudy corn beer from little gourds. Savory slices from a recently roasted goat were passed around in a tortoise shell. Cook, who didn't like offal, forced his morsel of liver down with a grimace. He knew that not to eat it would be seen as an insult. The prince pounded the ground with a shortened Spanish halberd. It was festooned in feathers and the skin of a pit viper had been wound around the shaft. The council of war could begin.

Everything had to be repeated three times; first from the chief, or 'Emperor' as the Englishmen called him, to Captain Andreas in Kuna; then from Andreas to Tom in Spanish; then into English; then all the way back again, three times, by the same route. This gave Tom and Andreas considerable power to influence the debate, especially since they were old friends and 'the Emperor' was Andreas' eldest son.

Coxon, the overall commander, began to speak for the raiders. The others grunted and fanned themselves with their hats, except Cook, who sweated beneath his French wig. Bartholomew Sharp stared disconsolately at the Dutch sea chart in his lap, shaking his head. The 1676 'Kaart van de Landengte van Panama' was magnificently printed on the finest Amsterdam rag paper and showed both the North and South Seas, but all the detail was on the upper coast. The interior indicated a road, the famous 'Camino Real,' a cobbled treasure trail crossing the isthmus from Panama to Porto Bello, but precious little else. Ranges of mountains and rivers with one or two islands in the 'Zuid Zee' told him absolutely nothing about their present position. All the compass bearings were in the 'West-Indische Zee' to the north. An engraved Indian couple under a palm tree occupied the southeastern corner. Sharp was tempted to throw the damn thing onto the burning cocoa in the rusty helmet. The mighty prince had merely stared at the chart upside down and handed it back.

Tom Sheppard, his Louis d'Or glinting, cleared his throat. "Gentlemen," he said gravely," I think I have an idea of what His Royal Highness wants."

"I know what I want," laughed Peter Harris, looking at the chief in a most friendly manner. "I want those bangles he's wearing! And that crown! There's a few hundred pounds right there. I'd put them in a sack and go straight back to the ship, and blast any little painted monkey in my path to hell." He bowed in the direction of the royal hammock.

"Now, now, Peter," said Coxon. "Any more of that and I'll squeeze the bloody flux out of your guts and pour it down your gizzard. We have bigger fish to fry. These painted monkeys will help us catch them." He too bowed at the chief and stole a glance at Andreas. Coxon suspected that the feathered old sly boots understood a little English.

"Let Tom tell us what Prince Golden Cap wants," growled Sharp, crunching the chart in his fist. "You can kill each other later. Tom! Get on with it, man."

"The nearest I can describe it, gentlemen," continued Tom, "is as a modern Trojan War. The prince's daughter has been abducted by a certain Spaniard called Gabriel. Just as the Greeks wanted their Helen returned, so the Indians want their woman back."

"What?" demanded Edmund Cook, his flabby jowls wobbling. "Helen? Trojan War?" He tore off his wig and wiped his sweating dome with a lace cuff. "Talk sense, man."

"Very well, Captain," said Tom quietly. "It seems we need them more than they need us. They will feed us and entertain us here while they assemble canoes to convey us rapidly to the South Sea. To march the army such a distance would take forever. There is a

Spanish outpost called El Real de Santa Maria at the mouth of the biggest southern river. It is a collecting point for gold panned in the streams. There is also a gold mine nearby at Espiritu Santo. The next shipment, about three-hundredweight, goes to Panama by boat eight days from now, regular as clockwork. I make that Friday the sixteenth of April. We have plenty of time. The Governor of Darien supervises the operation at Santa Maria with two hundred soldiers. Gabriel and the stolen Princess live within the compound. We surprise them and take the gold. The Indians rescue the Princess."

"And they all lived happily ever after! Trojan wars! Stolen princesses!" shouted Coxon. "What about Panama? That is the main prize. I've never heard of this Santa Maria. Why waste the element of surprise on a little outpost, when we can pounce on the city itself and get all the treasure of the Kingdom of Peru as well as a few nuggets and sacks of river dust? You say the gold is taken to Panama anyway. In effect, the Dons have saved us a lot of trouble by gathering it in one place."

Richard Sawkins, who had been quietly chewing his cigar, asked, "Tom, find out how far from Panama this Santa Maria really is. We might be able to take both places and ransom all the bigwigs into the bargain. If we secure the shoreline, nobody will be able to warn Panama before we attack. We could have both prizes and keep our Indian friends sweet for the return march. There would be more than enough gold and silver for everyone. We can depart as we came. Or else, we must round the Horn."

"Ah! You're a landlubber at heart," barked Coxon. "You don't know your poop rail from your binnacle box. I'll sail to Madagascar if I have to. We are always more effective at sea. We'll spin the Indians a yarn and go straight to Panama City. If you don't like it, Dick Sawkins, take your lousy crew elsewhere and be damned."

"No, I tell you what," snarled Sawkins. "I'll lead the attack on Santa Maria myself and show you how it's done properly, by real men."

Sharp tossed the Dutch chart into the air and let it fall at his feet. "Easy, brothers," he hissed. "Remember where we are. We might as well be on the moon. Show some fucking unity of purpose. It would be unwise to leave a hostile coast at our backs." He grinned at the Indians. "John," he said to Coxon, "you know the rules. You are our admiral. You command us in battle. Elsewhere we vote. We're not in the Duke of York's Navy, fighting Hollanders, now. We are the Emperor of Darien's soldiers of fortune, nothing more."

Coxon's face reddened with suppressed fury, but he bit his lip and sighed, "Very well. Ask them about this Santa Maria, Tom. God, what is this muck?" He raised his gourd and forced down the Indian beer, as if it were medicine. The prince said, "Napi!" and followed suit, calling for more. The medicine man produced a solid gold statuette of a frog, similar to the one Andreas had greeted on the trail, and held it in the cocoa smoke to bless their joint enterprise against Spain.

Kinki huddled in one corner of the council chamber with ten warriors while Prince Golden Cap and the buccaneer commanders continued to talk. Kinki laid out lines of corn grains on a plank of royal palm wood and gave the senior warriors instructions concerning food, lodgings, and canoes for the guests. The warriors had trouble calculating such large numbers, but the corn lines made the logistics clearer. Five warriors departed to assemble the dugouts downstream. It would not be easy. Prince Golden Cap's authority only extended for thirty miles around. Everything else depended on medicine men and family loyalties.

"The Empire of Darien," like "The Admiral of the Black," was a fiction employed by the buccaneers to increase their chances of avoiding the noose if they fell into the hands of unfriendly colonial governors. Since the fall of the Aztecs and Incas there had been only one empire on the mainland, defended by Spanish garrisons and their colonial militias. In the hinterland, the prehistoric laws and customs of the Stone Age prevailed, and in Darien they suited the buccaneers perfectly. Here everybody could call himself an 'emperor,' a 'king' or whatever he pleased, as long as he could back his claim with sufficient force. As for the Indians, they inhabited a Magic Empire that included the spirits of the clouds, plants, rocks, rivers, animals, and the dead. All creation was a supernatural miracle, even the smallest occurrence pregnant with meaning. Among the Kuna, nobody inhabited this spiritual dimension more completely than the 'Children of the Moon.'

As the sun began to sink in a red cloudy haze, streaked with yellow on the mountains, the buccaneers settled into their thatched houses and the Kuna albinos began to emerge. Since their skin could not tolerate sunlight, they were mainly nocturnal. They shielded their sensitive eyes from the blinding colors of the day in the shadows of their huts waiting for their mother, the moon, to appear. Simply being an albino conferred the status of a witch doctor. The villagers treated them with great respect, stepping aside to let them pass. To harm an albino, even inadvertently, would cause a terrible catastrophe to befall the offender and bring a curse on his entire family.

The sprawling village became the scene of a large party. The Indian warriors wanted cloth and metal objects, especially axes and cutlasses. In return they offered the services of their healers, food, endless quantities of their 'chicha' beer, and willing females.

Having finished his duties in the council house, the principal medicine man made a circuit of the narrow paths, calling on the spirits and declaring a carnival. A ghostly group of albino women followed in his wake, chanting and performing a running dance. The buccaneer musicians with their drums and fifes sat round a bonfire in the plaza. They had started to play a version of 'Greensleeves.' Kuna drummers supplied a thumping backbeat. The buccaneers introduced some faster Irish melodies, producing a savage combination of sounds with the haunting bamboo flutes. It was music to raise the dead. Dozens of warriors pranced around the fire waving spears, bows, and blow pipes. Circles of women swayed in the shadows, tossing their long hair and pausing only to drink more chicha. The light of the flames glittered from their nose rings and flickered over the snakes, turtles, crocodiles, and geometric shapes painted on their writhing bodies. The air was scented with coffee, tobacco, and cocoa. As the alcohol took effect, the occasional gunshot interrupted the animal calls from the surrounding trees. The whole countryside, including toucans and bearded howler monkeys, was awake, under a misty red moon. There was no danger; the nearest Spaniards were over fifty miles away.

Some exhausted buccaneers preferred to rest in the huts, eating mangoes and pineapples, putting their feet up in hammocks and rubbing greasy herbal pastes into their heat rashes. Most could not resist the temptation of sauntering into the fragrant tropical air to join the festivities. Rows of calabashes filled with chicha lined the edges of the plaza where the musicians were beginning to improvise a concert. O'Hare plucked his mandolin with gusto. Two fiddlers joined him, with a Northumbrian bagpipe player from Cook's crew, and half a dozen Kuna women stamping the ground with rattles round their ankles. The jigs, reels, and sea-shanties joined seamlessly with the soaring flutes and steady heartbeat of the pounding drums.

Malcolm, Joe, and Scarret picked up a calabash each. They felt marvelously light without their guns and bags, retaining only their swords.

"Christmas has returned! We go from feast to feast," laughed Scarrett. "I wish we had some of that rum left! This beer tastes like lizard's piss."

"You know as much about beer as you do about Christmas. It's not so bad after the first three mouthfuls," said Joseph. "I can feel the desired effect already."

Malcolm tipped a calabash to his lips and gurgled the contents down ferociously. "Ah, that's better!" He wiped the froth from his moustache. "I wonder what happened to Tom. He doesn't know what he's missing."

Two Kuna girls, springing backwards in their dance, crashed into Malcolm and spilled the chicha down his front. He tossed the empty calabash aside and slung his arms over their shoulders, kicking up his feet in time with theirs. The women stripped him to the waist, dropping his shirt and cutlass on the ground. This gave him an idea.

"Quick, Scarrett, lend me your blade. I've seen highlanders prancing about." He shouted, "I'll show ye how it's done properly! The wind hath blown my plaid away! I am the king of the glens today!"

Malcolm Munro crossed the two swords and performed a Highland dance, pointing his fingers over his head like a stag's antlers. The women circled round him, whooping and tugging his waistband. One had hooked crosses painted on her breasts, the other, jaguar spots all over her body.

"Don't be touching the blades, Mal," yelled Joseph, twirling his cutlass like a shillelagh. "You know that will bring a bloody curse down on your head, so it will!"

Malcolm did his best to step between the swords, but this became more difficult as the Indian women bent forward to lick the fresh sweat from his chest and unfasten his breeches. He lowered his hands, kicked the swords aside and retired to the shadows of a nearby hut with his playmates. Joseph picked up the weapons and turned to the Gipsy, who was strangely silent, staring at the silhouettes cavorting round the bonfire.

Joseph asked softly, "Is the beer not to your taste?"

"I don't even like English beer, let alone Scottish reels and Indian spittle," muttered Scarrett. "I think I'll go down to the river."

Joseph sighed. "Don't get lost, now. I will see you later."

He guessed what had upset his friend. Malcolm's two dark-haired women reminded the Gipsy of his sisters back in the stinking Port Royal tavern. On top of that, simply to be born a Gipsy was a hanging offence in Scotland. Suddenly, Joe felt tired. The music had become hectic, like a hasty, hand-over-hand shanty on the yardarms in a gale. He needed peace. He slid the Gipsy's cutlass into his belt, grasped Malcolm's forgotten sabre, picked up a fresh chicha calabash, and followed the nearest twisting path. Malcolm's shirt was being trampled into the dirt where it had fallen. Indian yells and pistol shots punctuated a chorus of "Blow the wind, blow!" The stentorian roar of a sleepless howler monkey answered from the jungle.

Joseph shuddered and scanned the sky for bats. He began to retrace his steps to their billet, but could not get his bearings. The paths had become a dark labyrinth. The alcohol did not help. There was no point in asking an Indian: he knew nothing of their language, and how would they know which particular hut he was after? He headed north-west from the plaza, trying to remember the general direction and hoping to bump into other members of Sharp's troop. Figures huddled in the shadows. Wrinkled Kuna couples sat in doorways like pairs of young sweethearts, offering each other chicha from tiny wooden ladles. They raised their nose ornaments with one hand and held the spoon in the other. An old man crooned a love song. An exhausted buccaneer snored by the wall beside him, surrounded with empty calabashes. Joseph found himself wondering whether he would ever see his wretched parents again, hauling plows on Barbados under the lash. They were probably dead, he concluded, which would be a blessing. Soon, he was completely lost near the outskirts of the settlement. The moon appeared and disappeared behind a sheet of rain clouds, which spread over the crouching outline of the surrounding forest.

Joseph leant against a tree and, on a whim, crossed the two swords on the ground in front of him. He let his back slide down the trunk, made himself comfortable, took out his tinderbox, and lit a pipe. The air hummed with insects. Fireflies danced in the smoke. The insistent whine of a mosquito stopped abruptly when he slapped his neck. Distant thunder rumbled in the west. The more he smoked, the more relaxed and carefree he became. Maybe it wasn't only the chicha. Scarrett had given him a little pouch of his strange green tobacco, acrid in the back of his throat, which seemed to lift his spirits. He imagined the shapes of animals in the outlines of the foliage. A group of three giant trees stood alone in wild cane field, their branches twisted together in a leafy mass.

"The Holy Trinity, like a giant shamrock," he smiled, and remembered his mother's stories of the fairies and wee folk that lived under toadstools in the old country. He took a long puff at his pipe. Something soft tickled the back of his neck. Fearing another little bloodsucking demon, he slapped it and was astonished to feel a downy clump of feathers under his hand.

Her name was Esamisi, "Silver Cat," a young albino woman, and she had stolen up quietly behind him. The feathers were part of a lightly woven cape she wore over her shoulders. She had been observing him for some time from her nearby cabin, and she knew he was the one. It could not be a coincidence. The crossed blades, quartering the world, were a sure sign. The magic was strong. His hawk-like profile, long fair hair, and muscular build clinched it for her. This big foreign devil would give her a mighty son, a great warrior, somebody to feed and protect her in the years ahead and lead his people to victory.

If Joseph had made an impression on Esamisi, it was nothing compared to the effect she was having on him. She appeared to float above him, in a haze of twinkling fireflies. Her long flaxen hair, pearl necklaces, snow-white skin, and feathered cloak made her resemble the Fairy Queen, complete with wings. His pipe fell from his hand as he tried to get up. He felt dizzy. It was easy for her to push him back against the tree with a gentle kiss. The savage music came in waves from the center of the village. He hadn't been with a woman since Port Royal's fish market. His breeches tightened instantly at the touch of her lips.

Joseph stared into her blazing, pale eyes, reached for her nipples with his tongue, smelled cocoa butter, and sank his teeth into her leather thong. She hissed, "Emiski pani ukkur mesesisunna!" tugging off his waistband and belt. He seized her by the buttocks and gorged himself between her thighs as if licking out a guava. To do this to a dirty Port Royal whore would be unthinkable. He hardly heard the nearby crackle of thunder, but he saw her stark and white in the lightening flash that followed, tossing back her mane of yellow hair and moaning as she sank down onto him. He felt as if he was in the center of a whirlwind, being ridden through the sky. His fingers clawed into the grass and he erupted to a louder crash of thunder immediately followed by torrents of cool rain. She rocked on top of him, her hair and feathers plastered to her alabaster skin, water coursing down between her breasts. The music had come to an abrupt halt. The soaking couple gathered up the pipe and swords and ran to the shelter of her cabin. Later, while Joseph slept like a log in her hammock, Esamisi lit a fire in front of some wooden effigies and strung the smallest figure round his neck. She hid Malcolm's precious sabre under a stack of baskets. Esamisi would give it to their child when he came of age and name him "Son of Thunder."

While Joseph settled down for the night and the April rain extinguished the hissing bonfire in the square, Thomas Sheppard ducked into the shelter of his old friend Captain Andreas' house. The two interpreters had met in 1671 and were about to enjoy a late supper of collared peccary with Andreas' two wives. Several children lay, two and three to a hammock, in the total darkness at one end of the long smoky hut, pretending to sleep but occasionally stealing a glance at the blue-cheeked, hairy visitor with the coin in his ear. Andreas removed his shirt and headdress. He knotted an ocelot pelt over his shoulders. The women, one much older than the other, shared a pipe and a bowl of chicha while the men feasted on the roasted wild pig. They sat on flat grey stones encircled by scallop-shell oil lamps. A grey curtain of water fell outside the doorway. Droplets filtered down through the thatch.

Tom grinned and smacked his lips. "Wettar bueno! Good!" he said, praising the food in a garbled mixture of Kuna, English, and Spanish.

"Peeg good-good, si!" agreed Andreas.

Dessert consisted of baked bananas washed down with grenadillo juice, Tom's favorite. As well as tasting delicious, he believed the juice warded off the scurvy. He drank as much as he could at every opportunity, and had never suffered from that dreadful illness, although dozens had perished around him.

The men lit their pipes. Tom produced a set of stoppered Murano perfume flasks, protected in leather pouches, from his knapsack. He had found them on their last day in the Portobello mansion, along with a beautiful Moorish lady's dagger. He presented the weapon to Andreas who grinned appreciatively with a sparkle in his obsidian eyes. Tom pointed to the largest flask and said, "Waiye, Andreas, escucha. This one for nele sampulakkwa, eh?"

Captain Andreas nodded. They had discussed Tom's requirements. For the large flask, Tom wanted a carefully balanced brew of a hallucinogenic cascabel vine mixed with coarse Mapacho tobacco leaves and ground-up roots. He had tried some on his last expedition to Darien under Andreas' guidance, and knew that one dose affected him after three hours. A small sip of the bilious liquid was enough to transport him into a waking dream of kaleidoscopic shapes, while thoroughly purging his bowels, worming him like a dog. It could also snap him out of the depression known as cabin fever on an exceptionally tedious voyage. Slipped into unsuspecting enemies' strong coffee or thick chocolate, a few more drops would send them laughing over the side of a ship, claiming to be able to fly like seagulls. Tom had dispatched more than one dangerous nuisance to the sharks in this fashion. He called it his 'Mind Expanding Elixir and Purgative.'

The medium-sized flask was to be filled with an even more dangerous concoction called "Hell's Bells." Made from a common ditch weed with white tubular flowers known as Angels' Trumpets, this foul-smelling sauce had been used to great effect against the king's guards by rebelling indentured servants and African slaves in Jamestown, Virginia, four years earlier. After going temporarily blind, the soldiers began to talk to invisible friends, strip off their clothes, climb over the furniture like squirrels, and pull faces as if trying to win a gurning competition. Some dislocated their jaws. Some attempted to bugger each other and then daub themselves with feces. Judiciously applied to pungent sea food or rotting cheese, Hell's Bells could render an entire crew insane for days. Andreas added pig grease, mashed centipedes, and a pinch of chili to the mixture, for texture and flavor, before securely inserting the cork stopper.

The third, smallest flask was to contain a specialty of the region: the quickest and deadliest poison on earth. Extreme caution was required while preparing it, and Andreas asked Thomas to light more lamps and bring them closer. One stray droplet could be fatal. It was the poison used to tip blowpipe darts, especially when hunting monkeys. The victims fell paralyzed out of the branches and were dead before they hit the ground. They became perfectly edible once the venom had reacted with the blood, as Kinki had proved to Malcolm on the beach.

Andreas produced a sealed Spanish wine bottle from the shadows. It contained several recently suffocated luminous frogs, lying in the slime of their final bowel movements. Each frog was smaller than a man's thumb. Their transparent outer membranes glowed cobalt blue over a layer of black spots. The froglets were miniature versions of the medicine man's figurine in the parliament house.

Tom took the bottle and gasped. He held a burning wick up against the glass. "The little blue guardians of Darien!"

Andreas sprinkled a pinch of gunpowder into a wooden saucer, adding salt and oil. He grunted at Tom to give him the bottle, which he briefly warmed over the flame before whisking the frogs into a creamy purple paste with a twig through the bottleneck. Their eyeballs resembled tiny eggs. Whining a ritual song, he slowly tipped the deadly slime into the saucer and stirred. He was apologizing to the animals, knowing that, if they ever became extinct, it would herald the end of the world. The old hunter then carefully coaxed the resulting cream into the smallest Venetian scent flask. He immediately burned the twig while Tom screwed down the stopper with a sigh. His chemical armory was complete. The airtight seal would preserve its potency. Now it was his turn to fulfill a promise to his host.

Andreas had never stopped pestering Tom about the fate of John Gret, the unfortunate tribesman killed in Jamaica. His ambition was to travel and see more of the world, all of it, if possible, before he died. This was unusual for a member of the self-contained Kuna people, but Andreas was an exceptional man of great curiosity. Thomas knew his friend thought the world was a tiny fraction of its actual size. He imagined the fabled kingdom of England to be just over the horizon from Barbados. Thomas agreed to give Andreas a lesson in modern geography, with a little politics thrown in for good measure. Andreas had a lively intellect, but it would not be easy.

A great weariness spread behind Tom's eyes until his entire body was sapped of strength. Andreas understood and indicated a hammock. The geography lesson would have to wait until tomorrow.

"Mañana!" grunted Tom, wearily heaving up his feet. Andreas whispered, "Mañana," and blew out the lamps. Gradually the rain petered out and the wisps of smoke stopped curling into the sky from the Indian town. Even the noise from the jungle abated. The nearby river gurgled over the rocks and the low buzz of the insects was interrupted by the occasional cough, the creak of a hammock, or a female giggle. A hand slapped a mosquito. Then silence. The moon slid behind a misty mountain and the night became pitch black. Big cats, vipers, bird-eating spiders, and bloodsucking bats went stealthily about their business.

The sky was a brilliant blue overhead, long before the sun cleared the high eastern ridges. The men, both Kuna and English, seemed to have decided to enjoy a long lie-in. Women and children bustled about, fetching wood and brewing cocoa. Scarrett had, by some natural homing instinct, found his way back to his hut. He sat among Joe and Malcolm's possessions. He gratefully accepted a bowl of cocoa from a young woman before filling his pipe with his special weed. Within a few minutes he was ravenous and his eyes were bloodshot. He pointed to his mouth and was given a ripe plantain. He lit his pipe again and admired the spider, the size of his hand, which stared at him from the wall with four of its eight eyes. The little Gipsy called to the Kuna girl and pointed at the beast. She nodded, crushed it with lightning speed on the end of a stick, roasted it in the fire, and offered it to him as a snack. He ate the hairy legs; they tasted like prawns, but more bitter. He could not bring himself to chew the head or belly.

In a hut near the square, Malcolm woke up with a raging thirst and, much to the delight of his Kuna lady friends, a serviceable erection. While the Jaguar woman poured a fresh calabash of chicha down his throat, the other one gave the engorged crown of his penis a cursory lick and then proceeded to straddle his hammock and ride him like a wild horse. A leathery grandmother shooed three children into the street and observed the proceedings, with a nostalgic smile under her nose ring, while smoking her pipe, stirring cocoa, and muttering. A warrior looked in at the door and discretely vanished.

Malcolm didn't know if he was in heaven or in hell, and he didn't care. Jaguar woman's hair irritated his face, so he tugged it back with one hand while she gargled chicha and forced it into his mouth, following it with her tongue. He couldn't breathe. He yanked her head back and panted. Two ripe breasts with hooked crosses painted on the nipples bounced before his eyes. The pretty young face above them contorted into a snarling mask. Gasps turned to moans and moans turned to a high-pitched, "Ay! Ay! Ay! Ay! Ayiiiiiiiiihh!" The hammock crashed from the wall posts, but she carried on until they all collapsed in a laughing, chicha-soaked heap.

The captains had lodged in the council chamber, since it was the airiest building. Sharp and Cox occupied the central area, to keep Coxon away from Harris and Sawkins. Edmund Cook spent the night huddled quietly in a corner. The Indians made him nervous.

Strolling within earshot of Malcolm's orgy, John Coxon, Grand Admiral of the Black, with Captain Sharp at his side, winced and shouted at his musicians, "Play some tunes, you dogs! Drown out those squealing bitches in heat! Spread yourselves about the place!"

Impromptu concerts with buccaneer and Kuna participants soon established themselves all around the settlement. Coxon turned to Sharp, "I tell you, Barty, it's a blessing we have no stronger liquor here than that Indian dishwater. Things would not be so peaceful."

"You are not wrong, John," agreed Sharp. "There would be at least a dozen throats slit after a night like that in Port Royal."

More calabashes of chicha appeared, but the tempo was relaxed compared with the previous evening. The Indians were constantly singing little dirges to their spirits, so they presumed their guests were doing likewise when they intoned songs of lost love and gloomy ballads of vengeance from the Scottish borders.

A pall of smoke rose from the thatched roofs. The smell of cocoa, tobacco, and coffee intensified. Shortly before noon, great balls of cumulus cloud began to tower over the forest to the south. Within an hour, the sun had vanished and the buccaneers emerged, en masse, hatless and in their shirtsleeves, to wander about and enjoy the sensation of not having to march in the blazing heat for a few precious hours. Many went to the river to paddle and gulp down the clear water.

Joseph had no idea where he was when he awoke. For a few seconds he imagined he was swaying in his hammock below decks until the shafts of sunlight, wood smoke, and bird calls brought him into the day. The albino girl turned to meet his gaze with her colorless eyes. Esamisi's white skin, yellow hair, and pink lips and nipples startled him. He hadn't seen her properly in the dark. Apart from her lack of color and a tendency to squint, she was quite attractive, with little dimples playing at the corners of her mouth. He held his forearm against hers. His deeply sun-burnt skin seemed African by contrast, like a log of wood on a bed of snow.

Joseph saw that there was an entire family in the long, thatched cabin. He had been too exhausted to notice them the previous night. He lurched out of the hammock, pointed to the nearby trees and went to relieve himself. On his return, a little boy stood in the doorway with a bowl of water, like a human wash stand. He splashed his face and rinsed his hands under the child's solemn scrutiny. Chocolate and cornmeal porridge awaited him inside.

Esamisi insisted on painting a simple geometric bird over a pair of zigzags onto his forearm. A wrinkled grandfather hobbled forward and pricked the design into Joseph's skin using a sharp fishbone. The family tried to make Joe understand, in sign language, that this mark would guarantee his safe passage through Kuna territory in future. When he asked for the missing sabre, however, they merely shrugged. Finally, he planted a kiss on Esamisi's brow, slung his baldric over his shoulder, and retraced his steps to the plaza, swinging his arm to let the air harden the scabs on the tattoo.

Nobody noticed Kinki, the prince, and two other braves, painted and equipped for the hunt, walk quietly to Andreas' house. Without his crown, cape, and bangles the prince looked like any other Indian. He thrust his head inside the door and saw his father Andreas squatting with a couple of children in front of Tom, who was slowly tracing intricate shapes onto a round calabash, using bright vegetable dye and a chewed twig. Andreas glanced up and saw Kinki with his companions over the prince's shoulder. He grunted, nodded, and turned his attention to Tom's painting again. The prince escorted the hunters to the edge of the forest south of the village. He patted the little pouch of corn grains hanging from Kinki's quiver and watched the three men slip into the shadows before returning to the village.

Tom had started his lesson by flattening out Sharp's Dutch sea chart, which he had retrieved from the floor of the council chamber. He made Andreas recognize the outlines of the Caribbean Coast, the San Blas Islands, and the South Sea beyond Panama.

"Now the world," Tom promised his host. "Ahora, el mundo!"

He forced his eyes to focus and copied the map onto a tiny central portion of the calabash as precisely as he could.

"Darien!" he stabbed the little area with a dirty fingernail. "Kuna tule, si?"

"Si," nodded Andreas, "Kuna tule."

From this small reference point Thomas gradually covered the entire globe, coloring the oceans green and leaving the land as the natural brown of the calabash. Europe, Africa, and the Caribbean were fairly detailed, then the coastlines and land masses became smoother, vaguer and somewhat lumpy, but the general form and scale of the planet emerged. For the first time in his life, Andreas began to get an inkling of the immense size of the earth and the tiny portion of it that he called home. The paint dried quickly, and he was soon handling and turning the calabash, muttering in amazement, constantly referring back to the original Darien section to get his bearings. He looked at his English friend and shook his head, marveling, "Todo esto!"

"Si," mused Tom, "todo esto. All that. But I'd still be lost twenty yards from the village."

For the rest of the afternoon, Andreas quizzed Tom about the homelands of the strangers who had been appearing in Darien in ever-increasing numbers since the time of Balboa. With dark pigment, the buccaneer showed the Indian London, Amsterdam, Paris, Lisbon, Madrid, and Rome. He drew arrows to indicate the direction of the Atlantic trade winds, which blew shiploads of black slaves from El Mina, Bonny, Calabar, and Gouida to the New World. Then he marked Hispaniola, Cuba, Jamaica, and Barbados. By the time the sun was setting, Andreas could absorb no more information. The Turkish attacks on Vienna, the Holy Land, Portuguese Goa, the Barbary Coast, the Silk Road, the Chinese Empire, and the Spice Islands were too far removed from his experience to register as more than strange-sounding noises.

Andreas proudly strung the calabash globe from the ceiling. He tied a crimson macaw feather onto the cord to indicate sacred knowledge. Tom began to dry out his gunpowder and sharpen his cutlass, while the Indian selected cruelly barbed war arrows for his quiver and the women flattened corn dough. Leaving his gear and weapons in order, Tom lit a pipe and strolled out for a walk in the smoky orange twilight.

His three young friends were relaxing outside the council house. They had met by the river. In the cool shallows, the water had rushed over their tired bodies. Now, they leaned against the wall of the house listening to the mandolin player. Malcolm's shirt was nowhere to be found, so he wore an embroidered waistcoat and neck cloth instead. He mourned the loss of his fine sabre. "I'll have to shoot a Dago, or club him to death, and take another sword at the earliest opportunity, but I'll never find one like that again."

"You can have my old hanger, so you can," said Joseph sheepishly. "I'm happier with an axe anyway."

"Most gracious of ye, Mr. Connolly," said Malcolm. "Now, when we enter the fray, I'll be in a better position to save yer life."

"Hats and swords seem to hate you as much as you love them. I'm sure I could obtain a stone axe for you," said Tom, "or a bamboo spear."

Bartholomew Sharp appeared in the doorway. "All set for tomorrow then, lads? Nicely rested?"

"Aye, captain," said Tom. "Are we to lead the procession again?"

"We retain that honor. We assemble here at dawn in the same formations as before. As you know, the prince and Captain Andreas will guide us. They have promised to bring along five dozen warriors, all the way to Santa Maria."

When Sharp had gone, Malcolm said, "Damn it to hell. More marching! How much further to this fucking place, and how come the savages skip along so easily while we flounder in their wake?"

"We walk like seamen," said Tom. "Steadying ourselves against the rolling deck. Everything goes crabwise, to the side, in narrow spaces. The Indians range over many miles a day, always going forward, but I've seen 'em fall like ninepins when they come aboard a big ship for the first time. It's horses for courses. You think the Moskito spearmen became fine sailors without a few spills? We'll be good foot soldiers after another day or two, you'll see. Better than the Dons, at any rate. The weaklings amongst us have already been weeded out."

The entire army paraded, with trumpets, drums, and flying colors, in the square, early on the following morning. Women and children stared at them solemnly. Sixty warriors, black paint around their eyes, fully equipped with bows, spears, and blowpipes, loped out of the village. The pirates swayed along behind them, struggling to keep up. They headed south along the riverbank. Vultures circled above the rear of the column in ever-increasing numbers, as if they knew what lay ahead.

12
THE GOLD OF SANTA MARIA

The octopus of the Spanish Empire had been feasting on American treasure for over one hundred and fifty years. By 1680, the beast was feeling its age, twitching defensively instead of grasping new prey. It was also sick in the head. The tentacles thrashed about when prodded, but could barely respond to messages from the monster's nerve center in a coordinated fashion. In fact, the head was trying to eat its own limbs.

Generations of inbreeding had placed a pitiful wreck on the throne. While England had her Merry Monarch and France her Sun King, Carlos the Second, 'the Accursed' King of Spain, was incapable of tying his shoes, let alone ruling an empire. His mother was constantly having him exorcised, offering rewards to anyone who could lift the evil spell. His protruding Hapsburg jaw prevented him from chewing properly. The swollen lower lip and permanently open mouth made him look like an idiot.

Scrofulous sores festered on his scalp under a flaxen wig. The skull was too large for the body. Two servants had to support him on his rickety legs when he walked. There was no chance that he would ever produce an heir out of his terrified young French fiancée. He was to be the last of his dynasty in Spain. Hiding from the public gaze, cowering in the shadows of his palace in Madrid, King Carlos the Accursed prayed for death. Death made him wait.

Spain went to rack and ruin. The nobility had become lazier and more parasitical. Under Carlos, their numbers quadrupled. Hordes of idle grandees sucked the treasury dry. They spent fortunes on clothes to wear in ceremonial processions. In an atmosphere of extreme orthodoxy, the Inquisition stepped up its Jew-hunts, looking for easy money. While the courts of London and Versailles abandoned themselves to gambling and fornication, Carlos' young lords fantasized about seducing nuns. The common people starved. Many turned to banditry and prostitution. Ravaged by malnutrition, the Peninsula's population declined. Portugal broke free. Catalonia tried to join France. The initial torrent of gold and silver from the Americas had dwindled to a trickle. Much of it was shipped straight to bankers in Milan to pay the crown's enormous debts. Increasing amounts lined the pockets of French, Dutch, Portuguese, and English slave traders. The colonists needed more disease-resistant laborers to work the fields and mines and construct elaborate fortifications against pirates. Every doubloon, every peso, was precious.

Nobody knew this better than Don Luis Carrisoli, Field Marshall of Darien and commander of the gold depot at El Real de Santa Maria. The outpost stood on the bank of a wide estuary in the Gulf of San Miguel. Tributaries, descending from the mountains in which the Spaniards made their slaves pan for gold, fed the mighty river mouth. Recently, climbing a gorge to the south, soldiers had spotted a glittering seam and followed it into an overgrown slope. Now the entire hillside was riddled with tunnels producing the purest gold in the Americas by the hundredweight. The location of the Espiritu Santo mine was a closely guarded secret, patrolled by lancers, musketeers, and Indian auxiliaries, deep in the wilderness.

Don Luis periodically showered the local Indian villagers with gifts of cloth and machetes, promising them a bonus for every runaway slave they captured. A larger reward was paid for living fugitives. These were put back into the mine after a good flogging. The dead were publicly hacked to pieces and scattered in the river.

The slaves, originally from the Fang tribe in the Bight of Biafra, were horror-struck. They traditionally kept the bones of their dead in boxes, as reservoirs of ancestral power, believing them to retain magic energy. To see their relatives' dismembered bodies thrown to the crabs in mountain streams was unbearable. A few escaped to join roaming bands of Cimarrons who supported themselves by hunting and fishing in an environment that resembled their West African home.

With his riding boots folded below his knees, his red velvet breeches, embroidered waistcoat, and coal black hair falling down his back, Don Luis' squat figure dominated the wooden quayside above the swirling torrent. The river was demonstrating its power. Tall forest giants, complete with roots, drifted in the current before his gaze. A piragua, its sail furled, strained on its hawsers awaiting the Easter consignment of gold, which was being weighed and counted in the strong room.

Don Luis heard heavy shoes on the boardwalk behind him. "Oh Christ," he muttered, "here he comes."

A badly-shaven young man wearing an oversized hat and a flapping robe approached. Ruperto Holzknecht, Santa Maria's Jesuit priest, wished to share his concerns with the Field Marshall.

"Good day to you, Padre," said Don Luis. "The Easter service was magnificent. You have trained those choirboys well. They sang like angels and made me forget all my troubles for a while."

"Thank you, Commander," the young Austrian wiped sweat off his nose. "They have good voices, but I found it difficult to prepare for Holy Week. I didn't want to disturb you at the time and cast a shadow over the rituals, but the witch doctors came into the church and planted all kinds of satanic bundles about the place. Some of them appeared to contain eagle claws and hawk moths, embedded in feces."

"How appalling, Padre. Do you know the culprits?"

"Yes," blinked the missionary, "I think I do. I suspect Lere Lorenzo and his friends. He seems to imagine that his filthy bundles will keep evil spirits out of the building on the night our Blessed

Redeemer descended into hell. Since his baptism, he claims he can do as he sees fit inside the church since he's been baptized. He encourages his friends to make a mockery of the Holy Mass, using chicha and plantain slices instead of the host and communion wine."

"I'll have a word with him," sighed Don Luis. "We will not tolerate such blasphemous desecrations."

"I sometimes wonder how Christian we are here, Don Luis," said the Jesuit. "Between baptism and extreme unction, I fear Satan presides over the rest."

"Satan, Padre?" growled the Field Marshall. "Here the King of Spain rules the roost in all His Majesty. He extends his protection to the faithful by force of arms. Bring Lere Lorenzo to the guardhouse and I will deal with him. What would you have me do? Make him eat his own shit bags?"

"No, no, Don Luis," the priest was alarmed. "He is but a child. Perhaps he will be convinced by the Passion and Resurrection of Our Lord if I explain it all to him again, patiently."

"I wish you luck, Padre Ruperto," smiled Don Luis wearily. He recalled that most Christian villages in Darien had reverted to witchcraft again after a few years. He bit his lip and turned on his heel as he walked towards the store rooms. The previous missionary, Fray Anselmo, who boasted about Saint Francis' conversations with birds and beasts, had been fed to the crocodiles. Poor old Anselmo thrashed about in the bloody water while the medicine men shouted, "Here's your chance! Talk to the animals now!"

Don Luis would never have carried out his threat to punish Lorenzo, but he had to appear zealous to the priest. The Jesuits were writing reports, which landed on His Excellency Viceroy Melchor Linian de Cisneros' desk in Lima. That nobleman was not only an Archbishop but had served his apprenticeship in the Holy Office of the Inquisition. Don Luis had to be very careful. His Spanish father, Don Julian, had been kidnapped and adopted by the Indians as the sole survivor of an ill-advised turtle hunt. It was no secret that Don Luis' mother was Kuna. He tried to turn this into an asset by insisting that she had been a native 'Empress of Darien.' Don Luis would challenge anybody who denied this 'fact' to a duel.

The half-breed warlord performed a delicate balancing act between the Spaniards and the Indians that corresponded exactly to the mixture in his blood. Don Luis gave everybody what they wanted, playing both ends against the middle. The Indians appreciated bolts of cloth and steel implements while the Spaniards counted the gold. Don Luis' trick was to make each side imagine it controlled the other. He walked a tightrope on the ill-defined border of an imaginary empire. He would tumble down if the true power beyond the frontier, the rule of an invisible network of medicine men, blew a bad wind in his direction.

As soon as Don Luis saw his cousin, Kinki, from San Blas, walking towards him with two painted hunters, he caught an ominous whiff of that bad wind. The Indians were escorted by six halberdiers wearing old-fashioned morion helmets and breastplates. The antiquated armor still proved effective against stone clubs, darts, and poisoned arrows on this frontier. The warlord told the guards to give the hunters food and ushered his cousin into the office beside the strong room. It was the only stone building in Santa Maria. Kinki shuddered after sipping a beaker of wine and poured three hundred and twenty-seven grains of corn onto the massive ironwood table. Don Luis counted the corn quickly.

"So many?"

Kinki nodded. "Nappira mai a."

The warlord groaned, "Almost as bad as Morgan."

Kinki swallowed more wine, indicated the pile of corn, drew a finger across his throat, and made a twirling movement in all directions. Don Luis recalled entering Old Panama with the Indian troops after Morgan's raid. He remembered the dead bodies bloating under smoldering beams, the stench, the buzzing flies, and the vacant eyes of the survivors. He took a rapier from the wall, presented it to his cousin, and summoned the sergeant of the guard.

"Todo el oro!" he shouted. "All the gold! To Panama! Now!"

Within forty minutes, the piragua was sailing towards the Gulf of San Miguel with its precious cargo.

Like many New World tribes, the Kuna's own name for themselves, 'Tule,' simply meant 'human beings.' They might squabble among themselves, but they hated the idea of Tule deaths at the hands of strangers. Their word for 'foreigners' was the same as that for 'enemies.' They would close ranks against outsiders at the drop of a hat. Don Luis knew that Kinki's purpose in warning him, apart from family loyalty, was to avoid a clash between Spaniards and buccaneers with Kuna warriors fighting on both sides. If the garrison's Indian auxiliaries suddenly decided to help Captain Andreas in the middle of the battle, Don Luis would lose all credibility in Panama. He had to stage-manage the coming fight carefully. A lesser man might have succumbed to panic.

At least the gold was safe. That was all the Spaniards really cared about. It was also the whole reason for the buccaneers' forced march, but Kinki had hardly given it a thought. Kuna blood was worth more than decorative yellow metal for nose ornaments and statuettes. Gold fever made the white men shed lakes of blood indiscriminately but was incomprehensible to the Indians. They were as eager to play the pale-faced lunatics off against each other, using gold for bait, as the European invaders were to divide and rule them.

The gold had gone. It was sailing to Panama with the urgent message that an overwhelming horde of pirates was pouring over the mountains from the north. Don Luis had exaggerated their numbers to six hundred, thrice his own strength. That would make any resistance seem heroic. He then called in his half-brother, Antonio, and explained the situation.

"Little brother," he said, "go with Kinki and tell all the Tule, especially Lere Lorenzo, to be ready to leave on an extended mission at the crack of dawn tomorrow. The valley up to Espiritu Santo must be guarded for at least two weeks. The men can take their families and stay in the village at Cania. We must not let the pirates find that mine."

"Very well, Lucho," said Antonio. "I'll go with them, of course."

Don Luis smiled. Clearly Antonio did not relish the thought of staying in Santa Maria to fight the buccaneers. "Of course you will go," he said. "I need somebody I can trust up there... and to take over here afterwards if I don't survive."

"Don't talk like that," Antonio embraced him. "You can rely on me. We will be gone at sunrise. This is a big one, eh?"

"Nearly as big as Morgan nine years ago, by the look of it," replied Don Luis.

"Dios! I hope you know what you are doing."

"I do. We will just have to weather the storm," said the warlord, as if trying to convince himself.

Antonio and Kinki went to look for the medicine man first. Then all three of them spread the word among the warriors to prepare for an early departure. Don Luis calculated that the enemy would arrive within two days at the earliest. The invaders would need scores of dugout canoes. He called again for the sergeant, Roque Alvarez, a veteran with a fierce moustache.

"Roque," he said, "hundreds of thieving heretical English dogs are about to descend on us. See that the men are ready. I will inspect the defenses this afternoon."

"A la orden!" said the sergeant. "What about lookouts?"

"The Indian scouts will patrol to the south. Tomorrow I want you to send the choirboys into the treetops. Position them upriver so that we can see their signals."

"Best to send them in pairs," said the sergeant. "Then they can be there day and night and signal with lanterns if necessary."

Don Luis pointed to a brass telescope lying on the table among his papers. "I'll leave this here when I'm asleep. Use it."

When Roque had gone, the warlord slowly drank three cups of dark Teruel wine. A little brown boy served him a steaming bowl of iguana boiled in coconut oil, complete with its cheesy yellow eggs, accompanied by mashed yucca. Don Luis bolted it down. The thought of action whetted his appetite. It also made him lustful. The boy returned. Don Luis asked him to tell his mother to prepare a sugared coconut dessert and bring it to him herself.

While Don Luis strained and sweated with the woman in the closet behind his office, the buccaneers cursed and heaved their heavy log canoes through the undergrowth to avoid rapids, boulders, and fallen trees. They were only twenty-five miles away, but the going was painfully slow. Sharp's vanguard had gone ahead in fourteen canoes while Sawkins, Harris, and the bulk of the army marched to another point of embarkation on a tributary in the jungle to the west.

The tension between Captains Coxon and Sawkins had become unbearable during their forced proximity in the village council house. Now Coxon and Edmund Cook sat in the leading canoe with Sharp, Cox, and two cabin boys. Andreas, Tom, Malcolm, Joseph, and Scarrett followed in the second canoe. At either end of the dugouts, Indians used poles, stemming them against the banks. At one point the ninety-eight-strong force had to drag the canoes over rough terrain for half a mile, to avoid a thundering waterfall. A family of spider monkeys, the babies clinging to their mothers' backs, screeched and pelted the column with fruit. A massive tapir stood in their path for an instant, gave vent to a high-pitched squeal, and crashed off into the dense foliage. Andreas imagined the feast such an animal would provide, but there was no time to hunt.

"What the devil was that?" shuddered Malcolm. "An elephant? A giant pig?"

They descended into a deep gully where the sun only touched the highest branches above their heads. Everything was covered in a fine white dust, bleached and dead in the moist shadows. Their legs sank into a thick carpet of mulch, which covered sharp rocks. Mushrooms crumbled underfoot. Leeches stuck to their shins.

"This is worse than the mountains," moaned Coxon, "and even slower."

Struggling with the canoe, Captain Edmund Cook kept glancing at the Kunas' conical penis sheaths from under his wig. He feared the worst. "I suspect the savages are splitting us into small groups in order to eat us and make off with our possessions. I'll blast them to smithereens at the first sign of treachery."

"Now, now, Ned," gasped Sharp. "If they had wanted to, they could easily have overpowered us in the village while we slept. Save your powder for the Dons."

"The powder will soon be caked and useless in this dampness," came the nasal voice of Quartermaster Cox. "We must sift and air it thoroughly when we get the chance."

Sliding his dugout over the moldy leaves behind the captains, Tom rolled his eyes and whispered, "Will you listen to that bunch of washerwomen, Joe?"

Joseph adjusted his grip on the slippery log. "It is murderous work, Tom. We haven't been afloat more than fifty yards at a time."

"It will be easier downstream," grunted Tom. "If an old dog like me can do it, it should be nothing for you frisky pups."

"I'll be glad when we are on board a real ship again," said Malcolm. "Even that tub we sailed through the storm now seems like heaven. We are seamen, by God's Guts, not mules. Furthermore, I am egg-bound. I haven't had a shit for three days." He spat and lost his balance, barking his shin painfully.

"Then you are the luckiest man in this army," said Joseph. "Everybody else is barely holding in their treacle."

"It's no joke," groaned Malcolm. "It feels like ballast rocks in my tripes."

"Ask the surgeon, Wafer, to dig it out for you," advised Tom. "He has the correct instruments. Compacted turds can be fatal." He lowered his voice. "Failing that, I'm sure Captain Cook over there would be delighted to do the honors with his purple plunger, pretty boy."

"I swear, Tom," said Malcolm, with gritted teeth, "if I wasn't carrying this bloody log, I'd knock yer yellow fangs out for that."

"Easy, son," said Tom. "As a last resort, I have a native remedy that might save your life, so don't offend me."

The lightly built Kuna warriors put their English allies to shame. They skipped over the slimy roots, bearing the heavy canoes, their toes splayed out in an effortless dance. The buccaneers seemed to be heaving battering rams at invisible doors. When they were finally afloat again things became easier. The water was deeper and the Indians abandoned their poles in favor of paddles. The pirates burned the leeches off their legs with fuses and reclined on their knapsacks, watching the tall trees slip past. Some lit pipes or dipped their black jacks into the current for a drink. Shafts of sunlight penetrated the canopy and lit up the steam that rose from the surface, making everything merge into overlapping shades of green and brown. Unseen flocks of birds chattered and shrieked incessantly overhead. Occasionally they glimpsed parrot feathers or the yellow bill of a toucan among the leaves.

In the middle of the afternoon they hauled the canoes onto a grassy bank. The Indians picked this spot because they knew the men were hungry. The surrounding country provided emergency rations of plantains, vine tubers, and oilseeds to make vegetable soup. Guavas and custard apples abounded for dessert. While half the Indians scoured the meadows, the others speared mountain mullet in the river. The buccaneers built shelters with palm fronds and wild cane. As the sun sank behind the trees, black kettles bubbled over a dozen campfires. Captain Edmund Cook clucked about like a pregnant turkey, reminding the raiders to sharpen their cutlasses, clean their guns, and sift their gunpowder. By eight o' clock everyone was fast asleep. There was a distant crackle of thunder. The palm leaves kept off the worst of the rain.

The Englishmen had come to realize that snakes only attacked when cornered. The trick was to shake any bags or bundles of clothes in the morning to avoid a nasty surprise. The Indians mixed wild garlic with their war paint, to repel snakes, mosquitoes, bats, and evil spirits.

Downriver, Don Luis Carrisoli stared at the teak beams holding up the ceiling of his bedroom. The shutters were wide open to let the warm breeze fan bundles of smoldering sage on the window sills and keep the insects at bay. He heard the plop of a submerging crocodile from the quayside and briefly remembered Fray Anselmo's martyrdom. The more he thought about it, the less he liked his chances against the invaders. El Real de Santa Maria was certainly not worth losing a single life for. With the gold gone, there was little to defend, except a few ramshackle huts and the rotten barn of a church. The stone storehouse, which contained his office and sleeping quarters, was empty except for a couple of flour sacks and ten large clay wine containers. The palisade, which he had inspected that afternoon, was a termite-riddled joke. A well-aimed kick would breach it. Tomorrow, after the departure of the Indian scouts, he would order the soldiers to help the slaves strengthen it with fresh logs and boulders. The worst thing now would be inactivity.

About fifty of the soldiers, a quarter of the garrison, were unfit for combat. They ran high fevers, some had ulcerated tropical sores, and one man's hip had been fractured by a kicking mule. Their white uniforms were patched and moth-eaten. Many of the brass buttons on the blue facings had been replaced with wood and bone. Their brave scarlet sashes had faded to pink in the sun, yet they still attempted to appear fashionable by tying scraps of lace under their knees. Battered straw hats, turned up at the front, sprouted red parrot feathers.

Every fifth man carried a pike and wore a breastplate and helmet. The pikes were effective against a cavalry charge, but useless against the guns and cutlasses of buccaneers advancing on foot. They would be shot and hacked to pieces where they stood. As for the musketeers, they hardly fired in anger from one end of the year to the other. Their lumpy, moist gunpowder was unpredictable. Only constant puffing and blowing kept the damp fuses alight. They considered themselves lucky if they managed to discharge the heavy matchlocks without losing an eye, let alone hitting a target. The garrison's war mastiffs looked fierce in their spiked collars, but would turn tail in battle. The dogs had only bitten runaway slaves. They were no longer the hellhounds of Balboa, Cortes, and Pizarro.

Any sensible commander would simply burn the place and retire into the forest. Unfortunately, this was not an option. Enemies in the Panama Audiencia hated Don Luis as a half-breed upstart and begrudged him his salary. His brother, Antonio, and sister, Isabel, were on the royal payroll too. His Spanish wife and children might be evicted from their estate near Puerto Nuevo. He had to organize resistance to preserve the family's reputation. He sighed and curled up against the round backside of the African woman beside him. She was letting out little snores. God, if only he could sleep like that.

Gradually, his mind relaxed, but this allowed his thoughts to wander into territory that he had been avoiding, back to Morgan's raid nine years ago. Old Panama had been razed to the ground. As a young man he had flanked the pirate army with his Indians, observing them but not daring to attack. The pirates had resembled ragged devils, armed to the teeth, with the strength and courage of the insane. When they were not mad with drink, they were even more delirious from lack of it. You had to shoot one of them four or five times before he would lie down. By then, the others would have carved you to pieces.

That wasn't the worst of it. Try telling them that there was no gold! Then the fun really started. The torturers of the Inquisition could learn new tricks from these animals! Don Luis wished he had not allowed himself to think of that. He smelled the woman's skin and felt a rigid urgency in his groin. He probed her from behind. After a sharp twinge of dry resistance, he slid in up to the hilt. For the third time that night, he rutted furiously and finally collapsed into sleep, leaving the woman gasping for air on the sodden mattress beneath him. She groaned and extricated herself with difficulty, but he no longer noticed. Flames and screaming demonic faces were dancing behind his eyelids in a red glow. He saw himself circling a palm tree while a bearded pirate held a torch to his backside. Don Luis' glistening intestines wound round the trunk like the stripes on a barber's pole. The pirate kept asking, "Where is the gold? Where is the gold?" His sister Isabel was being raped for the fifteenth time. Little brother Antonio was nailed inside a sugar barrel full of cockroaches and rolled into the river by a howling mob. His young sons were roasting on grills, like Saint Lawrence. Don Luis sank his teeth into the pillow. In the hot, dark bedroom, wisps of burnt sage hung in the air like smoke after a battle.

At noon the next day, the buccaneers were reunited. A loud cheer scattered birds in all directions. A mighty flotilla of canoes, the muskets and ammunition weighing almost as much as the raiders, paddled down the river. Meanwhile, Don Luis walked slowly around

El Real de Santa Maria. He looked at every detail; the goats grazing behind the church, the stone balls to tether the Africans, the termites eating the palisade, the pustulating sores of his soldiers. The Padre's choirboys kept lookout in the trees. Slaves heaved fresh logs and boulders into place. Musket fuses and gunpowder lay drying on the roof. The knotted red cross of Burgundy hung listlessly from the flagpole over the storehouse. He knew that all this familiar life would shortly cease to exist, and it made him study everything closely, as if he could stop time by concentrating on each passing second. He found that time only rushed along faster.

The current swept the buccaneers silently towards their destination. Before nightfall they had reached a muddy bank east of Santa Maria. They could see the palisade, and the red X of the Hapsburg flag, half a mile away in the twilight. They slogged and waded through the mire until they lay down, caked in dirt, with their hats over their eyes, shielding their gunpowder under upturned canoes. The word went round, to keep low and light no fires. The captains sat chewing plantains and discussing tactics. Richard Sawkins claimed the honor of leading the attack.

"I know you want to proceed directly to Panama, Admiral," he muttered hoarsely. "So it is only fit that I should lead my crew against this bastion. I'll charge straight in, to seal off the river."

"Bastion? That pile of twigs?" said Coxon, playing with the white plumes in his hat. "You should have been at Santa Marta! How can you call that a bastion, you whippersnapper?"

"Bastions, bastards, barnacles and bollocks, I've seen the lot, as you well know," said Sawkins, "and made cunts out of them too."

"All right," Sharp cut in. "These ain't the Havana ramparts, but there'll still be blood. You go ahead and enjoy yourself, Dick. We'll follow in your footsteps. Leave a couple of Dagos alive for the rest of us."

"I will surprise them in their nightshirts, at dawn, before they can even think about hiding the gold."

"If there is any gold. The Indians might have spun us a yarn," moaned Cook, not knowing how near the truth he was.

Sawkins cast a look of pure hatred at Cook. "We will bloody well find that out, won't we? Christ, why are we here at all? You will see me on the battlefield in the morning, gentlemen." He got up, spat, and strode off to inform his crew. They loaded up the cartridge tubes on their bandoliers with good powder and polished their guns. Old Watling, Sawkins' quartermaster, made sure that a dozen men with grappling hooks, halberds, and axes would be ready at the head of the column.

Sharp found Tom and Captain Andreas. "Tom," he said, "tell your Indian friend that we can't be having any singing or chanting tonight. If the savages want to croon to their demons, they must do it under their breath. No fires!"

"Don't worry, Captain," said Tom, "they'll be as quiet as mice."

A shout came from the dark thicket nearby. A red-faced buccaneer, his breeches round his shins, hopped out of the trees, frantically slapping himself around the crotch. He fell headlong into the mud, with his spotty white backside in the air.

"What, in the name of Christ, is the matter with you, Stevens?" hissed Sharp. "We are at battle stations. Do you want to warn the enemy? I'll have you buggered with a cactus!"

"God!" gasped Stevens, rolling in the red mud and fumbling with his breeches. "It couldn't be any worse than these ants, Captain. I didn't see them in the dark. They attacked my privates with stings worse than hornets."

When Sharp smiled, he looked evil. One side of his mouth went up, the other down. He dragged the man to his feet and sent him on his way with a kick. "Watch where you shit in future!"

The incident raised a general chuckle, which eased the atmosphere. Even so, the buccaneers hardly slept that night. After their epic march, they came within musket range of the enemy at last. Their blood was up. As the first hint of dawn colored the sky behind them, they began to stir. They scratched their mosquito bites and filled their bellies with water. Captain Andreas led Richard Sawkins' assault column, the sacrificial 'forlorn hope,' to the edge of the pasture in front of the palisade.

At the same time, Sergeant Roque Alvarez, on the roof of the storehouse, swung his spyglass along the treetops and saw two of the lookouts waving and pointing in the direction of the sunrise. The first blinding yellow rays made it difficult to distinguish the huddled attackers, but, when he lowered and focused the glass, he could see the glinting weapons of dirty, bearded pirates in the bushes. He raised his pistol and fired a shot into the sky. The drummer launched into a loud and protracted roll. It brought the soldiers stumbling out of their beds. The church bell rang incessantly. Bleary-eyed and half-dressed, the men scarcely had time to grab their weapons before Sawkins' forlorn hope came running across the field with a bloodthirsty roar.

Richard Sawkins led the way, striking heroic poses at every opportunity. He wore a scarlet jacket covered in golden thread and flourished a broadsword and a cavalry pistol. His hair stood on end with sweat. His boots and breeches, like everybody else's, were plastered with mud. The standard-bearer waved the captured Aragonese flag beside him. The drummer struggled to keep up and rattle out a rhythm at the same time, echoing his Spanish counterpart. The men with grappling irons soon overtook him. They flung hooks over the logs of the palisade and began to pull them down. Their comrades with axes chopped at the rotten timbers below. Any defender who poked his head over the barrier stood a good chance of having his face shot off.

The Spanish musketeers were having a bad morning. The sun blazed straight into their eyes. They fumbled with ramrods and fuses, forgetting to put wadding into the barrels. The balls simply rolled out when they aimed down at the attackers. The few shots that actually fired were hopelessly wide of the mark, lost in the buccaneers' smoke. The pike men fared no better. When they thrust their spears through the gaps in the logs, the pirates simply chopped the points off, blasted away with pistols, flung the guns at the Spaniards' heads, and then hacked into them with axes and cutlasses.

Faced with the fury of the onslaught, Sergeant Alvarez saw that his men were on the brink of running. Richard Sawkins came crashing through the palisade and cut through a pike, taking the man's hand off. The most desperate bunch of villains Alvarez had ever seen followed the buccaneer captain. White-haired Watling strode up to a group of pike men, fired his musket, used it as a club, threw it, pulled out two pistols, fired them simultaneously and threw them too, before finally advancing with a butcher's knife in one hand and a cutlass in the other. He swatted a pike out of the way and plunged the knife into a soldier's throat just above the rim of the breastplate. Then, with a satisfied grin, the grizzled veteran calmly wiped the blade on his victim's sleeve as the soldier sank to the ground among his dying comrades.

Alvarez looked about in despair. He had no way of knowing that Watling had once bathed in the blood of Catholics under Oliver Cromwell at Drogheda. Where the hell was Don Luis? A morning breeze cleared the musket smoke in front of the shattered defenses. Four times as many raiders swarmed across the field, banners waving. Once the fence was breached, a horde of shrieking Kuna warriors rose from a hollow. The situation was hopeless.

Sergeant Alvarez bellowed, "Basta! Nos rendimos!" and held his sword upside down. His men dropped their weapons. Instantly, Sawkins leapt over a corpse and grabbed Alvarez by the collar. Watling, the white-haired Ironside veteran, came forward with his knife.

"Quick!" shouted Sawkins, spraying the sergeant's face with spittle. "Where is the gold?"

Watling leered and pressed the point of the blade into the soft flesh under the sergeant's chin. "El oro! Rapido!" He spat through white whiskers framing his toothless gums. Alvarez sighed helplessly. Out of the corner of his eye he saw Don Luis and Padre Ruperto hurrying along the quayside behind the storehouse with a handful of men. He pointed at the running figures over Sawkins' shoulder. "Alli! Alli esta el oro! Gold, there!"

Sawkins swung round, releasing his grip. He saw the little group of fugitives. They seemed to be carrying a chest. The one in the flapping black robe was clutching a large, gleaming, golden crucifix.

"Shit!" he shouted and raced across the muddy street. "Come on! They are getting away with the treasure!"

A party of buccaneers reached the boardwalk just in time to see Don Luis' group furiously paddling a canoe towards the Gulf of San Miguel. Sawkins sat, helpless, on the edge, shaking his head and cursing. Don Luis, only forty yards away, taunted him, "No hay oro! Hijo de puta! Ladron! No gold for you! Thieving English son of a whore!"

This stung Sawkins into action. He turned to his men. "Quick! Run back and grab one of our canoes! Paddle it here as fast as you can! We'll catch those bastards yet!" Sawkins fired his pistol at Don Luis. The shot splashed well short. The Field Marshal of Darien had escaped.

His men were only gone for thirty minutes, but it seemed like an eternity to the fuming Richard Sawkins. Meanwhile, the bulk of the raiders entered Santa Maria. The captured garrison was herded into the street in front of the church. The Indians caught thirty soldiers who were trying to flee south and led them to the edge of the forest. They stripped them naked. Some were tied to trees for target practice. Others were chased through the thorn bushes and speared like wild pigs. Tom saw what was occurring. He did not like it.

"Can't we stop that? Paramos esto?" he asked Andreas. Malcolm and Joseph backed him up.

"Claro. I stop," shrugged the war chief. As they approached the woods, a naked young Spaniard came racing towards them, his feet torn to ribbons. Three warriors loped behind him, laughing and aiming their spears like javelins. 'Hunting' was in progress all around them, with horrible screams announcing a kill. The garrison's pack of mastiffs lay on the ground covered with arrows like pincushions. Spanish soldiers hung from the trees; dead, dying, or awaiting a fatal arrow with urine running down their legs.

Tom pulled the lock of his pistol back. He fired a shot in the air. Captain Andreas blew a booming note on his conch shell. He cut some of the human targets free. Soon Thomas had half a dozen whimpering Spaniards grabbing at his knees and begging for mercy.

The warriors gathered round them prodding them with the shafts of their spears. Andreas shouted, "Weti ipikarye a?"

A warrior with black paint covering his entire face was about to answer. He wore a spiked mastiff's dog collar round his neck. Andreas glared at him coldly and walked over to a Spaniard who was strapped to a tree, pierced like Saint Sebastian. The man was screaming and writhing in agony. One of the arrows had punctured his liver. The chief pulled out his hunting knife to cut his throat. Blood gurgled down the man's chest and the screaming stopped. Andreas buried the blade in the tree trunk and announced, "Pela. Perkusa!"

The warriors lost interest in further tortures after that. They began to skin the mastiffs for breakfast. The surviving Spaniards gathered their shirts and breeches. They followed Thomas back into Santa Maria, like chicks behind a mother hen. When they joined their comrades outside the church, they kept their heads down, shooting nervous glances at the forest.

Richard Sawkins fretted on the boardwalk. Two buccaneers, who understood a little Spanish, approached him with a nervous young captive.

"What have we got here?" asked the captain.

"This is Gabriel," said one of the men. "He reckons he knows the most likely course of that canoe you are after. He also says he knows the location of the gold stores in Panama and all the secret hiding places. He would be pleased to assist us."

Sawkins scrutinized the trembling young man, who was chewing the points of his moustache and constantly glancing over his shoulder.

"He's definitely scared of something back there," said Sawkins, "but I haven't the time to find out what it is. Here comes the canoe, at last. We need a pilot. Take these muskets. Get in, the three of you."

The men hesitated. "Hurry! We're after the gold, you swabs!" shouted Sawkins. "We'll catch those Papist dogs yet!" They eased themselves into the rocking dugout and began to paddle hard into the middle of the current. Gabriel took a last look at the quayside, with visible relief.

There was no need to keep a close watch on the prisoners in Santa Maria. They were terrified of venturing into the surrounding countryside. Bands of angry Indians descended from their gold-panning drudgery in increasing numbers. The buccaneers rifled the church, storehouse, and cabins, finding very little of value. They drank wine and threw a few stray coins and silver communion cups into a chest. Then they tore any rings and medallions from the captives and prised the golden halo off a statue of the Virgin Mary. Only two of the raiders had been slightly wounded. One had lost half an ear to the careless swing of a comrade's cutlass; the other had a musket ball in his left buttock. It had not penetrated very far. Lionel Wafer was able to pop it out like a pea with his thumbnails. Some thirty Spanish corpses began to bloat behind the ruined palisade. When Sergeant Alvarez asked permission to give them a Christian burial, he was told, "Don't bother. We'll cremate them soon enough."

Word had spread that Sawkins was in hot pursuit of the fabled gold. This information spared the prisoners from any further interrogations. Captain Andreas and Prince Golden Cap located the Kuna Helen of Troy in a shack near the river. She was heavily pregnant and showed no emotion as she rejoined the tribe. Twenty African slaves, six of them women, were locked into a cabin with the smaller children and a barrel of water. They began to make a hideous wailing noise. Coxon got fed up with it and suggested killing them.

"What for?" asked Sharp. "Why not let them out? They can't do any harm. They can serve us. The women might be fun. They say it cures the pox."

"Do what you like," said Coxon. "So long as the caterwauling stops."

Sharp saw Tom emerging from the store with a fancy plumed beaver hat on his head and brand new rapier in an embroidered baldric. The old buccaneer was examining the dog lock on a brass-mounted horse pistol. He wore a clean starched shirt with billowing sleeves, purple satin breeches, and shiny riding boots. His greasy leather jerkin, wampum pouch, hunter's rifle, and tarpaulin knapsack remained the same.

"My, my, Tom Sheppard," said Sharp. "You've done yourself proud. You look more like a captain than I do."

"I think I found a general's wardrobe. There are a couple of excellent French periwigs left, if you want one. Of course we'd all sooner have gold, you know."

"There will be gold presently, I promise you. Meanwhile I'll take a wig for Captain Cook. That shoddy shit he wears would look cheap on a scarecrow." Sharp paused. "Ah, yes. Before I forget, take a couple of men and let those noisy niggers out, before the admiral has them shot."

"With pleasure," said Tom. He found Joe and Malcolm exchanging their torn muddy clothes with some prisoners in the street. The buccaneers began to look more presentable, while the Spaniards turned into tramps.

"Come on, you two," Tom said. "Another mission of mercy."

They prised the lock off the cabin door with the point of a halberd. The slaves fell silent and backed away into the dark overcrowded shack. The place smelled fearful. The Africans refused to come out.

"What's 'free' in Spanish?" asked Joseph.

"You should know that by now. It's 'libre,'" said Tom. He opened the door wide and gestured, "Libre! Libre! Anda! Fuera! Come out!"

An older man stepped forward. His cheeks were covered in dark blue zigzag tattoos, which were common among Indians, but not slaves. A line of oval lumps ran across his upper chest. He blinked in the light and asked, "Libre? Free?"

"By God," said Malcolm. "He speaks English!"

"Free! Yes. Lower your weapons, lads," said Thomas. "They think we are about to kill them."

The tattooed slave came cautiously over the threshold. The buccaneers gave him room. Gradually the others followed. They stood in the road silently, staring at their feet. They tried not to look at the wild scene around them. Their former masters slunk about timidly, like ragged beggars, and did not give them a second glance.

Mortally wounded soldiers crawled into corners to die. Fierce, hairy men, bristling with weapons, strutted up and down, laughing and cursing.

"Well we kinna just leave them standing here," said Malcolm.

"We can. We can do whatever we like with them. They're worth at least fifty pesos each," said Joseph. "Pick a couple of ladies, Mal. Pick three or four. Enjoy yourself like the Duke of Buckingham. I'm having this one, so." The Irishman was unnaturally excited. He took a buxom young woman, with firm breasts pointing up under her cotton shift, by the wrist and pulled her towards him. A little boy, with snot running down his face, seized the hem of her dress.

"Looks like you've got an instant family there, Joe, like your saintly namesake. Find yourself some pleasant accommodation," said Tom. "Let's hope you prove to be a good stepfather. What about you, Malcolm? You're not usually so bashful."

"Not this time, old man," groaned Malcolm. "I can hardly walk. My guts are solid. I'm going to find the surgeon."

"Well," said Thomas, "our friend with the decorated face interests me." He turned to the tattooed man and asked, "Tu nombre? What is your name?"

"Name?" the man pointed to his scarred chest. "Zaqueo. Me Zaqueo."

"You speak English?"

"Zaqueo savvy English, Francois, Spaniol. Zaqueo Calabar Ibibio."

Tom took Zaqueo by the arm and led him away. The remaining slaves started to follow. Tom waved them back with his new hat. "Free! Libre!" he shouted. "Shoo!" The woman and child plodded along obediently behind Joseph. Malcolm was using his halberd as a crutch. Other buccaneers began to take an interest in the slaves. A woman let out a shriek and ran behind the shacks, pursued by a limping scoundrel in a short cape. A group of six African men and a woman found abandoned pikes and daggers under the swelling corpses near the palisade. They picked them up and sprinted towards the tree line.

Provisions appeared from every corner of the outpost. Coxon, Cook, and Sharp set up their headquarters in the church. Cook was wearing Don Luis' beautifully curled wig, which Sharp had given him. They used the altar as a dining table and reclined on the pews, like Romans at a feast, while the cabin boys danced attendance. A pirate orchestra sat in the stalls recently occupied by Padre Ruperto's Easter choir. The paltry treasure of Santa Maria, the coins, goblets, and the Virgin's halo, lay inside a giant clamshell that served as a font. It was far too little to divide. Coxon said, "Leave it where it is until Sawkins returns."

"What if he comes back empty-handed?" asked Cook.

"We'll throw dice," said Coxon.

"Give Sawkins the Virgin's halo," said Sharp. "We can throw for the rest now. It will relieve the boredom while we await his return."

Dirty crockery was smashed against the wall and the altar became a gaming board. Sharp produced five ivory dice from his coat pocket, "Here," he said, "test these to see if they are true. I bought them from a Guinea man in Port Royal; real elephant tooth."

The captains threw the dice along the altar. Coxon reckoned, "They fall nicely." He turned to a cabin boy. "Bring more wine and put that driblet of pelf on the table. Jump to it, you monkey."

"Shouldn't we call Peter Harris?" wondered Cook.

"Fuck Peter Harris," said Coxon. "He can wriggle his tongue in my ass. He thinks he's too good for us. If he ain't here that's his lookout."

The boy dumped the loot onto the table with a crash. Coxon removed the halo and put it aside, muttering, "That is solid gold; too good to waste on the likes of Sawkins."

"Let him have it anyway, John," said Sharp. "He carried the day this morning."

Coxon lowered his thick, black eyebrows and reddened. "I'll let him have it, Barty, don't you worry. As for this morning, a gang of Quaker housewives could have taken this pile of dried-out twigs. Why didn't you fools listen to reason and head for Panama? Oh no! The Brethren of the Coast had to vote!" Coxon brought his fist down on the loot. "See what we've got for our trouble! Where's that wine? I'll have it in this cup!" He picked a silver goblet from the top of the pile and snatched the flagon out of the boy's hand.

Edmund Cook was staring at the carved Jesus nailed to the cross above them. He called the cabin boy back. "Shin up there, lad, and take it out of here."

The boy clambered over the altarpiece and brought the wooden Christ smashing down onto the floorboards. Sharp swung round and Coxon almost jumped out of his skin.

"What in bright blue blazes is going on here?" shouted the admiral.

"Easy, John, easy," said Sharp. "It's only an effigy. They burnt them by the thousand under the Lord Protector."

"So? Is that a reason to startle us out of our wits?" demanded Coxon as the boy dragged the crucifix towards the door.

"In my opinion," said Cook, "it can only bring bad luck to throw dice under the cross like Roman soldiers." He turned to the boy. "Leave it there, son. At least it ain't hanging over our heads."

"God's Death!" growled Coxon. "You are a strange one, Eddie! Scared of a Papist doll! Can we please proceed?"

The musicians were ordered to play tune after tune or risk a flogging. The mandolin player, O'Hare, led them into a series of reels, which produced an endless, circular melody. The dice began to roll. A bedraggled Spaniard wandered past the door of the church, peeped inside, crossed himself, and hobbled away.

Captain Peter Harris made himself comfortable in Don Luis' bedroom. He wanted to be the first to greet Sawkins on his return. The rest of the buccaneers barged into any cabin that took their fancy. Every square inch of the outpost was turned over. When they found a mulatto woman they raped her gleefully. It became too much for one recently married Spanish soldier and he hammered on the door. He was dragged inside and forced to watch before being tossed into the river with his guts falling out. When the pretty young bride started trying to slash her wrists with a shard of broken pottery, the rapists snapped her spine over a barrel and threw her into the water after him. They returned to find a full wineskin hanging in the cabin and amused themselves by squirting the contents into each other's mouths.

Goats and chickens were being roasted in the street. Half a dozen cows had been found in a nearby field. The buccaneers tied them to crossed pikes and butchered them. A pair of Scotsmen decided to pass the time by making tropical haggis with maize, yucca, and chili peppers stuffed into the stomach bags. Oxtail and cow foot soup bubbled in cauldrons over open fires. Any remaining offal was thrown onto the ground in steaming heaps for the Spaniards. It was quickly covered in blue flies. Sergeant Alvarez sat in the dirt, wearing a filthy old pirate's shirt and tattered breeches, with tears rolling down his cheeks. He cursed Don Luis between sobs. His men huddled in the shade, trying to avoid a random kick, and pretended not to hear the outraged screams of the women.

A drunken Captain Sharp staggered briefly to the doorway of the church and ordered his cabin boy to fetch the Hapsburg banner down from the flagpole. He wished to use it as collateral in the game. Don Luis' flour supply was kneaded into dough and consumed as damper. In the shade of the trees, the Indians digested the dogs and turned their attention to the dead Spaniards before the ants reduced them to skeletons. None of the raiders went hungry that day.

Tom and his companions settled into a relatively clean cabin containing four cots. Lionel Wafer came in. He prodded Malcolm's belly. "When did you last have a movement?"

Joseph answered, "We had the privilege of witnessing a most glorious bowel evacuation on the beach ten days ago, remember?"

"That sounds about right," said Malcolm.

"Incredible. Your guts are so hard, I would have said three weeks. You've had no quicksilver up there for the grand pox?"

After letting some blood, Wafer told his patient to lie face down on a cot and relax. His apprentice held Malcolm's buttocks apart while Wafer tried to get a grip on a hardened turd with a pair of tapered steel tongs. Only a few small fragments of leathery black excrement came out. Wafer rummaged in his toolbox and produced something that resembled a marrow knife. "Hold still," he advised, "I don't want to wound your lower gut." He carefully gouged into the center of the problem, gave a little twist and quickly extracted the instrument. A thin sliver of dry ropey paste lay in the hollow of the scoop. "We need to dig out more than a strand of clinker," he said. "Give a good push."

Malcolm strained and cried out in pain, "God! It's like broken glass down there!"

"Try again," said the surgeon. Thomas, Zaqueo, Joseph, Andreas, the slave woman, her child, and a red-eyed Scarrett watched attentively. Malcolm groaned. "It's no use. I'm clagged to the gunnels. Nothing is moving."

"Can't you squirt something up his ass?" wondered Joseph.

"I'm afraid it's too solid for that," said Wafer. "He's packed tight from stem to stern. He needs a radical purge to liquefy the obstruction from above. I have a small quantity of Senna pods and licorice that I could grind up, with opium and aqua vitae, but I fear it would not be enough." He patted Malcolm's rear. "You can't push at all?"

"Not without splitting myself," said Malcolm. "Tom, ye said ye had a cure for this."

Wafer turned to Tom. "If you have a remedy, use it or this man will die. I have never encountered such compacted shit. It's harder than the walls of Portobello. I bled some poison out of his veins, but the shit has passed the point of no return. It will petrify to rock, from his ass to his stomach."

Tom took the largest of his three flasks out of his bag and gave Andreas a meaningful look. The Indian nodded.

"Leave your new breeches off, Mal," said the old buccaneer, "unless you want to squirt foul slime into them. You won't need the shirt either. You'll be sweating like a pig. Take a good swig of this. Force it down. Your guts will be clear in the morning, I promise, but we must tie you to the bed. This stuff can addle your wits. You won't know friend from foe."

"What?" shouted Malcolm. "So I am to become a lunatic? Why

don't ye just shoot me and have done with it?"

"Trust me, Malcolm, Andreas gave me some of this same brew when I was here with Morgan," said Tom. "I sprayed fountains out of my asshole and buckets of bile from my throat. I saw God in all his glory and the devil dancing in hell, but it was all over on the next day. My mind was as clear as my bowels. Would you rather wait until your innards turn to granite and you roll on the deck begging somebody to end your misery?"

"Ye had better be right, Tom," sighed Malcolm. "Give me the damn stuff."

Tom passed him the flask. "One good swallow," he said. "No more. Remember, I cured that clerk on the Caernarvon Estate."

The spectators leaned forward expectantly. Even the snotty little boy was gripped by the drama. Malcolm raised the concoction to his lips and took a gulp. Tom snatched the flask away from him as he clenched his fists and choked.

"Hold it down, man," shouted Tom. "Hold it down!"

The patient screwed up his face. After a minute he gasped, "It is down. By God's bones, I have never tasted such evil muck."

Lionel Wafer took the flask off Tom and held it to his nose. "Phew!" he winced. "That smells worse than a dead rat! A Smithfield mountebank would be hard pressed to sell it." He handed the medicine back, wiped his instruments on a rag, and tossed them into the box. "That will either kill or cure him. If it works you must give me the recipe, Thomas."

Tom shrugged. "The ingredients come from vines in the forest." He turned to Captain Andreas and asked, "What is the name of the vine? Que vinia?"

"Cascabel," replied the chief.

"Cascabel?" said Wafer. "Never heard of it. I will visit the sufferer in the morning."

"Well," said Malcolm when the doctor had gone, "are ye going to tie me up then?"

"In a while," said Tom. "It takes an hour or two to start working. Lie back and breathe slowly."

Joseph noticed that the scab on Malcolm's throat seemed to have grown. He examined it closely. "You didn't get that from a woman the other night, did you?"

Malcolm felt around the little wound. "No, I think I had a scratch there before. It is strange, but there appears to be a hard lump growing underneath. Why do ye ask?"

"Oh, nothing." Joe remembered the vampire bat, but kept his thoughts to himself. Malcolm had enough worries for the time being.

The street outside was as noisy as Port Royal. A tipsy buccaneer with an impish sense of poetic justice swaggered about, accompanied by an African and a Kuna warrior. He made the black man lash out at the cringing Spaniards with a bull hide whip while the Indian shouted, "El oro? El oro?"

"There!" yelled the pirate. "Haha! The boot is on the other foot now, you Dago dog! How do you like a taste of your own medicine?"

Drum, fife, and fiddle music, drunken roars, female screams, wood smoke, and the smell of roasting meat came in through the bamboo blinds. Santa Maria had never been as crowded and lively as she was in her final hours. Scarrett, lying on his cot in a cloud of pungent pipe smoke, announced, "I am starving! I could eat a horse! Watch my gear!" He picked up a basket and headed for the roasting pits, slamming the door behind him. Joe turned his attention to the woman and discovered that she was menstruating. The blood, combined with her lice and the boy's running nose, put him off. He ran out after the Gipsy.

Tom began to strap one of Malcolm's wrists to the bed frame, but Captain Andreas waved him back. The Indian produced a feathered rattle and shook it while chanting and blowing tobacco smoke over his patient. Tom beckoned Zaqueo to follow him out into the street. The child gaped at Andreas' performance from behind his mother's skirts. She had slumped into a corner and began to sleep. Soon all was quiet inside the cabin except for the boy's sniffs and the steady shaking of the rattle, like boots crunching on gravel, accompanied by Andreas' low crooning.

Malcolm found himself dozing off. His heartbeat kept time to the rattle and the steady chanting regulated his breaths. The room became dim. The hubbub from the street faded into the sound of waves and seagulls. He tasted salt. He was a young lad again, a cabin boy, catching his first glimpse of the palm trees swaying in the West African breeze. Deep bass drums boomed along the shore and gaudily dressed warriors were herding lines of naked black figures over the white sand. As they came nearer, he heard whips cracking and screams. He saw branding irons pressed into dark skin and smelled burning flesh.

The drums grew louder, his heart pounded faster, hurting his chest. Warm seawater pumped through his veins, throbbing in his temples. The rigging cut into the palms of his hands. He held onto the mainmast for dear life, unable to escape the hideous stench emanating from the bowels of the ship. It rose like a foul mist around the crow's nest. The light from the sand burned his eyes. Saliva accumulated in his mouth.

Searing pains popped his eardrums. A burning wave of nausea erupted from the pit of his stomach. He felt sweat coursing down his face, neck, and sides. He thought he would never stop vomiting. His heart seemed to be trying to escape out of his skull. A hand gripped his shoulder firmly. Hot gasps of brandy-laden air panted behind him. A jaunty Dorset squeezebox melody mingled with curses, rattling chains, and Ibo women's shrieks. A sharp stake was tearing into his backside, searching for a knot of unbearable pain, finding even more pain. The old Quaker captain's face was shining beetroot red, his wig askew, as he repeated, "Lord forgive me! Lord forgive me!" over and over, finally shouting, "Jeeeeesus! Sweet fucking Jeeesus!" Malcolm's guts shuddered, exploded, and boiling peppers ran down his legs, wrenching out a scorching jellyfish of pure agony in their bloody wake. Snotty tears streamed from his chin. Everything went white.

Malcolm tumbled down towards the deck past a blur of sails and ropes, crashing through the planks, into darkness and oblivion. Captain Andreas cleaned him and settled his unconscious body in a comfortable position.

Next day, Saturday morning, April the 17th 1680, the gold depot at El Real de Santa Maria stood in flames. The timber shacks exploded in showers of sparks. The broken palisade burned fiercely, interrupting a great gathering of vultures. One fat bird was so reluctant to abandon the feast that its tail feathers ignited.

Forty canoes, each carrying between five and ten men, swarmed downstream, like angry wasps. The pirate horde had swollen in size. It now included Spanish prisoners, a few African slaves, and the more adventurous of the Indians. The river, twice the width of the Thames, was crowded. Bartholomew Sharp's men were the last to leave. Behind them, desperate Spaniards occupied the final two canoes, slapping the water with their bare hands. Their stranded comrades howled in dismay. Gangs of Indians finished the garrison off with stone clubs, in choking clouds of smoke. The raped women were dragged into the woods to become concubines of the Kuna tribe. Vultures circled overhead and alligators slid towards the quayside. The leaves of the tall Imperial palm near the church blazed like a great torch. The bell crashed out of the collapsing tower with a resounding knell.

"Truly a vision of hell," remarked Tom. "Peace to their ashes."

"No mercy for the merciless!" muttered Joseph as they paddled away. Malcolm sank back against Toms' knees, smiling feebly. His guts were clear, but his heart thumped and needles of pain stabbed at the back of his eyes. Tom tied his sash over Malcolm's head after wetting it in the river. Scarrett worked his paddle in a trance. His pipe, filled with weed, never left his mouth. He hardly spoke these days, and when he did, the words oozed out in a muddy drawl. Captain Andreas knelt in the stern, steering as he paddled. From the waist up he was dressed as a European, with a broad beaver hat and red jacket. His cheeks were black with paint. A nose ring glittered above a golden crescent hanging from his lower lip. Below the waist, the chief still sported a penis sheath and nothing else. In the prow, Zaqueo would have looked at home fishing in the Bight of Biafra. Only a leather strap concealed his genitals. He dipped the spear-shaped paddle into the current unhurriedly. Sitting low in the water, filled with bags, pistols, swords, and muskets, they overtook the less efficient canoes on their way to the Great South Sea.

Tom had sailed through many storms, from the Newfoundland Banks to the coast of Brazil, but the thought of the South Sea made his heart beat faster. Only Sir Francis Drake, and a handful of other brave Englishmen, had ever dared to venture into this secret Spanish ocean. Getting back meant circumnavigating the globe or risking an eastward passage through the Magellan straits. He remembered how Sharp had casually discarded the Atlantic sea chart in the Indian village. 'One way or another,' Tom thought, 'This will be my final cruise.'

Sharp's red plume bobbed along ahead of them. He sat in the middle of the canoe with Edmund Cook. The captains were taking an interest in a pair of Father Ruperto's choirboys while their men paddled. The children trembled but tried to ingratiate themselves with their captors. These showed the youngsters how to stuff and light pipes. Cook was delighted when one of the boys donned his new periwig and sang the 'Te Deum' in a shaky, unbroken voice. The sacred music contrasted with the wild surroundings. Even the alligators on the bank seemed to be listening with open mouths.

Tom said, "It is the voice of a sad angel."

A strong wind, loaded with grey clouds, swept up behind them. The pall of black smoke over Santa Maria vanished. They were being pushed to starboard towards the twisted mass of cable roots that anchored a red mangrove swamp. The roots began to vanish as the flood tide drowned them in salty water. Herons took to the air followed by clouds of recently-hatched mosquitoes.

"Paddle hard to port!" shouted Tom. The waxy leaves of the top branches were uncomfortably close. They fought a massive incoming surge. "Thank Christ we have the wind at our back."

The flotilla scattered. Three canoes floundered into the maze of branches and were never seen again. Others turned turtle, losing all their weapons before they could be righted. The wind pushed the top layer of water towards the sea. The tide welled up beneath. The wide estuary fanned out into the marshes on either side. It was pointless to paddle. Suddenly the water level had risen by twenty feet and the banks were on the horizon. The currents were irresistible, deep and cold. Spring rains announced their arrival by making the surface of the sea hiss. They were floating in the Bay of San Miguel, soaked, and desperately bailing out their unseaworthy craft.

Fortunately, a cluster of tiny islands was sprinkled across the river mouth. They were within shouting distance of each other. The raiders scrambled ashore. Mangroves covered the islands on one side and patches of sand and shingle on the other. Rain collected in pot holes among the rocks and provided drinking water. Sharp's men shielded their muskets and powder flasks under upturned canoes. Some attempted to construct crude shelters with mangrove branches, but most sat quietly under their broad-brimmed hats, leaning against tree trunks with pipes in their mouths.

Joseph expressed the general mood of despondency. "We have come all this way. We have found no gold, not even silver. We are marooned on a savage shore without a ship. This is the most miserable expedition ever undertaken, so it is."

"Don't be an old woman, Joe," said Malcolm. "We are fighting-fit and well-placed to carve into King Carlos' underbelly. All the galleons from the mines of Peru pass this way. Pieces of eight will spill out by the hundredweight."

"That's brave talk, Mal. Are you still beside yourself? How's your own underbelly?" asked Joe. "Softer?"

"Much softer," said Malcolm, "but now I know what a woman suffers in childbirth. I was shitting hot cannonballs."

"Captain Andreas asked if you had any visions during the purge," said Tom. "You were screaming at things only you could see. Did any animals or people appear in your mind's eye?"

"No animals but seagulls, nor any people but slaves. I thought I was back on the Guinea Coast. Ever been there, Tom?"

"No," scowled Thomas, "but I've been near enough to those damn ships to catch a whiff. The stench always blisters the inside of my nostrils. By the bloody wounds of Christ, that's one cargo they can keep." Tom glanced over at Zaqueo. A linen sheet covered the decorative lumps on the African's chest. The zigzag tattoos on his cheeks shone blue in the grey light.

"Hey, Zack!"

"Yessah, Massa Thomas?"

"Pass me some of that pisco."

Zaqueo rummaged in a sack. Tom flashed his yellow teeth. "Our new amigo, Zack, found three jars of this firewater in Santa Maria. Pass it around, lads, but don't be obvious, or it will all be gone in seconds. We have a long, damp night ahead."

The clay jar traveled from hand to hand. Captain Andreas poured a few drops onto the ground before forcing the clear liquid down with a grimace. Zaqueo sipped it tentatively, shuddering. Soon they were all chasing it with gulps from Toms' water skin, making increasingly stupid toasts.

Joseph growled. "Here's to guts on my blade and silver in my purse!

Malcolm rejoined, "To my cock in a crimson cunt!"

Scarrett muttered something about King Charlie Stuart's death. The African and the Indian intoned the names of their respective gods. Eventually, Tom reckoned it was time to toast their captain. He raised the jar to his lips and said, "To the cack-stained britches of snake-eyed Sharky!"

A cloaked scarecrow, with a sodden red plume drooping from his hat, stepped towards them through the rain. "Ah, here you are Tom," said Bartholomew Sharp. "I'll drink my own health, if you please, you miserly dog."

Sharp squatted down and grabbed the drink.

"Help yourself, sir," said Tom. "It'll warm your bones."

The captain took a long swig. His neck twitched and he hissed, "Ah! That's better! So, are you all ready for the attack on Panama?"

Joseph reached for the jar, but Sharp held on to it.

"I don't know if we have enough men," said Tom. "We are barely a quarter of old Harry Morgan's strength. How far is Panama from here, d'you reckon?"

"Two or three sleeps, paddling hard," replied Sharp. "If we

surprise them at a weak point with our entire force, we have a good chance. We'll pepper them with musket balls and carve them to shreds. Then we'll squeeze all the treasure of the Indies out of their eyeballs." He nodded at Captain Andreas and took another gulp of pisco. "Here's to fortune and fellowship, Big Chief! By God, that's good! I think I'll share this with Ned Cook. I'm sure you sneaky devils have some more squirreled away."

Sharp patted Tom's shoulder and sloped off into the undergrowth, still clutching the pisco. Tom motioned to Zaqueo, who produced another jar.

The morning sun at low tide revealed a vast expanse of sandbanks dotted with black rocks. Herons poked their bills into the mud. The mangrove roots were covered in oysters and barnacles. The beach came alive with crabs. Sharp walked around with a filthy messenger from Coxon's crew who had splashed through the narrow channel from the adjoining island.

"Shipmates," Sharp announced, "we will depart during the slack water. The ebb will pull us over the banks. Sawkins has a Spanish pilot on board who knows the course to Point San Lorenzo. Follow his sail and be prepared for a long paddle."

The buccaneers busied themselves lighting steaming fires with damp timber. The sun dried the shirts on their backs. They ate cornmeal porridge on sticks and prised open oysters. Mosquito eggs were strained out of the rainwater in the potholes. Crabs bubbled and reddened in the kettles. Scarrett entertained his friends by slowly eating a hairy spider, legs, body, and head. Captain Andreas quietly chewed a boiled mudskipper.

As soon as the tide steadied, they hauled the dugouts into the sea. The flotilla headed northwest, chasing the Richard Sawkins' sail like the tail of a comet. Sawkins clung to the idea of capturing Don Luis and preventing him from raising the alarm in Panama. He set a merciless pace. Nobody paddled harder than young Gabriel, anxious to find favor with his captors. When Point San Lorenzo appeared, he turned to Sawkins with a satisfied smile.

"Mira!" he shouted happily. "La Punta!"

Gabriel was still grinning when Prince Golden Cap seized his ankle and tipped him over the side. It was a matter of family honor. During the night, the prince had learned that Gabriel had abducted and impregnated his sister. She was the famous 'Helen of Troy,' and the man who had defiled her could not be allowed to live. Gabriel's cries grew fainter as the salt water washed into his drowning throat. Sawkins quickly pushed the rudder around. "We need him!" He hauled the bedraggled Spaniard back on board. Gabriel coughed and spluttered for a minute before cowering in the stern. The prince paid no more attention to him. There would be other opportunities. Instead, he turned to Sawkins and pointed due north. The pirate captain understood immediately. The Indian shared his instinct for concealment. It was also wise to hug the shoreline in case the sea became too choppy and swamped the canoes. The jungle stretched endlessly to starboard. The mountains they had crossed crouched astern, shrouded in clouds. Land breezes and currents from swift rivers threatened to scatter them again. The piragua's sail was furled to allow the others to catch up. Parrots exploded out of the trees as the buccaneers approached a wide beach in the dying rays of the sun. They leapt into the surf to lift the canoes through the breakers. At nightfall, Basil Ringrose suddenly appeared in a big canoe full of Indians. He had narrowly escaped from a crowd of stranded Spaniards on a half-submerged sandbank.

That night, the rains held off. The beach blazed with a hundred fires. Tom was summoned to the captains' conference. He thought it wise to bring Zaqueo, Andreas, and the remaining jar of pisco. Upturned canoes served as benches. Coxon had one to himself. Prince Golden Cap, Sawkins, and Harris sat opposite. Cook and Sharp, attended by the pair of nervous choirboys, occupied the middle ground. Thomas completed the circle with Andreas and the African.

Sharp pointed at the dark waves. "Ringrose has just caught up with us. I feared him drowned. I would hate to lose such a fine navigator."

"We are all blind navigators in these waters," muttered Cook.

"We have no charts."

"Basil is making his own charts, Ned," said Sharp. "They'll be handy if we come to this coast again. The Dutch map was useless."

"Oh, we'll come back all right, loaded with gold and slaves!" Coxon eyed Thomas' cheek and Zaqueo's tribal scars. "Trust old blue-chopped Tom here to get himself the ugliest nigger in creation, with a face to match his own!"

"He has his uses, Admiral," said Thomas. "He speaks Spanish and a kind of pig English. I reckon he was a trader in Guinea, maybe a chief who ended up being sold himself. He found this Spanish liquor from Peru. See what you think."

"Hmm," Coxon took a small sip. "Looks like Dutch Geneva, but tastes like nothing on earth." He took a bigger mouthful. "Phew! Hits the spot, it does. It'll do."

Prince Golden Cap declined. He passed the jar to Sharp who winked at Tom as he swallowed. Edmund Cook dipped his finger and made the choirboy on his knee lick it, laughing at the child's grimace.

"The babe hasn't been weaned yet, Eddie," Coxon cackled. "Offer him one of your tits. They're juicy enough!"

Cook opened his mouth to reply, thought the better of it, and passed the jar to Harris. Then, he took the boy's hand and walked off to a dark corner of the beach. "More for us!" laughed Sharp, tousling his own choirboy's hair. "I'll inform Ned of any decisions."

"The first decision," said Peter Sawkins, unable to restrain himself, "must be to catch that bloody governor, before he raises a general alarm along the coast. He can't be far ahead. He might be sitting on the next beach, as we sit here nattering like old spinsters."

"Either we catch him, or we don't," shrugged Coxon. "As it is, we are rushing as if the devil were behind us. Do you suggest we grow wings and fly?"

"A few good men could do it," said Sawkins, "with Indian guides, in my pirogue, paddling through the night." He drank a good measure of pisco and handed the jar to Captain Andreas. Tom managed to stop the chief from pouring a libation onto the sand.

Andreas scowled and went to join his tribesmen round another fire.

"He doesn't want to upset the spirits," explained Tom.

In the dancing firelight, Tom studied the admiral closely, trying to fathom what lay behind that angry red mask with its beetling eyebrows. Sawkins was right, but Coxon opposed him at every turn. Perhaps, thought Thomas, it boiled down to simple jealousy. Coxon was a veteran basking in the glory of his famous Santa Marta raid, but Sawkins saw a leader who had lost his appetite for the fight. Sawkins wanted his own bigger and better version of the Santa Marta victory. He wanted to become the new Morgan. Meanwhile, Sharp was everybody's friend, playing a waiting game. Tom took a third swig of pisco.

"Hey, Mr. Rifleman," said Coxon, "you're hogging the drink, Sheppard. I'm dying of thirst here! Thank you!" He snatched at the jug. "Let us have your opinion, you old dog!"

"Captain Andreas," said Tom, "told me that the Spaniards are rebuilding Panama, a couple of miles away from the ruins. This time they are using stone rather than wood. Shiploads of slaves have been at it for nine years."

"Portobello was stone," said Sawkins. "It still fell."

"Look at it this way;" suggested Tom. "Sir Harry attacked a timber town from the rear with four times our strength. I know. I was there. So were you, Barty. Remember how the Dons drove a herd of cows against us? They were desperate. Now, we are about to attack stone ramparts from the sea. The garrison is four times stronger than it used to be. We have no hope of success."

"If they are still building," said Sharp, "there must be holes in the defenses."

"The Dons are no cowards," spat Sawkins, glaring at Coxon, "and if there are so many of them, the only way we can do this is by pouring through a gap where they are unprepared. We need to catch them off guard. That means the Governor of Santa Maria must not escape."

"Go on then, Dick," taunted Coxon. "Hop into your canoe and after him! Maybe we can hold the bastard to ransom as well."

Richard Sawkins' fist tightened on the hilt of his sword. "We are all too tired tonight. I say we depart at dawn and leave all these confounded Spanish prisoners on the beach. Nobody would dream of ransoming such mean rogues, that's for sure. They slow us down and add to the risk of discovery. I don't care if the Indians kill them all."

"As you wish," said Coxon. There was a chorus of ayes. Sawkins took Tom and the prince on a tour of the shore and threw five canoes onto the flames. The Spaniards would not need them. They huddled together in a mass, casting nervous glances at the Indians. For the Kuna, this was not a raid but part of a war of extermination. While the pirates rested, the tribesmen began to assault the prisoners. The Spaniards defended themselves with rocks and pieces of driftwood before fleeing into the forest. Then, at last, the Indians sang their evening songs and lay down next to their snoring allies. Another day of strenuous paddling lay ahead.

Geronimo Cobarrubias, a senile veteran of the Mapuche wars in Chile, manned the watchtower on the Punta de Platanos beyond Cape San Lorenzo. He had not slept since Don Luis Carrisoli and his fugitives had beached their canoe and warned him of the enemy approach; "Hold them back with all the men you have!" The Field Marshall had only stopped long enough to slake his thirst from a jar of fresh water.

Geronimo's men amounted to a dozen bored slaves and a mulatto overseer. They quickly melted into the green shadows, leaving Geronimo alone, perched on his wooden scaffold, with a keg of fortified wine and a telescope. The rising sun caught him napping. He was snoring when Sawkins climbed the ladder and tickled him under the chin with his rapier.

"Come, grandfather, talk! Where are they?"

Geronimo picked the sleep out of his eyes. He saw the sweating Sawkins, Prince Golden Cap, and Gabriel, looming above him on the platform. Urine oozed into his breeches. Suddenly, he was wide awake. The shore teemed with pirates and Indians.

"Se fueron hace doce horas! A Panama!" He screamed, "They

left for Panama twelve hours ago!"

Sawkins resisted the temptation to drive the point of his sword into the old man's neck. He leaned back on the railings with a sigh. The prince stepped forward to seize the telescope, twisting it and, finally, breaking it apart. He threw the broken pieces at Geronimo's head. Sawkins bit his lip; the precious instrument was ruined. Gabriel reached for the wine keg, but Sawkins held his wrist, growling, "I think you'll find that's mine now, you cack-arsed canary! Now, ask this Methuselah where we can get fresh water around here!"

There was a spring five hours away in the jungle, among bands of runaway Cimarrons, many snakes, and Indians hostile to the Kuna. The nearby rivers offered brackish water that would drive a man crazy. Geronimo recommended another beach, six leagues further east, which boasted a well and a plantain grove. A little further, the island of Chepillo had plenty of wood and water. He was sure Don Luis would head for it. The men were given a brief rest.

Basil Ringrose aimed his quadrant at the noonday sun and scribbled the position onto a piece of parchment. Meanwhile, Sawkins and Harris ordered the men to get ready to depart. Peter Harris made sure the remaining water was shared out equally, to the last drop.

Tom noticed Zaqueo gazing wistfully across the bay. "Been here before, Zack?"

"Yessah, Tom. Zaqueo perla fisherman; long time for island over dere." The old slave tapped the lumps on his chest, wheezing painfully, and pointed to the horizon. "No aire, no aire; go for Santa Maria. Work for Don Luis."

Tom turned to Captain Andreas. "Perlas? They have pearls over there?"

In a jumble of three languages, with many hand signals and puffs on his pipe, Captain Andreas recounted the history of the Pearl Islands. There had been a tribe of peaceful Indians in a village on the Isla Del Rey in the time of his grandfather. They traded with the Kuna. Occasionally, beautiful rose-tinted pearls with an inner glow changed hands. This glow symbolized the Great Spirit who lived in all creation, even the rocks. When the Spaniards arrived, they tied five chiefs to stakes in the main square and set their big war mastiffs on them, in front of all the people. When the chiefs had been torn to pieces, the Indians were forced to dive for pearls all day long, over the oyster beds. A Portuguese trader made them dive; men, women, and children, deeper and deeper. Their lungs burst and their brains died. The Spaniards were delighted; a good pearl was worth more than a diamond. Soon there were no Indians. Africans like Zaqueo replaced them. It was amazing how the blacks survived such a life and managed to produce offspring. The Kuna would never let anything like that happen to them. Nor would they eat an African. Too tough. However, they loved to eat the Spaniards' hearts and their hellish dogs, reduced to a spicy soup.

"Buena sopa," grinned Andreas, rubbing his belly and making a slurping noise. "Good soup!"

Pearls! The baubles were becoming scarce in the Caribbean Sea. Tom remembered his own grandfather's stories. Old Queen Elizabeth had gone to her grave gleaming, wrapped in strings of perfect white pearls from head to toe. Most of them came from Sir Francis Drake's chests. Queen Bess thought this would please God, because it betokened her chastity. Sir John Hawkins and Sir Thomas Cavendish rattled with pearls as they walked. Sir Walter Raleigh always wore one as an earring in the royal presence; he knew the Virgin Queen loved them above all else. Tom stroked his beard, felt the gold coin hanging from his earlobe, smiled to himself, and muttered, "This Louis d'Or will do me fine; look what happened to Old Sir Walter. Still, a lustrous yellow pearl might set off Captain Sharp's jaundiced complexion to advantage."

"What," asked Malcolm, who seemed completely recovered, "are ye burbling to yerself, Tom? Come, we are shoving off!"

"Don't you talk to white men anymore?" wondered Joseph.

"Och, Joe," said Malcolm. "Let him be. Lately, he's in a world all of his ain. Barely knows we exist."

Tom was grasping at straws. Perhaps, he pondered, he could persuade Sharp to separate his crew from the rest of this lunatic expedition. They could seize a fortune in pearls from the nearby islands and return to Golden Island independently, retracing their steps through Kuna territory. It would have to wait. Tom sighed and helped to haul a canoe into the water.

The buccaneers left Geronimo Cobarrubias in the sand, staring at his blazing watchtower. Wisps of smoke and sea hawks followed them along the coast in the chasing wind. Tom envied the birds their wings, which could carry them over the mountains and far away.

The next beach looked promising, until Sawkins dropped the bucket into the well. "By the Crown of Christ!" he screamed. "Will you come and look what the swine have done to the water!"

The well was stuffed with rotten plantains, fish guts, and a dead dog. A top layer of stinking human feces buzzed with insects, steaming in the heat of the day. They could see the remains of a fire, footprints, and the lines of a canoe in the sand. The buccaneers filed past the well, shook their heads, and collapsed. They were too exhausted to be angry and too thirsty to curse. Only Coxon's rasping voice disturbed the peace. He was berating Sawkins, who worked his jaw muscles and stared at a hole in the toe of his boot. A group of men vainly attempted to sift the salt out of seawater through a felt hat.

Tom urinated into his leather mug and examined the contents. "Too damn thick and yellow," he said, throwing it away. The beach under his feet was the last solid link to their ships and his dreams of Europe. Why the hell didn't the buccaneer captains turn back now? They had found exhaustion, thirst, foul odors, and no gold. Sawkins was leading them to certain death. Tom looked at the footpath leading inland.

"Are ye that weary of life?" asked Malcolm. "On yer own, with luck, ye'd last quarter of an hour in there."

"Yes," said Tom, "and I'd be well out of it."

Bartholomew Sharp wandered past, ignoring his men, silent under the wide brim of his hat. His red feather drooped listlessly behind him. He approached a lone coconut palm at the far end of the cove. Four yellow globes were clustered under the fronds. Sharp looked around for similar trees, but saw none. He called a Jamaican boy over and told him to shin up the trunk with a cutlass and cut the coconuts down. The lad was nearing the top when he stopped. "Captain, a sail!"

Sharp's crew lurched mindlessly towards their canoes, too tired to think. Their captain tripped and sprawled on the sand. Joseph was quickly by his side, helping him up.

"Quick!" screamed Sharp. "I want that boat!"

As usual, Destiny was calling Tom in the wrong direction. The hungry western horizon wanted to swallow him and his shipmates until they were a fading red stain on the skyline after sunset, a bloody memory of a passing scourge, a temporary pestilence. With his remaining strength, born of helpless rage, Tom stabbed the pointed paddle into the waves as if he was attacking Neptune himself. He was just a murdering pirate, no more, no less—another damned thief in a world of thieves. Nothing made sense any more but the rhythm of his paddle, the charge in his firearm, and the outline of his next target, bobbing up ahead. He had come fully into the present. He knew he'd better stay there or go mad. For the moment, never mind gold or pearls. In those endless churning wastes, he'd be happy to settle for a few drops of drinkable water before his brain fried. The rest could take care of itself.

ABOUT THE AUTHOR

Mike Hawthorne was born in Manchester, UK, 1954 and was a visual artist for 30 years (see www.mikehawthorne.net) before concentrating on writing, after he graduated with first-class honours in Creative Writing at Roehampton University, London in 2012. This is his first book, one of a planned series of three volumes. See author's blog 'Smoke Signals' at uniquearoma.blogspot.com.

Excerpt from *The Unholy Trinity...*
The next exciting installment of
Pirates of the Pacific Trilogy.

Zaqueo retrieved the knife and raised it high. Then, to Tom's surprise, he rose to his feet and stuck the blade into a tree trunk. Tom spluttered. He sucked the clammy air into his lungs. Sweat poured down his face.

"What...what..." He could not force the words out. He heard a gurgling gasp in the undergrowth. It dawned on him that Zaqueo had not been trying to murder him, but had aimed at something else. He raised his hand in a sign of peace. Zaqueo returned the gesture with a weary, red-gummed smile. He came closer and gingerly extracted a furry splinter from the crown of Tom's hat. It was a poison dart. They advanced slowly to pull back the branches. A strange figure stared back at them with dead eyes. The straight hair and high cheekbones were Indian, but the skin was very dark. The bloodstained lips and nostrils looked African. Zaqueo's spear stuck out of his chest. The man wore nothing but a breechclout and a necklace of jaguar claws. A rattan hunting bag, a trade axe and a long blowpipe lay beside his body.

"Un Lobo Cimarron," said Zaqueo, yanking out the spear and looking around anxiously, "Mother Indio, father Negro."

"More here? Hay mas?"

There was no way of telling. The possibility of more Cimarrons in the vicinity made Tom consider turning back at once. They left the hunting bag undisturbed, for fear of pricking their fingers on more darts, but Zaqueo took the necklace and the axe. Behind the steady cicada chorus, they heard gull cries and waves breaking against the rocks to the west. Tom's curiosity got the better of him. Soon, they stood on a flat stone washed by the foaming swell, with their backs to the wall of trees and the green mainland, stretching south to misty Punta Chama. A little dugout lay nearby, with a single paddle. The wild man had come on his own, to look for pigs, just as they had.

Experience Other Books by Fireship Press

MacHugh and the Faithless Pirate
by William S. Schaill

Robert MacHugh is a late 17th century Scots wine merchant and smuggler in New York who finds himself (not totally willingly) chasing pirates, perfidious French persons, angry Native Americans and others as a "favor" for a very powerful London power broker. A story filled with straining canvas, roaring cannons, spies, crooked Dutch patroons, Maroons and pretty girls, among other things.

The Ramage Companion
by Tom Grundner

Between 1965 and 1989, the British author, Dudly Pope, wrote the 18-volume Ramage series of nautical fiction novels. With its publication Mr. Pope joined C.S. Forester and Patrick O'Brian as one of the giants of the nautical fiction genre. While companion books have been written for the Forester and O'Brian series, no one has yet written a companion book for Ramage...

Until Now!

The indispensable guide for the Ramage fan. Written in a light and entertaining style, it provides snapshots of the people, places and events that shaped Nicholas Ramage and his times. It's a treasure trove of information not only for the Ramage devotee, but for anyone interested in 18th and early 19th century naval warfare.

For the Finest in Nautical and Historical Fiction and Non-Fiction
www.fireshippress.com

Interesting • Informative • Authoritative

All Fireship Press books are available
through FireshipPress.com, Amazon.com and
other leading bookstores and wholesalers worldwide.

Lightning Source UK Ltd.
Milton Keynes UK
UKOW02f0105240816

281370UK00004B/182/P